WHERE WEREWOLVES FEAR TO TREAD

BY ALAN GORDON

ISBN 978-1-945247-16-3

WHERE WEREWOLVES FEAR TO TREAD

A Thurston Howl Publications Book
Published by Thurston Howl Publications
thurstonhowlpublications.com
Knoxville, TN

jonathan.thurstonhowlpub@gmail.com

Edited by Sherayah Witcher
Cover artist and designer: Tabsley

Printed in the United States of America
10 9 8 7 6 5 4 3 2 1

Dedication

So, I WAS AT THIS CONFERENCE, and Toni comes up to me all breathless and without any preamble asks, "Have you ever thought about werewolves?" And I said no, and she says, "Well, Charlaine and I are putting an anthology together and we thought you'd be good for it," so I said I'd think about it, and she walks away, and ten minutes later I had this really cool idea.

After the story was done, I showed it to Mitchell, my agent, and he says, "Good story. Now write the book." And I said, "Seriously?" and he says, "Seriously. You write the book, and I'll sell it." So I did, and he did, and here we are.

This book is affectionately dedicated to Toni L.P. Kelner, Charlaine Harris, and Mitchell Waters.

Once or twice in a lifetime,
a man or woman may choose
a radical leaving, having heard
Lech l'cha — Go forth.
> God disturbs us toward our destiny
> by hard events and by freedom's now urgent voice
> which explode and confirm who we are.
We don't like leaving,
but God loves becoming.

—Rabbi Norman Hirsh, "Becoming"

CHAPTER 1

CRAWFORD PLACED A SHEET of tissue paper around the last button on his jacket, dipped the corner of the cloth in the tin of silver polish, and gently rubbed the button until it gleamed in the early morning sun. He wiped it clean, then held the jacket up and inspected it with satisfaction. He removed the tissue and slipped the jacket on, regarding himself in front of the mirror.

The Army expected him to buy his own polish—a petty expense that rubbed him the wrong way every time—but all things considered, they had taken care of him. As they damn well should have, given what he had done for them. Still, he had finally scored an off-base house, small as it was, and could now spend the rest of his career recruiting dumb-ass kids to go risk their necks, the way he had been recruited once upon a time—

Once upon a time, when he was a dumb-ass kid, and Pastore had found him, like Pastore had found them all.

He sighed. There was a high school fair at ten in Goldboro, an easy drive from Fort Bragg, and it would be over by four, which would get him home before traffic hit. Sunset was at nineteen seventeen. Plenty of time.

He loaded the box of forms, the posters, and the cool-looking compasses that they used for giveaways into the back of his Jeep, then programmed the school's address into his GPS and hit the button for the garage door. He pulled out slowly and stopped at the end of the driveway, watching for kids on bikes the way he once watched for hostiles in the Hindu Kush. He reached for the garage button, then the tightness began in his chest—the familiar tightness, so familiar that he didn't even think it was all that odd.

Then he looked up at the morning sun and knew that it was very odd.

1

Beyond odd. Extremely dangerous.

His chest heaved and swelled. He grabbed at the door handle and threw himself out of the Jeep. His jacket, his beautiful dress uniform, designed to impress and seduce impressionable and desperate teenagers into signing their lives over to their country, burst open at the seams. He tore at his laces, getting the boots off before his feet were crushed inside them. His belt, shiny and made from black leather, snapped with a report like a rifle shot. He fell to his knees. His neighbors—were they watching? He had to get to cover. He loped on all fours into the garage and hit the button to close it, then reached awkwardly into what was left of his jacket pocket with two claws and pulled out his cell. It took him three tries to enter Pastore's number, as his hands—no, his paws were shaking so badly.

"Joe," said the werewolf. "It's Crawford. Something impossible just happened."

Behind him, silver buttons caught the morning sun where they had fallen, scattered in the grass by the side of the driveway.

Kerry turned on the grinder and watched it pulverize nine scoops of beans into a fine brown powder, mesmerized like she used to be, back when she was little and Daddy would take her to the plant to watch the rock crushers; back when there still was a working plant nearby; back when Daddy was still with them, not with his skank of a girlfriend in Miami.

She poured the coffee into the coffee maker, then filled the container with filtered water and turned it on. She tightened the sash on her pink kimono, walked to the foot of the stairs, and called, "Coffee's ready! Rise and shine, Delta Girls!"

Groans drifted down in reply. She grinned, skipping up the stairs and down the hall.

April and Missy were in the first guest room. April pulled her pillow over her head as Kerry pounded on the door.

"You can't be serious," muttered Missy, taking her watch from the night stand and looking at it blearily. "It isn't even ten yet."

"Coffee tastes best in the first five minutes after it's brewed," chirped Kerry. "Y'all got about four minutes left. Come on down."

She moved to the next door and pounded on it. "Rise and shine, Ginny!" she hollered. "The sun is out, the birds are singing, the turtles are snapping, and the local boys are flexing with their shirts off."

"Go away," moaned Ginny.

Kerry opened the door and turned on the light. Her college roomie had pulled the blanket over her head, so Kerry sat on the edge of her bed and pulled it back down, revealing a disheveled blonde, squinting in disbelief. Kerry bent over and put her lips near the other girl's ear.

"I will tickle," she whispered.

"No, no, no," protested Ginny weakly.

Kerry held her hand over the sheet, just above Ginny's ribcage. "You have been selected by the Claw," she intoned, and she dug her fingers into Ginny's side.

Ginny shrieked and bent in half. "Stop, stop, I'm up!"

Kerry ceased, and returned to the kitchen.

April was the first one down.

"Good morning, Sunshine," she said to Kerry. "How the hell do you have so much energy after last night? You drank more than any of us."

"Because I'm home, and home is a happy place," said Kerry. "It's a beautiful day in Trion, the most beautiful place in the world, and I am not gonna miss a single minute of enjoying it."

"So, this is where you grew up," said April, staring out the window. "Tell me I didn't just integrate this town."

"Not quite," said Kerry. "There's a few Black families, and lots of Latinos. There's an okay Mexican place if you want to check it out later."

"Coffee?" mewled Missy as she staggered in.

"Would you like a cup?" asked Kerry sweetly.

"Cup's too small," said Missy. "I need one of those things that's bigger than a cup."

"Mug?"

"I was thinking tureen."

"Start with a mug," suggested April. "Refills are free."

"Ginny!" called Kerry. "Won't stay hot forever."

"I will, too," said Ginny as she entered, having managed in a short time to get her hair brushed and her makeup applied.

"How do you do that?" marveled Missy.

"Fast hands."

"That's why all the boys like you," said April.

"So true," sighed Ginny. She poured herself a cup, and raised it in salute. "To the Tri Delts."

"To the Tri Delts!" cried the others, banging their cups together.

Kerry looked around the table happily as the Executive Committee of the Emory U chapter of the Delta Delta Delta sorority dug into their muffins and coffee. Missy, the treasurer from Tennessee, small, White, and brunette, with an anxious demeanor that lent itself well to monitoring their finances; April, the secretary, Georgian like Kerry, but a big city girl from Atlanta, tall and Black, with a set of braids that took half a day to reset; and Ginny, her veep and wing-woman, who came from New York money and whose mom was some high-placed player in the State Department.

Kerry couldn't remember the last time she sat with three happy people at her family table. Not since she was a child eating with her family, before the realities of her parents' marriage surfaced, before she found out about Tom . . .

She shook her head clear of the memories and gaveled her coffee mug on the table. "Okay, first order of business: did we get Senator Castor for the annual dinner?"

"I got a tentative yes," said April. "She put it on her calendar, but it depends on what votes are coming up that week. We should keep a backup speaker just in case."

"Ginny could talk about makeup," said Missy.

"Or Missy could talk about how to mix drinks and not throw up," retorted Ginny.

"Both are good ideas," said Kerry. "Now, there's initiation of the rushes."

"Got any thoughts?" asked April.

"I do," said Kerry. "There's a place I know. Wear your bathing suits and pack the cooler, ladies. We're going out."

"Very mysterious," commented Missy. "I am intrigued."

They loaded the cooler with the three B's—burgers, buns, and beer—then hustled up to change.

Kerry was back down first, wearing cutoffs and an Emory T-shirt over her bikini. She grabbed a set of keys from a rack in the kitchen, then went into the living room. The photos on the mantle over the fireplace caught her eye. She hadn't looked at them since she had come home. She didn't want to, but they drew her toward them anyway.

There they all were. The happiest of families in the nicest of homes. So long ago.

April came up behind her and rested her chin on Kerry's shoulder. "You were a real tomboy, weren't you?" she observed, noting the younger Kerry in her soccer uniform, her brunette hair in pigtails, smiling through her braces. There was a young man in uniform next to her, his arm wrapped affectionately around her shoulders. "Is that your brother?"

"That was him," said Kerry. "Big brother Tom."

"Handsome," said April.

"Sure was," said Kerry. "That was the last time he was home: Thanksgiving, 2009. I was fourteen. It's been seven years. I still miss him like crazy."

"I'm sorry, Sunshine," whispered April, giving her a quick hug.

The other two came in, holding the cooler between them.

"Ready," said Missy.

Kerry led them to the garage where the Jeep awaited them.

"It doesn't have a roof," said Ginny, looking at the Jeep dubiously.

"It does," said Kerry, pointing to where it was hanging on the far wall.

"What if it rains?"

"Then we get wet. Usually happens at 2:30 on the dot."

"Cozumel," sighed Ginny, climbing into the backseat. "Cancun. Could be there right now, a Mai Tai in each hand, making love on a balcony with some muscular boy whose name I would not quite remember. But instead, I come here, where the entertainment will be dancing at the Friday night social with some inbred redneck named Cooter."

"You're not being fair," said Kerry, opening the garage. "Cooter is a wonderful dancer, and I don't think his parents were any closer than third cousins, so that barely counts as inbreeding round these parts."

She kept her face straight for as long as she could hold it while Ginny looked at her in horror, then burst into laughter.

"Let's go, ladies," said Kerry, turning the key. "Adventure awaits."

They drove through town, which took all of a minute.

"What's that over there?" asked April, pointing to some heavy-duty fencing dotted with guard towers.

"State prison," said Kerry.

"Yuck."

"Gotta put 'em somewhere."

"They ever escape?"

"Officially, no," said Kerry, "but you hear things."

"What kind of things?" asked Missy nervously.

"That they escape. But, I never saw one."

"I am so relieved to hear you say that," said Ginny. "So, what's your great plan for initiation?"

"Take 'em to Corpsewood Manor," said Kerry.

"There is no such place."

"There is too, my hand to God."

"What's Corpsewood Manor?" asked April.

"An old ruin in the woods on the ridge," said Kerry in her spookiest voice. "Scene of a dark and horrifying murder thirty-five years ago."

"A murder?" gulped Missy.

"Two murders. Four, if you count the dogs."

"They killed the dogs?" wailed Missy.

"And that's what upsets you?" laughed Ginny. "Who were the people?"

"Some professor type from Chicago and his lover," said Kerry. "They bought forty acres on the ridge and built the place themselves. Called it Corpsewood Manor, which was just asking for trouble."

"If they called it Immortality Acres, would they be alive today?" asked April.

"Probably not," said Kerry. "Story goes, they were homosexuals—"

"Which must have freaked out the locals," said Ginny.

"Never interrupt a scary story," said Kerry sternly. "Anyhow, people didn't bother 'em since they were up in the woods, not ramming headboards in the apartment next door like they do in wicked old Manhattan."

"Hey!" protested Ginny.

"But rumors were, they were also Satanists and served homemade wine spiked with LSD."

"Sounds like one of DU's parties," said April.

"So, some of the local boys would participate in any and all of these alleged activities, and two of them decided to have a little fun. That fun ended up with the local boys killing them."

"How horrible!" exclaimed April.

"But, what about the dogs?" persisted Missy.

"Couple of bull mastiffs," said Kerry. "They shot 'em just to keep 'em quiet. The boys went to prison, and soon after, Corpsewood Manor got looted and burned out. They say it's been haunted ever since."

"That's ridiculous," said Ginny.

"People have seen stuff there, especially at night," said Kerry. "Weird emanations, mists that move against the wind. Giant dogs that walk upright."

"Giant dogs," breathed Missy.

"Sounds like a load of hooey, as my granny would say," laughed April.

"Well, it's a spooky place no matter how you look at it," said Kerry. "You'll see."

"That's where we're going?" asked Missy nervously.

"Oh, no. Right now, I'm taking y'all on a picnic at a swimming hole I know."

"Oh," said Missy, looking relieved.

"I'm taking us to Corpsewood Manor *tonight*. Full moon, should be perfect. You can tell me if it's hooey or not. Feeling brave, ladies?'

"You're on," said April.

"Can't be scarier than New York," said Ginny.

Missy was silent.

They drove on, eventually coming to an intersection. Kerry stopped. "That way's Alabama, that way's Tennessee, and that way's to both Carolinas. This is the crossroads of the universe, right here."

"So impressed right now," yawned Ginny.

Kerry turned right.

"Which Carolina we going to?" asked Missy.

"Neither," said Kerry. "Hold on." She abruptly veered off the paved road into a field of high grass, whooping as the other girls screamed.

"Are you crazy?" shouted Ginny.

"Little bit," said Kerry, and they came through it onto the remnants of a dirt road that hadn't been visible from the main road. They bumped along, then came up to a dilapidated chain link fence, about ten feet high, topped with razor wire. An old sign, weathered and cracked, still hung from it, its faded letters reading, "Cheller Quarry."

"As in Kerry Cheller," said April.

"That's me," said Kerry. "This was the family business for a hundred and fifty years, till Daddy decided to diversify." She pulled up to the gate and turned off the ignition. Grabbing the keys, she got out and went up to the chain keeping it shut.

The padlock was missing.

"Huh," she said, and looked around. She spotted it lying at the base of the fence and picked it up. Someone had clipped it apart.

"What's wrong?" called April.

"Looks like someone broke in," said Kerry. She slid open the gate, then got back behind the wheel.

"Shouldn't you be calling the police?" asked Ginny.

"To do what?" returned Kerry. "I haven't been here in a year, and whoever did this must have done it months ago."

"How do you know that?" asked Missy.

"Look at the road," said Kerry, pointing ahead. "If they needed the gate, they must have been driving something, 'cause there's plenty of holes in the fence you could get through if you were on foot. But, the grass on the road came up undisturbed, so nobody's driven here since winter. And, since it is now June, I figure they're not here anymore."

"Freakin' Sherlock," said April, impressed.

"I don't know," muttered Ginny. "I think you're planning to get us all raped and murdered."

"Yes, that is my plan exactly," said Kerry, and she drove ahead.

The road took them through a forest of oak and hemlock.

"This all belongs to your dad?" asked Missy.

"Until the divorce gets finalized," said Kerry. "Daddy thought he could develop it, make a new suburb, but Mom wants it more. She's thinking about giving it to the Nature Conservancy."

"She's a nature nut?" asked Missy.

"No, she just knows that would piss off Daddy more than anything."

"Where is your mom?" asked April.

"Probably in Cozumel, making love on a balcony with some muscular boy who got tired of waiting for Ginny to show up," said Kerry. "Okay, here we are."

They came out the other side of the forest.

"How lovely!" exclaimed April.

The folding of the quarry business had left a massive hole which, without the giant pumps sucking out the rainwater, had gradually filled up. The surviving granite rose high on two sides, the walls perfectly perpendicular to the surface of the water, a light coating of lichen dotting them at several points.

At the far corner, the runoff spilled into a nearby stream that vanished into the woods.

"Used to be two hundred men working this hole in the ground," said Kerry as she drove down to the far edge. "Almost nobody knows about it anymore. I thought we could take the girls here, picnic, swim, sunbathe, and start telling 'em stories. Then, we take 'em to Corpsewood and scare the hell out of them."

"Sounds like fun," said Ginny.

"Okay, Ginny and Missy, y'all go get us some firewood, and we'll get everything set up here," said Kerry, hauling the cooler out of the back of the Jeep.

"Firewood? Is there some place where they sell it?" asked Ginny.

"Okay, city girl," said Kerry, rolling her eyes. "Those things over there are called trees. They are made of wood, which in its dry, dead state is flammable. Go get some."

"Right, I knew that on some level," said Ginny, heading toward the woods.

"And watch out for poison ivy, poison oak, and poison sumac," said Kerry helpfully.

Ginny stopped dead in her tracks. "Oh, like I know what they look like. Sorry, forgot to take that advanced ethnobotany course this semester."

"Come on, Ginny," said Missy, tugging at Ginny's hand. "I know what they look like."

They headed into the edge of the forest and started searching for fallen branches.

"This is all payback for me teasing her about bringing only two pairs of shoes when she visited New York," grumbled Ginny. "I'm probably gonna get eaten by an alligator or something."

"Gators are on the coast," said Missy. "We're too high up for gators."

"That's one less thing to worry about, then."

"Bears, on the other hand . . ."

"Just shut up now, will you?" snapped Ginny.

"I was just—"

"I mean it," whispered Ginny, motioning for her to be quiet. She was staring intently into the woods.

"What is it?" whispered Missy.

"Thought I heard something," said Ginny, still looking. "Got this feeling something's watching us."

"That's because you're a New York paranoid."

"Kept me alive this long."

"I don't see anything," said Missy. "Let's get back to the others."

They came back to the quarry, where Kerry and April were already in the water.

Missy waved to them, then giggled. "Well, you're both as naked as a pair of jaybirds, aren't you? What if someone sees you?"

"No one around for miles," said Kerry, floating on her back. "Come on in."

"You got a hatchet for the firewood?" asked Missy.

"In the back of the Jeep."

"Okay, I'll get it," said Ginny. She looked in the Jeep and saw it, its blade encased in a leather cover. There was a latched wooden box next to it. Curious, she opened it to see a .45 automatic nestled inside. She closed the lid immediately, then grabbed the hatchet.

"What's with the gun?" she asked, coming back to Missy, who took the hatchet and began chopping the larger pieces of wood down to size.

"In case of rattlesnakes," said Kerry.

"It just keeps getting better, doesn't it?" shuddered Ginny.

"They don't swim," said April. "Come on in."

"Any other predators I need to know about?" asked Ginny as she stripped off her clothes. "Snapping turtles?"

"Not a chance," said Kerry.

"Why not?"

"It's a quarry pond. There's no fish for them to eat."

"You convinced me," said Ginny, before she kicked off her bikini bottom and dove in. After she came up for air, she shrieked, "Cold!"

"You'll get used to it," said Kerry, then she ducked as Missy cannonballed over her.

Once they were done swimming, Kerry got a fire going in a ring of stones while the others sunbathed.

"These are organic burgers, aren't they?" asked Ginny.

"Um, sure," said Kerry as Missy hid a smile.

They dug in with an appetite

"How deep is it?" asked April, sipping on her beer and looking out over the pond.

"Pretty deep," said Kerry. "We used to jump off that ledge over there and not hit bottom."

"You jumped off that," said Ginny, shaking her head in amazement. "That has to be forty feet up."

"About that," said Kerry. "I was nine and fearless the first time, my big brother cheering me on."

"I could never do that," said Ginny.

"I could," said Missy, knocking back her third beer.

"No way."

"Twenty bucks says I will," she said defiantly.

"You're on," said Ginny.

"Okay, here I go," said Missy.

She had to scramble up a tumble of rocks to get to the ledge. The other girls stood and cheered as she inched carefully forward until she was at the edge. She took a deep breath, then gathered herself and jumped before she could change her mind. She squealed, pinwheeling her arms on the way down, and sent a plume of water shooting up around her as she disappeared feet first below the surface.

"Not exactly a rip, was it?" commented Ginny.

Missy resurfaced, spluttering and choking.

"What's going on?" asked April.

"Something's wrong," said Ginny, but Kerry was already diving in.

She kicked hard to the middle of the pond where Missy was floundering, her face contorted in pain.

"What's happened?" asked Kerry as she grabbed her.

"I thought you said it was deep enough," gasped Missy.

"It is—I know it is. What happened?"

"I hit something down there. Something metal."

The other two girls swam up.

"Are you all right?" asked Ginny.

"I hurt my ankle," said Missy, "and you owe me twenty bucks."

"Help her back," said Kerry. "I want to check this out."

She swam to the spot where Missy first hit the water and peered down. There was something large and black resting on the floor of the pond.

"I can't believe this," she called back to the others. "Someone dumped a van here. That's disgusting."

"Maybe you can get someone to haul it out," said Ginny.

"Hell," muttered Kerry. "I'm gonna take a look."

"Wait!" called April, but Kerry took a deep breath and dove down.

It was a cargo van of some kind.

Looks pretty new, she thought. *Wonder why anyone wanted to get rid of it.* She swam down further, saw that the front windows were both open. *Helped to sink it quicker.*

The water was still pretty clear at this depth, and the sun high overhead gave her enough light so she could peer right into the passenger window.

And the man in the passenger seat looked right back at her, except he had no eyes left. Just the dark holes where they used to be in the unnaturally white chunks of flesh that were still clinging to the skull.

She managed to hold the screams back until she broke the surface.

CHAPTER 2

S ALLY SPINELLI SPED ALONG the road, her legs churning the pedals as hard as they could. She was wearing faded, hand-me-down, blue denim overalls over a Georgia Tech T-shirt that was way too big. With her hair cropped short for the summer, she was frequently mistaken for a boy—something she didn't mind at this point in her life. Things were going to change, she knew. Her mother had sat down and given her "The Talk," as she called it, with a dark, ominous look that Sally knew was a put-on. Her body was going to change, her moods were going to change, she might even find that boys were good for other things than sports and video games.

Although, her mother had conceded, they were still pretty useless overall.

Sally wasn't sure she wanted to change just yet. She liked herself the way she was. She liked her friends, male and female, without the complications. Maybe she would like boys in a different way someday. But in the meantime, there was something she liked—no, loved—more than boys, more than college football, more than Christmas, maybe even more than her family.

Sally loved dogs.

Waldo had arrived last Christmas, a young Doberman Pinscher that her Dad had bought at Sam Lehrmann's place. Waldo was a guard dog, but Sam trained his guard dogs to be family dogs as well. Before he even let them take Waldo home, the entire family had to train with the dog for a month. Sandy, her little brother, was scared of him at first, but Sandy was scared of everything.

Sally was scared of nothing.

Her visits to Sam's continued after the dog had become part of her family. She constantly pestered Sam with questions about the different types of dogs, what they were used for, where they were first bred. Sam, a good-natured man who knew everything about them, indulged her, and she, in turn, knew when to be quiet if he had a customer or was in the middle of training. She began helping him on Saturdays, which was bath day for the animals. Her parents, after sitting through a couple of these messy sessions, decided that there was no safer place to entrust their daughter. They would drop her off in the morning and take Sandy downtown for his lessons, then return in the afternoon to collect their soapy, sodden, and completely exhilarated older child.

So, when school ended, she asked Sam if she could help part-time on a daily basis. He conferred with her parents, who agreed, relieved that she would be earning some money rather than costing them another summer camp tuition.

"Are you sure you don't have a crush on Sam?" teased her mother. "He's kind of handsome."

"Don't be silly, Mom," she said, wrapping her arms around Waldo. "I love Waldo, and only Waldo."

The Doberman thumped his tail on the floor in agreement.

It was about ten thirty when she turned into the driveway to Lehrmann's Dogs, at the converted warehouse where he raised and trained them. She kicked her right leg back over the seat while still moving, and coasted the last thirty feet standing on the left pedal, jumping to a run at the last second.

The dachshund at the end of the row of cages barked a greeting.

"Hi, Arnie," she said, waving.

"Hey, Sally, what about me?" called Sam from the pit, a hurt look on his face.

"Arnie noticed me first," said Sally, wheeling her bike over to the office, letting the air conditioning flow over her.

"You bike all the way in this heat?" asked Sam.

"Yessir," said Sally.

"Then there's a big old Cherry Coke with your name on it in the ice box," said Sam. "Don't even think about doing a lick of work until you drink it."

"Yessir!" she said happily, then went into the walk-in refrigerator.

There were two sides of beef hanging on hooks, something that had unnerved her the first time she worked there. But, that was what Sam fed his dogs, and if that was what made them happy, she felt she could make the adjustment. She pulled a Cherry Coke from the case by the wall, dropped her lunchbox by it, and closed the door carefully behind her. She stuck the bottle in the metal opener bolted on the wall, then flipped the cap off and brought it to her mouth in one fluid motion before it fizzed, just like Sam always did.

"Coke tastes better in the summer," she said. She walked back into the main room and rested her elbows on the top of the padded wall encircling the pit.

"I always thought so," said Sam. "Used to ride my bike down to the soda fountain, get a Cherry Coke fresh made and drink it at the counter. Sipped it slow so it would last forever, but it never did."

"Where'd you grow up?" she asked.

"North Carolina. Small town like this one, up in the mountains."

"Was it nice?"

"It was all right," Sam said shortly. "Pretty boring."

"Sounds like here."

"Yeah, only I like boring now."

"How can you like boring?" asked Sally.

"Boring is something you come to appreciate when you get older," said Sam.

"You're not boring," said Sally. "You got the best job in the world. You get to work with dogs all day."

"That is a compensating factor," said Sam. "Well, let's put you to work at this best job in the world. Take Arnie and the Russells out to the pen and put them through their paces."

Arnie, hearing his name, jumped up and down and barked.

"Calm down, Arnie," said Sally, getting the leads.

"Not what you say, Sally," called Sam.

"Right, sorry," said Sally, holding her hand out, palm down. "Arnie, sit." Arnie sat.

"Good boy, Arnie."

She opened his cage and attached the lead, then led him out. She looped the end of the lead around a hook, then turned her attention to three Jack Russells who sat together, looking at her expectantly.

"Roz, sit. Jane, sit. Nipsy, sit," she said, even though they were already sitting. She leashed them, grabbed Arnie's lead, and said, "Dogs, heel."

They followed her obediently, and she opened the door to the outdoor pen. Once it was closed, she jogged with them once around the perimeter, then unhooked the leashes.

"Dogs, perimeter," she commanded.

The three Jack Russells immediately scooted to the fence and began trotting around it. Arnie took his time.

"Step it up, Arnie," said Sally.

But it's hot.

"I don't care if it's hot," said Sally crossly. "You have to . . ."

She stopped.

Arnie glanced at her, then trotted to the fence and followed the Jack Russells.

"Weird," muttered Sally. She took them through more basic commands, but that was that. After treating them to some cold water—which they lapped up eagerly—she then took them back inside.

Sam was working with Bert and Nan, a pair of Dobermans in the indoor pen. She leaned on the rail and watched.

"Sam, can dogs hear our thoughts?" she asked.

He took the question seriously, one of the things she liked about him. "I don't know of anything anyone's ever done scientifically to prove that—and I've read up on it, believe me. But, it wouldn't surprise me if it was true. Of course, it also might be that dogs are just good readers of our body language and expressions. They evolved in close proximity to us, so it might be a developed trait. You know what evolution is, right?"

"Sure."

"I'm not teaching you anything your folks wouldn't want you to know, am I?" he asked, grinning. "My old man refused to believe in evolution to his dying day."

"Your daddy's dead?" she exclaimed in dismay.

"Afraid so," said Sam. "Smoking got him young."

"I'm sorry."

"Happens. What put that into your head, by the way?"

"Nothing, really," said Sally. "It's just that sometimes I think Waldo knows what I'm thinking. And, there was that time on Christmas Eve—"

Waldo became agitated and strained against the leash, nearly pulling Sally off her feet.

"Waldo, come!" she said.

He looked at her resentfully.

"What's wrong?" she asked.

He whined.

Sally squatted to look into his eyes. She studied them for a long time, then reached down to unclip his leash. "All right, but you have to come back soon."

"—I thought he was trying to tell me something."

"Now, when you can hear the dogs talk, that's when they call you crazy," laughed Sam.

"Yeah, I suppose," she said. "What should I do now?"

"Take the shepherds, same thing."

"Okay."

Sam watched as she led them outside. Sally, the Alpha Girl.

Boss? called the dachshund.

Yeah, Arnie? he replied.

I think she heard me. For a moment, she actually heard me.

Did she? Interesting, said Sam.

Sheriff Boudreau drove his Jeep carefully down the road to the quarry, mindful of its suspension. Two police cars, an emergency services van, and an ambulance were already there, a paramedic carefully examining the swelling ankle of a petite, young woman while three others stood around her. They were all wearing bikini tops and cutoffs, he noted with approval. He parked and got out.

"Which one of you is the Cheller girl?" he asked.

"That's me, Sheriff," said one with a brunette pony tail. "I'm Kerry."

He looked at her. "You grew up nice. Last time I saw you, you were just a spit of a girl."

"Thanks," said Kerry. "These are my sorority sisters from Emory: Ginny, April, and Missy. Missy's the one on the ground."

"How do, ladies," said Boudreau. "I'm Sheriff Boudreau, Chattooga County Police. What's the damage on Missy?"

"Ankle looks broken, Sheriff," said the paramedic. "Gonna have to take her to County."

"Shoot," said Missy. "I'm gonna miss all the fun."

"Who saw the body?" asked Boudreau.

"I did," said Kerry.

"Wilkins, you got your gear?" called Boudreau.

"Gettin' it now, Sheriff," said one of the troopers, pulling scuba gear out of the rear of the van. He removed his hat, then peeled off his shirt, attracting the immediate attention of the girls.

"Wilkins, you want for me to put on some music?" asked Boudreau. "The ladies here might have some singles they could stuff down your pants."

"Sorry about that," said Wilkins. He hauled his gear behind the van and continued changing.

"No apologies necessary," called Ginny.

"Now, Miss Cheller, I need you to answer some questions for me," said Boudreau.

"All right," said Kerry.

"This is still your family property?"

"Yessir."

"When's the last time you were down here?"

"Would have been end of last August, right before classes started."

"And who else would be coming down here?"

"Basically nobody but us since the business closed down, and that was years ago," she said. "We had the padlock keys at the house, but the padlock was busted when we got here this morning."

"Which way is the van pointing?"

She turned and looked at the water.

"To the right," she said. "The man was in the passenger seat. Had his seat belt on."

"Didn't save him," said Boudreau. He looked at the pond, then up at the quarry wall rising to his left. "Danny, take Jared and check up there. Van must have gone off that side to land where it did."

"Right, Sheriff," said a trooper. He and another got into one of the police cars and drove off.

"Sheriff, Doc Oliveras is on her way," said Wilkins, emerging wearing a wet suit and scuba gear, holding a mask and a camera. "She said we shouldn't touch anything."

"Then don't touch anything," said Boudreau, "but go down there and get a look. That thing work underwater?"

"The camera? Sure does."

Boudreau looked back at Kerry. "Y'all were skinny dipping, weren'tcha?" he asked.

"How'd you know?" asked Kerry, blushing.

"Your suit's dry, but your hair's still wet," he said.

"This is private property," she said. "We weren't breaking any law."

"Nope," he said. "Just showing off my detective skills. Where's that padlock?"

"Back by the gate," she said. "Must have been broken back last fall or winter."

"How do you figure?"

She explained the condition of the grass.

"Makes sense," he said, nodding. "That helps. Good to narrow down the time frame in a murder investigation."

"Murder?" gasped April. "Why murder? Could have been an accident, a drunk driver, or a suicide or something."

"You said this feller was in the passenger seat," said Boudreau.

Kerry nodded.

"See a driver?" asked Boudreau.

She shook her head.

"Murder," he pronounced with satisfaction.

"Why are you so happy about that?" asked Kerry.

"Something to do, ain't it?" beamed Boudreau. He turned back to Wilkins, who was wrestling with an inflatable boat from a storage space at the top of the van—wrestling and losing.

"Do you need help with that, Wilkins?" he asked.

Wilkins nodded.

Boudreau walked over, reached up with one hand, and flipped open the metal fastener that kept the boat safely stowed inside. "Should be a mite easier now," he observed.

"Thanks, Sheriff," said Wilkins, sliding the boat out. He hauled it to the water, where he, Boudreau, and another officer got in.

"Don't bother with the motor," said Boudreau, grabbing a yellow oar.

They paddled out to the spot Kerry had pointed out and peered over the edge. The van was dimly visible through the murky waters.

"Take a look see," said Boudreau. "Get a plate number. VIN, too, if you can read it off the dash."

"Right," said Wilkins. He fixed his mask and mouthpiece, picked up the camera, then tumbled backwards into the water and disappeared.

"He remembered to turn on his air, didn't he?" asked Boudreau.

"Think so," said the other trooper.

"Well, I guess he'll figure it out soon enough if he didn't," sighed Boudreau.

Wilkins was under for five minutes, then surfaced in a flurry of bubbles. He handed the camera up to Boudreau, then held out his hand and was hauled back up to the boat.

"Got the plate and the VIN," he said.

"Good," said Boudreau. "How about the body?"

"Right where she said he was," said Wilkins. "Here's the thing. He ain't alone."

"What?"

"There's more floating in the back. I could see them through the windshield. No other windows, though."

"How many?"

"Three, I think, but it's hard to tell exactly."

"How come?"

"Well, there's some assembly required," said Wilkins, grinning weakly. Then, he leaned over the side of the boat and vomited.

"You might have waited to do that back on land," said Boudreau sternly. "Especially since I will be sending you back down there once the ME arrives."

"It floats," said Wilkins. "I can get around it. Won't be the least pleasant thing I'll be doing today, looks like."

"Looks like," agreed Boudreau.

"Don't say nothing about it in front of the girls."

"You're an idiot," said Boudreau. "They been watching us the whole time. Might want to use some mouthwash 'fore you get too close. Okay, let's go back and run those numbers. Give us something to do until the doc shows."

They paddled back.

"Did you see him?" called Kerry.

"Yup," said Wilkins.

"And here's the interesting thing," added Boudreau. "He has some friends with him."

"There's more?" asked Kerry.

"Yup."

"Drug runners," said April. "Gotta be."

"Thinking along those lines myself, but until we get that van out of there, won't be able to say for sure." said Boudreau. He looked at the ESU truck. "That winch strong enough to pull the van out of there?"

"Doubt it," said Wilkins. "No real slope on the edges 'cause of it's being a quarry and all. Too steep."

"There should be a ramp over yonder," said Kerry, pointing to the right. "They used to get trucks down there."

"So it's just a question of maneuvering it into the right spot," said Boudreau. "Think you can manage that? Otherwise, I'm gonna have to call in for some heavy equipment."

"We can try," said Wilkins.

"All I ask," said Boudreau. "Let's run that plate."

A small group of officers gathered around the remaining squad car while Boudreau punched the plate number into the computer.

"Plate was stolen," he said. "Reported in Savannah, December 22nd. So that gives us a back end. Gimme that VIN number."

He typed that in and waited—and waited some more.

"I'm getting no response," he said. "What the hell?"

He retyped it. Same result.

"Show me that camera," he said.

Wilkins thumbed the toggle on the back until the image of the VIN on the dash popped up.

"Number's right," said Boudreau.

"Must be using a fake VIN," said Wilkins.

"That the case, I'd still be getting that from the computer," said Boudreau. "Well, gonna have to check the one on the engine block, see if it matches up. Until then—good, there's the doc coming with the meat wagon."

Oliveras, the medical examiner, drove her truck down the road and parked it by the others, then hopped down to the ground. She was a short, stocky woman with jet-black hair and a tan that she worked on every moment she wasn't required to be cooped up in a lab. She was wearing jeans and a faded plaid cotton shirt.

"Hey, Sheriff," she called. "Did I miss seeing Wilkins with his shirt off?"

"You did," said Boudreau.

"It was something," called Ginny.

"Well, probably get to see it again later," said Oliveras, unbuttoning her shirt.

"Now, Doc," began Boudreau.

She reached both hands to the front of the shirt and pulled it open to reveal the wetsuit underneath. "What exactly were you expecting?" she asked.

"Pretty sure I'm not allowed to say," said Boudreau. "What the hell you doing?"

"Got to see the scene of the crime, don't I?" Oliveras said, hauling scuba gear out of the truck. "Lucky you got the only underwater certified ME in the state of Georgia."

She finished suiting up, then hauled a body bag out.

"Forgot to tell you," said Boudreau. "There's three more of 'em, give or take."

"Well, crap," she said. "Gonna be an all-nighter."

She grabbed three more body bags, then joined Wilkins and another officer in the boat. The two men paddled out to the spot while she leaned out over the bow, watching for anything.

"Sorry about the floating vomit," said Wilkins. "That was me."

"Just go around the other side of it, would you?" directed Oliveras. "Where in the van is everyone?"

"One in the passenger seat, three in the back."

"Fine. I want to get pictures, then we take the passenger out first. I'm gonna need some water samples, and we need to bag them down there and seal them up tight. Can you handle that without losing your lunch again, Wilkins?"

"That lunch is history," said Wilkins. "It'll be breakfast next."

"Just don't faint on me," she said, tossing him some latex gloves.

"Do my best," he said, putting them on.

They went under. Wilkins turned his lamp on, and they kicked down to the van. Oliveras uncapped a plastic flask and let it fill, then recapped it and put it in a pouch at her waist. Then, she went to look at the passenger.

His head lolled about slowly as she displaced the water around him. *Definitely male,* she thought as she took a few shots. *Fair amount of flesh on him, although adipocere formation has claimed it, giving it a grayish white appearance. Eyes, nose, lips, ears—all gone.* She took a shot of his head. Some marks were present on the right side of the neck. She zoomed in.

Looks like it was torn away, she thought.

The windows were open. She reached for the door handle and pulled it up carefully. Fortunately, the door wasn't locked. She opened it slowly, trying not to disturb the corpse with the motion.

He was wearing a thick, black sweater and jeans—or at least the remains of them. Sturdy, black leather boots, still intact. There were holes in multiple places in the clothes. *Natural decay underwater? No,* she thought. They looked like tears, and several were large enough that she had a good view of his torso. Actually, a good view of the ribs underneath. *Entry gained to the interior,* she noted. *Gonna be a royal mess inside.*

She took more pictures, then slowly lifted the sweater, trying not to peel the flesh off with it. There was an odd set of marks on his side. She braced herself inside the door frame to steady the camera and got a close-up. Then, she gestured to Wilkins to hand her the body bag.

They had to cut through the seatbelt to free him. She carefully maneuvered him into the bag, trying her damnedest not to shake anything loose. Despite her best efforts, one arm detached slightly, but was held in place by the remains of the sweater.

Wilkins' complexion was taking on much the same color as the corpse's, she noticed. She gave him a questioning look, and he gave her a thumbs up in reply. She didn't believe it for a second.

She was about to seal the bag when something caught her eye. She lifted one of his feet and examined the boot, then took another picture. She sealed the bag, and the two of them floated back up to the surface with it.

"Everything okay?" asked the officer in the boat.

"Despite my best efforts, I was unable to save him," she said solemnly. "Take him back to the wagon, tell Ernie make sure the seals are tight and the fridge is on full blast. We're going back down."

"How do you wanna get them?" asked Wilkins. "Open up the back?"

"And let everything float out of there? I don't think so," she said. "We'll go through the front. Don't worry about matching up everything, we'll just get all the loose pieces and sort 'em out later."

"We meaning you," said Wilkins. "Okay, let's do this."

They dove back down. Oliveras, who was smaller than Wilkins, motioned for him to stay at the van door. She maneuvered her way into the van with difficulty, her air tank banging into the door frames. She shined her light into the rear. Another eyeless man floated in front of her—armless, too. She took a few pictures, then reached forward and grabbed his belt. She brought him forward carefully, tilting him sideways and passing him on to Wilkins, who was doing better.

He took the body and slid it into the bag like he did this every day of his life.

She went back in, filled another flask, and looked around. There were the remains of several arms rising and falling as she came in, as well as one fairly intact body and one that was mostly torso. She spotted the head in the corner. She looked around to see what else was in there, and got her first surprise of the day.

The van was filled with electronic equipment. Computers, microphones, monitors, and speakers—and there were guns scattered on the floor.

Not drug dealers, she thought with a pang of dismay. *More like the guys who watch the drug dealers.* She looked around in case any wallets or IDs were loose, but saw nothing. That would be for the police, not her, she decided.

She moved the pieces out in order of size. Wilkins kept shoving them into the body bags, sealing them as they became full. She counted hands to make sure that they were all accounted for, then went back into the van to make one more sweep. Something glittered in the corner where the head had been. She picked it up and held it under the light.

A dog tag. Gunked up so she couldn't read the name, but Army all the way.

She stuffed it in her pouch, then came out of the van, closing the door behind her. Wilkins had the three body bags clipped together. She checked the seals, then gave him a thumbs up. They surfaced, dragging their gruesome cargo between them.

Arnie looked up from his cage and barked a greeting. Sally glanced out the front windows to see Mona's Prius pulling into the parking lot.

"Mona's here, Sam!" she called.

"Thanks," Sam said from the office. "Be right out."

Mona Havelka came through the front door with Nicky, her Rottweiler, trotting after her. Mona and Sam were in the on again cycle of their relationship, having reunited during the previous Christmas Eve. Mona was a computer consultant who worked out of her home in town, Nicky guarding the threshold against the rest of the world. Being a slender brunette with skin as pale as a full moon in winter was not an easy thing to maintain in the Georgia summer sun. She favored expensive clothes and blood-red nail polish to match the rubies she wore on her ears and at her throat.

Mona was sober, noticed Sally, but it was still early in the day.

"Hi, Nicky," said Sally. "Hi, Mona."

Mona looked at the girl, a touch of irritation on her face. "You know, Short Stuff, when you get out into polite society, you're gonna have to learn to greet the humans before the dogs," she said.

"Then I don't want to be in polite society," said Sally.

"Now, that's what I call a plan," said Sam, emerging from the office. "Hey."

"Hey, yourself," said Mona, smiling as he kissed her.

"Yuck," muttered Sally.

"Something else you're gonna learn someday," said Mona as she broke free.

"No rush," said Sally.

"And on that note, time for you to skedaddle on home," said Sam.

"So you can kiss her some more?"

"Yes."

"Now, that's what I call a plan," said Mona.

"And still yuck," said Sally. She walked down the line of cages as the dogs came up to sniff her good-bye. "Bye, Arnie. Bye, Jane. Bye, Nipsy . . ."

She continued down the line until she had named then all, then turned to the two humans and the Rottweiler. "Bye, Nicky," she said, grinning mischievously. Then, she left.

"That little . . ." began Mona.

Sally stuck her head in the door. "Oh, bye, Mona and Sam. See y'all tomorrow."

"See you, kid," said Sam. "Thanks for the help."

Sally closed the door. A moment later, they saw her peddling her bike down the farm road.

"Now, where were we?" said Mona. She wrapped her arms around him and kissed him more thoroughly.

"Right about there." he said.

"You smell like dog."

"Hazard of the profession, ma'am," he said. "Hi, Nicky."

In polite society, it is customary to greet the dog first, said Nicky.

In your society, you sniff each other's butts, replied Sam.

What's your point? said Nicky. *And what's wrong with smelling like dog?*

Sam grinned, and hit a button on the wall. The doors to the cages opened.

"Playtime!" he called.

The dogs bounded into the pit, racing and tumbling over each other. A few came over to Mona and Nicky to sniff or nuzzle a greeting. Arnie galloped up, then growled and bared his teeth menacingly as only a dachshund could.

"That was very good, Arnie," said Mona, petting him on the head.

Yeah, said Nicky. *Keep it up and you might actually scare a small animal. Someday.*

Screw you, said Arnie.

You'll need a ladder, said Nicky, looking down at him.

"Cut it out, you two," ordered Sam. "Go play with the others."

The two dogs trotted away.

"Who was teasing who?" asked Mona.

"They both got their digs in," said Sam.

"Arnie's not given up on being a watch dog yet?"

"Still hoping."

"He'd make a good pet for someone," said Mona, watching the dogs romp around.

"He's not a pet," said Sam. "He's a guardian. A warrior, tiny but fierce."

"You're very loyal," said Mona. "Can I help with anything right now?"

"You want to clean the cages or cut up the meat?"

"Let me rephrase that," she amended herself quickly. "Can I whip up some dinner while you clean the cages and cut up the meat?"

He looked at his watch. Ninety minutes. "That'd be nice," he said.

Ernie, Oliveras' assistant, and one of the troopers trundled with the body bags to the truck. Wilkins went to change out of sight of the others, to the evident disappointment of the girls. Oliveras came over to Boudreau.

"Sheriff, you may have a bigger case than you thought," she said quietly.

"More than four bodies in there?" he asked.

"Far as I can tell, there were not quite four bodies in there," she said, "but that's not what I'm talking about."

"What then?"

"Van was loaded with electronics in back," she said. "Looked like surveillance equipment, top of the line, state of the art. Not my field of expertise, but drug dealers don't carry that stuff."

"Ah, shit," he muttered. "Feds. Find any ID?"

"Didn't see any wallets, and I still have to check the clothes, but I found this." She handed him the dog tag.

He held it up to the light. "Army. Can't make out the name, but we should be able to dig it out. That on one of them?"

"Not exactly," she said, "but I'm guessing it used to be. It was near a head."

"Any preliminary guesses on what killed them?"

"Take a look at this," she said, thumbing through the pictures on her camera screen.

He winced as he saw the carnage slideshow.

She stopped at the boot from the passenger and magnified the image. "Look at the marks."

There were two lines of punctures, almost parallel to each other.

"And here," she said, showing him the marks on the side of the body. "Same pattern."

"Teeth?" he guessed.

"That's what I think."

"You saying he was bitten by his killer? We got a guy running around biting people to death?"

"Ain't human. Human bitemarks leave a semicircular pattern. See?"

She bared her own teeth, then snapped at him suddenly. He flinched, and she grinned.

"Animal, then," he said. "What kind?"

"Looks canine to me."

"Can you tell what kind?"

"Not an expert on that, either," she said. "Gonna have to get one."

"Know anyone?"

"Not in Georgia. I'll have to check."

"Shoot, that's gonna lose us time," he said. "Hey, Cotter?"

"Yessir?" replied one of the troopers.

"Who's that feller we get our dogs from?"

"Sam, something—Lehrmann, Sam Lehrmann. He's got a place over in Dalton."

"Maybe he can take a look for us first," said Boudreau.

"Sam Lehrmann?" said Kerry, looking puzzled. "I know that name."

"You own a dog, Ms. Cheller?" asked Boudreau.

"Not in years," she said, "but I know him."

"Tom!" she cried, sliding down the bannister and bounding into his arms. He swept her up and swung her around.

"Hey, sis," said Tom. "Look at you, getting all grown up. Damn, I have missed you more than anything in the world. Hey—I want you to meet my bud."

She looked over his shoulder to see another young man in uniform standing in the doorway, a duffle bag slung over his shoulder. He smiled at her, and her heart nearly stopped.

"This is Sam Lehrmann," said Tom, letting her slide gently down, her knees going a little wobbly when her feet hit the floor. "He was in Basic with me. He's gonna stay with us for a week."

"How do you do, Kerry?" said Sam.

"Oh, my goodness, Tom," whispered Kerry. "If that's what you brought me for Thanksgiving, then I can't wait for Christmas!"

"He knew my brother," said Kerry. "He was in the Army with him in Afghanistan. Came for a visit when they were on leave, Thanksgiving, 2009. I didn't know he was in Georgia."

"When's the last time you heard from him?"

"Right after we lost Tom," she said. "December 28, 2009. We got a sympathy card from Sam a week later. Haven't heard from him since."

"Well, I need to know about these bitemarks," said Boudreau. "I'll run over there in the a.m."

"Sheriff?" called Cotter. "There are some reporters up at the front gate. Local news. They want to know what's up."

"Tell 'em I'll give a statement soon," said Boudreau. "Meantime, you boys figure out a way to get that van out of there pronto."

"You authorizing overtime?" asked Cotter.

"If I can't justify overtime for a quadruple homicide, then no point in being me, is there?" said Boudreau. "But, don't abuse it."

"Yessir!" said the troopers happily.

Sam put the last set of bowls in the cages, then whistled.

"Dinner!" he called, and the dogs scampered back to the cages. "Hey, Nicky! You don't live here anymore."

Nicky came out of a cage looking embarrassed. *Sorry, Boss. My old training kicked in.*

There were barks of derision from the other dogs.

Mona leaned out of the office doorway.

"Dinner," she said.

"Woof," said Sam. He closed the cages and followed Nicky in.

She had take-out fried chicken warmed up in the microwave, paper plates and a couple of cold beers laid out on his desk. Sam put an extra dinner bowl on the floor for Nicky, then glanced at the clock. Thirty minutes.

"You nervous?" he asked.

She took a long swallow from her bottle. "Yes, but this is helping. You nervous?"

"'Course I'm nervous," he said. "You seeing me like this."

"I've seen you after."

"Yeah, but the change itself—not easy to accept."

She reached across the desk and held his hand. "Nothing worth doing is ever easy, Sam. I'm glad you're letting me see it."

A German shepherd wandered in, nuzzled Nicky who responded in kind, then began eating.

"Hi, Carson," said Mona.

The dog nodded at her—somewhat curtly, she thought.

"He doesn't approve," she observed.

"He's a creature of routine," said Sam.

"And this is a break in the routine."

A big one, said Carson.

She earned it, replied Sam. *She has a right to be here.*

So you've said, responded Carson. He finished eating quickly and began his patrol around the building.

"I'm going to check the doors," said Sam. "Then I'll be ready."

"Okay," said Mona. "I'm going to drink more beer. Then, I'll be ready."

Sam checked the locks, then the security system. He passed Carson twice, but the dog paid him no mind. Sam checked his watch. Ten minutes. He returned to Mona.

"Here we go," he said. He started unbuttoning his shirt.

"I'm liking it already," she said, leaning back in her chair and idly swirling the beer around in its bottle.

He hung the shirt on a hook, then kicked his boots off. He unbuckled his belt, then gave her a quick, shy grin. "Not used to you watching like that."

"Get 'em off, soldier," she said. "Drop trou."

"Sir, yessir," he said, and pulled his jeans and boxers off in one swift motion. He hung up the jeans, then tossed the boxers over to her.

She caught them and twirled them around her finger. "Smells like a sweaty man in here. Much better than dog."

"Okay, follow me."

There was a large cage set apart from the rest, empty except for a beat up leather easy chair. There was a large screen blocking the cage from the view of the dogs, a recent addition. Sam stepped inside, then pulled the door shut. A minute later, an electronic lock clicked into place. Carson trotted by to inspect it.

"All good, buddy," said Sam to the dog.

Carson trotted away.

"A naked hunk in a cage," said Mona. "Best zoo ever."

"Don't tease the animal," said Sam, sitting cross-legged in front of the chair.

He glanced at the clock. Three minutes. He had cut it close this time. Careless, getting distracted like that. He took a deep breath, let it out, then repeated.

"Om," he chanted.

She watched in fascination. He had never allowed her to see him change before. She had seen him afterwards, starting with that wonderful, terrible Christmas Eve . . .

"Om."

. . .when she found him lying on his storeroom floor, nearly dead of aconite poisoning, the dogs running around loose, fearful, frantic, not knowing how to help him . . .

"Om."

The night that she learned that he was a werewolf—and the night she chose to save him.

"Om."

Outside, the sun dipped below the horizon.

"Om."

His voice grew hoarse. The muscles around his chest rippled and swelled.

"Om."

Crackling noises came from the cage. She drew in her breath sharply as the hair sprouted from every inch of his skin. His arms—they actually grew longer. His shoulders expanded, his chest becoming massive.

"Om," he chanted, his eyes closed.

Claws thrust out of his fingers and toes. His jaw jutted forward, the lips stretching around the fangs forcing their way between the human teeth. From the other cages, some of the younger dogs whined fearfully, running in circles. Arnie yawned.

"Om," Sam whispered one last time, then he opened his eyes and rose.

A werewolf stood inside the cage, its gray fur shimmering in the moonlight streaming through the windows, looking at her with Sam's eyes.

"Does it hurt?" she whispered.

"Yes."

"Do you get used to it?"

"Never," he said. "Will you?"

She stepped up to the cage in response and pressed her hand against the mesh. "You're still Sam. Underneath it all, you're still Sam."

"Still Sam," he echoed, placing a massive paw against the inside of the mesh opposite hers, "but not underneath. It's not something I put on. It's what I am, all the time and especially now. Can you accept that?"

"I did from the moment I first found out," she said. "How long until the lock opens?"

"I have it on half an hour."

"Why do you lock yourself in at all? I thought you had it under control."

"It's never entirely under control."

"When's the last time you lost it?" she asked.

"Years ago," he said, "but I don't want to risk it happening again. It also takes a while for my eyes to adjust to artificial light. I have night vision as a werewolf."

"Do you weigh more?" she asked, suddenly wanting to know all the little things.

"Never thought about it," he said. "Probably. I'm bigger."

She looked him up and down. "You sure are," she said, grinning. She unbuttoned her blouse.

"What are you doing?" he asked.

"Getting ready for playtime," she replied, slipping off the blouse.

"I don't think that's such a good idea," he said, watching as her skirt slid down around her feet.

"Part of you thinks it's a very good idea."

"That ain't the part that's good at thinking," he said. "You really want to make love to me when I'm like this?"

"I want to try," she said, unhooking her bra and dropping it to the ground. *Ugh, she's so hairless.*

"You might want to come closer to the cage," said Sam.

"Why? The better to see me, grandma?"

"I ain't the only one getting the free show right now."

She glanced at the other cages, stuck out her tongue, then stepped up so that the screen hid her from view.

Thank you, called Arnie. *Some of us are trying to get some sleep here.*

"Will they hear you?" she asked.

"Only when I speak their language," he said, "but they can sense me, even when I don't speak."

"How long is their range?"

"About a quarter-mile during the day, more at night, and really far when the moon is full."

"Maybe we could go someplace where they can't reach you," she said, sliding off her panties.

"Let's see, you're naked, I'm a werewolf," he said. "How we gonna explain that to the cops when they pull us over?"

"If I'm naked, they sure as hell won't be looking at you," she whispered.

It's not like we want to hear this, complained Jane.

Yeah, right. Like we ever get any, muttered Elsie.

You should talk. What about you and Ignatz the other night?

Shut up! You weren't supposed to tell him about that!

All of you shut up, said Sam. *Next one to talk gets spayed.*

There was silence.

"Sure got quiet all of a sudden," observed Mona. "That must have been some threat. What do we do now?"

He glanced at the timer. "We wait."

An eternity later, the timer chimed. The gate unlocked. Mona grabbed it and pulled it open.

"Your office?" she asked.

"Sure as hell ain't doing it out here," said Sam, stepping out of the cage.

She stepped into his embrace. "Your fur's so soft. That's a nice perk."

"Good thing," said Sam. "Cause there ain't enough conditioner in the world otherwise. You keeping those sneakers on?"

"When did you mop these floors last?"

"Umm, not sure."

"Keeping them on, sir," she said, leading him into the office. "Now, stating the obvious: No biting, no clawing."

"Yes'm," he said. "How about this?"

"Oh! That tickles."

"How about that?"

"No, that doesn't tickle at all. Mm, do that some more. Do that a lot."

Carson paused outside the office door, listened for a moment, shook his head in disgust and continued his rounds.

She curled up in the crook of his arm on the couch after. "You were holding back."

"I didn't want to hurt you."

"Have you ever done it with a human when you were like this?"

"Never. Apparently, I've been missing out."

"Ever done it with another werewolf?"

"That, I have," he grunted.

"Bet you didn't hold back with her."

"Let's just say the fur flew and leave it at that. Mona, if I lost control and bit you, you'd become like me."

She stroked his chest. "Maybe I'd like it. The last barrier down."

"Maybe not the last. Everyone has barriers. There's always something else getting in the way. Don't rush it. I'm still adjusting to this."

She kissed the top of his nose and looked into his eyes. "Think about it, okay?"

"Okay. Want another beer to cool you down?"

"Love one."

He grabbed two, opened them on the bottle opener on the wall, and handed her one. "Hey, want to hear something weird?" he asked.

"It's all weird," she said. "What?"

"Arnie thinks Sally heard him talk."

"Short Stuff? She can hear Arnie? Does that mean she's a werewolf?"

"Why would it mean she's a werewolf?"

"Because she can talk to dogs."

Sam looked at her in confusion. "Wait. You thought that was a werewolf thing?"

"It isn't? I just assumed it was part of the deal."

"I'm the only werewolf I know who can do it," he said.

"Fine, forgive me," she said. "I'm still adjusting to all this, too."

She laughed suddenly.

"What?" he asked.

"You mean even among werewolves, you're a freak?" she asked.

"I guess," he replied, and then he started laughing with her.

They drank some more, cuddling on the couch. Sam picked up the remote.

"You're gonna watch television?"

"Catching the news," he said. "Force of habit."

The local channel came on. A field reporter was standing in front of a chain link fence, a faded sign reading "Cheller Quarry" behind him. "A shocking discovery has the Chattooga County Police working through the night. While details are sketchy, we know that four bodies have been found in a submerged van in the abandoned quarry beyond the fence behind me. The Sheriff has no comment other than that they are treating this as a multiple homicide, but our sources believe that the crime may be drug-related."

"Sam," whispered Mona.

"Damn it," he said, staring at the screen. "Damn it all to hell."

CHAPTER 3

BOUDREAU WAS UP BEFORE dawn the next morning, driving his Jeep to Trion from Summerville. The Medical Examiner's Office was on the grounds of Hays State Prison, something that he suspected terrified the inmates. The guards liked to spread rumors of bizarre experiments that needed involuntary test subjects. It was one way to keep people in line, he supposed. He parked and grabbed the take-out from the passenger seat before buzzing the intercom.

"Who is it?" asked the doc.

"Breakfast, with a side of law," said Boudreau.

She answered the door herself. She looked disheveled, her hair tied back in a messy bun, her eyes tired behind her glasses.

"You're up early," observed Oliveras.

"Had a date with a cute lady pathologist," he said, holding out her cappuccino.

"Don't tell your wife," she said, taking it and inhaling gratefully. "That from Helen and Bill's?"

"A four-corpse special: omelette with chorizo, peppers, and Monterey jack."

"Gimme," she said. "Come on in, Sheriff."

They ate at her desk, the breakfast smells barely managing to overcome the formaldehyde fumes that drifted in from the examination room.

"What do you want to know first?" she asked.

"Date of death, as near as you can figure it," he said.

"Very tough," she said, swiveling her computer screen so he could see it.

"Bodies underwater are a bitch to figure out. Not a lot of serious work done on it, and there's a zillion variables to take into account. Plus, it's a quarry pond."

"How does that change things?"

"Relatively pristine environment compared to, say, a river. Remember that car y'all pulled out of the Chattooga two years ago with the guy in the trunk?"

"Sure do."

"Well, he'd only been down there a couple of weeks, and the local fauna still managed to get inside and chow down on him. But, there aren't any fish or large crustaceans here, and the van was down too deep for any insect activity."

"So nothing eating at them?"

"Still got worms," she said, shoveling a mouthful of potatoes into her mouth. "The worms go in, the worms go out, they go in thin and they come out stout."

"That ain't the version I learned. The worms play pinochle on your snout."

"Not as useful as mine. So, worms got to them, but fairly late in the game. We had a cold winter, but no freeze, then we had a cold spring pretty much through the end of April. Which means the bodies were pretty well preserved up to that point."

"But they were in pieces."

"Yes, they were, and underwater decomposition didn't account for that, but that's the second question," she said. "I'm still dealing with time of death. The skin was off their hands entirely. Usually you get washerwoman's hands early on, then the skin peels off, so that's an indicator. And, that stolen plate narrows things down considerably. So."

"So?"

"So I used a program that the FBI came up with a few years back. Allowed for depth, pH balance, average daily temperature, worm infestation, yada yada, then you wave a magic wand and click your ruby slippers three times. If the front end was December 22nd, then the back end was late January, and that's the best I can do on that."

"That's a start," said Boudreau. "Cause of death?"

"Rapid loss of blood," said Oliveras. "Every one of them."

"And what made them bleed so rapidly?"

"They were torn apart," said Oliveras. "Either dogs or wolves, can't tell which, but they were torn apart. Bite marks are consistent, and chunks were taken out, mostly at the necks."

"How many dogs?"

"I said dogs or wolves. Why not wolves?"

"'Cause there ain't no wolves in Georgia," he said. "Not in years."

She shrugged. "Whatever they were, there had to be a bunch of them. Bite marks were different sizes. I made photos to scale, and I got at least eight different sets."

She pulled out the photos on screen, sending them to different parts of it. Next to each bite mark was a small ruler. "Six incisors," she said, pointing to them. "Incisors hold the prey down, then the premolars and molars gouge out the flesh. Then gulp. That's how dogs and wolves do it."

He looked at the photos carefully. "You keep saying wolves. Why?"

"Just can't exclude them yet, speaking scientifically. Doesn't have to be wild ones. Someone might be raising a wolf pack on a farm privately. Maybe not here in Georgia. Could have been Carolinas, or Florida, and they drove the bodies here to dump them in our laps."

"Long way to go with one strapped into the passenger seat. Even Highway would have noticed that," he said. "My feeling is, this is relatively local. And, the killer knew about Cheller's Quarry."

"How many people worked for Cheller over the years?" she asked. "How many kids snuck in there to skinny dip once the place closed down?"

"Didn't say it would be easy," said Boudreau. "You got hard copies of those bite marks?"

"Right here," she said, handing him a large, manila envelope.

"Those fellers' DNA survive underwater?" he asked.

"Sure," she said. "I already sent Ernie down to Decatur to the GBI lab with samples. I also got some good dental x-rays. Teeth and jaws were all intact, so if we can find the originals, we should get some good matches."

"Here's hoping," he said, standing up.

"You barely touched your eggs."

"Thought I had an appetite, but I must have left it somewhere."

"Do you mind?" she asked, reaching for his plate.

"Be my guest," he said, putting on his hat. "Thanks, Doc."

Dawn was breaking as he got back into his Jeep.

Mona awoke with the sunrise, watching as the claws on the fingers against her breast retracted. The fur vanished like mist, and Sam was human again.

She shivered suddenly. She was naked on a sofa bed and no longer had a large furry creature pressed against her body. Leaning over the edge of the bed, she grabbed the blanket which had been kicked off during the night.

She was sore in a number of places. Despite his efforts to be careful, there were scratches, mostly on her back. She looked over her shoulder, trying to see how bad they were.

Sam rolled over the other way, and she gazed at him, his taut, muscular body still a thrill for her in human form. There were fresh scratches on his back as well. She checked her nails, then grinned.

"The difference between you and me is that during the day, I'm still dangerous," she whispered.

He snored.

The events of the previous night came back to her then, and she didn't feel so dangerous anymore. She got up, looking around for her clothing, before remembering her striptease act outside the cage. She opened the office door softly and peered out.

Carson sat up, looking at her guiltily. Nicky was curled up by his side.

"Guess I wasn't the only one who got lucky last night," she said.

He bared his teeth in acknowledgment, then got up and walked away.

She retrieved her scattered clothing and dressed, feeling grungy as all hell. Her back smarted as the fastener of the bra rubbed against a scratch.

Six months. Six months since she had learned his secrets. Six months of waiting for him to let her see him change. Six months of dreaming what it would be like to have him like that.

It was terrifying. It was brutal.

It was incredible.

She was stiff from sleeping on the thin mattress of the sofa bed, and when she walked, she felt—*well,* she thought, *there are consequences to making love with a werewolf, and if you want the night before, you have to accept the morning after.*

God, she wanted a shower.

"Hey, Nicky, wake up," she said.

Nicky sat up with a start, then looked embarrassed.

"You and me both, girl," said Mona. "Let's go for our jog of shame."

Carson passed them as they came up to the front door.

"All clear?" she asked.

He nodded.

She keyed the combination to deactivate the alarms and went outside. It was already hot and muggy, so her halfhearted attempt at jogging lasted all of ten minutes.

She retrieved the morning paper from the mailbox by the farm road and walked back, reading as she went. The discovery of the corpse-filled cargo van was the headline.

The dogs were stirring in their cages when she came back in. Arnie was wide awake, watching her with interest.

"Sam, tell me you installed a shower while I was out and I will marry you right now," she called.

"Sorry on both counts," he said, appearing in the doorway. "I made coffee. What does that get me?"

She came up and kissed him, then grimaced. "Do you at least have an extra toothbrush? My breath must be a horror."

"In the washroom," he said. "Bought specially for you."

"You're a sweetie," she said, handing him the paper. "Here. Some friends of yours are in there."

"Never really got to know them all that well," he said, taking it.

Carson trotted by. He and Nicky exchanged a glance. Then, she followed Mona into the washroom.

"Oh, ho," said Sam to Carson. "And exactly who was guarding the premises when you were occupied with the divine Miss Nicky?"

Did anyone break in? asked Carson.

"No."

Then mission accomplished. Good dog, Carson. I'm going back to sleep.

"Good dog, Carson," said Sam. "See you tonight."

He went into the washroom, reading the article while Mona brushed her teeth.

"Nothing that wasn't on the news last night," he said.

"So what do we do?" she mumbled through the toothpaste.

"We do nothing. There's nothing in that van that's gonna connect anything to me."

She spat and turned to look at him. "To us, you mean."

"You didn't do anything," he said. "You're safe."

"I helped clean up. I destroyed evidence," she said. "I am an accessory after the fact."

"I'm not letting you take any of this on yourself."

"I didn't ask you, Sam Lehrmann, I volunteered. We're in this together."

"No. If the shit hits the fan, I'm taking the blame."

"You can't shut me out, Sam. Not now."

"You're not spending your life in prison on my account."

"It was self-defense. Can't you explain that to them?"

"Don't like that approach," he said. "Means I have to explain a few other things about my life, and that gets real messy real fast. And, given how I disposed of the bodies after, I'm thinking a jury ain't gonna be real sympathetic."

"What about the van?"

"It's been underwater for six months," he said. "Washed clean of sin. I promise you, Mona, there is nothing there that's gonna link up to us."

Boudreau pulled into his reserved space at the station house and got out, carrying the photos. Wilkins met him as he came in the door.

"You got the van out okay?" asked Boudreau.

"It was a real bitch, but we did it," said Wilkins. "That ramp helped, but the wheels don't exactly turn no more. Undercarriage was shot to hell."

"Where is it now?"

"In the shed out back. I figured you'd want it where we could keep it locked up."

"You figured right. Good," he said. "Check the rest of the VIN's?"

"Yessir, both on the door and the engine block. They all match the dash, and the computer is still registering nothing. I called down to the State Police, and they got the same result."

"Don't understand that," muttered Boudreau. "Anyone taking inventory?"

"Cole's doing that right now, along with that Homeland Security feller."

Boudreau stopped short and turned to face Wilkins, who flinched when he saw his boss' expression.

"What Homeland Security feller?" asked Boudreau softly.

"He showed up about twenty minutes ago, said he'd been called in," said Wilkins rapidly. "His ID checked out. I just figured . . ."

"You're batting .500 with the figuring this morning," said Boudreau. He tossed the photos onto his desk. "Come with me—and draw your weapon, son."

"My weapon?"

"I am referring to your sidearm, issued to you as a police officer for emergency purposes involving a potential threat to human life."

"Yes, yessir!" said Wilkins, drawing his gun.

Boudreau had his out already. He went through the back door at a run, with Wilkins scrambling to keep up with him.

The van was sitting on three flats and a rim in the garage next to the emergency services van. Cole was in the back with a large man who was squatting in front of one of the computers, working on it with a small screwdriver.

"Hey, Mister G-Man, would you mind stepping out of there for a minute?" called Boudreau.

The large man turned to see two guns leveled at him. He smiled a big toothy grin.

Cole looked at her boss in shock and backed quickly out of the line of fire, reaching for her own weapon.

"Don't mind at all, Sheriff," the large man said easily. He stepped out of the van, his hands raised. "Where do you want me?"

"Put your hands against that wall over there away from our vehicles," directed Boudreau. "I don't want to risk damaging county property if I have to start shooting."

"Glad to see you thinking about the taxpayers," said the man, complying.

"Left hand behind your back," said Boudreau. He cuffed one wrist. "Now, the other one."

He completed cuffing him, then patted him down.

"Holster's under my left armpit," said the man helpfully. "ID's at my waist."

"Right," said Boudreau, retrieving them. He flipped open the ID, then looked at the man. "Joseph Pastore, Department of Homeland Security—that you?"

"My friends call me Joe," said the man.

"Don't reckon that I count myself among them," said Boudreau. "Wilkins, put this man in lockup until I verify this."

"We ran the ID number," said Wilkins. "It's real."

"Ain't real until I say it's real," said Boudreau. "Lock him up."

"I should've checked with you first," said Wilkins sorrowfully.

"That would have been the right thing to do," agreed Boudreau.

"My fault," said Pastore. "I was very insistent."

"I don't give a rattlesnake's scaly ass what you did," said Boudreau. "Put him away."

Wilkins escorted Pastore inside.

Boudreau turned back to Cole. "You may put your weapon back in its holster, Officer Cole," he said.

"Yessir," she said. "I would be much happier if you did the same, sir."

"I doubt that I would have hit you, Lucy," he said, holstering his sidearm.

"I am relieved to hear that, sir."

"So, before my rude interruption, what the hell was going on here?"

"The guys wanted me to do the inventory because of all the gadgets," said Cole. "You know what a tech geek I am."

"Right," said Boudreau, stepping carefully into the van. "And this Pastore feller?"

"Just showed up, waved his ID, said he was here to help."

"Hmm," said Boudreau. "Was he helpful?"

"Yessir, indeed he was. He pointed out that this thing on the floor here was an infrared scanner, used for long-distance eavesdropping. I've read about them, but I've never seen one before, and this one's pretty corroded anyhow."

"And what was he unscrewing on that computer?"

"He thought there might be recoverable information on the disk."

"That possible? Whole shebang's been underwater for months."

"Maybe," she said dubiously. "The disk is optical, covered with a polyurethane coating. It might still be readable once it's dried out."

"Interesting," said Boudreau. "That gonna be true of the hard drives?"

"If the computer was on when the water hit it, then a whole lot of stuff's gonna get shorted out and fried," she said, "but the hard drive's supposed to be sealed. Only, the seals are gonna get leaky after a while."

"Nothing lasts forever," he said. "Any paper survive?"

"Nothing in the glove compartments, nothing in the van."

"Must have dissolved."

"No, sir."

"No?"

"Still has to be something left. It's just gone. Someone cleaned out everything before they dumped the van in the water."

"If they were smart, they burned it all," he said. "Let's hope they didn't think about the disks. Keep going on that. You need help, you call down to GBI for one of their tech boys. You can have some geek bonding time."

"Yessir," she said happily.

Boudreau walked back into his office, ignoring the questions from his staff. He closed the door and locked it, then unlocked a drawer at the bottom of his desk. There was a telephone inside. He pulled out his wallet, removed a card with a set of handwritten numbers on it, and punched one of them into the phone.

"State your name," came a digitized voice.

"William Thaddeus Boudreau," he said, overenunciating each syllable.

"Identification."

"Sheriff, Chattooga County Police."

"Number."

"Bravo bravo six seven three slash foxtrot."

He slid his card through a slot on the side. There was a pause, then a live voice came on.

"Good morning, Sheriff. This is Special Agent Cleveland, Homeland Security. What may I do for you?"

"I have someone here claiming to be one of your boys," said Boudreau. "Joseph Pastore. I am sliding his ID through the slot now."

He put Pastore's card through the reader.

"Checking now, Sheriff," said Cleveland. "Yup, he's ours. What's he doing in Summerville?"

"That's what I want to know," said Boudreau. "Thank you for your help."

"You're very welcome, and you have a safe day, Sheriff."

Boudreau rolled his eyes, then ended the connection and locked the phone up again.

There was a knock on the door.

"Come in," he said.

Wilkins poked his head in cautiously, looking ready to take cover. "I got something right."

"What's that?" asked Boudreau.

Wilkins held the dog tag up. "I did a rubbing and managed to get a name and serial number off the tag—or the Individually Carried Identification, as they call them. The Icy Eye."

"Did you now?" beamed Boudreau. "You might make a decent police officer yet. Who was the poor bastard?"

"Daniel Kenner, United States Army. Nine years in."

"Odd number. What happened?"

"Dishonorable discharge in 2012," said Wilkins. "Selling surveillance equipment on the black market in Kazakhstan."

"Surveillance equipment. Like the kind we got leaking fluids in that van."

"Yessir."

"Get everything you can from the Army on him. I am going to speak with our new resident expert."

"Yessir."

Pastore was sitting calmly on the bench in the holding cell when Boudreau walked in.

"Let me explain how things work around here," said Boudreau. "The Feds don't come in unless I ask them to. If you have an interest in a case of mine, you bring your interest directly to me before you do thing one about it."

"Unless I decide it's a matter of Homeland Security," said Pastore. "In which case, I take jurisdiction over any and all local authorities."

"The national office didn't even know you were here. You're not with the Atlanta office. I'm guessing you're a long way from home."

"Can't be a long way from somewhere that doesn't exist," said Pastore. "I saw the local news, thought I might be of assistance."

"And that's bullshit," said Boudreau. "You weren't anywhere near Georgia when that broadcast went out. Something about this raised a red flag on a computer somewhere, and you caught the next military jet down here."

"Did I?" mused Pastore. "What a colossal waste of tax dollars that must have been. What red flag alerted me, do you suppose?"

"The VIN number on the van. That's why it didn't come back as belonging to anything."

"Well, aren't you a smart one?" said Pastore, smirking.

"I wouldn't be making fun of a man who hasn't unlocked your cell yet."

"You don't have a reason to be holding me."

"Says the man from Homeland Security," retorted Boudreau. "You're right. This ain't Guantánamo. People still have rights here. Even Feds."

He unlocked the cell and tossed Pastore his ID. The Fed stepped out.

"My gun?" he asked.

"In my office," said Boudreau. He led Pastore in, unlocked his safe, and handed the gun back. "What can you tell me about all this?"

"Had an informant with a lead on some stolen military equipment, mostly surveillance stuff. Eavesdropping without bugs—that kind of thing."

"Was his name David Kenner, by any chance?"

"Never knew his real name," said Pastore, "but he was in on something nasty and spooky. He didn't tell me what, but he was working out of a van with a couple of other guys."

"Other guys Army?"

"Not current. Could have been freelance. How many turned up in the van?"

"Four," said Boudreau.

"How did they die?"

"I am awaiting results from the Medical Examiner," said Boudreau blandly. "I'll forward them along when I have them."

Pastore pulled a card out of his pocket and wrote a number on it. "Call me the minute you hear," he said.

"I'll be sure to do that," said Boudreau, standing. "Anything else you want to tell me?"

"That's all I got," said Pastore, getting to his feet.

"Then I thank you for your little visit," said Boudreau.

"You kicking me out?" asked Pastore.

"Have you imposed your big-ass Federal jurisdiction over my piddling little county investigation of a local crime?" asked Boudreau.

"Not yet."

"Then I am kicking you out. Have a safe trip back to the homeland."

Pastore gave him a bemused look, then turned to walk out.

"Pastore?"

"Yes, Sheriff?" replied Pastore, turning back.

"Who were they watching with all that surveillance equipment?"

"I'd like to know that myself," said Pastore. "See you around."

He left.

Wilkins popped in a minute later. "You let him go?" he asked.

"Yup."

"Was he for real?"

Boudreau considered the question at length. "He was who he said he was—but that was about the only thing he said that wasn't bullshit."

Mona left after finishing her coffee. Sam went back into the washroom. He scrubbed himself down the best he could, then pulled on his clothes from the day before.

The dogs greeted his entrance with a chorus of derisive sniffs.

Way to go, Boss!

So that's what human females smell like in heat.

Hey, Boss, you expect to sell any of us when you're reeking like that?

Do you really want to make fun of me before I decide whether or not I'm going to feed you? asked Sam.

Arnie looked at him quietly from his cage. *Something's wrong,* he thought to himself. *Boss got laid, but he's still not happy. There's something bothering him, something—*

Arnie looked at Sam more carefully, watching how he moved, how the human seemed unusually aware of sounds from outside. Something scared him, the dachshund realized in surprise, but he kept his thoughts to himself.

Sam's cell went off as he finished the morning feedings. He started at the sound, something that did not escape Arnie's attention.

"Lehrmann's Dogs," said Sam.

"Sam, it's Sally," came the voice. "I can't come in today. I have a sore throat, and Mom's taking me to the doctor."

"Sorry to hear it, kid," said Sam. "You get yourself better quick, y'hear?"

"Do my best," said Sally. "Say hi to the dogs for me."

"Will do," promised Sam. He ended the call. *Sally's sick,* he said.

There was a disappointed groan from the dogs.

I guess I'm not good enough for you anymore, said Sam in mock chagrin. *Okay, if we have any visitors, I want the pups to practice their readings. Older dogs stay out of it.*

He commenced the exercise and training routines. At about ten thirty, Jane pricked up her ears. *Car!* she called.

Car! Car! Car! several others joined in.

All right. Now, just the pups . . . Sam stopped suddenly, a puzzled look on his face. "Gus? That isn't possible."

What the hell? Arnie thought to himself as he picked up the bloodhound's call.

Who is Gus? asked Olga, the Russian wolfhound in the cage next to the dachshund.

I need everyone to be quiet, said Sam quickly. *And stay quiet until I give the order.*

Sam continued to work with the Rottweiler in the pit as the car pulled into the lot. He heard two car doors open and close, then a rear hatch. He pretended to be guiding the dog around the perimeter while the two men peered in through the front window. He only looked up when they came through the front door.

"How do, Mister Lehrmann," said Sheriff Boudreau.

"Hey, Sheriff," said Sam. "Long time, no see. Is that Gus?"

"Sure is," said Wilkins, bringing the bloodhound in on a leash.

"We were coming to see you on business," explained Boudreau, "and we thought you might appreciate a visit from old Gus here."

"Very kind of you," said Sam. "Be with you in a sec. Sugar, sit. Stay."

The Rottweiler sat. Sam gave him a chunk of meat from the leather pouch at his belt, then opened the gate to the pit, removing his gloves as he did.

"How's Gus been working out for you?" asked Sam, stepping forward to shake hands with the two policemen.

"Old Gus is a hero of the county," said Boudreau. "Last year alone, he found three bodies and four lost children. Best bang for the buck on the force."

"Is that right?" said Sam, squatting to face the dog. *What's going on?* he asked.

I was going to ask you that, replied Gus. *I'm working. I don't know on what.*

They want me to find something.

"Good boy, Gus. I'm proud of you," said Sam, rubbing the dog's neck affectionately. *I would appreciate it if you didn't find anything.*

Is there anything to find?

Shouldn't be, but if there is, I know you'd be on it. I really need you not to, said Sam. "So, what can I do for you today, Sheriff? Need another dog?"

Only for you, Boss, said Gus.

"Well, we might at that," said Boudreau. "If you don't mind, could Wilkins here take a look at what you got in stock?"

"Be my guest," said Sam, "but it sounds like you came for something else."

"What makes you say that?" asked Boudreau.

"You arriving without calling first."

"I apologize for that," said Boudreau. "It's been kinda busy the last eighteen hours."

"Yeah, I read the paper. Dope dealers, you think?"

"Maybe," said Boudreau. "What I came for was to pick your brain on something."

"My brain?" laughed Sam. "Sure. It's never done me any good, but whatever use you can find for it, pick away."

"You know anything about dog bites?"

Sam rolled up his right sleeve and showed some old scars on his forearm. "Firsthand knowledge."

"What did that?"

"A Doberman, back when I was learning how to train dogs," said Sam. "Learned a valuable lesson that day."

"How about bite marks?" asked Boudreau. "Know much about them?"

"Some," said Sam. "Why?"

"You got a strong stomach?"

"Depends—this ain't Mexican food, is it?"

Boudreau pulled Oliveras' photos out of the envelope and handed them to Sam.

"Jesus," whispered Sam, looking at them.

Nicely done, Arnie thought to himself.

The pups watched the interactions attentively, reading the men like the Sunday funnies.

Old one's in charge. Duh, easy. Obvious boss, just look at the hat. They're hunters. They work in pairs, sometimes in packs. They're hunting right now.

They're hunting the Boss!

Boss knows it, look how he's hiding inside himself. Showing the smile, like he was showing us to customers, only he's showing his shell, not himself.

Old one's trying to read him. Old one is playing, sending out lures, feinting with words.

Careful, Boss!

Boss can handle it, Olga thought to herself.

Wilkins was walking Gus by the cages as the other dogs looked up with interest. Some came to the front to try and engage him, but the bloodhound ignored them, sniffing the air with professional interest. Until he came to Arnie.

Well, said Gus. *Look who's still here. Can't say I'm surprised.*

Nice to see you, too, said Arnie. *And screw you.*

Don't know why the Boss hasn't been able to find a place for you as a guard dog after all these years, said Gus. *What with the tiny legs and the amiable attitude, I'd think you'd be a lock.*

Why are you here, Gus? asked Arnie. *They run out of garbage dumps for you to poke around?*

What are you doing here? demanded Olga.

Everything's cool, beautiful, said Gus. *I just want to know what happened here. I'm picking up human blood from the other end. It's old, it's faint, but it's there and it isn't the boss.*

Human blood? Here? asked Olga innocently.

Nice try, sister, said Gus. *Arnie, any ideas?*

All right, you got me, said Arnie. *I did it. I killed them all.*

Gus snorted.

It's true, insisted Arnie. *I am the Destroyer, the Dachshund of Death. Fear me! Once you've tasted human flesh, baby, you never go back. I'm savage, wild, feral . . .*

You're still stumpy, said Gus. *Keep dreaming, Arnie.*

"So what can you tell me about these marks?" asked Boudreau.

"Not a lot," said Sam. "Definitely canine."

"Wolf or dog?" asked Boudreau.

"Can't distinguish wolf from a large dog by the bite marks," said Sam.

"Why not?"

"Because dogs are basically a subspecies of wolves."

Subspecies?

Subspecies!

Oh, no, he did not just say that!

Outrage passed through the canine community, with one exception.

I am a wolf, Arnie thought to himself with smug satisfaction.

"Let me show you," said Sam. He went over to one of the cages and let out a Doberman. Then, he opened the gate and brought out the Rottweiler.

"Sugar, Bert, heel," he said, and he walked back to the sheriff, the dogs trotting behind him. "Now, sit."

They sat.

He took a muzzle in each hand and said, "Show."

They bared their teeth at the command.

"See?" said Sam. "Same pattern. You get a wolf, the only difference might be in size, but impossible to tell with the big dogs—and there ain't no wolves in Georgia."

"That's what I thought," said Boudreau, "but the ME was wondering if anyone could be raising wolves privately."

"Don't know of any round here," said Sam, "and that's the type of thing you hear about."

"What about that one?" asked Boudreau, returning to the photos. He pointed to some marks on a forearm. "Looks like there's a tooth missing."

"Sure does," agreed Sam. "If you found that dog, that could make for a match."

That was Errol, he thought. *Errol who helped save my life. Errol, who is now patrolling a used car lot in Calhoun, far from any dental comparisons.*

"What about DNA?" he asked the sheriff.

"From the corpses?"

"From the bite marks," said Sam. "If you got dog saliva in the bites—"

"The bodies have been underwater since last Christmas, thereabouts," said Boudreau. "Not a chance for that."

"Christmas. Huh," said Sam, secretly relieved.

"What about it?"

"Sad time to get yourself killed."

"Don't know a good one," said Boudreau. "Let me ask you this. Assuming these were dogs, were they trained or wild?"

"Trained. No question about it."

"Why?"

"Location of the bites," said Sam, pointing them out. "Thighs, to bring them down. Wrists, to disarm. Necks, to kill. And, there's a minimal amount of gouging. Wild dogs would have turned these guys into kibble."

"You said disarm," observed Boudreau. "I never said they were armed."

"The dogs went for the wrists," said Sam. "I was assuming the men were carrying weapons. Were they?"

"We found guns in the van," admitted Boudreau.

"There you go."

Boudreau looked over at the Rottweiler and the Doberman, who had been sitting patiently by Sam. "Do they bite?" he asked.

"Only if I tell them to," said Sam. "Or if I'm being attacked."

"But then they bite?"

"Yes, they bite—they bite very, very hard."

"Now, this was a whole pack of dogs," said Boudreau. "How many would you need to take out a group of armed men?"

"Me? How many men were there again?" asked Sam.

"Four."

"If I was training them," said Sam. "Four dogs."

"Against armed men?"

"Yessir. If I was training them, that's all I would need. Four men, four dogs."

Wilkins came back with Gus.

"See any you like?" asked Sam.

"How's the shepherd bitch on bringing down bad guys?" asked Wilkins.

"About a month away from perfect," said Sam. "I'll give you a government discount, have her ready by August."

"We'll think about it," said Boudreau. "What was Gus getting into down that end?"

"He and the dachshund seemed to be going at it," said Wilkins.

"Yeah, that's Arnie," said Sam. "He and Gus know each other from when Gus was here."

"You've got a dachshund for sale that long?" asked Boudreau.

"People don't think a dachshund makes for a good guard dog."

"I'm one of them," said Boudreau.

"Dachshunds are hunters," said Sam. "Smart as hell, and fearless."

Arnie swelled with pride.

Boudreau shuffled through the photos, then pointed at a bite mark on the thigh of one of the dead men. "Smaller dog did that. Could it have been a dachshund?"

Sam looked at it. "Could have been. Or a Jack Russell, or a bunch of different terriers."

"Not a Basset, though," said Boudreau. "Never seen one jump that high in my life."

"So, you feeding my Gus right?" asked Sam. "Still giving him raw meat?"

"Not every meal," said Wilkins guiltily.

"Why not?" asked Sam.

"I don't like handling it," said Wilkins. "Makes me squeamish."

"This from a man who spent yesterday hauling body parts underwater," said Boudreau.

"You did that?" asked Sam.

"Me and the ME, yessir," said Wilkins.

"Well, let me send Gus off right," said Sam, kneeling down and reaching into his pouch. "Here, boy." *And thanks.*

It took everything I had not to react, Boss. Goes against all my training.

I appreciate it. I truly do. Sam gave the bloodhound several chunks of beef, which the dog gulped down gratefully.

"Thanks for the help, Sam," said Boudreau. "We'll call you about the shepherd."

"I'll keep her available," promised Sam. "Gentlemen. Gus."

As they left, the bloodhound looked back over his shoulder. *By the way, you had sex last night, didn't you?* said Gus. *Way to go.*

Just no way to keep secrets around here, said Sam.

Yeah, there is, said Gus. *Good seeing you, Boss.*

The two officers put the bloodhound in back, then drove away. Boudreau looked back at the dog, who was curling up to sleep. "You don't suppose that a dog could be bribed by a chunk of beef, do you?" he asked.

"Gus is an officer of the law, Sheriff," replied Wilkins. "He is incorruptible. Like me."

"Hell, son, you could be corrupted by someone dangling a Snickers bar in front of you."

"I think you may be correct about that. Especially if that Cheller girl was the one dangling it. I got something I could dangle right back."

Boudreau snorted.

"Lucky about her remembering Lehrmann," continued Wilkins.

"Yup."

"He's got dogs."

"Yup."

"Bet he knows about the quarry. It was all over the news reports. And, he knew the Chellers."

"Yup," said Boudreau. "You'd think he'd've mentioned that."

CHAPTER 4

OFFICER COLE SAT IN THE wrecked van looking at the computer, wondering if it had anything left to share. It was a Scion 886, and her inner geek was bemoaning how such a prime piece of equipment could meet such a watery fate. She had been squirreling away her splurge money until she could buy one of the lower-end models, but this baby was way beyond her county-paid wages.

She had looked up the corporate website and zeroed in on the troubleshooting section. Supposedly, the 886 could survive a dunking—the website had a video of a clumsy nerd getting distracted by a hot blonde and falling into a swimming pool with one—but she was pretty sure they were contemplating a short-term spill, not several months under.

She rigged a pair of standing fans by the rear of the van and ran them top speed to dry the interior out, trying not to think about whether she had been stepping on any remnants of the van's previous occupants. She took the computer and tilted it forward.

Water streamed out the front, spilling onto her lap.

She sighed, anticipating the comments she would get when she walked into the station with wet pants. She consulted a manual, then poked through her tool box until she found a large paper clip, which she straightened out and stuck it in a small hole next to the slot where the disk would be inserted. It met no resistance.

She turned the computer around to open the back, then paused. Someone had punched three jagged holes in the rear panel before the van took its last plunge. She removed the panel and surveyed the damage. *So much for the hard drive,* she thought.

It didn't take much police acumen to know that the holes hadn't been made by a dog.

The disk drive nestled against the front of the interior of the computer, just below the monitor. She removed the clips holding it to the frame and eased it out, then unscrewed the two halves. It made a slight sucking sound as she popped them open: the seal hadn't been broken, but there was no disk inside.

The peepers Pastore had planted on the rearview mirror captured the whole examination. If Sam's dogs had been watching, they would have correctly identified Cole's disappointment from the slight slump in her shoulders—but it was Pastore who watched the video, standing by his monitor while brushing his teeth. His disappointment would have been more difficult to register, but it was there.

He walked into the motel bathroom and spat, then grabbed his cell from his belt and keyed a number.

"Yeah, it's me," he said. "No disk. Knew it was too much to hope for, but had to be sure. You have a green light."

Boudreau and Wilkins pulled into the precinct parking lot. As the junior officer opened the rear door to let Gus out, Boudreau looked at the dog and thought about its trainer.

"Know anything about Lehrmann?" asked Boudreau.

"Only about the dogs," said Wilkins. "He set up shop about six years ago, I think."

"How did we get on to him?"

"Someone recommended him," said Wilkins. "He had just come out of the Army—"

"The Army," said Boudreau. "The Cheller girl said he was in the Army with her brother. He seemed Army, didn't he?"

"He did, come to think of it," said Wilkins. "The way he stood when he was talking to us. Respecting the senior officer."

"You were Army, weren't you?"

"Sir, yessir," said Wilkins. "You?"

"United States Marine, soldier."

"Which means if you were my age, you'd think you could kick my ass."

"No, son," said Boudreau. "It means that I can kick your ass right here and now. Do some background on our dog supplier. See if he had any overlap with that Kenner fellow we found in the van. Throw Tom Cheller in there, too."

"Yessir."

"And while you're at it, see if he knew our new best friend Pastore," said Boudreau.

"Yessir."

Car!

    Car! Car! Car!

    Only need to hear it once, thank you, said Sam. *Pups, practice your reading.*

A man walked in wearing a light tan two-piece suit over a beige button-down shirt, his tie loose and his collar unbuttoned. "Hoo whee, hot one today," he said. "Worked up a sweat just walking from the car to here. Are you Mister Lehrmann?"

"I am, but call me Sam," said Sam, coming over to shake his hand.

"Larry Tennant," said the man. "Nice-looking bunch of dogs you got there."

The pups read Tennant as the two men spoke.

Athlete. Runs. Relaxed when he moves.

No kids. Fathers have that softness to them.

Married. Has a ring.

Not from here. New to the area.

"What type of dog are you looking for, Larry?" asked Sam.

"Well, we just moved into the area, and I'm looking for something to keep the missus company while I'm on the road."

Score on the new to town!

"Company or something more?" asked Sam. "Company's for pets. I provide guard dogs."

"There's that, too," said Tennant. "My wife gets nervous at night when I'm traveling, so something to reassure her—and protect her."

Olga looked up. *He's lying about the wife,* she said.

Confusion on the part of the pups.

But he has a ring.

How do you know that?

In his voice, she said. *There is no love in it. No concern. There is no wife.*

Maybe he doesn't love her.

But a man who buys a guardian for his wife cares for her, said Olga. *This man . . .*

Cares for nothing, said Otto, the Weimaraner.

The younger dogs looked at him in surprise. Otto rarely spoke.

The movement of so many dogs at once caught Tennant's eye. He twitched slightly, then relaxed. Arnie spotted it.

He's armed, Boss, called the dachshund. *Right-handed, something in the waistband to the rear.*

Thanks, Arnie, said Sam without changing expression.

"Well, in that case, you ought to bring her over to see who she feels comfortable with," said Sam. "If she'll be spending the most time with the dog—"

"I would, but she's feeling a little poorly," said Tennant. "She's expecting, and what with the heat and all."

"I'm sorry to hear that," said Sam. "About her feeling poorly, I mean. Congratulations on the baby. Your first?"

"Sure is," said Tennant, grinning broadly. He looked at Sam for a moment. "I know you from somewhere, don't I?"

Trap! cried several of the pups at once.

"Don't recognize you from anywhere," said Sam, "but I'm a common type, I hear. People keep telling me—"

"Were you in the Army?"

"Sure was," said Sam proudly. "Six years serving my country."

I love it when he does that, said Arnie.

Tennant snapped his fingers. "Kabul. You were in Kabul."

"Two rotations," said Sam. "You were there, too?"

"Affirmative. Three months there, then ten at the FOB in Khost," said Tennant, "but I'm pretty sure I saw you in Kabul."

"I was in the Quartermasters Corps," said Sam. "I probably issued you some gear."

"That must be it," said Tennant. "Small world, isn't it?"

"Sure is."

"See any action?'

"On a convoy once," said Sam. "We were in the third truck when the first got hit by an IED and out of nowhere I was in a shooting war. Didn't like it much."

"Bad?"

"Never good," said Sam. "Made Kabul look like a vacation spot after that, mortars, suicide bombers, and all. You must have seen some bad shit in Khost."

"Yeah, well, lived to tell about it," said Tennant. He looked at Sam some more.

"What?" asked Sam.

"I remember hearing something about you."

"Me?"

"Yeah," said Tennant, walking around him, looking at him from different angles.

Sam turned to keep him in view, stepping carefully to maintain his balance.

Are they going to fight?

They've been fighting for five minutes. Where've you been?

"You weren't really Quartermasters Corps, were you?" asked Tennant.

"Is there a problem here, Larry?" asked Sam. "Of course I was."

"I'm telling you, you weren't Quartermasters Corps."

"I was a Systems Supply Tech, worked my way up to Master Sergeant," said Sam. "What's it to you?"

"You were Special Ops," said Tennant. "That was the scuttlebutt. Nice cushy job sitting at a counter, handing out blankets and pillows, then you'd disappear for a few days to do some seriously weird shit in places no one else would go near."

"That's bullshit."

Tennant was now standing between Sam and the cages.

He has another man coming! called Olga.

"Tell you what," began Sam, then he lunged.

Tennant tried to sidestep him, but Sam was faster, clamping down on his right wrist. Tennant tried to throw him off, but Sam kept his grip and got behind him, twisting the other man's arm behind his back. He grabbed a gun from the back of Tennant's waistband and put it to Tennant's head.

"Stand down, soldier!" shouted Pastore, coming through the front door.

"Who the fuck are you?" Sam shouted back.

"Let him go, Sam," said Pastore. "He's one of mine."

"I repeat, who the fuck are you?" asked Sam, not budging.

"That is a direct order, Sergeant!" said Pastore, his voice edged with steel.

"I don't take orders, asshole, and my gun stays on your boy's head until I know what's going on."

Pastore nodded approvingly. "Absolutely correct," he said. "Tango bravo foxtrot three niner niner."

"Acknowledged," said Sam. "Charlie delta gamma two six eight."

"Acknowledged," said Pastore. "How've you been, Sam?"

Sam was in a cage. No, a jail cell. He was seventeen and scared shitless. They were going to find out. He was stuck in a jail cell, and there was one more night of full moon coming. Stupid, stupid, stupid.

Then the big man walked in, carrying a folder in his left hand. "You Sam Lehrmann?" he asked.

"Who are you?" asked Sam. "You a lawyer?"

"I've been called a lot of bad things in my life," said the man, chuckling, "but that may be the worst. No, son, I am not a lawyer. Are you Sam Lehrmann?"

"Yes."

The man pulled out a sheet of paper from the folder and looked at it. "Says you killed a couple of cows belonging to a Mister McTiernan."

"I was drunk," said Sam. "I'm sorry. I'll pay for the cows, plead guilty, whatever, but I got to get out of here. My old man—"

"Your old man wouldn't mind if you got a couple of years in prison," said the man. "Said it would teach you a lesson."

Sam was silent.

"How drunk were you?" asked the man.

"Must have been real drunk," said Sam. "I don't remember doing it. Woke

up in the pasture, and there's Mr. McTiernan comes running at me screaming with his shotgun."

"Lucky you didn't get yourself killed," said the man.

"Who are you again?"

"Now, here's the thing," said the man, pulling out another sheet of paper. "There have been cows killed before in this area."

Sam's heart sank.

"The attacks cover a fifty-mile radius," continued the man, "and here's the interesting part: they all took place on nights when the moon is full."

"Nothing to do with me," muttered Sam.

"Nobody thinks they did," said the man. "Except for me."

"Why?"

"Because McTiernan's cows were clawed apart and chewed up," said the man. "You were found with blood on your teeth and hands, but the hands and teeth I'm looking at right now could not have done that damage. It was pretty brutal stuff. The judge is thinking of remanding you for psychiatric evaluation. Do you think you need psychiatric evaluation, Sam?"

"Mister, whoever you are, I've got to get out of here," whispered Sam.

The man shrugged. "Everyone in jail thinks they have to get out. Not everyone should. I'm sure the local cattle population would have a radically different opinion on the subject."

"What do you want from me?" asked Sam.

"First sensible question I've heard from you," said the man. "I am a recruiting officer for the United States Army. I can get you out right now if you'd be willing to enlist in a specialized unit."

"Specialized?"

"I'm looking for werewolves, Sam," said the man. "You been one for long?"

Sam was silent again.

The man looked at his watch. "Three hours until sundown. If I'm getting you out on time, I have to know now. Are you a werewolf or not?"

"Yes," whispered Sam.

"Good," said the man. "My name is Joseph Pastore. Captain Joseph Pastore. You will call me 'Sir,' because I now own your ass for the next several years. One last question. Ever killed a human?"

"No!" said Sam, shocked by the question.

Pastore smiled.

"Would you like to?" he asked.

"Fuck you," said Sam, letting Tennant go.

"That's 'fuck you, sir,'" said Pastore.

"Not anymore, it ain't," said Sam.

"My weapon?" asked Tennant, turning and rubbing his wrist.

"Shut up, asshole," said Sam. "What's going on, Captain?"

The dogs were engrossed.

Did you see the Boss do that? said Nan to Bert.

I didn't know he could move like that when he's human, replied Bert, *but that big man—he's acting like he's the Boss' alpha!*

The Boss is acting like that man's his alpha, said Arnie in shock. *How could that be? He's the Boss!*

Pastore walked towards Sam.

He's a werewolf, said Otto. *He's an alpha werewolf.*

How can you tell? asked Arnie.

The way he moves, said Otto. *He moves like the Boss.*

"It's 'Colonel,' by the way," said Pastore. "Who made Tennant first, you or the dogs?"

"The 'hoo whee' should have tipped me off," said Sam. "Your man's been watching too many cartoons. But, the dogs made him first—including where he had his weapon."

"Jesus," said Tennant, impressed.

"I told you," Pastore said to him, "and you owe me fifty bucks."

"What was the bet?" asked Sam.

"That you could still take him, civilian softy and all," said Pastore.

"I caught him off guard."

"He's never off guard."

"Fucking werewolf reflexes," said Tennant. "They carry over even in daylight, don't they?"

Sam shrugged, then turned back to Pastore. "Why do I have the feeling that this isn't a social call?" he asked.

"I dunno," said Pastore. "Could be your extensive counter-intel training, or that I sent in an agent first—or that I have never made a social call in my life."

"That must be it," said Sam. "What do you want?"

"Ever hear about the Bogey Man?" asked Pastore.

"Rumors on the newsgroup," said Sam. "Some guy who killed werewolves for fun."

"Not rumors," said Pastore. "Truth. I've been looking for that bastard for years. Thought I had a lead last fall. Had an informant who may have been working for him. Then, the informant disappears off the face of the earth last Christmas."

"Maybe the Bogey Man found out about him."

"The Bogey Man had a pattern," said Pastore. "He always made a kill on the last full moon before Christmas."

"Sick."

"So, last Christmas, no kills," said Pastore. "Nothing since then."

"Thanks, Santa."

"Then this van turns up in a quarry pond not twenty miles from here," said Pastore. "My informant, at least most of him, is in the back."

"My condolences," said Sam. "Were you close?"

"Not as close as you were," said Pastore. "Only werewolf living anywhere in the vicinity is you. And, the only werewolf in a thousand miles good enough to single-handedly take out the Bogey Man and three highly trained mercenaries is still you. Throw in that they were killed by dogs, and I am very much in favor of it still being you."

"If true, then I did us all a favor."

"That doesn't quite count as a confession, does it?" commented Tennant. "And, you still have my weapon."

"Yes, I do, and don't interrupt," said Sam, pointing it at him. "So you came to investigate the Bogey Man's untimely death."

"Oh, it was timely," said Pastore, "way past timely. But, I'm here because I think that the Bogey Man had something he shouldn't have had."

"What's that?"

"The Book of Wolves."

"Want to run that by me again?"

"The Book of Wolves, Sam," repeated Pastore. "The United States government keeps a record containing information about every werewolf in the country."

"I didn't know that," said Sam. "Where is it?"

"Two places," said Pastore. "The first is in a secure room in the Pentagon. Two people have access to it: The Chairman of the Joint Chiefs of Staff, and me."

"My, my, my," said Sam. "You really have floated to the surface, haven't you? Why does the United States government care so much about werewolves?"

"Why did they intern the Japanese during World War Two?" returned Pastore. "The world is crazy and the government is paranoid. They are watching."

"Watching?" asked Sam. "Is that what Larry, the Boy Wonder, has been doing? Watching me?"

"Larry and I, along with a few others, collect data."

"On werewolves."

"Every time one is created, we know about it," said Pastore. "We gather intel, determine the level of danger it presents."

"And if it's dangerous?"

"We watch very closely."

"I'm dangerous," said Sam. "I used to kill people on behalf of the United States government."

"You were watched very closely for two years after you got out."

"And since then?"

"I was satisfied that you made the transition cleanly," said Pastore. "Until now. Now, there are four guys that look like chew toys in the Chattooga County Morgue, and I know you did it."

"How can you be certain?"

"Because you referred to the Bogey Man in the past tense."

"Did I?"

"'Some guy who killed werewolves for fun,'" quoted Tennant.

"Slip of the tongue," said Sam.

"Sheriff already has you down for a suspect," said Pastore.

"I know," said Sam. "He paid me a visit today. Another nonsocial call."

"Here's the thing," said Pastore. "He's good. He's very good. He's got the biggest multiple homicide in years on his turf, and he's not going to quit until he clears it. And, you made prime suspect inside of a day."

"Two places," said Sam.

"What?"

"You said this book was in two places."

"Good. You were paying attention," said Pastore. "The second place is in a lab in South Carolina. They have a copy on an encrypted disk."

"What kind of lab?"

"A very specialized lab," said Pastore.

"Whenever you say specialized, you mean werewolves," said Sam.

"Thanks for pointing that out," said Pastore. "I'll make sure I use different words more. Yes, a lab that studies werewolves."

"Who runs it?"

"They get funded through a discretionary fund that originates from Homeland Security, but passes through so many intermediaries, you'd never know it."

"You?"

"Me. And, they report directly to me."

"So, there are two places where this book exists, and you control them both."

"Control is a poor choice of words for the lab. I don't sit there and ride herd on them."

"You think they leaked it to the Bogey Man?"

"I do."

"How do you know it isn't the Chairman of the Joint Chiefs of Staff?"

"Because I keep very good tabs on him," said Pastore.

Sam slid the clip out of Tennant's gun, popped the remaining cartridge out of the chamber, then tossed the empty weapon to him. "Not my problem," Sam said.

"It's all of our problem," said Pastore. "If there's a leak . . ."

"You're the plumber, not me," said Sam. "I finished serving my country six years ago."

"There's something else," said Pastore. "You remember Crawford?"

The bullet took him through his left shoulder, punching through the body armor like it was paper and spinning him around before he fell. Pastore and Crawford dragged him back to the cover of the boulders . . .

"Sure, I remember Crawford. What about him?"

"I got a call from him yesterday. Funny thing happened."

"What?"

"He turned into a werewolf."

"Full moon last night. Nothing funny about that."

"It happened first thing yesterday morning. In broad daylight."

"What? That's impossible."

"Said he stayed that way for six hours, then turned back."

"How?"

"That's the thing," said Pastore. "I don't know—and I don't like not knowing."

"So, get this lab of yours involved."

"My worry is that they may already be involved."

"And you want to send me in to find out who? Jesus, don't you have anyone already working for you who could do that? What about Larry the Boy Wonder?"

"I'd appreciate it if you'd stop calling me that," said Tennant.

"They already know him," said Pastore. "I want to send someone they don't know. You —and a team of your best readers."

He means us! said Arnie.

"That dachshund's looking awfully bouncy all of a sudden," observed Pastore.

"You want me to use my dogs?" asked Sam.

"I know what you can do, and I know what they can do," said Pastore. "I can get you into the lab, and they can suss out who's lying or hiding something."

"Won't the lab folks suspect me?"

"Not with the cover story I'm giving you," said Pastore. "If that is the Bogey Man resting in pieces on that refrigerated slab, then he'll have been out of contact for six months. I doubt that the lab will have connected the discovery of the van to his absence."

"Look, I got a good thing going here," said Sam. "I don't want to disrupt everything to clean up someone else's crap."

"It's a nice setup," said Pastore, looking around. "Lucky you could get that loan from the bank at such a young age—and you got, what, four years left on it?"

"Three years, ten months," said Tennant. "With a whopper of a balloon payment at the end."

"Be tough if Sheriff Boudreau got in your face," said Pastore. "He's already poking around your Army background. Your cover should be secure, but you never know with the Army."

Sam's blood went cold. "You'd give me up?"

"I'm saying that there's a major shitstorm heading your way," said Pastore, "but I can provide you with a real good umbrella."

"How?" asked Sam.

"By imposing my bad ass self on their investigation."

"If I work for you."

"Yes."

"How long is the mission?" asked Sam.

"I figure a week or so," said Pastore. "If you can't find the leak, then I move in with the big guns and shut the operation down. But, I'd prefer not to do that."

"A week away from here? What about the rest of the dogs? What about their training?" asked Sam. "I do this for a living. If you expect me to—Good Lord, how many zeroes are on that thing?" He was staring at a check Pastore was holding up.

"Look at that, Larry," observed Pastore. "Here we are, using threats, subterfuge, and appeals to his better nature, and all we had to do was buy him."

"Guess we're out of touch with the common man," agreed Tennant. "As for the rest of the dogs—I'll take care of them while you're away."

"What experience do you have?" demanded Sam.

"We had dogs when I was a kid," said Tennant.

"And?"

"They're dogs. What's the big deal?"

Sam reached behind him and opened a cage. A pair of Dobermans stood, awaiting orders.

"Their names are Nan and Bert," said Sam.

"Hello, Nan and Bert," said Tennant, squatting to face them.

They growled.

"My, what big teeth they have," he said.

"In five seconds, I am going to tell them to use those big teeth on you," said Sam. "What are you going to do about that?"

"Ask you not to," said Tennant.

"Ask them."

"Nan, Bert, heel."

The dogs trotted over to him and took positions behind him. Sam took his reward pouch from his belt and tossed it to Tennant.

"What's in here?" asked Tennant.

"Fresh meat," said Sam. "How do we thank someone for not killing us?"

"Good dogs," said Tennant to Nan and Bert. He gave each of them a morsel of beef, then turned back to Sam. "Do I give one to you?'

"When it's not full moon, I like my steak medium," said Sam.

"Does this mean you accept?" asked Pastore.

"It means I'll think about it," said Sam.

"Let me know soon," said Pastore, looking at his watch. "We hit the road day after tomorrow—and don't even think about cashing that check until I hear a yes. Let's go. Sundown's in ninety minutes. I want to be someplace where I can do some howling."

Tennant followed him, but Nan and Bert stayed at his heels. He looked back at them, then at Sam.

"Nan, Bert, stay," he said.

The dogs stopped.

Tennant tossed the reward bag back to Sam, then chased after Pastore.

He's well trained for a human, said Arnie.

He's a soldier, said Sam, hitting the release button for the cages. *Everybody come here.*

The dogs emerged slowly.

Carson! You, too, called Sam.

Carson lifted his head. *What's going on?* he asked. *Did I miss something?*

You slept through all of that, Olga said in wonder.

All of what?

Dogs, sit, said Sam. *I need to explain a few things. I'm sure you were wondering about that man.*

What's he got on you, Boss? asked Arnie.

He got me out of trouble with the law when I was young, said Sam. *Then, he got me into bigger trouble. The human wars.*

The human wars are still going on, said Olga. *You don't fight them anymore. I did my share.*

But they want you to do more, said Olga.

This is a different war.

Are you going to fight it? asked Carson.

I don't know what I'm going to do yet, said Sam. *But if I do go, I'll be taking some of you with me—and it may be dangerous.*

The alpha didn't say anything about danger, said Bert.

He carries danger with him, said Otto. *Always . . .*

You got that right, said Sam. *Okay, playtime.*

But the dogs sat there, thinking about how the world had changed.

When Mona came in later, the dogs were still sitting. She picked her way carefully through them to find Sam sitting with his back against his cage, a beer in his hand, a few empties by his side.

"You started without me," she said. She went to the refrigerator and returned with more beer. "I'm not the chugging type, so you'll have to slow down for me to catch up to you."

She slid to the floor next to him, took a long swallow, and looked out at the field of dogs. "That's plain eerie, them sitting there like that. It's like the end of *The Birds,* where they walk out of the house through all the birds, and you're just waiting for the attack."

"Never saw it," said Sam.

"Is this some extended sit and stay training?"

"No."

"You gonna tell me what's going on?"

He stuck the bottle in his mouth and tilted it up.

"Point of information," said Mona. "Does getting drunk make the change easier or worse? Because sundown is coming real soon, and I'm kind of curious as to the answer."

Sam started taking off his boots. "Sheriff Boudreau paid me a visit today."

"That isn't good," said Mona. "How'd he find you so fast?"

"He was asking my expertise on dog bites," said Sam.

"Then maybe he doesn't think it was you," said Mona.

"Except he brought a bloodhound with him."

"You mean an actual dog, not a detective."

"I mean he brought a dog to sniff out human blood on the premises," said Sam, "but I got lucky. He was one of mine. He did me a favor."

"Jesus. You dodged a bullet."

"You can't dodge bullets, Mona," he said, unbuttoning his shirt and peeling it off. "They either hit you or they miss."

Her hand gently traced the small round scar on the front of his shoulder.

"There's something else," he said. "I had another visitor after that."

"Who?"

"My old C.O. from when I was in the Army."

She shifted to where she could see his face, but he was looking down into the neck of the bottle. She stayed quiet, waiting for him to talk. His time in the Army was the great blank space in her knowledge of his history: her questions had always been met either with silence or curt rejection.

"I was in a Special Ops unit," he said. "Five of us. All werewolves."

"All five? Why?"

"Extreme military service in exchange for the promise of being left alone once we got out," said Sam. "Which someone just broke big time."

"Extreme?"

"Mostly hunt and kill missions in Afghanistan, near the Pakistani border. Or Pakistan, near the Afghani border. No one paid much attention to where the border was. It all looked the same."

"You killed people."

"That's what soldiers do in a war."

"How many?"

"Didn't count. There were a lot of missions—and we were very good at what we did." He finally met her eyes. "I killed a lot of people, Mona—and the reason I was recruited is because they knew I would be good at it."

"You were a soldier," she said. "We were at war. Still are. Soldiers are still killing the enemy. If you're wondering how I feel—"

"I was."

She took his hand between hers. "I don't have a problem with soldiers fighting a war that should be fought."

He gripped her hand hard.

She winced slightly.

He saw it and let her go. "I'm sorry."

"You can't keep carrying secrets," she said.

"It was a classified operation," he said. "Still is. I could get you in trouble for telling you this much."

"You got me in trouble so many ways from Sunday, what's one more?"

The alarm went off.

"Shit," he said.

He staggered to his feet and stumbled into the cage.

"Get it closed!" he yelled, pulling off his pants.

She sprang to her feet. Carson was charging for them, barking a warning.

The change came faster than the first night, and he hadn't started his preparations. The panic hit as his chest swelled, and he had trouble breathing.

Mona froze as he fell to his hands and knees. "Sam!" she cried. "Are you all right?"

He turned to her, fangs protruding, eyes fierce. He howled suddenly, a harsh, despairing bay that echoed through the warehouse and drew fearful whimpers from the dogs.

Carson was barking furiously, trying to get her attention. She realized with a pang of terror that the gate to the cage had not latched. She reached for it.

Sam sprang toward her, claws extended. She screamed and threw herself back against the opposite wall.

He grabbed the gate and slid it into place, and the electronic lock engaged. He sagged to his knees. "I told you to get it closed," he whispered hoarsely.

"I'm sorry," she sobbed. "I'm so sorry."

Tell me what happened, demanded Carson.

I was drinking, said Sam. *I lost track. Everything's okay, buddy.*

The hell it is, said Carson. *I told you letting her be here was a bad idea.*

It ain't her fault, said Sam.

Yeah, but she's the one you'll end up hurting, said Carson. *Or me trying to stop you.*

"I would never hurt either of you," said Sam.

The man wouldn't, said Carson. *I'm not so sure about the wolf.*

Sam took a deep breath. "Are you all right?" he asked.

She stood, then walked up to the mesh. "Are you all right?" she asked.

"Getting there," he said.

She rattled the lock to make sure it was engaged. "I could use something stronger than beer right now."

"You know where it is," he said.

She walked into his office and closed the door behind her.

What's going on? asked Carson. *The last time you started drinking on a full moon was when she left you. That got scary and ugly—and I'm not talking about you being a werewolf.*

It isn't her this time, repeated Sam. *Let it go.*

I will when you do.

What's with you? You jealous of her?

I am your guardian! shouted Carson. *You raised me to protect you! To protect everyone here, including the woman you think you love and may end up slicing to ribbons if you lose it like it looks like you're going to.*

Do your job and patrol, said Sam.

But—

"Carson, patrol!" shouted Sam.

The dog looked at him with hostility, then turned and trotted down the length of the cages. The other dogs watched, mute questions in their eyes—except for Arnie.

Carson, what's going on with him? asked the dachshund.

Ask him yourself, said Carson.

Yeah, he put me at the far end of the cages so I can interrogate him more easily, said Arnie.

I've never seen him like this, said Olga.

I have, said Arnie. *Before your time. Mona's doing it to him again.*

He says it's not her, said Carson.

Sure, said Arnie.

The lock chimed. Sam slowly opened the gate and stepped out. He looked at the closed door to his office for a long time.

The dogs turned to watch him.

Anyone besides me think it's time for an intervention? asked Arnie.

Not yet, said Olga. *Look how he's standing there. Like he's been wounded.*

He has been wounded, said Otto.

Gee, you haven't said a word for weeks, and now we can't get you to shut up, said Arnie. *Of course, he's been wounded. We've seen the scars.*

I wasn't talking about the physical wounds, said Otto.

Neither was I, said Arnie.

A wounded wolf is most dangerous when he's cornered, said Otto.

He isn't cornered, said Olga.

Sam opened the door and went in.

Now, he's cornered, said Arnie.

She was sitting cross-legged on his desk when he came in, the bourbon in the bottle at a considerably lower level than he remembered.

"How much did you have?" he asked.

She held up her index finger, examined it closely, then raked the nail across her forearm. It left a deep, angry weal in its wake. She winced. "Not enough—I can still feel."

He took the bottle away from her. "Why be numb?" he asked.

"So I won't care what you're doing to me," she said. "So I won't think about it."

"I want you to feel it," he said. "Every pleasure, every pain."

"I don't want pain."

"You can't avoid it all the time."

"That's what bourbon is for," she said. "We can have this discussion when we're sober. I don't want to talk. I want to drink, and I want to fuck, so give me the damn bottle."

"My dad said never to take advantage of a woman when she's drunk."

"You listen to your daddy?" asked Mona, holding out her hand.

He looked at it, then gave her back the bottle. "Not much."

When she had enough, she pushed him back onto the couch and straddled him. She kept her eyes closed the entire time she was thrusting him inside her. He couldn't tell if she was feeling pain or pleasure, or anything at all. She cried out when she climaxed, then collapsed on top of him, sobbing until she fell asleep. He held her tightly, pressing the pads of his paws against her back, taking care that the claws never touched her.

At daybreak, when the change receded and he could breathe easily again, he gently rolled her off and pulled the blanket over her. He sat in his chair, watching her face in the early morning sunlight, the tear streaks dried on her cheeks.

He picked up the phone and punched in a number. A voice answered on the first ring.

"It's me," said Sam. "Yeah, awoo to you, too. Listen. I'm gonna cash that check."

CHAPTER 5

Danny opened his back door as quietly as he could and tiptoed through the kitchen. His mom was passed out on the couch, the television still on, an empty bottle on the carpet in front of her. Good old mom. The one thing he could count on when he was out on the prowl.

He went up to his room, stripped and showered, then threw his school stuff together. He shoved a change of clothes into his backpack, just in case Crazy Syl called. He sometimes hunted with her. Sometimes did other stuff, too, out there in the hills. Crazy Syl, his changer, his WILF.

It was so fucked up.

He brushed his teeth, then walked outside with five minutes to get to the end of the street for his bus.

The change hit him as he reached the street, his jeans, his brand-new jeans, shredding! Some kids were pointing and yelling. He ran back up his driveway, crashing through the door, screaming for his mother.

She woke to see a large, shaggy form bounding into her living room. She screamed and ran to the kitchen.

"Mom! No, Mom, it's me!" he howled, chasing after. "It's . . ."

The shotgun blast caught him full in the chest.

Mona shifted from sleep to wakefulness with a start, realizing that she was alone on the couch. Then, she saw Sam watching her from behind his desk, a cup of coffee cradled between his hands. He silently poured another, slid it to the edge of the desk near her, and sat down again.

She wrapped the blanket around her body and took the coffee, sipping it gratefully. "How long you been awake?" she asked.

"Never went to sleep," he said.

"Oh." She was very aware of being naked under the blanket. She glanced furtively at the clock on the wall.

"Six thirty," he said. "You got to go?"

"I want to grab a shower before work."

"I got a hose out back," he offered.

"Hot water," she said. "I need hot water right now."

"Yeah, I suppose you do."

Feeling unaccountably shy in the daylight, she clutched the blanket to her body and grabbed at her clothing. "Could you give me a little privacy?"

"As much as you need," he said, picking up his cup and walking out.

Carson trotted over to greet him. *Well?* asked the shepherd.

No casualties, said Sam.

Glad to hear it. The others filled me in on Gus showing up with that sheriff. You're lucky you've got friends.

Sure am, said Sam, rubbing the dog's neck.

Mona emerged from the office, dressed but disheveled. "Say something nice," she said.

"You look great," said Sam.

"Automatic, but it'll do," she said. "We should talk."

"Let's go for a walk," he suggested.

He opened some cages, the dogs inside snapping awake. He signaled to Nan, Bert, Olga and Ignatz to join them.

"You need protection?" asked Mona. "From who? Me?"

"Outside," said Sam. "Dogs, heel."

He opened the back door and led them outside.

"Where are we—" she began.

He held a finger to his lips and kept walking into the woods, the dogs at his heels. She followed him, curious.

About five minutes in, Sam stopped. "Dogs, compass," he said.

The dogs ran off in four different directions.

"Never saw that one before," said Mona.

"Making sure," he said.

"Of what?"

"Privacy."

Clear! called Olga from the north.

Clear! Clear! Clear! called the others.

"Okay, we're alone," said Sam.

"Paranoid much?" asked Mona.

"Times being what they are, not nearly enough," said Sam. "I told you about my old CO visiting yesterday."

"Yes. You didn't get to why he was here. Things got off track, conversation-wise. Everything got off track."

"I'm sorry. It got out of hand. I shouldn't drink on a full moon—I've known that for a long time."

"But you did it anyway."

"I frightened you."

"Terrified me. Werewolves? Scary. Drunk boyfriends? Scarier. The combination? Scary beyond belief."

"I'm sorry."

"But you stopped yourself, Sam," she said. "You closed the gate. However drunk you were, whatever was affecting you, you had enough control to do that instead of attacking me."

"That was lucky. It may not happen the next time."

"Next time, you don't drink. We'll be fine."

"That goes for you, too."

"Excuse me?"

"I don't like to not drink alone," he said. "I realize that anesthesia was needed for last night's procedure, but I like it better when you're all there."

She leaned against a tree, her arms folded in front of her. "I don't know if I want to be in this relationship sober."

"Let's give it a try. See how we like each other without the goggles on."

"I don't know if I like myself when I'm sober," she said. "You should be happy you're with a lush like me. Sober girls don't fuck werewolves."

"Maybe we should put a stop to that, too," he said. "We can give it a rest three nights a month."

"Total of six."

"There's always daytime," he suggested.

She grabbed the back of his neck and pulled him to her. "I like it when you're a werewolf," she whispered.

"It's dangerous."

"That's what I like about it."

"I'm going away for a while," he said, disengaging her gently.

"What?"

"A week, maybe a little more."

"Why? Where?"

"A mission. For my CO."

"A mission," she repeated. "Like an Army mission? Are you going back to Afghanistan?"

"Worse," he said. "South Carolina."

"Oh, God. That is horrible. What's going on?"

"My CO said he could take the local heat off me. Off us."

"But you have to kill someone first?"

"Ain't that kind of mission," said Sam. "Shooting folks in wartime is one thing, but I won't do wetwork."

"Is it dangerous?"

"Isn't supposed to be, but—"

"Something to do with those men who came to kill you, isn't it?"

"Yup. Loose ends need to be tied up."

"Then it's dangerous."

"So am I," he said softly, and she shivered despite the summer heat. He took her in his arms held her tight. "Don't worry—I'm taking Arnie with me."

"Oh, you are so screwed," she said, laughing sadly.

From the tree line across the road, Tennant looked through his binoculars. He had a very good view of a Russian wolfhound patrolling the woods where he saw Sam and Mona disappear. He couldn't chance getting any closer with the directional mike, and the peepers he had planted in the warehouse were of no use.

"Sheeit," he muttered, and waited for the two to reemerge.

"Can you remember this spot?" Sam asked Mona. "How we got here?"

"I think so. Why?" asked Mona.

"I'm about to show you something stupid."

He pointed to the trunk of a tree, where something was carved into it.

She peered at it closely. "Sam loves Mona," she read. "Inside a heart with an arrow through it. Jesus, when did you go back to fifth grade?"

"I made that right after we started dating."

"You went into the middle of the woods with a jackknife and carved a Valentine that nobody ever saw."

"Wasn't with a jackknife," he said, holding up his fingers and waggling them.

"Full moon and a werewolf in love," she said. "Those claws leave a pretty deep mark."

"They do," he said, trailing his fingers gently across her cheek, "but they're gone now. So are the fangs and fur."

"I have to go to work, Sam," she protested as he kissed her neck. "I need to go home and have a shower first."

"There's time," he said.

After she left, he brought the dogs back to the warehouse, then laid out food and water for the pack. Carson yawned and stretched, then began to head off to his bed.

Carson, wait, said Sam. *I need a consult.*

It's been a long night, Boss, said Carson.

Come outside with me. Arnie, you come, too.

Arnie glanced at Olga.

No idea, she said.

I'll fill you in when I find out, said Arnie.

The German shepherd and the dachshund followed out the back door, Carson squinting uneasily in the sunlight. Arnie looked around, automatically checking for threats.

Sam threw a towel, a clean shirt and a bar of soap onto the rusting grill that he kept back there, then started stripping down.

You brought us out here for this? asked Arnie. *I've seen enough naked human flesh in the last two nights to give me nightmares.*

Sam cranked up the garden hose, then turned it on himself. *This naked flesh is starting to reek,* he said, grabbing the soap.

No, it started to reek yesterday, said Arnie. *We tried to tell you.*

That's what I value you for—your honesty. said Sam. *Okay, here's the drill. I need to take a team of readers. Five should do it. You two are my top dogs, so I need to pick three more.*

Four, said Carson.

What?

I'm not going, said the shepherd.

But—

I'm not going, and that's final.

Sam looked at him while Arnie shifted his gaze back and forth between them.

Want to explain why? asked Sam.

You do know that every dog in that warehouse can hear us at this distance, said Carson.

Right. Let me finish up. Sam ran some soap through his hair and scrubbed hard. Then, he rinsed and dried himself off. *Better?*

Arnie sniffed the air. *You'll pass with humans.*

Always a critic, said Sam.

Ain't nothin' but a hound dog, said Arnie. *Excuse me for having a well-developed sense of smell.*

You're okay by me, Sam, said Carson.

Sheepdog, muttered Arnie disdainfully.

Race you ten feet, offered Carson.

Sam pulled on his clothes and boots. *Let's go,* he said.

The dogs trotted on either side of him as he walked back into the woods.

You think they bugged the place? asked Arnie.

Be surprised if they didn't, said Sam.

But human bugs aren't designed for dogspeak, said Carson.

Except these guys know I can speak to dogs, said Sam.

Can they translate what we say? asked Arnie. *Can any normal human?*

I doubt it, but I don't want to give them the chance. This ought to be far enough. Sam sat on a fallen tree. *Talk to me, buddy.*

You remember last Christmas Eve? began Carson. *When those men came?*

How could I forget it?

I was on guard that night, said Carson. *My one and only job was to protect you and the others—and I failed.*

There were four of them, Sam pointed out. *And they were armed.*

Which meant I attacked too soon, said Carson. *All these years of training and patrolling with nothing more dangerous than a pair of mice, and when the moment finally arrived, I failed. I should have fallen back and let you out first. Instead, I jumped the first guy to come through the door like an hyperactive puppy and got tranqed for my troubles. I screwed up.*

So did I, Carson, said Sam. *I didn't anticipate that kind of attack. You did exactly what I trained you to do. You can't keep beating yourself up over it.*

You never trained us to let stuff go, commented Arnie. *And you're not exactly a shining example of it yourself.*

What does this have to do with not coming with me now?

You need dogs who are more flexible than me, said Carson. *I'm an old dog. This is a new trick.*

Carson, you know I trust you with my life.

No, said Carson. *Take Arnie and four others. I'll stay here and guard the rest. It's what I do. It's all I know.*

Let it go, Boss, said Arnie.

You learn fast, don't you, Arnie? said Sam.

Always have, said Arnie. *So. Four more dogs.*

Olga, said Sam.

No question, said Arnie. *Great reader, great fighter, great dog.*

Absolutely, said Carson.

After that, tough to say who's the best, said Sam.

I like the Dobie twins, said Carson.

Really? said Sam in surprise. *Won't I just be listening to them argue all the time?*

That's what makes them good at reading humans, said Arnie. *They know how to get under each other's fur, so they know what makes humans react to each other.*

And you'll want the extra muscle if you're taking Stubbylegs, said Carson.

Hey! protested Arnie.

I mean it, Boss, said Carson. *Those two can fight. I'll feel better knowing they have your back.*

Fine, said Sam. *That leaves one.*

The two dogs shared a glance. Arnie nodded.

Take Otto, said Arnie.

Yeah, agreed Carson.

Otto? To read people? He hardly ever says anything, said Sam.

Yeah, but when he does, he's dead on, said Arnie.

He's got those spooky eyes, too, said Carson. *Otto knows stuff we don't.*

You're getting weird on me, said Sam. *Name one thing Otto ever did that I can't get from any of the others.*

He made your alpha as a werewolf, said Arnie. *Nobody else did that. Not even me.*

He did? How?

You'll have to ask him, said Arnie.

It's the spooky eyes, insisted Carson. *Let's get back. It's past my bedtime.*

Okay, said Sam.

Used to be we'd be getting back from a moonlight run around now, said Carson.

Things change, said Sam.

Yes, they do, said Carson. He perked up suddenly, his ears twitching. *Sally's coming.*

"Got some info for you, Sheriff," said Wilkins, poking his head in the doorway.

"Lay it on me, son," said Boudreau, leaning back in his chair.

"Our dog supplier was in the Army six years before he came here," said Wilkins, consulting a printout. "Spent five in Kabul. Started off in the Quartermasters Corp, then spent the last two in a canine unit. Silver Star, Bronze Star, Purple Heart."

"Decorated? How in the hell does a guy get decorated handing out blankets and playing with puppies?"

"He was in a convoy that came under attack," read Wilkins. "Ran through enemy fire to pull three guys out of a burning truck right before it exploded."

"How does one man pull three guys to safety?"

"He made three trips—the last one after taking a bullet through his shoulder. As for the playing with puppies, he trained and led dogs that would go through bombed buildings, looking for survivors and corpses. Report says he and his dogs got out more living folks than anyone else. I saw those guys once when I was there. Unbelievably dangerous, 'cause you never knew if the building might collapse on top of you, or if there were any backup booby traps left to take out the troops who came to investigate."

"I take it back," said Boudreau. "Our boy sounds like a real hero. Keeps it quiet. I didn't see a single decoration up at his place, and that's the sort of thing you brag about. It's good marketing around here."

"Maybe he keeps them at home," said Wilkins. "Tom Cheller was based in Kabul at the same time, but not in the same units."

"When was he killed?"

"December 12, 2009," said Wilkins. "Hey!"

"Hey what?"

"That's the same date that Lehrmann earned his Silver Star," said Wilkins, "but Cheller died somewhere in the mountains, body not recovered."

"They knew each other, they were friends, and Lehrmann sees his one significant piece of combat on the day his friend gets killed." said Boudreau. "Nope, not buying it. Sounds like the official version to me."

"And the official version is Army slang for bullshit," said Wilkins.

"It's what I'm thinking," said Boudreau. "What about Pastore and Kenner?"

"Kenner never served there," said Wilkins. "Pastore did."

"Same time as Cheller and Lehrmann?"

"Looks like," said Wilkins.

"But it says different units, doesn't it?"

"Yessir."

"Well, all we know is that there's something to know," said Boudreau. "Cracking the Army's secrets is gonna be a real bitch. Keep digging into Kenner's life. Let's see if we can work backwards from his final days."

"How long are you going to be away?" asked Sally.

"A week, give or take," said Sam. "If you're uncomfortable about working with a sub, that's okay. You can wait until I come back."

"He won't know the dogs like I do," said Sally. "I'll keep coming in."

"Okay, but check with your folks first," said Sam.

"What kind of job is it?" she asked.

"I'm giving a demonstration, using a team on site for a week," said Sam. "If they like what they see, it may be a regular contract."

"That would be good, wouldn't it? Means you'll be able to pay me minimum wage when I get old enough."

"This is an internship," he said. "I thought you did it for the love of dogs."

"I'm growing up," she said. "Does this guy Larry know what he's doing?"

"He'll keep them fed and clean," said Sam. "I'm counting on you to put them through their drills. Nothing more than basic commands, Sally. They can go a week without attack training."

"I could wear the padding," she offered.

"No," he said. "Emphatically, totally not. You're not old enough to get bitten."

"They wouldn't bite me. They like me."

"And that would screw up their training," said Sam. "They're learning to be guard dogs. One week being sweet to you, and they'll all be fluffy little bunnies."

"What about this Tennant guy?" she asked.

"They can bite him," he said. "I'm going to take the demo team outside. Work with the others in the pit, and holler if a customer comes."

He gathered the five dogs and brought them out.

"Dogs, sit," he commanded.

They sat in a semicircle around him, Arnie in the middle, Olga and Otto on his left, the twins on the right. From inside the warehouse, they could hear Sally putting the others through their paces.

You're the team, said Sam.

All right! said Nan and Bert.

Thank you, said Otto softly. *It is an honor.*

You may be reconsidering that before it's over, said Sam. *Now, apart from Pastore, no one knows about me at this place we're going to—neither about being a werewolf or a dogtalker. That stays secret.*

Who could we tell? laughed Olga.

They might have their own dogs there, said Arnie.

Right, Arnie, said Sam. *Full moon ends tonight, so at least I don't have to worry about the change, but when we're there, don't talk to me where other dogs can hear us. Remember, you're gonna be bringing everything you've got into play. Reading, scent, sound—whatever senses or instincts you have. Anything that bugs you, no matter how small, you tell me about it.*

What are we looking for, exactly? asked Nan.

Lying humans, said Arnie.

When they came back in, Sally was in the pit with Ignatz. She looked at the team.

"Cool," she said. "Those are the ones I would have picked."

"Seriously?" said Sam.

"Well, Carson, too, but he wouldn't want to leave, you know?" she said, then she turned her attentions back to Ignatz.

How old does she have to be before you make her a full partner? asked Arnie.

"What?" asked Sally. "Did you say something, Sam?"

"Just telling the dogs to get back in their cages," said Sam.

The five quickly got inside to back him up.

Sally left early in the afternoon to attend her brother's trombone recital. Around six, as Sam was cleaning up and feeding the dogs, a Jeep pulled into the parking lot, and a young woman wearing an Emory T-shirt and denim overalls came into the warehouse.

"I'm sorry, miss, but we're closed," said Sam.

She stared at him, taking him in so deeply that for a moment he was glad he had the dogs with him.

She knows him, said Olga. *She knows him from her past.*

"Is there something wrong, miss?" asked Sam.

"You don't remember me, do you?"

She loved him once, said Olga sadly. *He never knew.*

"Oh, that's a question that can only get me into trouble," said Sam, smiling. "I'm sure I would remember a pretty young lady like yourself if I had ever—"

He stopped. She had her hair in pigtails, like she had when . . .

"Got some pictures from Thanksgiving," said Tom. "Wanna see?"

"Sure," said Sam. "Let me finish packing my gear."

Water decontaminants. Uppers. First-aid kit. Enough MRE's for three days, then two days extra—it meant another two kilos, but you never knew. He closed it up, then came over to where Tom had his laptop open for one last look.

"There's a nice one of you," said Tom, pointing to a shot of Sam stuffing his face. "First time with food?"

"Felt that way," said Sam. "Your mom's a good cook."

"My mom doesn't even know where the kitchen is," said Tom, "but she knows how to hire a good cook. There's us at the quarry pond. Looking ripped, bro. No wonder Kerry—"

"Kerry Cheller," he said, shaking his head in wonder. "As I live and breathe, you're Tom's little sister."

"I guess I've changed in seven years," she said.

"Well, sure," he said, coming over to her. "All for the good."

He hesitated over what to do, then held out his hand. She shook it.

"This is your place," she said, looking around.

"Mine and the bank's," he said.

"How long you been here?"

"Six years."

"Six years," she repeated. "You've been twenty miles away for six years, and you never came by to say hello. Not once."

"I sent—" he began, then stopped. "It was awkward. I didn't know the right thing to do. I survived, and I didn't want to shove that in your face."

"I was waiting for you to rescue me," she said. "Stupid, sad schoolgirl with a crush on her big brother's handsome friend. Always thought you'd come back for me."

"You were fourteen," he pointed out. "I was twenty-two."

"Tom was twenty-one," she said. "Never saw twenty-two."

He couldn't say anything.

"I e-mailed you," she said. "A bunch of times."

"I know," he said. "It wasn't—I didn't know what to say, Kerry. I didn't want you to hurt any more than you already were."

"Not writing back hurt me," she said. "I had nothing else of Tom's but you. You were his only friend."

"I'm sorry."

"Please don't say that," she said. "When I found out from the sheriff that you were here—"

"That's right," he said. "You're the one who found those bodies in the quarry pond. Jesus, that must have been horrible."

"There is so much horrible in the world. I had put you out of my mind, I really had. No more Tom, then Mom and Dad started fighting, and there was a lot of that. They finally got divorced, and I went off to Emory, and everything seemed to be settling down into the ordinary daily horrible. Then, I saw that man in the water staring at me with his empty eyes."

She shuddered, wrapping her arms around herself. "They said he'd been down there since Christmas. Who knows if anyone would've ever found him? Complete fluke we did. So he's lucky. His family will finally know what happened to him. To them."

"That's a blessing, I suppose," said Sam.

"I still don't know what happened to Tom," she said softly. "Died in combat, some top-secret thing, still classified."

"I never knew, either."

"You're lying."

Oh, she's good, said Bert.

That wasn't hard, said Nan, dismissively. *He's all kinds of staggered right now.*

"Tom said you did missions together," she said. "Tom said you were—you were like him."

"I don't know what you're talking about," Sam said automatically.

She looked around furtively.

The dogs watched her, barely breathing.

"That you're a werewolf," she whispered. "Like he was."

"A what?" said Sam. "Did you say werewolf?"

She nodded.

"Okay, Kerry, I'm sorry I put you through anything, but that's nuts," said Sam. "There ain't no such thing as werewolves. That's movie stuff. Tom must have been teasing you."

"Tom was a werewolf," she said. "I saw him change. He told me we had to keep it a secret."

"This ain't exactly keeping it secret right now," said Sam.

"He said if anything ever happened to him, the one person I could trust was you," she said, starting to cry, "but you never wrote back."

"Aw, shit, Kerry," he said, coming over to hold her.

Bad move, said Arnie.

Very bad, agreed Olga.

"What happened to Tom?" she asked, still crying. "Please tell me the truth."

He hesitated.

"Get down!" shouted Pastore.

"No, sir!" Sam yelled, starting to clamber down the ridge. "Tom and Isaiah are still—"

The bullet took him through his left shoulder, punching through the body armor like it was paper and spinning him around before he fell. Pastore and Crawford dragged him back to the cover of the boulders as more bullets pinged around them, sending chips of rock in all directions. The mortar shells started falling at the base of the ridge.

"They'll have our range in thirty seconds," said Pastore. "Lehrmann, tell me you can walk right now or I'm going to have to put a bullet through your head and leave you for the buzzards."

"I can walk," gasped Sam.

A shell landed twenty meters away.

"How about running?" asked Pastore.

"Tom—"

"Tom and Isaiah are dead," said Pastore. "Let's move out."

"I don't know what happened to Tom," he said.

She looked up at him, tears glistening on her face. "Don't know? Or won't tell?"

"Don't know," he said. "I'm sorry."

"Tom was wrong about you."

She tried to kiss him suddenly, but he gripped her shoulders and held her away.

"Yes, he was," he said.

Um, Boss? said Olga. *Mona's standing in the doorway.*

"Hello, Mona," said Sam, releasing Kerry. *A whole room full of watch dogs, and that's the warning I get?*

"That's a very pretty girl you got there, Sam," observed Mona.

"Mona, this is Kerry Cheller," said Sam. "Kerry, this is Mona Havelka, my, my—"

"My, my," said Mona. "I can't wait to hear you complete that sentence."

"Girlfriend," said Sam.

"Hi," said Kerry, wiping her eyes with her sleeve. "Can I get a ten second head start before you kill me?"

Mona stepped to the side. "Since he wouldn't let you kiss him, I'll give you fifteen."

"I'm sorry about this, Kerry," said Sam.

"Stop saying that," replied Kerry. She walked past Mona. A moment later, the Jeep started up, then spun out of the parking lot so fast that gravel sprayed the front of the warehouse.

"Why did you make the pretty girl cry, Sam?" asked Mona.

"That was Kerry Cheller," he said. "Little sister of someone I knew in the Army."

"Didn't look so little to me," said Mona. "I wish I was little like that in a few places. Why was she here?"

"She was asking what I knew about her brother's death."

"Oh," said Mona. "Did you tell her?"

"No," said Sam.

"Why not?"

"I can't talk about it."

"Way to go," said Mona. "A weaker man might have shown some compassion in that situation. Can you tell me?"

"No. I already told you too much."

"Ooo, can you feel the love and trust in the room? Sure the pretty girl wasn't crying because you turned her down for something else? You must have rocked her world back then, big handsome stud like you."

"Nothing happened then, nothing happened now. I'd think you'd be happy about that."

"I'm a happy, happy girl," she said. "Happy and sober. Didn't even have a little something to take the edge off."

"Great."

"Which means the edge is still on."

The alarm went off. He walked towards the cage, stripping off his clothes. She followed him.

"Are we going to talk about this or not?" she asked.

"Let me get through the next half hour first."

Carson sat by the cage, watching.

"Carson, patrol," said Sam.

Carson didn't move.

What are you doing? demanded Sam.

My job, said Carson.

Leave.

When the gate closes, said Carson.

"What's with Carson?" asked Mona. "Which one of us is he worried about?"

Both, said Carson.

When did disobedience become part of your behavior? asked Sam.

When stupidity became part of yours, replied the dog.

"Carson, patrol!" snapped Sam.

The dog didn't budge.

"Jesus, could this day get any more crazy?" shouted Sam. He stormed into the cell. "Make sure that gate's secure, will you?"

It slid shut behind him.

74

Boss! shouted Carson.

Sam spun around.

Mona was inside the cage, leaning against the gate. She reached behind her and shook it with one hand. "The gate's secure, Sam."

"What the hell are you doing?" he asked, his breath starting to come in quick, panicked gasps.

"Being with you," she said, walking towards him. "Now, take some deep, slow breaths, Sam. You're going to be all right."

"Carson!" he shouted.

I'm on it, the dog called, running for the emergency switch.

"It's all right, Sam," she said. "We will get through this. It's—"

"You have to get out!" he shouted, grabbing her by the waist.

The change hit him hard and fast, his claws raking across her sides. She shouted in agony and terror as he shoved her against the bars, his muzzle against her throat, his fangs bared, primed to—

Now, Boss! called Carson, his front paw depressing the treadle that activated the release.

Sam grabbed the gate, slid it open, and pushed Mona out so hard that she slammed into the opposite wall. Then, he slid it back as Carson came running up. The lock engaged.

"What the hell were you thinking?" roared Sam. "Are you insane?"

She threw herself at the mesh and rattled it. "That's not the problem!" she shrieked. "This is the problem. It's the fucking cage, Sam. How can we be together when you lock yourself away?"

"If I hurt you," he began.

"You did hurt me," she said, holding up her hands, the palms covered with the blood from her sides. "You hurt me because you're afraid of hurting me. You have to stop being afraid, Sam. You have to stop holding back."

"But if I bit you," he said. "You'd turn. You'd be—"

"Like you, Sam," she said. "I'd be like you—and then you wouldn't have to be afraid of it anymore."

"You don't want this."

"I want you," she sobbed, collapsing against the mesh, "but you won't let me in."

He stepped back and sat down in his chair.

"First-aid kit's in the washroom," he said. "Get yourself taken care of, then leave. I don't think we should take any more chances tonight."

"Sam—"

"Go home, Mona."

She stood up stiffly and walked away. He heard her go into the washroom. He heard the cabinet door open and shut, and water running. Then, he heard her leave.

Carson went to check the front door, then came back to look at Sam.

I'm okay, buddy, said the werewolf to the dog.

Oh, that is so far from being true that the truth can't even see it from here, said Carson.

Tell you what, said Sam. *When the half hour's up, let's go for a run together.*

I'd like that, said Carson. *It's been a while.*

Tennant saw Mona come out, one hand pressed to her side. She climbed into her car awkwardly, then rested her head on the steering wheel for a moment. He jotted down her license plate number. He had heard everything that was said inside—said by the humans, in any case. He wished he knew what the conversations with the dogs were about.

He condensed the recordings into one burst of data and sent it along to Pastore. Then, he walked through the dark to where his own vehicle was concealed and drove to his motel.

CHAPTER 6

MYERS GOT BACK TO HER house at seven in the morning, hoping to grab a shower before heading off to the hospital. Her neighbor, Fred, was out in his driveway in his bathrobe, picking up his paper.

"Ho, ho," he chortled. "Coming in from a wild night, Ali?"

"You have no idea," said Myers, "and you never will."

"Oh, to be young and hangover-proof," he said, leering.

"Wasn't drinking," said Myers. "I'll leave the rest to your imagination. See you, Freddy."

She went inside. Her cell was charging on the kitchen table. There was a message.

"Ali," came a woman's voice, barely recognizable, "it's Sylvia. Call me the moment you get this."

She called immediately.

"Syl, it's me," she said. "What's wrong? Oh, no. Oh, honey, I am so sorry. He was such a cool kid. How did he—his mother? How horrible! The poor woman. Listen, Syl, I'm gonna see if I can switch my days off this week. I'll try to come up. Don't start drinking. All right, then don't drink any more, you hear me?"

She disconnected, glanced at the time, and sighed. She had just enough time to shower before work, get the night's run off her body.

She tossed her clothes onto the bed and started the shower. *Crazy Syl and her boy toys,* she thought as she shampooed her hair. *Never lasted, but this one—killed by his own mother when she didn't recognize him. Wait.*

Something Syl had said made no sense.

77

She rinsed quickly and dashed into her room, still dripping, to call her back.

"Sylvia, it's me again," she said. "When did you say this happened? I know—but what time? Syl, that's not possible. Are you sure? Okay. Okay, baby, stop crying. I'll be up there before you know it."

She disconnected, frowning. Then, she opened a drawer in her nightstand and poked through a bunch of cards until she found the one she wanted—no, didn't want, but he had to know. Protocol said she shouldn't use her cell. There was a payphone at the hospital.

She stuck Pastore's card in her wallet, then dressed and went to work.

"I've arranged for the butcher shop to make deliveries," Sam said to Tennant. "The refrigerator's here. The dogs get fed first thing in the morning and at the end of the day. You know how to carve up a side of beef?"

"I've done something similar," said Tennant.

"I don't ever want to know what that was," said Sam. "This mangy mutt in the corner is Carson. Carson, wake up and meet Larry."

Carson lifted one weary eyelid, took in the new guy—then went back to sleep.

"Carson's the night patrol. You let him out at the evening feed, put him back in the morning. He'll take care of everything else himself. By the way, you can have these back." He tossed a handful of peepers to Tennant, who caught most of them. "I swept the place this morning, as you probably know. I don't want to find any surprises when I get back. Are we clear about that?"

"I'm merely a humble dog-sitter," said Tennant.

"Yeah, fuck you," said Sam. "Here comes Sally. Pretend you're a nice guy."

"Morning, everyone," called Sally to the dogs as she came in. Tails thumped. "Morning, Sam. Is this the fresh meat?"

"Sally, I told you not to call him that to his face," said Sam.

"Sorry," she said. "I'm Sally."

"I'm Larry," said Tennant, holding out his hand. "I heard all about you, young lady."

She shook hands, perusing his face distrustfully. "You know what you're doing with dogs?" she asked him.

"Pretty much," he said, "but how about you introduce me around?"

She looked over at Sam, who nodded.

"All right," she said. "First thing you got to learn is their names. This is Ignatz—"

Sam left the two of them and went back into his office. He called Mona's number for the fifth time since daybreak. For the fifth time, he got her voicemail.

"Me again," he said. "I'll be out of here soon. Call my cell. I don't want to leave without talking to you."

He grabbed his duffle bag and walked out.

"Here," he said, tossing a set of keys to Tennant. "Run the van every day so it stays happy."

"Will do," said Tennant.

Car!

No, truck!

It's a van, dummy!

"Sounds like my ride is here," said Sam.

He loaded up the travel cages onto a dolly and trundled them outside to where Pastore was pulling up in a cargo van.

"Good morning," said Pastore, hopping out. "Have a good night?"

"You know damn well I didn't," said Sam. "Help me with these cages."

The two men loaded them into the van and secured them.

"I'll stay out here," said Pastore. "I'd rather the girl not see me."

"Fine," said Sam. "I'll get the team."

He went inside. He looked in on Carson. The dog was sound asleep, and he didn't want to wake him twice after wearing him out running all night.

Ignatz, tell Carson I said good-bye, he called.

Right, Boss.

He unlocked the cages and brought out his chosen five.

"Bye, Sam," called Sally, waving from the pit where she was surrounded by German shepherds.

"Bye, Sally," said Sam. "See you, Larry."

"Bye, Arnie, Olga, Otto, Nan, and Bert," called Sally.

With the exception of Otto, the team barked in response.

I call shotgun, said Arnie as they came outside.

You call cage, said Sam.

Rats, muttered Arnie.

"So, these are the best of the best," said Pastore, coming over to look at them.

"They are," said Sam. "Meet the soldiers."

Pastore looked down at Arnie.

"A dachshund? Seriously?" he asked.

"Arnie's the best reader I've ever had," said Sam.

"If you say so," said Pastore, shrugging.

I really don't like this guy, said Arnie.

Me, neither, said Sam. *Load up.*

The dogs hopped into the van. Arnie raced for the cage closest to the front.

Like we care, said Nan.

Sam tossed in his duffle and supplies, then closed the rear doors. Pastore got in and turned the ignition key.

Sam looked at his warehouse for a long moment, then climbed into the passenger seat. "The last time I went anywhere with you, it was in a chopper worth a hundred fifty million," he said.

"You saying we've come down in the world?" asked Pastore. "This is one of the finest vans ever made—in this country, anyway."

"We lost that chopper and three men on that mission," said Sam.

"Well, this baby's a rental," said Pastore. "If I don't return it, it's coming out of my credit card. Although I sprang for the complete insurance package."

"I feel safer already," said Sam. "Let's go. Where are we going, anyway?"

"Place called Hickory Grove in South Carolina."

"Never heard of it. What's it near?"

"It isn't near anything," said Pastore, consulting the mapfinder on the dash. "It's off 85 east of Spartanburg."

"And that gizmo's telling you to take 75 south to loop around by Atlanta, ain't it?"

"Yes, it is," said Pastore. "Your point?"

Sam, Tom, and Isaiah filed into the ready room. Crawford was already there, loading his spare clips.

"Yo," said Tom. "Where's the big man?"

"Right behind us," said Sam, coming to attention and saluting.

Tom turned to see Pastore filling the doorway. He nodded.

"I'm waiting," said Pastore.

Tom came to a kind of attention and gave him a lazy salute.

"When the full moon is over, you're gonna owe me some laps," said Pastore. "At ease."

"Yessir," said Tom.

"Everyone got their Odyssey charged?" asked Pastore.

The others held up the devices, gadgets the size of iPhones that contained detailed maps of the Afghan terrain.

"Coordinates for the extraction points," said Pastore, writing them on a chalkboard. "First one is at 0500. Second at 1030. Third at 1500."

"And the fourth is pray to Allah and run like hell," said Tom, keying in the numbers.

"Keep your Odysseys close," said Pastore, ignoring him. "After all . . ."

"They may save your life someday," the others chorused.

"You haven't changed," said Sam. "Still trusting computers to tell you what's what. Take 76 east. Slower road, but a straight shot across, the scenery's better, and we ought to find some food worth eating."

"I am here to make you happy," said Pastore, putting the van in gear. "How long before the dogs need a walk?"

"Two hours should be fine," said Sam.

He tried Mona's number again. Nothing.

"So, woman troubles," Pastore said when they reached the highway.

"Not talking about it."

"Weird having Tom's little sister showing up like that."

"Still not talking about it."

"Of course, dumping a van full of dead guys on her family property was a bonehead move," observed Pastore. "Made it easy to connect you."

"Didn't think it would be that easy," said Sam. "Haven't been in touch with the Chellers since Tom bought it."

"Did you know his sister had that crush on you?"

"Tell you the truth, I was too busy keeping his mama's paws off me."

"No shit," laughed Pastore. "Why did you resist? She looked pretty good in those pictures."

"Something in the Bible about not screwing your best friend's mother in the family home when she's still married to his father and has four gin and tonics fueling her pickup," said Sam.

"I am not familiar with that verse," said Pastore, "but I lack your religious upbringing. Still, using the Cheller quarry—almost like you wanted to get caught."

"Bullshit. I dumped them there because I knew the business was long gone and the water was deep."

"Wasn't deep enough," said Pastore. "I trained you better than that."

"You never trained us to dispose of bodies," said Sam. "Changing the subject—you got intel for me on this lab? And what's my cover?"

"Intel's here," said Pastore, handing him a file. "As for the cover, it's a stroke of genius, if I do say so myself."

"What is it?"

"You're going in as a dog trainer."

"That might work," said Sam, thumbing through the file. "Especially as how everyone at this place has a Ph.D. in something, and all I got is my associate's degree from community college. I'd have a tough time talking shop with them otherwise."

"Don't forget your Army training," pointed out Pastore.

"Forgot it as soon as I got out," said Sam. "What's a dog trainer supposed to be doing in a top secret lab full of werewolf specialists?"

"You are there to train your dogs how to identify werewolves in the field," said Pastore.

"Well, shoot, Colonel, they're the big hairy fuckers with the fangs and claws. What's so hard about identifying them?"

"You're training your dogs to identify them in their human form."

"Oh," said Sam. "Okay, I like that. I can work that."

You're not telling him about Otto? asked Nan.

No, said Sam.

Why not?

Because if Colonel Alpha Werewolf knows Otto can make him, he might consider Otto a threat, said Arnie. *And that could put Otto at risk.*

Right, said Sam.

Thank you, Boss, said Otto.

"Will there be any other werewolves at this place?" asked Sam.

"Not this week," said Pastore. "Full moon's over."

"They spend the full moon here?"

"Some volunteers," said Pastore. "For observation and tests."

"Tests?" said Sam suspiciously. "What kind of tests? Experiments?"

Pastore glanced over at him. "We're looking for a cure," he said.

"Holy shit," breathed Sam. "Do you think there is one?"

"We're still trying to figure out the mechanism of what goes on when a werewolf bites a human," said Pastore. "Makes your average autoimmune virus look like chicken pox. But, the eggheads will bring you up to speed."

"They'll give me the version for dummies, I hope," said Sam. *Okay, team. Is he telling me the truth?*

The dogs glanced at each other.

Not sure, said Nan.

Me neither, said Bert.

Yes, said Olga.

No, said Arnie.

Otto was silent.

Otto, your thoughts? asked Sam.

He thinks he's telling the truth, said Otto. *He may be telling the actual truth. He may also be a man who is capable of deceiving even himself in order to deceive others.*

Cool, said Bert admiringly. *That dog can sound deep without committing to anything. I'll stick with not sure.*

We don't have a consensus, Boss, said Arnie.

No problem, said Sam. *If you had, I'd be worried.*

They pulled over after two hours at a roadside barbecue stand where an elderly Black woman supervised a smoker made from scraps of sheet metal. Pastore ordered two platters while Sam let the dogs get their exercise and laid out their water bowls.

"Your dogs eat barbecue?" called Pastore.

"They never have before," said Sam.

Pastore bought a third platter, then divided it into five portions and placed them on paper plates. The dogs took one sniff, then gobbled them down.

You've been holding out on us, Boss, said Olga accusingly.

Okay, I like him now, said Arnie.

You're all too easy, said Sam.

"They look blissed out," observed Pastore, sitting on the van's floor, his legs dangling out the back.

"You have gained great face among them," said Sam. "They thank you."

"Least I can do for my new soldiers," said Pastore. "An army travels on its stomach."

"What will we do for fresh meat at the lab?"

"There's a butcher over in York," said Pastore. "I made the arrangements yesterday. It's a halal place."

"That brings back some memories."

Pastore reached behind him for a small bag and pulled out five dog collars. "When they're done, put these on them," he said.

Sam examined them. "Bugged?" he asked.

"You know it," said Pastore. "Voice-activated, and deactivated near the security trailer so they won't set off any alarms—and they repel fleas and ticks."

"Useful."

"See if you can get the dogs into situations where they're with the lab folks when you're not there. People might say things in front of them."

Sam put the collars on the dogs, transferring their tags.

"You still got your dog tag?" asked Pastore.

"Somewhere," said Sam. "Wherever I stowed my medals."

"You earned those," said Pastore. "You should display them with pride."

"Sure," said Sam. "Except two of them go with a cover story, and I have trouble faking the pride with that one."

"Be proud of the real story, then."

"The one where I killed lots of enemies, but couldn't save my friends? Yessir, I am real proud of that."

"You tried to save them. You got shot, and that saved your life. Tom went back for Isaiah and got himself killed."

"Tom was the best of us, Colonel."

"The best get killed the most," said Pastore. "It was a shitty war, Sam. Shit happened."

Sam collected the water bowls. "Dogs, inside," he said, and the team jumped into the van and settled into their cages. Sam tossed the bowls into their box and closed the rear doors. "Ready when you are."

"Let's go," said Pastore.

Boudreau's phone rang. He picked it up and held it several inches away as the screaming began.

"Goddamn it, Sheriff," yelled a voice at the other end of the line. "Why in the hell didn't you warn us what that shit was?"

"First of all, who is this?" asked Boudreau.

"This is Merritt, down at the GBI Chemlab. Do you have any idea—"

"Good afternoon, Mister Merritt," said Boudreau. "What seems to be the problem?"

"The problem is you sent us super deadly shit in an ordinary evidence voucher," said Merritt. "Thereby placing me and my team in danger."

"And when did I do that exactly?"

"Those dart guns from that corpse van you pulled out of that pond," said Merritt.

"Could you hold on one minute?" asked Boudreau.

"But—"

Boudreau hit the hold button, then keyed a number.

"Yessir?" came Officer Cole's voice.

"Officer Cole, I have an irate chemist on my main line screaming about some dart guns," said Boudreau.

"Oh, did they get the analysis done?" asked Cole.

"We have not reached that point in the conversation yet," said Boudreau. "Did I know about the dart guns?"

"It was in the inventory, underneath the other weapons recovered," said Cole.

Boudreau shuffled through his files until he found his copy. He read through it quickly. "Absolutely right, Officer. I missed it. Two dart guns—and you recovered intact darts?"

"Yessir. A full clip in one, and one dart in the other. I sent the darts off for analysis. Thought it might be a lead once we knew what was in them."

"Very good, Officer Cole," said Boudreau. "We might need to use some of them tranquilizers on the chemist. Thanks for bringing me up to speed."

He reopened the connection to the chemist. "I'm so sorry, Mister Merritt. We just assumed they were tranquilizers."

"And the ones in the full clip were," said Merritt. "It was what was in the other one that scared the shit out of me. Lucky we were using full-tox protocols."

"What did you find?"

"Aconite," said Merritt.

"What's that do?"

"It kills anything it touches, including chemists with crappy state-funded medical plans," said Merritt. "It's a neurotoxin. If we hadn't been working with it in containment, there'd be three openings at the GBI."

"My God," said Boudreau. "Who the hell puts that in a dart gun?"

"Someone who really wants to make someone else dead," said Merritt.

"I've never heard of this stuff before," said Boudreau. "Where do you get it? Is it commercially available, or do you have to have permits?"

"It's not used for anything in this country," said Merritt. "Anything legal, anyway. It's a folk remedy in some parts of Asia where they don't know shit, but anyone who has it around here is making it himself."

"That's useful to know," said Boudreau. "How does one go about making this stuff?"

"Comes from a family of plants," said Merritt. "They all have different names, but most of them are known as wolfsbane."

Boudreau almost dropped the phone. "You said wolfsbane?" he asked in disbelief.

"That's what I said. So you advise whichever idiot bagged this sucker that he's lucky he kept the dart intact."

"She," said Boudreau. "She's the lucky idiot. All right, I'd appreciate you sending me that report pronto—and any thoughts on where we can find a wolfsbane farm would be helpful."

"Oh, sure, I'll get right on that, Sheriff," said Merritt. "As soon as my heart gets down to normal."

He terminated the call with a slam at his end.

Boudreau called Cole.

"Yessir?" she answered.

"Be very glad you're still breathing, young lady," he said sternly.

"Sir?"

"You and Wilkins come on in here," said Boudreau. "You're not gonna believe this."

"You know," said Pastore. "If we had taken 75, we could've saved half an hour."

"But I would have missed sharing it with you," said Sam.

"Well, welcome to Hickory Grove," said Pastore. "There's your general store, there's the other store—and that was Hickory Grove, population 517, give or take. The lab is outside a few miles. There are four churches, two A.M.E., one Baptist, one Methodist. Nearest bar is in Sharon. Nearest titty bars are in Charlotte."

"Am I keeping the van?" asked Sam.

"'Fraid not, son. I told you it's a rental."

"Great. So I'm stuck here."

"Yeah, I was only telling you about the titty bars for the extra frustration," said Pastore. "I'll be heading straight out to them once I get you settled."

"What about police?"

"They'll be at the titty bars, too, most likely."

"In case of emergencies."

"Town's covered by the York Police, but the lab has its own security people."

"I saw that. Five men, five dogs, bunch of cameras."

"And a bunch of computers monitoring everything."

"Which you trusted."

"I did," said Pastore, turning onto a dirt road into the woods, "but I don't anymore."

"What do you trust?" asked Sam.

"You, at the moment," said Pastore.

Lie, said all five dogs.

He's never trusted anyone in his life, said Sam. *No surprise there.*

They drove through trees for about three kilometers. Then, the trees opened up into meadow. Ahead was a double fence, made of steel mesh and topped with razor wire, and beyond it were a pair of trailer offices.

"Electrified?" asked Sam.

"Only at night," said Pastore. "Not a lethal voltage, just enough to immobilize someone for questions."

"What kind of questions?"

"Haven't thought about that," said Pastore. "Hasn't ever happened."

They drove up to the gate. Pastore slid an ID card through a slot, and the gates slowly slid open. A man walked out of a trailer that sat on the other side of the fence.

He was about to salute, said Olga. *His arm twitched, then stopped.*

"Good afternoon, sir," said the man. "We were expecting you about an hour ago. Any trouble?"

"No," said Pastore. "It was such a nice day, we took the scenic route and got sidetracked by some barbecue."

"Barbecue will do that," said the man. "Is this the dog man?"

"It is," said Pastore. "Meet Sam Lehrmann. Sam, this is Jim Bolton, Head of Security here."

"How do you do, Mister Lehrmann?" said Jim. "I'm gonna have to ask you to step out of the van for a moment, and remove any bags from the vehicle."

"No problem," said Sam, getting out. He pulled his duffle from the van and handed it over for inspection.

"Come inside for a moment," said Bolton.

Sam followed him into the trailer, where another man was seated, watching an array of monitors displaying the perimeter fence.

"That's Carl," said Bolton, and the man waved without looking. "I'm gonna scan your bag. Anything metal I pick up, I will ask you to remove for inspection."

"Got an electric razor," offered Sam. "Nothing else."

He took it out. Bolton scanned it, then ran the scanner over the duffle.

"That should be fine," he said. "Stand next to the grid for your ID."

Sam smiled pleasantly as his picture was taken. The plastic card slid onto a tray moments later.

"Came out nice," said Bolton, inspecting it. "I'll need your cell phone."

Sam handed it over. Bolton put it in a small lockbox and gave Sam the key.

"Any calls you need to make go through our designated lines," said Bolton. "You planning to walk your dogs on the grounds?"

"Unless you have a designated area for them," said Sam.

"Then bring them back out here to meet my dogs when you're all set up," said Bolton. "We'll introduce them to each other so there won't be any trouble later."

"Will do," said Sam. "Marine?"

"Hell, no," said Bolton. "Never gonna risk my neck for chicken feed."

"Good call," said Sam.

He walked back out to the van and waved his ID at Pastore. "I'm official," he said, hopping in.

Pastore drove another half a kilometer. A low, concrete building came into view, consisting of three rectangular slabs radiating from a central hub, the top of which was the dome of an observatory.

"Biology's on the right," said Pastore as he pulled into a parking lot in front. "Physiology and psychology is in the central wing, living quarters on the left."

"No kennels?"

"I thought you'd want the dogs with you in your rooms," said Pastore, "but there's kennels for the guard dogs back at the trailers."

"Looks like we're bunking together, team," said Sam.

Wonder what it's like to sleep without a cage, said Nan. *It's going to feel weird.*

Got to start sometime, said Bert.

A lean, weathered man in his fifties wearing a dingy, gray jumpsuit sauntered out. "Hey, Colonel, welcome back," he said. "Need a hand?"

"We can manage, but come meet Sam Lehrmann," said Pastore, shaking his hand. "Sam, this is Sid Coleridge. He's the facilities manager."

"Means I'm a hi-tech maintenance man," said Coleridge. "One step up from a janitor. Only, we ain't got a janitor, so I do that, too."

"Nice to meet you," said Sam. "Come meet the dogs."

"Are they friendly?" asked Coleridge.

"If I tell them to be," said Sam. He let the team out of their cages. "Let them sniff you, but don't pet them. They're on the clock."

Coleridge squatted and held out his hand.

"Dogs, sniff," said Sam.

The team trotted over to Coleridge and stuck their noses close.

"Dogs, heel," said Sam. "You're good."

"Really got them trained, don't you?" said Coleridge.

"That's what I do," said Sam.

"Now, if you need any special equipment, you let me know and I'll run it up from the shop," said Coleridge.

"Can't think of anything, but thanks," said Sam, grabbing his duffle. "Joe, want to grab that box for me?"

"Sure will, Sam," said Pastore.

The entrance hall was round, with double doors at the four compass points. Coleridge waved his ID at a sensor by the set on the left, and they opened. "This way," he said.

"Can you fix up ID cards for the dogs?" asked Sam. "I'll need them free to roam. Otherwise, they'll be a pain in the ass."

"Sure thing," said Coleridge. "I'll have them ready for you in ten. We're putting you in here. One room for you, an adjoining room for them."

Sam's room could have been plucked from one of the nicer hotel chains, with a nice, king-sized bed against the far wall.

Dibs, said Arnie hopefully.

"You guys are in there," said Sam, pointing to an adjoining room which had a couple of old mattresses tossed on the floor.

Olga walked in, sniffed them critically, then rested one paw on them. *Looks safe enough,* she said. She stepped onto the mattress, walked in a circle three times, then curled up and groaned happily. *Boss, may we live here?* she asked.

Me next! shouted Bert, bounding onto the one next to her, his sister right behind.

Arnie was still in Sam's room, eyeing the bed.

There was a knock on the door. The dogs immediately sprang to alert position.

"Yes?" said Sam.

"It's Sid Coleridge. I've got those ID tags for your dogs."

Sam opened the door and Sid came in, nodding approvingly at the array of canine attention he was drawing.

"You're a well-protected man," he observed, handing Sam the tags. "Doctor McKenna told me that he's getting everyone together to meet you and the dogs in the conference room in ten minutes. That's across from the cafeteria."

"Be there in ten," said Sam. "Thanks, Sid."

He attached the tags to the dogs' collars, then turned to Pastore. "You scanned the room?" he mouthed.

Pastore nodded, pulling a small device out of his pocket. "We're clean," he said.

"Anyone in particular here raised your hackles?" asked Sam.

"Not sure where my hackles are," said Pastore. "Any or all of them. Be careful."

"I can take down a scientist most days," said Sam.

"The security team is top notch," said Pastore. "Don't go picking any fights. This is strictly an intel job."

"Got it, Joe."

"I'm not used to you calling me that, son."

"I'm not in the Army anymore," said Sam. "Don't forget that."

"But I am," said Pastore. "Don't forget that. Now, let's go meet the nice scientists."

"Wolfsbane? Are you kidding?" laughed Wilkins.

"Aconite," said Boudreau. "It's made from wolfsbane."

"Wolfsbane was an X-Man—or X-Girl, wasn't she?" asked Wilkins.

"A what?"

"New Mutant," said Cole. "Then she bounced around. Excalibur, X-Factor, X-Force . . ."

"Right," said Wilkins. "Remember in Age of Apocalypse, she got stuck being a wolf?"

"That was so sad," agreed Cole. "But, she was one hell of a tracker."

"What the hell are you two talking about?" demanded Boudreau.

"Wolfsbane," said Cole. "Marvel Comics. She was a werewolf, basically."

"Went from being this itty-bitty Scottish chick to like this eighteen-foot wolf," said Wilkins.

"Wasn't anywhere near eighteen feet," said Cole. "That's just stupid."

"Speaking of stupid, could the two of you go back to being grownups?" asked Boudreau. "Officer Cole, you apparently put yourself unnecessarily at risk with that dart, along with a bunch of whiny lab techs."

"Sorry," said Cole. "But, wolfsbane? For real?"

"Do you know anything about it that isn't related to comic books?" asked Boudreau. "For that matter, do either of you know anything about anything that isn't related to comic books?"

"About aconite? No, sir," said Cole, "but I will find out what I can."

"Wolfsbane is also what they use to kill werewolves," offered Wilkins. "Got that from this book I read back in junior high."

"Extremely helpful, son," said Boudreau. "Answer me this: if that comic-book girl was supposed to be a werewolf, why was she named after something that's poisonous to werewolves?"

"It sounded cool," explained Wilkins. "Gotta admit, kinda spooky it being wolfsbane when those guys were torn apart by wolves, ain't it? Maybe they were hunting werewolves, and the werewolves got them first."

"I say they were killed by dogs, and I'm the feller in charge," said Boudreau. "I also say that you're a couple of Goddamned morons and I'm wondering why I ever hired you. Get out of here and do some police work, will you?"

"Yessir."
"Yessir."

Pastore held open the door to the conference room until Sam and the dogs went through. Sam stood at ease facing a group of six people—four White, one Black, one Latino—seated around a large, black oblong table. Coleridge, sitting closest to the door, nodded to Sam and winked at the dogs.

"Dogs, flank," said Sam, and the team took up positions on both sides— Arnie, Olga and Otto on his right, the twins on his left.

"Why aren't they leashed?" asked a blonde woman sharply. "You can't walk in here with a bunch of animals unleashed like that. It's—"

She broke off and sneezed abruptly, then again. "Shit," she gasped, grabbing at her purse for a tissue and an inhaler.

"They're not leashed because they're trained, ma'am," said Sam.

"So they're safe?" inquired the man at the far end of the table.

He was White, with close-cut brown hair, graying at the temples, and sat straight up in a chair designed for comfort. He was stocky, but Sam thought it might be muscle rather than middle age.

He's the alpha, said Olga.

"They're safe," said Sam. "Unless I tell them not to be. Or if they encounter a situation where their training tells them not to be."

"But we're getting ahead of ourselves," said Pastore. "Folks, this is Sam Lehrmann, the dog trainer I told you about. I first met Sam when he was with the Canine Corps in Kabul. He had a remarkable success rate with bomb-sniffers and rescue dogs during his time there, and has continued in civilian life as one of the top guard-dog trainers in the South. He is now here to get as much information as you can provide to turn these animals into werewolf hunters."

"Excuse me, but is that a dachshund?" asked the man at the end.

"Yes, sir," said Sam. "That's Arnie."

"He's a guard dog?"

"A very good one."

"Ridiculous," muttered the man.

"We could demonstrate," offered Sam.

"How? Have him bite me on the ankle?"

"And straight through the tendon," said Sam. "That takes out one leg. If you insisted on hopping around after that, he'd take out the other leg, and then you're down. If you kept going after that, he'd have his choice of targets— but the jugular's the quickest."

"A killer dachshund," said the man dubiously.

"Not yet," said Sam, "and hopefully never. I take it you're Doctor McKenna."

"That's right. Sorry, it's been a while since we've had a guest, and I'm a little rusty on the social skills. Eric McKenna. I'm the chief here. I'm a microbiologist."

Micro, hell, said Arnie. *He's a full-sized asshole.*

"Lisa Kudowski," croaked the blonde woman, tears pouring down her cheeks. "Evolutionary genetics and neurology and allergic as hell right now. Can we get this over with? I'm dying here."

"Juan Sanchez," said a balding, nervous man. "I'm analyzing the reproductive mechanism as well as the physiological aspects of the transformation. Nice to meet you."

"And you," said Sam.

"Sandra Buenaventura," said a brunette woman in a mellifluous voice that made Sam look at her more closely. She had almond eyes that looked at him the way he had seen his dogs look when they were reading humans, and an amused smile. "I'm a psychiatrist."

"Uh, oh," said Sam, smiling back, and there was a chuckle from the table.

Uh, oh, said Olga. *She's trouble.*

For sure, said Nan.

The last to be introduced was a woman in her thirties who looked unaccountably sleepy. "Valerie Burton," she said. "Astrophysicist."

She yawned abruptly. "Sorry. This is the middle of my rest period."

"Doctor Burton works primarily at night," explained Doctor McKenna.

"Makes sense," said Sam. "That's when the stars are out."

"I'm not watching the stars," she said. "I watch the moon."

Sam's pulse quickened for a second. "Of course. It's werewolf research. Well, folks, I am here to learn from all of you, and I am looking forward to finding out what all those big words mean. I am trying to find anything that you have that will help my dogs identify werewolves in their human state."

"For what purpose, exactly?" asked Doctor McKenna.

"So we can locate them and monitor them," said Pastore. "Particularly immigrants who might be enemy operatives infiltrating—"

"Paranoid delusions," snapped Burton.

Pastore smiled at her. "I expect your full cooperation," he said. "Continue, Sam."

"The dogs must be free to roam the facilities," said Sam.

"Why?" asked Buenaventura.

"Because that's how they will work in the real world once they are trained," said Sam. "They have to become accustomed to it. However, these are guard dogs, so I am going to ask that each of you come up so that they can get your scent into their brains. Once there, you will have no problems with them."

"Oh, no, no," said Kudowski, turning pale. "This is as close as I can stand."

"I'm sorry, ma'am," said Sam. "Just hold your breath and hold your hand out. They won't touch you."

Clutching her tissue against her mouth and nose and almost laughing in spite of her predicament, Kudowski stood and quickly came forward, her free arm out like she was going to stiff-arm a tackler.

"Dogs, sniff," commanded Sam, and Kudowski flinched as the pack came up to her and stuck their muzzles close to her hand.

So tempted to lick right now, said Bert. *Just to see how she freaks.*

You'll do nothing of the kind, said Arnie sharply. *Obey your orders.*

"You're good, ma'am," said Sam, and she scooted back to the far end of the table.

"May I go now, please?" she begged.

"Fine," said Pastore. "Nice to see you, Doctor Kudowski."

She fled the room. Seconds later, a series of explosive sneezes echoed from the hallway.

"Might as well line up," suggested Sam.

The ice broken, the scientists lined up and presented their hands one by one for canine assessment.

"Are we all friends now?" asked Buenaventura. "Can I pet them?"

"Well, I'd rather you—" began Sam.

She immediately squatted down and rubbed Arnie's neck. "You are so cute!" she cooed.

The other four dogs looked at Arnie and snickered, something that could only be heard by them and Sam.

Hate her, said Arnie. *This is completely—actually, this feels really good. Could she get that spot?*

"He particularly likes it behind the ears," said Sam.

Look at him wag, marveled Nan.

Seriously, guys, you gotta try this, said Arnie.

You are such a slut, said Olga.

I know, said Arnie happily.

Pastore's cell went off. He looked at the screen, then stepped into the hallway and answered it softly.

Something just freaked him out, said Nan. *Before he even answered.*

That's him freaking out? asked Sam. *He barely twitched.*

It's all relative, she said.

Pastore disconnected and motioned for Sam to join him.

"There's been another one," he mouthed. Then, he clapped Sam on the back. "Okay, now that you've been introduced, I'm taking off. Errands to run, dry-cleaning to pick up, you know. I'll be back in a week. You can give me a progress report then."

"Good enough, Joe," said Sam. "Safe trip."

Tennant finished hosing down the last cage, then consulted his checklist. He was exhausted. The dogs didn't like him. That kid didn't like him, even though he was doing his level best to be nice to her. She watched him like she thought he was going to steal a stapler. He didn't know if she didn't like him because the dogs didn't like him, or if the dogs didn't like him because the kid didn't like him. Maybe he just wasn't likable.

At the moment, he didn't give a shit.

"Which one of you is Carson again?" he called.

The entire pack looked up resentfully from their dinner bowls. He sighed.

"Carson, heel," he said, and a German shepherd detached itself from the group and trotted forward.

"Carson, patrol," he said.

The dog started walking along the walls.

"Damn, that actually worked," Tennant muttered. "Dogs, cages."

The pack went into their cages, and Tennant went down the line, closing them.

"Right," he said. "Time to work."

He went into Sam's office and started with the desk, upending the contents of each drawer and sorting through them. He sensed a presence and turned to see Sally looking at him from the doorway.

"I thought you went home," he said.

"I left my lunchbox here," said Sally.

She went into the refrigerator and retrieved it. "What are you looking for?" she asked.

"Invoice forms," he said.

She looked at him, then walked over to a filing cabinet, pulled open a drawer, and handed him one.

"It says so right here," she said, pointing to a label on the drawer.

"So it does," said Tennant. "Thanks. Good night, Sally."

She left without saying anything. He heard her saying goodnight to the dogs, then waited for the outer door to close before resuming his search. Then, he heard a noise at the door.

"Look, Sally—" he said, turning.

Carson stood in the doorway, looking at him.

"Carson, patrol," said Tennant.

The dog didn't move. Tennant considered throwing something, then simply closed the door.

What was he doing? asked Ignatz from his cage.

Searching the Boss' office, said Carson.

What's he looking for?

Something he won't find, said Carson.

Sam walked out of the building, the dogs following. As they approached the security trailers, he could hear conversation.

Only two females.

The wolfhound's mine. She's hot.

Hey, he's got a pet dachshund!

Arnie growled.

"Easy, Arnie," said Sam.

Bolton stood in front of the trailers along with the rest of the guards and five German shepherds, straining at their leads and barking ferociously.

Ooo, scary, giggled Nan.

"Don't you think your dogs ought to be leashed?" asked Bolton.

"Mine are trained," said Sam.

"Mine kill," said Bolton. "Come meet the team. People first. Carl, you met inside. These are Henry, Priscilla, and Floyd."

"Nice to meet you," said Sam.

The guards nodded without speaking.

His people are trained better than his dogs, commented Olga.

What's it to you, bitch? said the largest of the shepherds, a powerfully built animal with part of his right ear missing.

"Now, this big ol' brute is Sarge," said Bolton, grabbing the dog by the collar and bringing him up to Sam.

Sam held out his hand for the dog to sniff, then pulled it back quickly as the dog lunged for it. Sam's dogs all took a step forward.

"Stay!" Sam said immediately.

"Sorry about Sarge," said Bolton. "He doesn't like strangers."

"Then tell him I'm not one," said Sam. "Otherwise, there'll be problems."

"Sarge, friend," said Bolton, twisting Sarge's collar until the dog whimpered. "Hold out your hand."

Sam held it towards the dog's muzzle. The dog sniffed it this time.

"All right, once you got Sarge on your side, you'll be okay with the rest," said Bolton. "These are Tito, Franz, Benny, and Jasper. Let's have the dogs get acquainted."

The two packs inched towards each other until they were muzzle to muzzle.

Which one is the alpha? sneered Sarge.

I am, said Arnie.

Since when? objected Bert.

Shut up, Bert, said Arnie.

Oh, this is precious, said Sarge. *The lapdog is in charge. Guess I should be terrified.*

We'll be working inside, said Arnie. *We'll be out of your way.*

Our way is anywhere I want, said Sarge. *Which means I am your alpha now. Got that?*

No dog is my alpha, said Arnie. *Got that?*

Sarge stuck his muzzle in Arnie's face. *That means you're mine if it ever comes to a fight,* he said.

I know what it means, said Arnie. *And you'd better pray it never comes down to that, crotchlicker.*

"Aw, that's sweet," said Bolton, watching the two. "Sarge is making nice with the dachshund."

"Arnie has that calming effect," said Sam. "Is there a place where I can let my dogs run?"

"Rear of the compound," said Bolton. "About a mile run from here. The dogs should smell it right away."

"Good enough," said Sam. "Nice talking to you. Dogs, heel."

He started jogging along the fence, the dogs keeping pace.

What's all this about you being alpha? asked Bert.

Shut up, said Arnie.

But—

Shut up until we're out of range, said Arnie.

Bert quieted down, but looked offended.

The fence extended around an expanse of lawn. Someone had planted vegetable gardens, including a patch of corn that stood high in the late afternoon sun.

I can't hear them anymore, said Olga.

Right, said Arnie, standing in front of Bert. *I will say this once. Don't you ever question my authority again, either in front of other dogs or in private.*

Why are you the alpha? objected Bert.

I'm the oldest, and I'm the smartest, said Arnie.

But you're the smallest. Any one of us—

Bert, you submit to him or I will take you out right now, said Olga.

You leave my brother alone, growled Nan, standing at his shoulder.

Otto sat by Sam's feet, watching.

Protocol demands that our pack have an alpha, said Arnie. *This is a job where we have to be smart, not strong. But even if it called on us to be strong, I'm still the alpha, because I am the meanest one here.*

You only talk tough because you've got Olga backing you, said Bert.

We can go at it right now, said Arnie calmly. *I will show you what experience does. Make your move, Bert.*

The two stood muzzle to muzzle, Bert glaring, Arnie still. Then, the Doberman slowly lowered himself until his body was on the ground, his front legs out in submission.

Good dog, said Arnie.

CHAPTER 7

INITIAL IMPRESSIONS, SAID Sam. *Start with McKenna.*

Defensive, said Nan.

We're on his turf, said Bert. *He doesn't like outsiders. He wants to be the master of his kennel.*

He attacked right away, said Arnie. *And he picked on the smallest dog first, so he's a bully. It's how he maintains control.*

Or thinks he does, said Olga.

Otto? Any thoughts? asked Sam.

A man who is truly in control doesn't need to be defensive or attack at the first sight of an intruder, said Otto. *A scientist would have more curiosity.*

Scientists are no different than other people, said Sam. *They depend on funding that's always uncertain from year to year, they have to show results to justify their efforts, and they always wonder if their lives are just a waste of time.*

Sucks to be human, doesn't it? said Arnie.

I wouldn't know, said Sam. *Is McKenna only asserting dominance, or is he hiding something?*

Can't tell yet, said Olga, as the other dogs nodded their agreement.

Fair enough, said Sam. *Kudowski.*

Hard to read a body when the body keeps on sneezing, said Bert.

I hate sneezing, said Arnie. *I keep whacking my muzzle on the floor.*

She was sooo funny to watch, said Nan.

Can someone be allergic to dogs, but not to werewolves? asked Otto.

Oh, shit! exclaimed Bert admiringly as the other dogs looked at the Weimaraner with respect.

Helluva point, and I don't know the answer to that, said Sam. *I'll have to ask. Sanchez?*

Hiding something, said Arnie immediately. *Did not like talking about himself at all.*

He didn't like being in the room with the rest of them, said Olga. *I don't know if it's because he doesn't like them, or if he doesn't like anyone.*

I like him as the person to start with, said Sam. *He's the most logical choice for our cover . . .*

Otto growled a soft warning.

Sam stood up and brushed himself off.

"Dogs, heel," he said, then he turned to see Bolton jogging toward them with Sarge on a leash.

"Dinner's at five thirty," called Bolton. "Thought you might have lost track of the time."

"Guess I did at that," said Sam. "Thanks for coming to get me."

"Oh, Sarge and I make our rounds now anyway," said Bolton. "I was watching you for a while on the monitors. You really have these puppies trained. Pretty impressive."

"Thanks," said Sam.

"That wolfhound's your best werewolf hunter?" asked Bolton.

"I'm working with a mixed pack," said Sam. "Different skills for different scenarios."

"Like an Afghan guerrilla unit," said Bolton.

"Wouldn't know about that," said Sam. "I wasn't in the field much. Were you?"

"Iraq. Private contracting out by the Basrah oil rigs," said Bolton. "Our job was to shoot anyone who looked suspicious before they got close enough to blow anything up."

"How did you know which ones looked suspicious?"

"They all did," said Bolton. "People stopped coming by once word got out. Which dog's the fastest?"

"Olga," said Sam.

Damn straight, said Olga.

"Tito's my boy for speed," said Bolton. "Maybe we could set up a race for fun. Be nice to break the monotony."

"Sure," said Sam. "How about tomorrow sometime?"

"We're here 24/7," said Bolton.

He continued on, Sarge giving Olga the once-over as they passed.

"Don't respond," muttered Sam as she tensed. "Keep walking."

They ambled back to the compound.

Clear, said Otto as they went in.

Thanks, said Sam.

Bolton was checking you out, said Arnie.

He's Security, said Sam. *He's supposed to be checking me out.*

Even with the Colonel vouching for you?

Yup. Although I wonder who told him I was in Afghanistan.

All the scientists know, said Arnie. *Any one of them could have told him. Probably McKenna.*

Let's continue this after dinner, suggested Sam. *Stay here. I'm going to the kitchen to reconnoiter.*

Barbecue, please? asked Olga.

When we go home, said Sam, *but don't tell the others. I can't afford it on a regular basis.*

He found the cafeteria. No one had arrived yet, so he pushed open the door to the kitchen. A young woman with hair the color of light straw was tending to a couple of pots on a stove.

"Smells good," said Sam.

She gave a small shriek and dropped her ladle.

"Sorry, didn't mean to sneak up on you," he said, retrieving it. "I'm Sam Lehrmann. I arrived today."

"Knock whenever you come in here," she said, taking the ladle from him and washing it. "I'm Bonnie Whitfield. You're the man with the meat?"

"Um, yes," he said. "It's for the dogs."

"Goddamn waste," she said. "Can't give 'em regular dogfood instead of taking up space in my fridge?"

"These are very special dogs," he said, pulling some packages of beef out of the refrigerator. "Could I have a bottle of soap for the bowls?"

"Over the sink," she said, turning back to her pots.

"You should come introduce yourself," he said.

"You think you can get me into your room by using a couple of puppies, you got another thing coming, mister," she said. "I am a married woman."

"Nothing like that, Ms. Whitfield," he said. "It's so they won't think you're a stranger when they meet you. I'll bring them into the hall if that will make you more comfortable. Won't take but a minute."

She looked at her pots for a moment, then wiped her hands on a dish towel. "All right," she said. "One minute."

She followed him down the hall to his rooms.

He opened the door and said, "Dogs, heel."

They came out, and Bonnie softened. "They're beautiful," she said, smiling.

"Hold out your hand," he said. "Dogs, sniff."

She did, and giggled as five noses swarmed around it.

"Dogs, inside," he said. "You're good. Nice meeting you—and I promise to knock from now on."

"All right," she said. "Nice meeting you, too."

She left, and he went inside.

Now, that was a nice lady, said Bert.

She's the cook, said Sam.

I knew I liked her for a reason, said Bert.

Read anything about her? asked Sam.

She smelled of fresh herbs, said Otto dreamily. *Sage and rosemary.*

She likes dogs, said Olga. *And she's happily married.*

How do you know that? asked Sam.

Human women usually react when they see you, Boss, said Olga. *Kudowski and Buenaventura both checked you out like Bert does his dinner bowl. This lady didn't.*

Buenaventura's married, noted Sam.

Not happily, said Nan. *And her husband isn't here.*

What about Burton? asked Sam.

She just woke up, said Olga. *She wasn't reacting to anything. Probably needs coffee.*

Sam laid out the dogs' dinners, then went back to the cafeteria. Four of the scientists, along with Coleridge, were seated around the table.

"Join us, Mister Lehrmann," said McKenna, waving him over.

"Thank you, Doctor," said Sam. "I usually don't get to sit at the smart kids' table."

"Were you a jock in high school?" asked Kudowski.

"I sat with the guys from auto shop," said Sam. "One table over from the stoners, although there was a fair amount of mixing."

"You're among nerds here," said Buenaventura.

"Then I'll shut up."

Burton staggered in, still looking tired.

"Jeez, Val, you look awful," said Sanchez.

"Thank you, O Master of the Social Arts," muttered Burton. "I'm still thrown off from having to meet the Dog Man. Hello again, Dog Man."

"It's Sam, and I apologize for disrupting your schedule."

"Right, Sam," she said. "No problem. Not your fault."

Whitfield came out and began ladling chicken stew into bowls for all of them except Burton. "Cereal or waffles?" she asked.

"Waffles, please," said Burton. "Thank you, Bonnie."

"Waffles?" asked Sam.

"Breakfast time for me," explained Valerie.

"That's why we call her the Vampire," said McKenna.

"Don't be silly, there's no such thing as vampires," said Kudowski immediately.

They broke into tired laughter at what Sam guessed was an old joke. He tasted the stew.

"This is good," he said. "I'm tasting sage and rosemary?"

"That's right," said Bonnie, surprised and pleased. "I'll be back with the collard greens in a minute."

"So, Mister Lehrmann," began McKenna.

"Please, it's Sam."

"Very well, Sam. We have a little tradition here for new arrivals."

"Hazing?"

"Oh, no," said McKenna, "but we deal with matters here that most people don't even believe exist. They've become routine to us, but it's useful to remind ourselves once in a while how strange they truly are. So, we always ask our guests to tell us what it was like when they first realized that werewolves were actually real."

They all were leaning towards him, Sam noticed, their faces eager, almost hungry.

"I saw my first werewolf when I was thirteen," he said slowly.

"So young," murmured Buenaventura.

"I don't like talking about it," he said.

"You'll find no audience more sympathetic, I assure you," said McKenna. "There will be no disbelief or derision here."

"I was camping out in the woods with my best friend, Billy," said Sam. "Cooking up a couple of rabbits we had shot with our .22s, telling ghost stories under a full moon. Billy suddenly said he heard something moving in the trees. I thought he was just trying to scare me, and I laughed it off, but he told me to shut up and grabbed his rifle and walked to the edge of the firelight. I still thought he was joking. I kept waiting for him to turn and go, 'Got you!' Then the thing attacked."

"Madre de Dios," said Sanchez, crossing himself.

"Billy couldn't even get a shot off. The thing was on him, tearing at his throat. I fumbled for my own gun, and then it looked at me, the blood dripping from its fangs. Billy's blood. I screamed, and it kept looking at me, and then it smiled—it fucking smiled, and I kept screaming. Then, it picked up Billy's body and ran into the darkness."

"What did you do?" asked Buenaventura.

"I ran home, screaming all the way. My dad had been drinking, so he was passed out, and there was nobody else. I called the sheriff, and they came down, but when I told them what happened, they didn't believe me."

"They never do," said McKenna.

"They brought a bloodhound at daylight and found Billy's body—what was left of it. Ripped apart, eaten. I told them over and over that it was a werewolf, but the sheriff decided it was a bear. They sent out hunters for a week, but they never found it."

"Probably a transient," said McKenna. "Hit and run."

"Is that why you became a werewolf hunter?" asked Buenaventura.

"Yes'm. I went looking for it at the next full moon. I made my own silver bullets—"

"You're kidding!" laughed Burton. "Everyone knows that's a myth. Well, everyone that knows anything about werewolves."

"That's still just a handful of people," said Buenaventura. "You couldn't expect a thirteen-year-old to know that."

"No, ma'am," said Sam.

"Did you ever find it?" asked Kudowski.

"It took me a few years, but I did," said Sam. "I read everything I could on them. Most of it was bullshit—excuse my language—but then I read this book by a guy named Adler—"

"Adler," sighed Kudowski. "I remember when I first read him."

"So out of date," said McKenna, shaking his head. "He was good in his day, but we know so much more now."

"What did you do when you killed it?" asked Burton, awake now. "Did you bring it to the authorities?"

"No, ma'am," said Sam.

"Why not? It would have validated your story."

"Because when I shot him, it was after a full night of tracking," said Sam, "and the sun had just come up."

"You shot him when he was in human form," breathed Kudowski.

"Awkward," said Sanchez.

"Couldn't exactly go to the authorities and explain how I was justified in shooting an unarmed naked man in the woods with a silver bullet," said Sam. "So, I buried him there."

"How old were you by this time?" asked Buenaventura.

"Fifteen," said Sam.

"Still young," she said.

"Maybe," he said, "but I felt old when I was done."

"Now, you understand that the werewolf you killed was atypical," said McKenna. "Most of them adjust to their condition and lead peaceful lives."

"I'm here because of the ones who don't," said Sam. "That's what the Colonel needs, and that's what I want."

Whitfield came in with a covered plate.

"Sweet potato pie," she announced to cheers from the table. "And, with that, I'll be going, Doctor McKenna. Leave your dishes in the dishwasher, and I'll run it in the morning."

"Will do," said McKenna. "Thank you, Bonnie, for another excellent meal."

"Thank you, Ms. Whitfield," said Sam.

She smiled at him and left.

"Well, Sam, what exactly do you expect from us while you're here?" asked McKenna.

"As you pointed out, my knowledge is out of date," said Sam. "I want to get a crash course and learn everything I can. Especially things that might help me train the dogs."

"So you can kill even more werewolves?" asked Buenaventura.

"So I can locate them, ma'am," said Sam. "Once located, I'll leave it to the Colonel to decide if the subject is—atypical."

"How many have you killed?" asked Kudowski.

"As I said, that's not my job anymore," said Sam.

"You didn't answer my question."

"No, ma'am, I didn't."

Mona unlocked the door to her townhouse.

Nicky sat inside the foyer, her leash in her mouth.

"Can I put my bag down first?" asked Mona.

The dog waited while she dumped her stuff on the hall table and leafed through her mail.

"Right," said Mona, grabbing the leash. "Let's go."

The Rottweiler dragged her through the door. They took their regular route around the block, with Nicky stopping to sniff trees, bushes, and mailboxes.

"He called ten times," said Mona as they turned the corner. "Ten times in one day. I have had stalkers who've called me less. Crazy men who made me run to the courts for orders of protection."

Nicky ignored her, taking a moment to growl at a cat who watched them from the safety of a picture window.

"So the question is, you unfeeling beast, how long do I let him stew before I return his calls?" asked Mona. "Or should the answer be never?"

Nicky looked at her, and she could have sworn the dog shrugged.

"Then there's the crying girl," said Mona. "The very pretty, younger, crying girl with her crush on Sam—and the bitch of it is, I feel sorry for her. She's got a dead brother, and he's all tied up with her unrequited love for my suddenly-available boyfriend, and I've got this weird urge to help her. Is that altruism on my part, or my way of sussing out the competition? Or is this another trip to the Land of Low Self-Esteem?"

Nicky sniffed the base of a parking sign.

"Fat lot of help you are," sighed Mona.

Get yourself attacked, and I'll be on the guy's throat in an instant, said Nicky. This stuff, you've got to work out for yourself.

Unfortunately, Mona couldn't hear a word she was saying.

Sam opened his door, then stopped. "What do you think you're doing?" he asked.

Arnie looked up guiltily from the middle of the bed. He tried, *Um, guarding? The bed is secure, Boss. I'll be going, now.* He jumped down.

"Laps in the morning for you," said Sam.

If a black and tan dachshund could have turned pale, Arnie would have.

Sam picked up the bowls and washed them in the bathroom sink.

Olga came to the door. *The patrols stay by the fence,* she reported. *They go by every fifteen minutes. There is only one stretch that's close enough for them to hear us, so we've decided to maintain silence when that happens.*

Bert wanted to yell rude things, but Arnie told him to stop, said Nan.

It's clear now, said Otto.

Turns out Otto has the longest range for dogspeak, said Olga.

Is that so? said Sam. *Never knew that. You keep surprising me, Otto.*

Otto gazed at him solemnly with his light amber eyes, but said nothing.

Sam refilled the water bowls and set them out, then stretched out on his bed. There was a television. He turned it on.

Could we watch CNN tonight? asked Arnie.

Sure, said Sam, finding the channel. The dogs drifted into the room and watched as some politician gave a press conference.

Lie, said Bert. *Lie. Lie. Lie . . .*

Keep it to yourself, said Sam.

Olga sat by the bed and rested her chin on the quilt.

Sam reached over and rubbed her neck.

You look sad, she said.

Some old memories came up at dinner. They wanted to know about my first encounter with a werewolf.

Did you tell them the truth?

Told a story about a friend named Billy who was carried off and killed by a werewolf. Said I hunted the creature for two years before I finally killed it. That part was true.

Was that when you were bitten? she asked. *When Billy was killed?*

Yes.

And that's when you started talking to dogs?

No, said Sam. *That started when I was twelve.*

Otto turned to look at him. *You talked to dogs before you became a werewolf?* asked the Weimaraner.

Yes.

Interesting, said Otto. Then, he turned back to the news.

Do you like being a werewolf? asked Olga.

Doesn't matter much whether I like it or not, said Sam. *I'm stuck with it.*

If they succeed in developing this cure, will you accept it?
I don't know, said Sam.
Do you think Mona will like you better if you're not a werewolf?
She likes me more as a werewolf, said Sam. *I think that's part of the problem.*
What's the other part?
Doesn't matter, said Sam. *I think she's through with me.*

Kerry came through the doors and glanced around uncertainly. The brunette sitting at the end of the bar raised a glass in greeting. Kerry went up to her.

"I wasn't sure what you looked like," said Kerry. "Only saw you for a moment, and I was crying—and running."

"I remember you just fine," said Mona. "What are you drinking?"

"Blue Moon would be great," said Kerry.

"Hector, a Blue Moon for my friend," Mona said to the bartender. "Same again for me."

"She old enough to drink?" asked Hector.

"She looks old enough to do anything," said Mona.

"Here," said Kerry, sliding her driver's license over.

Hector slid it back without looking at it, then poured their drinks.

"What shall we toast to?" asked Mona.

Kerry was silent.

"Well, then I'll start," said Mona. "To Sam, and may the best woman win."

"Is that what this is about?" asked Kerry.

"Sam has never cheated on me," said Mona. "At least, not with another woman."

"No way he's gay," blurted Kerry.

Mona snickered. "No, he certainly ain't that—but he's awfully devoted to those dogs. But, as far as he and I are concerned, it's been rocky but regular. So, you can imagine how I felt—"

"I'm sorry," said Kerry immediately.

"Yeah, that's nice," said Mona. "I've heard that said before, and it's always said too late. He told me why you were there, or why you said you were there."

"I was . . ."

"What I need to know is what you really want," said Mona. "If it's to find out what happened to your brother, then I am your friend and ally, and I will help you. If, on the other hand, it's to go after my boyfriend, then I am your enemy in all things. Which is it?"

Kerry downed her beer. Hector was back unasked with refills.

"I was fourteen when I met him," said Kerry. "Do you remember what fourteen was like?"

"Not as long ago as you think," said Mona. "It was horrible."

"Tom brought him home for Thanksgiving. For a week. I knew Sam for a week, and I knew I loved him, and that he must love me."

"Did he say or do anything?"

"Of course not. I was fourteen—I was practically invisible. He and Tom went trolling for college girls every night, and I'd stay up looking out my window over the driveway, hugging my pillow."

"Jesus," said Mona, shaking her head.

"But he talked to me," continued Kerry. "He talked to me with respect, like I was a real person, and that was the best—and then they were gone. I e-mailed him. It was always being nice to the soldier stuff, you know. Then, Tom was killed, and everything went under for a long time."

She drank. Mona watched her.

"I know there's no way," said Kerry. "It was just a shock hearing he's been this close all this time. Like he was watching over me, but wouldn't do anything until the time was right."

"I don't know whether that sounds romantic or creepy," said Mona.

"Romance is always a little creepy, isn't it?"

"Oh, more true than you know," shuddered Mona.

Then they both started to laugh. Somewhere in the middle of it, more drinks appeared.

"God, I was fourteen, and I thought someday I'd grow up and marry him," said Kerry, somewhere between a giggle and a sniffle. "How sad is that?"

"I was twenty-six," said Mona. "I thought someday he'd grow up and marry me."

"And you'd have furry little babies!" cried Kerry.

Then she gasped as Mona clamped down hard on her wrist.

"And what exactly do you know about that?" Mona asked softly.

You know, huffed Arnie in the morning, *dachshunds are not meant for chasing around above ground.*

We haven't done one lap yet, said Sam. *The others aren't even breathing hard.*

Sure, but I have to work twice as hard to cover the same distance, said Arnie.

Dachshunds hunt, said Sam. *They chase rabbits, badgers—*

In holes, said Arnie. *You show me a burrow, I'm your dog. A dachshund delving the depths, the dark, the danger, disregarding his own safety—*

I have never doubted the courage and loyalty of dachshunds, said Sam.

And this isn't a farm, said Arnie. *So I don't get why we have to be up at the butt-crack of dawn—*

It's seven thirty, said Sam. *Dawn was two hours ago. And, we need to keep in shape—especially those of us who run to fat.*

Are you referring to me? asked Arnie indignantly.

I just don't want you to get stuck in one of those burrows, said Sam. *I'd have to yank you out by the tail.*

Arnie glanced back at his tail, standing high and bouncing merrily behind him.

Sneezelady dead ahead, called Bert. *Request permission to freak her out.*

Denied, said Arnie.

"Dogs, heel," called Sam, and the four large dogs fell back behind him.

Otto growled. The shepherds were in hearing range.

Lisa Kudowski was stretching her legs, preparing to run. She had her blonde hair plaited and was wearing a faded Johns Hopkins University T-shirt over a pair of blue jogging shorts.

Nice legs for a scientist, Sam thought to himself.

"Good morning, Doctor Kudowski," he said as he approached her.

She glanced back and scowled when she saw the dogs. "Keep them back, please," she asked, taking off.

"Dogs, fall back and follow," said Sam, catching up to her.

They ran by the security trailers. She waved to Floyd who had Benny on a leash. Floyd waved, Benny barked.

"You run every day?" she asked.

"At least five miles every morning," he said. "Lot less than what the Army made me do, and I'm not carrying a pack."

"That's two laps here," she said. "I usually do three."

"I always figured scientists as strictly brains," he said. "Got to change my thinking. You're in good shape, apart from the allergies. Don't the German shepherds bother you?"

"The guards keep them at a distance," she said. "If I get too close, I clog up, run inside, take my medicine, keep a lot of tissues handy, and sniffle through it. How come you don't have any shepherds?"

"Oh, I work with them all the time," he said. "I just didn't have any suitable for this assignment at the moment."

"How did you get into training dogs for werewolf hunting?"

"Given my early experiences, seemed like a natural fit," said Sam, "and once Pastore found out about me, I started getting the occasional call. How about you? What brought you into this territory?"

"Eric did," she said. "Doctor McKenna, I mean. I was his graduate student. He suggested I get into this particular discipline, and then told me why. I thought he was insane the first time I heard about it. Oh, God!" She came to a halt and started sneezing.

Sam held the dogs back with a gesture.

"Must be downwind," she muttered, her eyes reddening.

"How do you cope with werewolves when you're so allergic?"

"What do werewolves have to do with allergies?" she asked, pulling a tissue from her fanny pack.

"But you're allergic to dogs."

"Werewolves have nothing to do with dogs," she said, blowing her nose. "The name's a misnomer, based on the superficial physiognomic resemblance."

"The fizzy what?"

"They've been called werewolves, wolfmen, whatever, because they have fangs, claws, hair, the whole package," she explained, "but genetically—well, you can get all that info from Eric, but they are completely unrelated. A whole other hybrid. Hell, that's not the best word. Eric tells it better. Anyhow, I'm not allergic to them, but I've got to get inside. I'm sorry. Good running with you."

"You, too," said Sam, watching as she dashed away.

He turned to see the dogs looking at him in dismay, except for Otto.

"What?" he asked.

We just always assumed—began Nan.

You know, said Olga.

Assumed what?

That we were related somehow, said Bert. *You and us. Werewolves and dogs. Cousins or something.*

We never were, said Otto. *You would know that if you had listened.*

Listened to who, Otto? asked Bert.

Your mothers, said Otto. *So much has been lost.*

What the hell are you talking about, Spooky?

But Otto only growled. Benny and Floyd were coming into range.

Boudreau's computer pinged. He looked up to see Doctor Oliveras' image in a corner of the screen. He clicked on it. "Morning, Doc. Whatcha got for me today?"

"DNA hits on three of the four," she said. "The one you got, plus two more."

"Excellent. Which database?"

"Two from the military, one from CODIS by way of the Maryland Criminal Justice database."

"One's got a record," said Boudreau. "So we can rule out the Feds, unless they've changed their hiring practices. What about the fourth?"

"Nothing," said Oliveras. "He was one of the ones in back. The one who sustained the most damage, interestingly enough."

"I thought the one with the detached head was the one with the dogtag."

"He was."

"But he wasn't the one with the most damage?"

"His head came off because they went at his neck, and then the worms did the rest," said Oliveras, "but the unidentified deceased was chomped all over by the largest number of canines. That's what I meant by most damage."

"I wonder if the dogs considered him to be the biggest threat," said Boudreau.

"No way to conclude that from my end," said Oliveras. "Maybe he was the tastiest."

"Any other way of identifying him?"

"Only if we find some DNA to match up with," she said. "Or dental records. Sorry, Sheriff, but that's all I got. I'm sending it to you right now."

"Hey, Doc, what do you know about aconite?" he asked.

"Heard of it," she said. "Neurotoxin, plant-derived. Why?"

"They had some in a dart gun," he said. "Ever read of any bodies found with aconite poisoning?"

"No, but I'll post the question to the national newsgroup," she said. "I'll let you know the minute it comes in."

"Thanks, Doc," he said.

She winked at him and disappeared from the screen.

He printed out the info she sent him. "Wilkins and Cole, front and center," he yelled.

The two came in a minute later.

"Doc came through," he said. "We know three of the four names. Wilkins, you take the other Army guy. His name is Forrest Edwards. Cole, meet the late Ramon Hidalgo, also known as Ramon Juarez. An occasional guest of the Maryland criminal justice system."

"You want us to talk to their families?" asked Wilkins.

"It's my job to break it to them," said Boudreau, "but I'll need to know who to call, first up. And, I want all their cell phone records. If we can get some common numbers, maybe we can figure out who Mystery Guest Number Four is. Now, git."

Sam knocked on the door to Sanchez's lab. It opened as he did, and he saw the scientist hastily type a command on a keyboard. The monitor went to deep blue, leaving a momentary glimpse of an exceedingly hairy arm.

"Morning, Doctor Sanchez," he said. "This a good time?"

"No good time, no bad time," said Sanchez. "No deadlines on pure research. That's one of the joys of the job. Come in, please."

He doesn't sound joyful, said Nan.

Sanchez looked uncomfortable when he saw the dogs following Sam into the lab. "I wasn't expecting them to go everywhere with you," he said.

"For this job, they do," said Sam. "Never know when something might come up that I have to incorporate into their training."

"They must interfere with your social life," said Sanchez.

Don't get us started, said Arnie.

"Don't have much of one at the moment," said Sam.

"I'm surprised," said Sanchez. "A young man in his prime like yourself. I would think you would do quite well with the ladies."

"Nah, they all go for the science types," grinned Sam.

"Would that that were true," laughed Sanchez, running his hand over his pate.

"What do you do for fun at this place?" asked Sam. "You're really isolated here."

"We're all single, except for Sandra," sighed Sanchez. "The security is very tight. Quite embarrassing what you have to go through just to leave the campus. Most of us just gave up. It wasn't worth the bother."

"Yeah, I read the instructions," said Sam. "Don't fancy the strip search every time I want to grab a beer."

"They bring beer here," said Sanchez, "but I agree. Our cook, young Mrs. Whitfield, found it quite humiliating to go through it on a daily basis, but times being what they are, she needs the money more than her dignity—and I hear that Priscilla, who searches the women, is very thorough."

His eyes went dreamy for a second.

He's thinking about the cook being strip-searched by the lady guard, said Olga.

So is the Boss, said Arnie, looking up at Sam.

Sam cleared his throat. "Sorry—inhaled something while I was running earlier. So, tell me about what you're doing here. I gather you were looking at the specific changes werewolves go through."

"As much as one man can," said Sanchez. "There are so many things happening, all within the span of a minute. Bones lengthen, muscles shift, claws extend, fangs descend, hair—and these are just the obvious external changes. Internally, the lungs and heart enlarge, the circulatory system itself expands to carry more blood—"

"Why more blood?" asked Sam, fascinated to hear what he had gone through for so long described in a way he had never heard before.

"Because the change happens on a cellular level, and each cell requires more energy and more oxygen to effectuate it," explained Sanchez. "And the digestive system! My God, what it does in the werewolf form, the amount of food it has to process, and the type of food. Werewolves prefer raw meat, of course, in amounts that normal humans—"

He stopped, his face distressed. "I'm so sorry—how could I speak of that after hearing about your friend?"

"That was a long time ago," Sam reassured him, "and I need to know all of this if I am going to complete my mission."

"Your mission," repeated Sanchez, rubbing his head again. "Of course. You're a military man. You carry out your orders without question."

"I'm not Army anymore," said Sam. "I'm allowed to ask questions. Here's one—what do you do in this lab?"

"Observe the changes, analyze them," said Sanchez. "For example, the fangs—what is the biological mechanism that causes them to descend and withdraw? There are very few parts of the human body that have that much movement."

"I can think of one," said Sam. "In the male, at least."

"What?" asked Sanchez. "Oh. The genitalia. Of course. Very good example for both genders, when you think about it. But the fangs—there actually are structures above the maxilla that force them down and lock them into place."

"Like muscles?"

"More like cartilage, but it's something different," said Sanchez, becoming enthusiastic. "It hardens to compress the space around each fang, so that the only way they can go is through the gums and into the mouth. Then, it softens at daybreak, and it's like rubber bands pulling them back up. It's remarkable. No other fanged creature has anything like it."

"Not like a snake's, then?"

"Similar only in its ability to inject—well, we call it venom, but it's not a venom, exactly. The werewolf fangs are hollow like those of the viperids and elapids—"

"The whats?"

"The two families of fanged snakes. The fangs of the viperids do rotate, of course, but—"

Sam held his hand up. "Werewolf fangs are only present when the change has happened," he said.

"Correct."

"So, this information won't help me find them in their human form, will it?"

"Well, there is some damage to the gums," said Sanchez thoughtfully. "Although they heal within a day."

Sam reflexively ran his tongue over his upper gum before he could help himself. Sanchez noticed it immediately.

"Hah! You see?" chortled Sanchez. "Everyone does that whenever I tell them about it, werewolf and human. How'd you come out?"

"Human," Sam lied. "So, if I am lucky enough to see someone's gums the day after he's changed, then I can make him as a werewolf."

"Exactly," said Sanchez triumphantly.

"And how am I to get in position to do that?" said Sam. "Practically speaking?"

"Practically speaking? Well, you could—no, maybe—hmm. I see your point. That isn't the most useful example, is it?"

"Unless we can get the government to authorize French kissing at roadblocks," said Sam. "I'll give Pastore a call, see what he can set up."

"The frightening thing about Pastore is that he probably could," said Sanchez.

"That's nowhere near the most frightening thing about Pastore," said Sam.

"You mean that he's a werewolf."

"One of the meanest ones I've ever seen."

"It's surprising that a werewolf hunter like you would work with someone like him," said Sanchez.

"I get to do what I want and the Feds have my back," said Sam. "If I've got to deal with a devil in wolf's clothing to do it, then I deal."

"Have you ever killed a werewolf who wasn't himself a killer?" asked Sanchez. "Before you became more—enlightened?"

"Maybe," said Sam. "Who knows, who cares? Don't matter much now, does it? They all had such lousy lives, when you get right down to it. I just put them out of their misery."

"I've met many who've led peaceful, productive lives," said Sanchez. "The ones who volunteer here, for example."

"Yeah, how do you find those?" asked Sam. "You got a Rolodex or database or something?"

"Doctor McKenna does," said Sanchez, "but he's the only one who has access to it."

"I'll have to chat him up," said Sam. "So. Which parts of the change back to human leave traces behind besides the fangs? Claws?"

"The wounds they cause seem to close up quickly. I'm not sure how. Let me show you." He tapped on his keyboard, and the monitor showed a close up of a werewolf's paws, the claws extended. "This is just before daybreak. Watch."

The claws receded under the fingernails, the skin closing around them as they vanished. The fur retreated. Within a minute, the hand looked completely human.

"Now, if you x-rayed the fingers, the claws would be visible, nestling against the bones like collapsed police batons," said Sanchez, showing the image.

"But I can't carry around an x-ray machine and ask people to stick their hands inside," said Sam.

"When I was a kid," said Sanchez, "I always wanted to get the x-ray specs they advertised inside the back covers of comic books so I could, you know, look at the pretty girls and see through their dresses. But, I never got up the courage to buy a pair—and now I know that they didn't work."

"Okay, so we've ruled out fangs and claws," said Sam. "Let me ask you this. I'm working with dogs. The thing they do best is smell. I figure with all the changes werewolves go through, especially with all that extra hair growth, they must still carry some scent in human form that a dog could pick up."

"Interesting thought," said Sanchez, rubbing his head again.

Does that make him think better? wondered Nan. *He keeps doing it.*

Something's making him nervous, said Bert.

"Werewolves have extra glands in the skin that secrete oil," said Sanchez. "I suspect to keep the skin from getting irritated by the hair sliding in and out. I've never noticed if it had a particular smell, but I wouldn't, would I?"

"You don't happen to have any samples of that oil lying around, do you?" asked Sam.

"Come with me," said Sanchez, standing. "I may have something in cold storage."

He opened a metal door, similar to the one on the walk-in refrigerator at Sam's warehouse. Sam followed him.

"Let's see," said Sanchez, sliding open a drawer in a cabinet. "No large amounts, nothing fresh. I have a few swabs from volunteers, but it's been some time since I last had the opportunity to—you know."

"What?"

"Dissect a specimen," said Sanchez.

Boss, said Otto softly. *Up on that shelf.*

Sam looked over Sanchez's head. Stuffed in a corner, partially concealed by stacks of files, was a large jar. Inside, floating in formaldehyde, was the head of a werewolf, eyes still open, staring at a point over Sam's head.

He felt nauseous. "You've dissected werewolves?" he asked, feigning enthusiasm.

"Only a few," said Sanchez. "We don't often get the chance. To obtain one who has been killed in his changed state takes a lot of luck. There is something that makes them decay rapidly once dead, so if they're not preserved right away, forget about it. One last defense mechanism that allows them to stay—concealed, I suppose. Even after death, they hide from us. But now that we have you, perhaps I shall have another opportunity."

"Here's hoping," said Sam.

CHAPTER 8

That guy really needs to get laid, said Arnie as they left Sanchez's lab.

You play your role well, Sam, said Otto. *Have you hunted werewolves?*

I've done a lot of things, said Sam. *Crowded life, considering I'm still at the tender age of twenty-nine.*

That—head, said Olga. *Was that someone you knew?*

No, said Sam. *I haven't met that many werewolves, to tell you the truth. Especially since I left the Army.*

Why not?

Safer that way. You never know who's watching—and that's before I found out about our friendly national government surveillance. So, apart from the sexual frustration, what did you see in Sanchez? He was a talkative guy once he warmed up.

All of his talk was a screen, said Nan.

Yeah, said Bert. *The more he talked, the further he got from what he was hiding.*

Which was what?

I don't know, said Bert. *It was hidden.*

Duh, added Nan.

He shut down what was on his monitor as you came in, said Otto.

Yeah, I noticed that, said Sam. *Got a glimpse of a werewolf's arm.*

Seems like the type of thing he'd be working on, said Arnie. *So why block that from you? He had no trouble showing you that paw changing.*

No clue, said Sam. *I'm going to start letting you guys wander around on your own. Let's see what happens when they think they're unobserved.*

We can't exactly sneak up on them, said Arnie.

Why not?

Linoleum floors, said the dachshund, tapping his toenails for emphasis. *They'll hear us coming.*

We can fix you up with some little booties, offered Olga.

And a sweater! snickered Nan. *Something Christmas-y!*

Shut up, growled Arnie.

You guys are missing the point, said Sam. *You don't have to sneak up on anyone.*

Why not? asked Bert.

Because they don't know that we can understand them, said Otto. *Or that we can talk to Sam.*

So all of us cute little puppies can wander about, said Arnie. *And if they look at us funny, we'll just wag our cute little tails.*

They came into the lobby. Coleridge was waxing the floor. He waved. "Almost done," he shouted over the whirring. "Hold up for a second."

"No problem," called Sam.

Coleridge shoved it along the last strip of floor until he had it gleaming, then switched off the machine.

"You weren't kidding about being the janitor, too," said Sam.

"Fortunately, not much to maintain," said Coleridge. "I stay out of the labs except for when they need the equipment fixed, and with only five of them wandering about, not much cleanup after. Although, now I got your dogs shedding all over the place."

"That shouldn't be for long," said Sam.

"Makes no difference to me," shrugged Coleridge as he unplugged the waxer and coiled up the cord. "Those tags working?"

"Everything's fine, thanks," said Sam.

"Right, then back down the rabbit hole for me," said Coleridge. He opened a door and disappeared into an elevator on the other side.

Lunch for me, said Sam. *You guys can wander. Remember, after lunch, Olga is racing Tito.*

Think you can beat him? asked Nan.

Please, said Olga. *No shepherd alive can take me.*

"Goddammit, slow down!" yelled Tennant as Ignatz and Sugar took off around the outside pen, yanking him along. "Dogs, uh, heel? Come on!"

Sally stepped into the doorway and watched with what he hoped was concern. He had a feeling it was amusement.

"You're not doing it right," she said.

"I figured that out," gasped Tennant, "but they aren't listening. I don't want to hurt them."

"Ignatz, walk," she called sharply. "Sugar, walk."

The two dogs slowed down immediately.

"Why didn't they do that for me?" demanded Tennant.

"Ignatz and Sugar need to hear their names," said Sally. "They're still learning. You do know their names, don't you?"

"There are twenty something dogs in there," said Tennant. "I haven't had time to memorize them."

"Twenty-eight dogs," said Sally. "Their names are on their cages—also on their tags. They like to hear their names. It makes them feel like you care about them."

"Take over these two, kid," said Tennant.

"I like to hear my name, too."

"Take over, Sally."

She looked at him impassively.

"Please," he sighed. "I need to get some water."

"Sure," said Sally, holding her hand out for the leads. "Ignatz, Sugar, heel."

The dogs fell into step behind her.

"How do you do that so easily?" he asked.

"Next to Sam, nobody knows these dogs better than me," she said. "It's all about trust."

Tennant glared at the three of them and went inside.

"You should be nicer to him," said Sally to the dogs as they jogged around the enclosure. "You can't take advantage of someone just because he's new. How are you going to work with your new people when you keep acting like this?"

It was fun, said Ignatz.

Yeah, agreed Sugar.

Sally looked at them sternly, and they hung their heads in shame.

The phone rang inside Sam's office. Tennant picked it up.

"It's me," said Pastore. "How goes?"

"No luck," said Tennant. "I looked for hidey holes, ran through my old visuals, got nothing."

"Has to be somewhere," said Pastore. "We need to step it up. There was another daylight transformation. I've spent the better part of a day doing clean up."

"Where?"

"A kid in North Carolina."

"Crawford's in North Carolina. Think it's related?"

"Wouldn't surprise me."

"Maybe you should get your lab involved."

"May have to," said Pastore. "The kid already was in decay. If we can get someone into a cold morgue early enough, then I can get the lab on it."

"Good luck with that. Want me to come help?"

"No, you keep searching. Sam's my boy, so it ain't gonna be easy. Have you tried the house yet?"

"Tonight, after I finish feeding the mutts," said Tennant. "They must have taken a vote to make my life miserable. They're running me ragged. I haven't worked this hard since basic training."

"How about the girl?" said Pastore.

"They like her," said Tennant. "Thank God for that."

"She suspect you?"

"She doesn't like me, but she doesn't think I'm anything other than what she sees. There's one dog that acts like he suspects me."

"Don't worry about the dog," said Pastore. "Just find the disk. By the time Sam gets back, you'll be long gone, and he can deal with them."

Tennant disconnected, then saw Sally standing in the doorway.

"How long you been there?" he asked, irritated.

"I'm done with Sugar and Ignatz," she said. "What do you want me to do next?"

"Whatever Sam would do," he said.

"Right," she said.

"Any man who hates dogs and children . . ." he muttered as he watched her walk away.

"I heard that," she said.

So did we, said Ignatz.

"You ever bet on the greyhounds?" asked Bolton as he brought out Tito.

"No," said Sam. "I don't like how they treat them."

"All they know how to do is run, and that's what they get to do," said Bolton. "Nothing wrong with that. Not any different from what we're about to do."

"This is for fun," said Sam as he unclipped Olga's lead. "Not a daily thing."

"Depends on what you think is fun," grinned Bolton. "I was going to suggest a friendly wager."

"What do you consider friendly?" asked Sam.

"A hundred?"

"I don't mind taking you for that much," said Sam, holding out his hand.

Bolton shook it. The other guards, with the exception of Carl, drifted out to watch, each with one of the other shepherds. Sarge looked at the rest of Sam's team and bared his teeth. The dogs ignored him.

"Once around the perimeter," said Bolton. "She'll do that, won't she?"

"She'll do whatever I tell her to do," said Sam, "but how are we gonna watch? I need to know your dog isn't taking any shortcuts."

"Our cameras cover the entire campus," said Bolton. "We can monitor from inside the trailer. And, there's air conditioning."

"All we need is a cold one," said Sam.

"That can be arranged," said Bolton. "Priscilla, get us some beers."

He sat Tito by Olga.

The German shepherd glanced over at the Russian wolfhound. *Maybe we could have a bet of our own,* he leered. *I win, I get to do you.*

And if I win? she asked.

You get to do me.

The other shepherds snickered.

Olga looked at him coolly. *Let's play for real stakes,* she said. *I win, I get to bite something off you.*

You serious? he said in shock.

I haven't hunted anything in a week, she said. *I'm losing my touch.*

You're crazy, he said.

Maybe. Only one way to know for sure. Game on?

No way!

Didn't think so, she sniffed.

"Tito, up," said Bolton.

"Olga, ready," said Sam.

The two dogs stood, tensing. The men looked at each other. Bolton silently counted down from three on his fingers.

"Perimeter!" they yelled.

The dogs took off.

Bolton, Sam, and the rest of the guards quickly crammed into the trailer. Carl had the monitors set up sequentially. Olga and Tito disappeared from the first and immediately appeared on the second.

"And they're neck and neck coming into the first quarter-mile," intoned Bolton. "Maintaining an easy pace . . ."

You better over sprints or distance? asked Tito

Both, said Olga.

They passed into the stand of trees at the rear of the compound.

The image shifted from the sixth monitor back to the first as Carl tapped a key.

"Rounding the turn, still even," called Bolton. "Any side bets? My boy Tito is doing me proud."

"She's just making him feel like he's doing well," said Sam.

The dogs went from the first monitor to the second.

"Halfway point," said Bolton.

Tito was pounding away. Olga maintained an easy lope. She glanced over at him.

Do you want to stop and rest? she asked sweetly.

Screw you!

Only if you win, remember? Oh, wait. You didn't want to make that bet.

Screw you again.

You know the real difference between you and me?

What?

You herd sheep. I hunt wolves.

They disappeared off the second monitor as they reach the edge of the trees. A few seconds later, they appeared on the third.

"Still even," said Bolton.

"Watch," said Sam.

They hit the three quarter mark. Tito was breathing hard. He glanced over at Olga.

Gotta hand it to you, babe, he said. *You're a beautiful creature when you run.*

Thank you, kind sir, she said.

And you got great legs, he said.

Thank you again, she said. *I have been told that my haunch is also quite attractive.*

Haven't had a good look at it, to tell you the truth.

You're about to.

She took off.

"Holy shit, will you look at that?" said Priscilla.

"Atta girl!" shouted Sam.

Olga stretched her lead over Tito until their images were three monitors apart. The humans filed outside and cheered as she came into view on the east side of the complex. Sam stood in front, applauding. As she came up to them, she left the ground and soared into his arms, knocking him back and over. He laughed after he caught his breath, and she licked his face.

"Get a room, for Chrissakes," said Bolton, tossing a pair of fifties on top of them.

He turned and glowered at Tito, who trotted to the finish line shamefaced.

"Stupid son of a bitch," muttered Bolton. He lifted his arm and gave the dog a backhanded slap that sent him staggering.

"Git your sorry ass inside!" yelled Bolton, gesturing at the kennels.

Tito slunk away. Sam's dogs watched in disgust.

"That wasn't right," said Sam, getting to his feet.

"Don't tell me how to run my dogs," said Bolton. "You don't discipline them, they don't learn."

"What did he learn?" asked Sam. "That to lose to a faster dog means a whipping?"

"Next time, he won't lose," said Bolton.

"Not gonna be a next time," said Sam. "Dogs, heel."

They walked to the lab without turning back. Behind them, they could hear Sarge berating Tito.

Bert walked through the halls, keeping his weight on the pads of his paws to avoid the noisy linoleum. The door to lobby opened silently before him. He passed through it, then watched with fascination as it closed again. He gave in to temptation and passed through it two more times before continuing on.

He could scent McKenna and Kudowski at the entrance to the wing containing their labs. There was a soft murmuring of voices in the distance. He went through the doors and paused halfway down the hall, listening.

"What have you been doing in your Fortress of Solitude?" asked Kudowski.

"I was curious about our new friend's first werewolf encounter," said McKenna. "I was looking up old news stories about any young boys being killed by bears around that time period."

"And?"

"I found one in a regional weekly in North Carolina. I took a look at the Book. There was a transient werewolf popping up in that area who disappeared about two years later. He had been flagged as a suspected predator, but he had been careful."

"Careful until Lehrmann got him," said Kudowski. "Impressive, getting his first kill at fifteen. He could be useful."

"If he's legit," said McKenna. "That might have been a cover story based on someone else's facts. We can't really verify it."

"You don't trust him?"

"Trust one of Pastore's people? I may be a brilliant scientist, but I'm no fool. I need to know more about him before I—"

They entered the hall from a door on the right. Kudowski saw Bert.

"Gah!" she exclaimed. "Go away! Shoo!"

Shoo? said Bert. *Seriously?*

"He won't hurt us," said McKenna. "Remember?"

"According to the man you don't trust," said Kudowski, reaching for her Kleenex. "Make it leave."

"I'm not sure how to do that, exactly," said McKenna, peering curiously at the Doberman.

"Thanks, brilliant scientist," muttered Kudowski.

The doors opened behind him. Bert turned to see Sam.

"There you are," Sam said to him. "Everything okay here? Bert behaving himself?"

"Keep him back," begged Kudowski. "Please."

"Bert, out," said Sam.

But I want to . . .

Shoo, said Sam.

You did not just say that.

Said it. Meant it.

I need to talk to you about what I heard.

You can. Just tell me from the other side of the door.

Oh. Right.

Bert slunk out.

"A contest of wills, eh?" observed McKenna.

"Part of the process," said Sam.

He was checking out your story, Boss, said Bert from the lobby. *He found that werewolf you killed in the Book.*

"You hear about the race?" asked Sam.

"Your Borzois beat one of the guard dogs," said McKenna.

She said something about a Fortress of Solitude.

"Tito," said Sam. *That's a joke. A nickname from* Superman. *It means he has a secured room in his lab.*

There are supermen? exclaimed Bert. *You never told us that!*

"I had an interesting talk with Doctor Sanchez this morning," said Sam. *A comic book. I'll explain later.*

"That makes you the first," said Kudowski. "Dullest man on the planet."

"Please, Lisa," said McKenna. "Who is next on your mission?"

"Thought I'd talk to you," said Sam.

"I should be last," said McKenna. "I'm the one who will tie it all together for you."

"All right," said Sam. "Doctor Kudowski, I am dog-free at the moment. And, I showered, so there shouldn't be any residual hairs or dander. Could you spare me some time?"

"You need me for anything?" she asked McKenna.

"Not at the moment," he said. He went back into his office.

"And good-bye to you," said Sam. "Abrupt, ain't he?"

"He's not used to being around people," she said.

"You're a person," he said.

"Thanks for noticing," she replied wryly. "Welcome to my lab."

He followed her inside.

"Sheriff?"

"Yes, Marlene?"

"Got that call from North Carolina for you."

"Thank you, darlin'," said Boudreau, tapping a button on his phone. "This is Sheriff Wayland Boudreau of Chattooga County, Georgia."

"This is Sheriff Barnard Johnson of Wilkes County, North Carolina."

"How do, Sheriff? I appreciate you're gettin' back to me so promptly."

"Never a problem—and first off, call me Barney."

"Thank you, Barney—and call me Wayland. I assume that you received my request?"

"I did, Wayland, and I've got the file right here."

"Very quick work, Barney. I'm impressed."

"Now, you understand that this case was sealed."

"I do understand."

"But my mouth sure ain't, and I don't need any file to remember this one," continued Johnson. "Sam Lehrmann was a dumbass kid from Moravian Falls. He got drunk and killed a bunch of cows on a dairy farm. The owner found him naked and asleep in the middle of a pile of carcasses, blood all over him. One of the most disgusting things I ever saw."

"How did he kill them?"

"Gouged 'em apart, far as we could tell. Never found the weapon, but there was no question he did it. Judge was all set to teach him a good lesson when some Army recruiter showed up and saved his ass."

"He did well in the Army, apparently."

"Guess he finally manned up," said Johnson. "Surprised the hell out of me. That boy was destined for prison or an early grave, far as I could tell."

"He ran that bad?"

"Not like he was hanging out, running drugs or nothing," said Johnson. "But, a kid who kills animals like that—well, that was messed up. Mom died young, dad was a mean drunk. Only had but the one friend, and he was killed when Sam was thirteen."

"Killed?" exclaimed Boudreau, leaning forward in his chair. "How?"

"Two of 'em were camping out by Scott Reservoir," said Johnson. "Bear goes after them, kills this boy Billy, mauls Sam pretty bad. He manages to get away, screaming like a maniac. I wasn't sheriff then, but I was on the search party that found Billy, or what was left of him."

"Definitely a bear that did it?" asked Boudreau.

"Yeah, I know what you're thinking," said Johnson. "ME said it had to have been a bear, given the size of the claw marks, but we never saw any other signs of it. Usually you find scat, bark on trees sliced up, that sort of thing. Some of our boys tried tracking it from where we found the body, but came up empty. Sam wasn't right in the head after that, which was understandable. County sent a social worker to try and help, but the old man didn't believe that the boy needed anything more than a good whipping, so he told her to take a hike."

"Poor kid," said Boudreau. "He do anything else? Juvy stuff?"

"Never got caught," said Johnson. "When the cattle thing happened, it got me thinking. There had been a cow or two disappearing in various parts of the county, but nothing we could pin on Sam. Did all right in school, except he'd disappear every now and then. They figured he was hiding from his old man, but he never said nothing against him."

"Do you think he killed Billy?" asked Boudreau.

"I will wonder about that until the end of my days," said Johnson. "Wouldn't surprise me none."

Two sheriffs sat silently for a minute.

"This is about them folks you found in that quarry, isn't it?" asked Johnson.

"Yes, it is," said Boudreau.

"Tell you what," offered Johnson. "I can dig up the ME's report on Billy. Might be something in the photos you can compare to what you have."

"That is a splendid idea, Barney," said Boudreau. "I'd be obliged."

"Shoot, this is what we're supposed to be doing, ain't it?" said Johnson.

"Yes, it is," said Boudreau. "One more thing—do you know the name of the Army man who recruited him?"

"Well, that would be in this sealed file, wouldn't it?" said Johnson. "Oops, clumsy me."

"What happened?"

"I accidentally dropped it on a letter opener. That seal must have been old. Came apart right in my hands."

"That is unfortunate," chuckled Boudreau.

"Well, since it's already open, no harm in taking a little looksee. Here it is. Recruiter was a Captain Joseph Pastore."

"Sonofabitch," said Boudreau.

"How much school have you had?" asked Doctor Kudowski.

"Got an associate's degree from county college," said Sam. "Army training, whatever I've done on my own."

"What I do is pretty advanced," she said. "It's over the heads of most graduate students. I'm not sure how much I can explain. Do you know anything about genetics? Evolution?"

"Everything about it that relates to dogs," said Sam. "You name a breed, I can give you its history, its forebears, which traits are recessive, which are dominant, which location on the DNA needs to be turned on to express that trait. They decoded the canine genome a few years ago. I may only be a hick dummy with an associate's degree, but I've got a doctorate in dogology."

"I don't think of you as a, as a hick or a dummy," she stammered, turning red. "I'm sorry if it came out that way."

"It's okay, I am a dummy about a lot of things," he said. "Women being at the top of the list, according to every woman I've ever met. Let's talk about werewolves. You said this morning that they weren't really wolves. What are they?"

"They're human."

"Most of the time, then kaboom. So, they're human, but they aren't."

"The DNA is identical," she said. "Every single werewolf we've tested, the same thing. One hundred percent human DNA."

"Then what makes them change? Full moon, yeah, got that, but what goes on in the body that gets them all fang-y and furry? I know it ain't Gypsy curses."

"Do you know what a symbiote is?" she asked.

"Uh, you got me."

"Symbiote, as in symbiotic," she said. "Two organisms living together and off of each other. Please skip the obvious joke about marriage."

"You stopped me just in time, Doc. Living together like how? Like bacteria in the stomach?"

"Perfect example," she said. "Bacteria help us digest, we keep them alive. A mutually agreeable arrangement that's evolved over time. If you traced the genetic development of those bacteria, you'd find that they changed to accommodate us and vice versa."

"So you think that people turn into werewolves because of some weird bacteria?"

"Close, but not quite," she said. "You look inside the human cell, you'll find all sorts of stuff floating around there. We're still sorting through what everything does. For a long time, we thought that werewolves became that way because of a section of what was considered junk DNA in normal humans."

"Junk DNA?"

"There are sections of the human DNA that have no observable function," she said. "They may have had one somewhere in our ancestral past, but became obsolete over time."

"But that's not what makes werewolves."

"No."

"It's this symbiotic thing, whatever it is."

"It turns out that werewolf cells contain a second set of—well, not DNA exactly, but something that interacts with human DNA."

"Interacts? You mean this other . . . thing changes us?"

"Us?"

"People," said Sam. "This thing changes people into werewolves?"

"The change is on a cellular level," she said. "Every werewolf we've tested has this structure—or organism, or whatever it is—in most of their cells. It's like almost nothing else in nature. It's not bacterial, not viral, not a prion.

We've only found it in humans, although—"

She smiled. "You're going to like this," she said.

"What?"

"There is something similar in dogs."

"They'll be pleased to hear it," said Sam. "What does it do to dogs?"

"I don't know yet," she confessed, "but here's another odd thing. We only find it in a minuscule percentage of humans, which is why there are so few werewolves. But, most dogs seem to have it, which leads me to believe that dogs pass it down genetically."

"And humans don't," he said.

"It's not directly chromosomal, so even if two werewolves were to mate and reproduce sexually, the offspring is not a werewolf."

"Why do you think that is?"

"Because the symbiote is found in most of the werewolf's cells, not all. It's not in the reproductive organs. For whatever reason, this symbiote is not meant to reproduce sexually."

"You're the evolutionist," said Sam. "Don't all living things need to reproduce?"

"To survive, yes," she said. "Some are more efficient at it than others. Sexual reproduction is only one method."

"But it's the most fun. You have to give me that."

She laughed. It was a nice laugh, he thought.

"It's fun because nature wants us to reproduce," she said, coloring again. "Werewolves are driven to reproduce, too. By a method that isn't so much fun."

"The bite," he said. "The venom."

"Yes, only what you call venom is not a venom. It's a concentrated dose of the symbiote. We find that werewolves are most likely to bite a victim on the third night of the full moon. They spend the first two nights feeding, building up the manufacture of the symbiote in the glands, for lack of a better word, that supply the fangs. We've milked our volunteers on each night, and the levels of symbiote on the first two are not enough to turn a victim. But, if someone gets bitten on the third night, they're doomed."

"Doomed," he repeated. "So the hunting, the slaughter—"

"All part of the old biological imperative," she said. "Feed, reproduce, survive. Now, as for your project, the main behavioral characteristic I'd look for would be someone whose appetite is high during the first two night's full moon, even by day."

"I can't go after every glutton I see, not in this country," he said. "How easy is it to do this cellular test?"

"If you had the right equipment, you could test everyone," she said. "But, it's expensive, and you'd have to train people to find the symbiote. We can't just take blood samples from everyone and run them through electron microscopes."

"Can the symbiote be destroyed? Or removed?"

"Can a werewolf be cured, you mean?"

"Yes."

"That's what we're working on," she said, then she started, staring over his shoulder at the door to the hall.

Bert was sitting there, watching the two of them.

"I thought you told him to stay away," she said.

"He must want to be walked," said Sam, standing up. "Doc, you said you were an evolutionist."

"Yes."

"If this symbiote thing isn't anywhere else in nature, how did it get in humans? Did werewolves just evolve from humans?"

"Hard to say. Doctor Sanchez told you about the rapid decay after death?"

"Yes."

"That means we don't have old werewolf samples to compare. But, if we look at canine evolution—assuming the symbiote evolved simultaneously in both—we can get an approximate date of when it first appeared."

"When?"

"About twelve thousand years ago," she said, walking him to the door. "Only yesterday, evolutionarily speaking.

"Well, thanks, Doc," he said, turning to shake her hand.

She pulled back. "Have you touched any of your dogs since your shower?" she asked.

"Yes," he said.

"Then forgive me for not shaking your hand," she said, turning to go back to her desk. "Good-bye."

"Good-bye, Doc," he said.

He walked down the corridor, Bert pacing beside him.

She lied to you, he said.

I know, said Sam. *Which part specifically?*

That she's working on a cure.

Ah.

Are you disappointed?

I'm not sure, said Sam. *I wanted it when it first happened. When I changed for the first time. But, I've been living with it for so long, I suppose I'm used to it.*

Boss?

Yeah?

You said you knew she was lying, said Bert. *How did you know?*

Remember how she introduced herself yesterday? asked Sam. *She said she was researching evolutionary history and neurology.*

So?

So she gave me a whole lot of evolutionary history and not one mention of neurology. I guess she thought my poor hick brain would be too overwhelmed to notice.

What she didn't say made you think she was lying, mused Bert. *Something I wouldn't pick up because I'm watching and listening to the things she does say. Tricky. That's such a human thing.*

Sam laughed suddenly.

What? asked Bert.

Say there was some creature that could bite you and turn you human for three nights a month, said Sam.

Like a reverse werewolf, said Bert.

Right. Would you like it?

Sure, said Bert. *Then, I could work the remote control myself.*

Sam's house was a modest split-level, the last house in a cul-de-sac bordering the woods.

Perfect place for a werewolf to live, thought Tennant as he approached the back yard from the cover of the trees. He stopped just before they petered out and scanned the house with his binoculars. Sam lived alone, he knew, but Tennant was a man of careful habits.

He checked his intel, then looked around until he saw the stump. There was a hole on one side of it. Tennant reached in and pulled out a small oilcloth packet: inside was a key. He removed it and replaced the packet, then made a quick dash to the back door. The key fit, and a second later, he was in the house.

He searched it slowly and methodically, checking the edges of the carpet to see if they pulled up, flipping through the pages of books and checking their bindings. He pulled out a magnetic locator that produced three-dimensional images, a stud-finder on steroids, and ran it over the walls, looking for strongboxes, safes, and hidey holes.

Nothing.

He went upstairs. There were two bedrooms. The smaller one doubled as an office and library, stacked with books and magazines. Every cover depicted a dog. Hunting dogs, herding dogs, show dogs, lap dogs, smiling dogs, growling dogs, dogs at work, dogs at play, and one devoted entirely to circus dogs wearing ruffles and four-legged clown costumes.

"You have a boring house and a boring job, Sam Lehrmann," Tennant sighed. "You're even a boring werewolf."

He ran the locator over the stacks. No luck.

The main bedroom was next. A full-sized bed with a polished maple headboard was against the far wall, a battered and well-traveled trunk at its foot. Tennant knew without looking that the sheets would be creased and folded with military precision at the corners, that the shirts in the drawers, even the T-shirts, would be clean and pressed, that the socks would be arrayed in identical pairs, and that the shoes in the closet would be burnished. He almost hated the mess he was about to make in this soldier's life. He certainly hated that he was going to have to restore the room to the same state in which he had found it.

He reached for the first dresser drawer, then froze. A car was pulling into Sam's driveway. He stood by the corner of the front window and peered down.

Mona was getting out of her car, a set of keys in her hand. She walked around to the other side and opened the door. A Rottweiler bounded out, looking glad to be on solid ground after her driving.

The girlfriend and her dog, thought Tennant as the front door opened downstairs. *Great.*

He decided to stay where he was, hoping he wouldn't have to do anything about the two of them—then he heard the damn mutt growl. He thought quickly, then stripped off his shirt.

"What is it, Nicky?" Mona whispered.

She had decided to water Sam's plants. It didn't mean she forgave him, she thought. It was merely a nice thing to do. A friendly thing. Neighborly. No one should come home to dead plants.

But now Nicky was tensed, all of her canine senses focused on the stairs to the second floor. She gave a soft growl.

Mona immediately reached into her handbag and grabbed her gun.

A burglar. Sam had told too many people he was going to be away. No time to call the police if she was going to catch the bastard. She wasn't afraid. She had fourteen rounds and a well-trained Rottweiler on her side. She'd show the little—

Upstairs, the shower went on.

"What the hell?" she muttered.

She crept silently up the stairs, Nicky staying at her side. The bathroom was between the two bedrooms, and vapor was drifting out from under the door. She could hear a man humming.

Sam never hummed in the shower.

She pushed the door open carefully, took a deep breath, and pulled back the shower curtain.

"Hey!" shouted the man, turning, his hair lathered with shampoo. Then, he saw the gun. "Jesus! What the fuck, lady?"

He put his hands up, then wiped his forehead as the lather began to run into his eyes.

She wished at that moment that his hands had gone in the other direction—or that she could sink immediately into the earth.

"A lady with a gun and a Rottweiler," said the man as soon as he got a good look at her. "You have got to be Mona."

"I've got to be," she said. "Who are you and what are you doing here? This is a forty caliber Glock 23 asking the questions."

"Yes, ma'am, I recognize the weapon," he said. "I would appreciate it if you would point it elsewhere, as I am not wearing any body armor at the moment."

"Name. Purpose."

"Name: Larry Tennant, ma'am," he said. "Purpose: Cleanliness, ma'am. Next to godliness, ma'am. My eyes are stinging. You mind if I rinse out my hair?"

"Oh, for God's sake," she said, lowering the gun. "I'll be outside. I'm leaving Nicky here to keep an eye on you. Nicky, guard."

The dog sat by the tub and watched Tennant. Mona went to Sam's room. There was a pile of clothes on the floor. She picked up his pants and felt the pockets, then removed his wallet and went through it.

There was a short bark. She walked back to the bathroom to find Tennant standing with his arms folded, still standing in the tub, trading glares with Nicky.

"Would you instruct your watchdog to allow me to grab a towel?" he asked.

"Take two," she said, tossing them to him. "I'd appreciate it if you'd cover up right away."

He wrapped one around his waist, then started drying his hair. Then, he noticed the wallet in her hands.

"I didn't know this was a robbery," he said.

She held up his driver's license. "Says 'Lawrence Tennant,'" she said.

"I prefer Larry," he replied.

She held up another card. "You were Army," she said.

"Four years, yes, ma'am," he said. "That's how I met Sam."

"Old Army buddy?" she asked.

"Canine Corps," he said. "We both liked dogs. We kept in touch. He asked me to fill in for him at the kennel while he was away."

"Why are you in his house?"

"He wanted me to water the plants," said Tennant. "I was all sweated up from the dogs, decided to grab a shower. Didn't know that was a capital offense in Georgia."

"We are the unwashed state," said Mona, She put her gun back in her bag. "Come on, Nicky."

"That's it?" he asked, following her into the hallway.

"I accept your explanation," she said, walking down the stairs as Nicky bounded ahead of her. "I'm sorry I scared you."

"Did I scare you?" he called. "Tell me I scared you a little."

"I'm embarrassed enough, thank you," she said. "Take good care of those plants. Come, Nicky."

The door closed. Tennant grinned, got dressed, and resumed his search.

CHAPTER 9

Whitfield was bringing in cherry trifle for dessert when Burton made her appearance.

"Sorry, everyone," she said, yawning. "Bonnie, could I get a side of bacon with my waffles today?"

"Sure thing," said Whitfield, "and I'll save you some trifle."

Burton sat down next to Sam, looked at him blearily, then brightened. "Sam, right? The Dog Man."

"That's right, Doctor Burton," said Sam. "How are you?"

"Looking forward to work," she said. "Clear night tonight."

"I wouldn't think this part of the world would be a great place for an observatory," he said. "What with the humidity and the low elevation and all."

"You know something about astronomy?" she asked.

"Just what I learned in school growing up."

"Well, you'd be right if I was looking deep into the cosmos," she said, "but I'm looking at the moon, so I don't need anything that powerful in the way of a scope, and this area works fine."

"Mind if I come for a visit?" he asked.

"Only if you bring the doggies."

From the other end of the room, the Dobermans bristled with indignation.

Doggies, puppies, said Nan. *Where's the respect?*

Where's the fear? added Bert.

Quiet, said Arnie. *Sarge is in range.*

Hey, runt! called Sarge from patrol outside. *How are all the little doggies doing?*

Warm and toasty, thanks for asking, replied Arnie. *Mind the ticks.*

"Done," said Sam. "What time?"

"After dark would be best," she said, smiling. "Don't you think?"

"Makes sense."

Mckenna and Kudowski exchanged a glance that Sam missed but Olga and Arnie didn't. Sanchez stared moodily at his trifle, while Buenaventura, as always, watched all of them, leaning back in her chair.

"Sunset is at 8:10," said Burton. "Come by about nine. Everything should be set up."

"It's a date," said Sam. "Um, how do I get there, exactly?"

"Same elevator that I use," said Coleridge. "Press the Up button."

"I would have figured that out," said Sam. "Eventually."

He finished his trifle, picked up his dish, and brought it to the kitchen, being careful to knock before he entered.

Whitfield turned and smiled gratefully. "How was everything tonight?" she asked.

"Terrific," he said. "That trifle reminded me of the one my grandma used to make."

"Got the recipe from mine," she said. "The cherries are local. We put 'em up in May, and they start getting a little tart right around now, which I like."

"Hope you saved some for your husband," he said, putting his plate in the dishwasher.

"He gets the best leftovers in the county," she said, holding up a plastic container.

"Lucky man."

"See you tomorrow," she said.

He turned to see the dogs watching him from the doorway.

"Looks like it's time for a walk," he said.

No one spoke until they were outside and clear of the patrols.

Okay, what? asked Sam.

You were flirting with her, said Nan.

I was not, said Sam. *I was complimenting her on her cooking. I was being polite.*

Boss, your body language was blatant, said Olga.

She's married, said Sam. *Happily, I believe you pointed out.*

Which is why she's not flirting with you, said Olga.

Just the opposite, said Otto. *She knew you were flirting with her, so her defenses were up.*

She didn't seem like her defenses were up, said Sam.

That's how good they were, said Otto.

And now you got a date with another lady in a dark room, said Nan.

It's not a date, said Sam. *It's an interview.*

With a lady, Nan repeated. *In a dark room.*

Is everything with you guys about sex? asked Sam.

We wish, sighed Arnie.

Tennant restored the last pair of socks to its place in the array, then called Pastore.

"The house is clean," he said.

"You always did like a challenge," said Pastore.

"No, I hate challenges," said Tennant. "I like things easy and quick. Time to take it to the next level. Maybe the level after that."

"You've got maybe three days," said Pastore.

"All I need is one night," said Tennant.

Sam stretched out on his bed, the alarm set for sunset. The dogs were sacked out in their room. Except for Olga, who sat by Sam's bed, watching him.

Have you called Mona yet? she asked.

Not since I've gotten here, he said. *She never called back yesterday.*

Maybe she did after they took your phone, said Olga.

You think I should call her.

I do.

Even if she continues not picking up.

Yes.

How many times do I do this?

Until she picks up.

This is why we don't let dogs have phones, said Sam.

He picked up the headset from the room phone.

"Yes, Mr. Lehrmann," said a voice on the other end.

"How do I make an outside call?" he asked.

"You give us the number and we connect you," said the voice. "All calls are monitored."

"Monitored as in computer listening for key words?"

"Monitored as in we listen to the call," said the voice. "Just so you know up front."

"Puts a damper on the phone sex," said Sam.

"Some people get turned on knowing that we're listening," said the voice encouragingly.

"I ain't one of them," said Sam. "Put me through to Mona Havelka. She's on my list."

"She is your list," said the voice. "Pathetic."

The phone rang—and rang. Eventually, he got her voice mail.

"Pick up next time," said Sam. "Okay. I'm done."

"Pathetic," said the voice again.

He hung up. *Satisfied?* he asked Olga.

Are you? she replied.

He glanced out the window. It was dark. He woke the other dogs. *Time to visit the astronomer,* he said.

What do they do, exactly? asked Bert.

They look at the sky, said Otto.

And they get paid for that, said Bert in amazement. *Humans. They're just weird.*

Tennant drove into town, following the directions from his cellphone. Not that he would have needed them, he thought. This lady was all too predictable.

He spotted the bar and parked half a block away. As he neared the entrance, he saw Nicky tied to one of the poles supporting the awning in front. The Rottweiler saw him and growled. He wanted to growl back, but suppressed it. He stepped around the dog and went in.

Mona was seated at the end of the bar, watching the news. He slid onto the stool next to her.

"Not interested," she said without turning.

"Usually I buy a woman a drink before she gets to see me naked," he said. "Things got all mixed up today."

She snorted, then spluttered, grabbing at a napkin and clutching it to her face. "Goddamn, that stings when it goes through your nose," she gasped.

"Let me buy you one you can actually drink," he suggested. "What's the bartender's name?"

"Hector," she said.

"Hector, another one of whatever she's drinking," he said, "and a Corona for me."

"One ice tea, one Corona," said the bartender.

"Ice tea," repeated Tennant. "As in Long Island?"

"As in Lipton's," she said, wiping her nose. "Two sugars, one lemon, and a sprig of fresh mint."

"Must be the lemon that stung you," he said. "Not drinking the hard stuff?"

"I've cut back."

"Strange place to do it."

"One bad habit at a time."

"Huh," he said. "I was sort of under the impression that you had dropped another one recently."

She eyed him carefully, still dabbing at her nose as Hector brought the drinks over. "I'm leaking snot like a five-year-old, and you're hitting on me. What kind of desperate are you?"

"You aren't the kind of woman who draws the desperate," he said.

"That's right, I get the psychopaths and the suicidal. Which one are you?"

"Must be the second," he said, grinning, "but what a way to go."

She clicked her glass against his bottle. "How long you known Sam?" she asked.

"We met in Kabul," he said. "Worked together in the Canine Corps for five months, which is like five years anywhere else."

"Sounds like rough work," she said.

"Saw a lot of bodies," he said. "Saved some people. That was the good part."

"Did you know him before he was in Canine Corps?"

"No, ma'am."

"Did he ever talk about what he did before?"

"A little," he said, wondering where she was going.

"Here's the thing," she said. "I'm worried about him. He's got something going on in his head, and I've been reading up on post-traumatic stress syndrome and wondering if that's it."

"Could be," said Tennant. "I'm no expert, but there's enough crazy in the Army to go around."

"Did he ever talk about someone named Tom? Tom Cheller?"

Ah, he thought. "Name rings a bell, but I don't remember the exact conversation. Who's he?"

"A friend of his. Killed over there."

"We all had friends who got killed," said Tennant, trying to look mournful.

"Sorry," she said, clinking her glass against his. "This is a name that's been coming up."

"Come to think of it, he might have said something. I'll check the memory bank after the hangover wears off. Anything comes up, I'll give you a call."

"Okay," she said. "I'd appreciate that."

"I'm gonna need your number to do that."

"Oh, that was smooth, Army," she said, smiling.

She opened her purse, pulled out a pen, and wrote it on a coaster. "Don't start hoping," she said sternly as she handed it to him. "This is just for the information."

"How long were the two of you together?"

"What makes you think it's past tense?"

"Got that impression from Sam before he left," said Tennant. "Sorry, but it wasn't hard to see. He was getting philosophical already."

"Great," she sighed. "Yeah, I suppose we'll have the Talk when he gets back."

"If you want to try it out on me first, I'm a good listener."

"I've got a better one," said Mona.

"Maybe, but you tied her to a post outside," said Tennant, "and I can throw in some sympathetic grunts when the monologue slows."

"I can pet her," said Mona.

"You can—"

"Stop immediately. You just got into town, you don't know me."

"I'd like to. And, I'm only in town for a few days, so I'd be out of your hair after."

"You think I need rebound sex? Or revenge sex?"

"I'm not particular," he said. "It could be random, unmotivated sex if that's what you want."

"What I want," she repeated. "What I want is to figure out what I want."

"How long is that gonna take? Because—"

"You're only in town for a few days, I know. I heard you the first time." She finished her ice tea, then gave him a look he couldn't figure out. "Come with me, Army."

He knocked off the last of his Corona, threw some money on the bar, and followed her out.

She stood by Nicky, looking into the dog's eyes.

Nicky turned and looked at Tennant, then bared her teeth and growled.

"Nicky's in charge of vetting my men," said Mona. "Sorry, I guess it ain't your night."

"Given that Sam trained her, this really doesn't seem like a fair test," said Tennant.

"She ain't Sam's dog, she's mine," said Mona, "and there were plenty of times she was like this with Sam, believe me."

"You're a grown woman, Mona," he said. "You don't need to let a dog do your thinking for you."

"That may be true," she drawled, "but letting my dog do the thinking is a damn sight better than letting your dick do it. Good luck getting laid, Army."

She untied Nicky's leash. The dog gave Tennant a look of disdain as they walked away. Mona never looked back at all.

"Goddamn," muttered Tennant. He walked back into the bar.

Hector looked at him sympathetically. "Coulda warned you there'd be no luck there," he said. "Another beer?"

"Might as well," said Tennant.

A blonde sidled up to him as he drank. "Looking for company?" she asked hopefully.

"You a dog person?" he asked, giving her a once over.

"Ooh, I love dogs," she cooed.

"Not interested," he said.

She looked at him in disbelief, then stormed away. He finished his beer and left.

The dogs followed Sam into the elevator, looking around in trepidation.

What's wrong? he asked.

We've never been in one of these things before, said Arnie.

It's safe, said Sam.

*But in that movie—*began Bert.

That was a movie, said Sam. *Movies aren't about reality.*

Then why do you watch them?

Humans don't like reality, said Otto.

That's pretty much it, said Sam.

He hit the button marked "Observatory," and the doors closed.

What do the other buttons do? asked Arnie.

That one takes you down to Maintenance. That one stops the elevator. Door open, door closed, alarm.

Got it, said Arnie.

Great, said Bert. *Only you'll need to climb on one of us to press them.*

And it's gonna be you, said Arnie.

The doors opened, and they stepped into the observatory. The dome was closed and the lights were on, so their attention was immediately dominated by the giant reflecting telescope that was mounted on a swiveling base like a cannon pointed at the sky. There was a cluster of consoles to the right.

"Hello?" called Sam.

"Good evening, Sam," said Doctor Burton, bobbing up from behind the consoles. "Hello, doggies."

"Dogs, sit," said Sam.

They sat.

"What other tricks do they do?" asked Burton.

"They don't do tricks," said Sam. "They obey commands."

I'll roll over if that would make her happy, offered Arnie.

"Although Arnie will roll over if you ask him nicely," said Sam.

"Arnie, roll over," said Burton, squatting in front of the dachshund.

Arnie did a clumsy barrel roll and scrambled to his feet.

"Not his best trick, is it?" observed Burton.

Piss poor, commented Olga.

Hey, I've never done it before, said Arnie. *Takes some practice.*

"He's a watch dog, not a trick dog," said Sam. "He's very good at what he's trained to do."

"You don't waste time on frivolities, do you, Sam?" asked Burton.

"It ain't a frivolity if I like to do it," said Sam. "And, if I don't like to do it, it's a waste of time. So, I'm guessing that huge thing there is a telescope."

"Very good," she said. "It's just a baby compared to some of the ones I've worked with, but it helps. And please don't make any of the obvious size jokes. I heard them all in freshman astronomy, and that was a long time ago."

"With all due respect, it couldn't have been that long ago," commented Sam.

Burton smiled for a moment.

You're doing it again, warned Nan.

"And you look at the moon through that scope and do what, exactly?" asked Sam, ignoring her.

"I use it to help guide those suckers over there," said Burton, pointing to a smaller array of mirrored dishes mounted on a platform near the top of the dome.

"What do those suckers suck in?"

"My life's work," she said. "My great theoretical contribution to science, only it's classified. The folks here and your boss know about it, and no one else in the world. Or, at least, on this world. Ever have a secret so huge that you want to scream it to the skies, or you'll burst?"

More like I want to howl, thought Sam.

"I've had one or two," he said. "Nothing earth-shattering. But, since I am now cleared to know yours—"

"Werewolves," she said. "What do we know about werewolves and the moon?"

"They change when the moon is full," he said. "Three nights out of every twenty-eight."

"Why?" she asked. "Why the full moon?"

"Well," he began, then he stopped. "I don't know."

"Right," she said. "No one does. Or no one did. Such a fundamental question, and no one ever asked why. Why only the full moon? Why only at night? A physiological change that profound, triggered the exact same way in thousands of werewolves who are otherwise different. The old way of thinking was that it had to be psychosomatic, that werewolves bought into the myth that the full moon was the source of their power."

"Isn't it?"

"One of the things we did here, early on, was to take some werewolf volunteers and induce comas," said Burton.

"Jesus," said Sam. "Why?"

"To take the lunar cycle out of the equation," she said. "We put them into an artificial environment underground and woke them without letting them know what day it was. They couldn't see the night sky, they didn't know when sunset was, or when the full moon rose. They were then shown daily videos of the moon and told that it was accurate to the minute. Some of videos were accurate, some weren't. If the effect of the full moon was psychological, then the transformation should have taken place when the werewolves believed it was present—but it didn't. Even when they thought the moon was presenting its dark side, the change took place if it was really full."

"Wow," said Sam. "Clever experiment. Who thought that one up?"

"Sandra and I did," said Burton. "I expected that result."

"Why?"

"Because I'm a scientist," said Burton. "I don't believe in magic, or Gypsy curses, or any of that crap. Lycanthropy is physical. It is triggered by the full moon. Cause and effect. Therefore, there had to be something coming from the full moon—"

"Coming from the moon?"

"When you look at the moon, what do you see?"

"Um, craters? A man, a lady, a rabbit?"

"And how is it that you're able to see it?"

"Because it's lit up by the sun."

"Which means we see it how, Dog Man?"

"Because it's light out in space?" guessed Sam. "I mean, without the sunlight, there'd be no way of seeing the moon."

Duh, said Nan and Bert.

"Okay, I'm sounding like a moron," said Sam. "What am I missing?"

"Nothing but this," said Burton.

She walked over to a console and pressed a button. Music came through speakers mounted on the walls. A big band, swinging gently.

"Do you know it?" she asked, swaying to the beat with her eyes closed.

"Sounds familiar," he said. "An oldie."

"But a goodie," she said.

"All you need is a mirror ball and we've got a party," he said.

"I've got something much, much better," she said. She pressed another button, and the dome split open, the two halves sliding down with a low rumble, revealing the night sky.

Oh, sighed Nan. *The stars are so beautiful.*

My God, thought Sam guiltily. *They haven't been out at night in months.*

Burton glided towards him. "Dance with me, Dog Man," she said.

Before he knew it, she had slipped inside his arms, and they were foxtrotting under the stars.

Uh, Boss, said Olga. *Remember the other day when I said Burton wasn't reacting to you? She's reacting to you now.*

Gee, you think? snickered Arnie.

"You can dance, Dog Man," observed Burton.

"Learned a lot in the Army, ma'am," he said.

"You 'ma'am' me one more time and I will hurt you," she said. "Badly. My name is Valerie. Not Val, Valerie. Three syllables, with a soft, feminine ending. Do you know the song yet, Dog Man? 'It had to be—'"

"Moonglow," he finished. "Should've known it right away. It was in some movie."

"Picnic," she said. "William Holden dancing with Kim Novak when they were both young and sexy."

"Yeah, I remember," he said. "Saw it on TCM once. She was something. No Valerie Burton, but not bad."

"Now we're talking," she said as he twirled her.

"You are the prettiest astrophysicist I've ever met."

"And the only one."

"And the only one. Tell me about the moonglow. It's reflected sunlight— that's the answer I was supposed to come up with."

"Correct, Dog Man," she said. "Sunlight does nothing to werewolves by itself, but bounce it off the full moon, and kapow! No one ever wondered about that. How is moonglow different from sunlight? How does the moon transform it? Why only during the full moon?"

He dipped her, bringing his face close to hers. "You scientists enjoy asking me questions that you know I can't answer. Nobody likes a tease, Valerie."

She grinned up at him. "My favorite version of *Moonglow* is the one by K.D. Lang and Tony Bennett. The harmonies kill me every time."

He pulled her back up. As they danced on, he asked, "Why is moonglow different than sunlight? Aren't they both just light?"

"No such thing as just light," she said. "Light is the spectrum of electromagnetic radiation that our eyes evolved to see. Other animals can see different parts of it, either deeper into the ultraviolet or out past the infrared."

"So moonglow isn't just light?"

"Sunlight isn't just light," she said. "It has a whole range of radiation at different frequencies. But, when it bounces off the moon, something happens. It creates a pulse, a regular beat out in the high end of the spectrum. It's like the moon is a giant lens, bending solar radiation into this new frequency. And, with the right equipment, the pulse can be measured."

She pressed herself against him. "You'd be amazed what you can do with the right equipment," she murmured.

The music ended, and he extricated himself as gently as he could.

"Thank you for the dance," he said. "Tell me about the pulse."

"I'm wondering if you have one."

"I'm on duty."

"Right, so am I," she sighed. "Come with me."

Sam and the dogs followed her to the consoles. She sat down, clicked on a file, and a graph appeared. She indicated a stool next to hers, so he straddled it and sat.

"Here's the frequency, isolated over time," she said. "It stays low, then, two days before the full moon, starts to climb rapidly. At full moon, it hits a peak and stays there for the duration, then drops over the next two days."

She slid her finger across the screen, expanding the timeline. The little bell-curves marched across the x-axis, repeating with boring regularity.

"Why isn't it measurable during daytime?" asked Sam.

"Regular sunlight interferes with it," she replied. "Effectively wipes it out."

"And that pulse—how does it cause the change?"

"Not my department," she said, "but nature is full of mechanisms that evolved to react to different frequencies in the EM."

"And that's it," he said. "The big secret."

"Not even close," she said, grinning broadly. "Care to dive into the deep end of the crazy pool?"

"You go first."

She pulled up another file. "I've been using the radioscope to isolate the sources of the pulse—to see if there was anything special about the type of rock or surface that causes this change."

She opened the file, then tapped on an icon. It expanded to fill the monitor with an image of the full moon. "Turns out that the pulse emanates from several specific locations. I can't quite pin them down, but I have their approximate areas—" She typed, and several red circles popped up on the picture.

"Notice anything about them?" she asked, swiveling in her chair to face him.

He peered over her shoulder at the screen. "I count twelve," he said.

"Very good, Dog Man," she said.

"They taught me how to count in the Army, too."

"What else do you notice about them?"

He looked more closely. The twelve circles were all near the perimeter of the visible moon. "It's like someone drew a clock on the surface," he said. "They're—wait."

"Deep end, Dog Man," she whispered. "I'm already swimming below the surface. You can jump in and do the dog paddle."

"They're regularly spaced," he said. "Equidistant."

"Bingo," she said, and they sat silently staring at the screen.

I don't get it, said Bert. *What's the big deal?*

She's saying it isn't possible, said Otto.

"Could this be a natural phenomenon?" asked Sam. "Some accident? A fluke of the universe?"

"Could be," she said. "But, say you wanted to bathe the earth with a regular pulse with this particular frequency and amplitude three nights out of the lunar cycle. Say you wanted to use the lunar surface as a giant lens to focus it. You would want to put your transmitters—"

"Transmitters?"

"For want of a better word," she said. "You'd want them in a circle, solar powered, and angled so that only the full moon would bring the signal into play. You'd also want them a safe distance inside the perimeter of the sunlit surface."

"Why?"

"To allow for the moon's natural oscillation," she said. "If you put them right on the line between light and dark, then the slight perturbations would take some of them out of play part of the time. But, these locations are all about ten kilometers inside that line, guaranteeing them constant exposure."

"You're saying someone put them there."

"I'm saying someone put them there."

"Who?" asked Sam, shaking his head like he was trying to come out of a drunken stupor. "Why would someone do that? What does it have to do with werewolves?"

"I don't know," she said softly, "and I gotta tell you, I'm afraid to find out."

CHAPTER 10

THE DOGS GOT ON THE elevator like they had been doing it all their lives. Arnie watched as Sam pressed the button for the lobby.

The buttons are stacked in the same order as the floors, he said.

Right, said Sam.

That makes sense, said Arnie, *but what if the building is big? Wouldn't the buttons stack up higher than the elevator? And how would you be able to reach them?*

They put them in a grid, said Sam. *And they're numbered when there's a lot of floors.*

Of course, said Arnie, nodding wisely. *I'm gonna have to learn how to read numbers.*

They're the same ones as the ones on the remote control, said Sam.

They are? Cool.

You don't have to know how to work an elevator, said Sam.

And you still can't reach the buttons, said Bert.

I can reach yours, offered Arnie, baring his teeth.

The door opened. Coleridge stood there, a rolling cart piled with cleaning products at his side. "Evening, Sam," he said. "How'd you like our observatory?"

"Impressive," said Sam as he led the dogs out.

"And how did you like our observer?" grinned Coleridge.

"Even more impressive," said Sam. "Good night."

Coleridge pushed the cart into the elevator. Sam thought he heard him chuckling as the doors closed.

The dogs suddenly turned as a unit to face the doors to the central wing. A second later, Sanchez emerged.

"Hey, Doc," Sam greeted him. "Burning the midnight oil?"

"It's only ten o'clock," said Sanchez, glancing at his watch. "I was getting some work done. Nothing else to do. Not all of us get to dance under the stars."

"You heard the music," said Sam.

"Same damn tune, over and over, every night," said Sanchez. "The woman is obsessed."

"Unlike anyone else in here," said Sam.

"Look where we are, look what we do," said Sanchez. "Normal hasn't left the building—it was never here in the first place."

"I assume it's all worth it."

"Debatable. The science is groundbreaking, but the circumstances—I don't know anymore."

"Is the money good, at least?"

"Beats working in a university," said Sanchez, rubbing his head.

Moonglow drifted down from the observatory. Sanchez gazed upwards, then closed his eyes wearily.

"You can have the next dance," suggested Sam.

"She won't dance with me," said Sanchez. "Good night, Mister Lehrmann."

He walked through the doors to the residential wing.

Are all scientists lonely and crazy? asked Nan.

Can't say I know that many, said Sam.

Scientists are people, said Olga. *People are lonely and crazy.*

That may be true, said Sam. *Let's turn in.*

All the dogs but Nan immediately settled into their beds. Nan took up position at the base of Sam's bed, facing the door.

What are you doing? he asked, sitting by her and taking off his boots.

We're guard dogs, she said. *I'm guarding you. It's my turn tonight.*

Who decided that?

We all did. You said this might be a dangerous assignment.

I'm touched, he said. *I mean that. But, who exactly do you think I need guarding from?*

She glanced at the door, her ears perking up. *At the moment, her,* she replied.

There was a soft knock at the door.

Let me guess, said Sam. *More dancing.*

If that's what it's called, said Nan.

He got up and opened the door. To his surprise, Doctor Kudowski was standing there. She looked down the hallway in each direction before whispering, "May I come in for a moment?"

"If you can hold your breath long enough," he said, stepping aside to let her through.

"There was this guy in grad school I liked," she said. "Smart, good-looking, great in bed. I was crazy for him. Only problem was, he had a dog. I thought to myself, Okay, this a biological problem, and I'm a scientist. I started experimenting with different combinations of antihistamines and inhalants. The trick was to find the balance between breathing and knocking myself out. Once I got it, we had some pretty mind-blowing experiences, and he still kept the dog."

"What happened to him?"

"I wanted to take it to the next level," she said, "but that meant full-time canine exposure, and there's not enough medication in the world. I told him, me or the dog. I came in second."

"There's a point to this story?"

"Fifteen minutes ago, I took my antihistamines," she said, glancing at Nan, who was watching her intently. "Ten minutes ago, I hit the inhaler. I am good to go for the next twenty minutes, then I'll either start sneezing or get really groggy or both, which is a really attractive combination, so I want to suggest that we quit gabbing and get going."

"I wasn't the one who was gabbing," said Sam, "but what makes you think—"

She stepped forward and kissed him.

"Why do—" he tried again.

She kissed him harder.

"Nineteen minutes," she whispered. "Who's gabbing now?"

"Doc, I'm flattered, but I've got a girl—"

"Who isn't here," said Kudowski. "You're in our bubble, Sam. When you live in a bubble, you have to grab everything you can get."

She tried to kiss him again. He held her away and disentangled himself.

"Wrong time, wrong place," he said gently.

"This is the only time and place I've got," she said.

"I'm sorry," he said, reaching forward to wipe a tear from her cheek. "I didn't mean to make you cry."

"I'm not crying," she insisted, reaching up to feel her face. "I'm—oh, shit."

She looked through the connecting door to see the other four dogs, lying in their beds, silent but wide awake. She started to sniffle.

"Didn't allow for—" she mumbled, then sneezed violently. "It's a variable, not a constant. Five dogs, not one. Underestimated the impact—."

She started wheezing.

"Got to—" she gasped, clawing at a pocket. It was empty. "Shit! Shit, shit, shit."

"Come on," he said, guiding her out into the hall. "Dogs, stay."

She doubled over, coughing violently, then gasped for air. He caught her and picked her up.

"Which room?" he said.

She pointed, and he ran with her cradled in his arms.

Sanchez stuck his head out of his room. "What's going on?" he called.

"Allergic reaction," answered Sam as he reached her door. "Key?"

She fished out her card. He grabbed it and opened her door. He carried her inside and placed her on her bed.

"Where's your inhaler?" he asked.

"Won't be enough," said Sanchez, coming into the room. "Lisa, where's your kit?"

She pointed at her dresser drawer. Sanchez opened it and took out a small, metal case. He removed a syringe and pulled off the cap, then tossed a small, sterile package to Sam.

"Swab her bicep," he said.

Sam tore open the package and dabbed at her upper arm. Sanchez sat next to her.

"Here we go, Lisa," said Sanchez, injecting her. "Should be good in a minute. Just relax."

He held her hand tenderly until the adrenaline took effect and she began breathing more easily.

"Thank you, Juan," she said hoarsely.

"I'm always here for you," he said. "You know that."

She pulled her hand away. "I'm sorry," she said, starting to cry for real. "I'm sorry, I'm sorry, I'm sorry."

Sam had no idea who she was saying it to.

"Do you want us to—" Sanchez began.

"Leave me alone," she said, rolling away so they couldn't see her face. "Please."

"Okay, Lisa," said Sanchez, getting to his feet. "You call if you need anything."

Sam put her card on the night-table, and they walked into the hall, closing her door behind them.

Sanchez blocked his path. "What happened?" he asked.

"She wanted to talk to me about something," said Sam.

"In a room full of dogs?" snapped Sanchez, his anger rising. "What was so important that she'd want to talk to you there?"

"Never found out," said Sam.

"You listen to me, my friend," said Sanchez. "I don't care who you are or what you're doing here. You'd better watch yourself."

"I'm not trying to cut in on your play, Doc," said Sam. "I can't help it if the ladies like me more than you."

Sanchez swung at him clumsily. Sam blocked the blow and caught his arm.

"Not a good idea, Doc," he said, squeezing until Sanchez winced. "I've got a lot more experience in this than you do."

"Brute force, that's all you people know," growled Sanchez. "Let me go."

Sam released him.

Sanchez rubbed his elbow. "This isn't over," he muttered.

"It never even started," said Sam. "Go to bed, Doc."

Sanchez stormed into his room, slamming the door behind him.

Sam walked back to his, wondering how many denizens of the lab were listening on the other sides of their doors. He went into his room. Nan was standing by the door, poised for combat.

Nothing I couldn't handle, said Sam.

I know, said Nan. *I would have been out there if there was.*

Thanks, said Sam.

Weird her coming on to you like that, she said. *Second one tonight. I thought they were supposed to be smart.*

Thanks again, he said.

The point is, Boss, you're not that attractive.

It keeps getting better and better with you, doesn't it?

She was trying to get something from you, persisted Nan. *And it wasn't your hot loving. Well, some of it was, but she was after something else.*

I know, said Sam.

Were you going to have sex with her to find out? asked Nan. *That's what spies do in those movies we watch with you.*

I'm not—well, I guess I am a spy, said Sam, *but I wouldn't sleep with her for that.*

How about to get back at Mona?

You see too much sometimes, said Sam.

Never had the opportunity to watch you full-time, she said. *It's been educational.*

Great, he said.

He stripped off his clothes and toppled into bed, but couldn't sleep, thinking about Kudowski; thinking about her runner's body, her smooth legs; thinking that if the dogs hadn't been there, he damn near might have gone along with it, and what did that mean about Mona and him?

At some point, he heard Nan pad off into the other room. He turned to see Otto sitting by his bed.

Your shift? he asked.

My shift, said Otto. *Hope you don't mind. I like this time of night.*

What's your take on my love life? asked Sam.

Otto looked at the door. *This place is like a kennel for humans. They're trapped here. Dogs have grown accustomed to sleeping in cages, but humans haven't. It makes them act oddly.*

So my success with the ladies is due to that?

Nan was right about Kudowski, said Otto.

Was she doing this on her own, or because McKenna told her to?

Not enough information to say, said Otto, *but those two do whisper a lot. They are the only ones who share an alliance. There is no team among the scientists, not like us. Sanchez and Burton are dominated by McKenna.*

And Buenaventura?

She watches. Always from the outside. Not under anyone's control, but powerless. There's something else about Burton.

What?

She's frightened. She was reaching out to you for help. That was what that dance was all about.

She said she was freaked by the signals from the moon, Sam pointed out.

It's more than that, said Otto. *She wants to tell someone something that scares her. She might tell you. She was trying to find out if she could trust you.*

All right, Otto, said Sam. *I'll talk to her again.*

He started to drift off.

Sam?

Something on your mind? asked Sam drowsily.

Always, said Otto.

What?

Different things at different times, said Otto.

How about right now?

Otto seemed to be looking at him from some other world. *This man, Pastore—your alpha.*

Former alpha, Sam corrected him. *Former commanding officer.*

Your alpha, repeated Otto. *How did he find out that you could speak to us? Why did you trust him with that?*

Sam closed his eyes.

The sun broke through a gap in the Hindu Kush, and three soldiers staggered barefoot where three werewolves had just been running.

"Break here, fifteen minutes," croaked Pastore. "Crawford, take lookout. Lehrmann, let's see that shoulder."

Crawford crawled to a position on the rocky ridge where he could stay hidden while watching in all directions. There were no trees in this section of the mountains, barely any vegetation at all. This meant little cover for any pursuers. It also meant little cover for them once they began moving again.

Sam sank to the ground and pulled his canteen out of his belt with his right hand. He gripped it between his knees and wrestled it open while Pastore peeled the dressing off of his shoulder.

"Clean so far," Pastore pronounced. He sprinkled more sulfa on the wounds, then put on a fresh dressing. "I'm gonna leave this one on for the duration, because we don't have many more. You need morphine?"

"Save it," said Sam. "I'd rather be awake and hurting than asleep and dead."

Pastore buried the old dressing and the package from the new one, then looked east. One mountain loomed over the rest, casting a giant shadow over the range.

"The Tirich Mir," he said. "Means the King of Shadows."

"Let's not go there," said Sam.

Pastore focused on the mountain with his binoculars, then pressed a button and read the numbers that came up. He checked them against his Odyssey.

"Sixty kilometers due east, which puts us near the Pakistani border," he said. "We made thirty-five since the second extraction point. Pretty damn good, even for werewolves."

"Nothing like fear to bump up the speed," said Sam, digging his boots and socks out of his pack. He pulled them on one-handed, then looked at the laces helplessly.

"Jesus," said Pastore, squatting down to tie them for him. "Didn't they teach you how to do this in kindergarten?"

"Something about a bunny diving under a log," said Sam.

"I figure no way those assholes kept up with us," said Pastore.

"You figure wrong," said Crawford. "I got one tracking party to the east, one to the west, both heading right at us."

"Fuck me!" exclaimed Pastore as they scrambled up the ridge to join him. "That's impossible."

"Nevertheless," said Crawford, pointing. "I'd say they're two hours away."

"We came from the south," said Pastore. "How is it we're getting flanked? If anything, they should be coming from the south."

"Maybe they phoned ahead," said Crawford.

Pastore pulled out his Odyssey. "Okay, so we're here," he muttered, looking at the screen.

"Turn it off," said Sam.

"What?"

"Turn it off. It's the Odysseys, it has to be. They were waiting at the first extraction point, they were waiting at the second extraction point, and now they're making a beeline right for our position."

"These things are untraceable," argued Pastore.

"Says the Army," said Sam. "You got a better explanation? You, us, the pilot, and the general were the only ones with the locations. The Odysseys have been compromised. Turn them off, get rid of them, and let's get the fuck out of here."

"We'll be traveling blind," said Pastore.

"Pick a direction. We'll do it the old-fashioned way. Compasses and the stars."

Pastore punched in some coordinates. "East is a whole lot of bad road followed by no road. Northeast is hostiles from here to China. Including China—it's all Uighurs out there. South and west are covered. My guess is they'll be expecting us to go northwest toward the NATO outpost in Fayzabad. So we go due north and hope we can outrun them."

"How far?" asked Crawford

"As far as we can," he said. "We bypass Eshkashem, then cross the Panj into Tajikistan. Ought to find a friendly face there."

"Long walk," said Crawford.

"You know what Sharia says about werewolves?" asked Sam.

"Can't be nothing good," said Crawford. "I like long walks."

"Give me your Odysseys," ordered Pastore.

The two soldiers handed them over. Pastore turned them on.

"What the hell are you doing?" asked Crawford.

Pastore heaved one to the left, a second down the mountain, and a third to the right.

"I hope they follow them into a ravine," he said. "With my luck, I'll get court-martialed for letting top-secret equipment fall into the enemy's hands. Grab some rations while you're walking."

They skidded down the ridge, found a small pass that looked like it hadn't been traveled recently, and jogged north. After an hour, Sam's head was swimming and his shoulder was throbbing.

Crawford looked over at him and silently beckoned for his weapon.

Sam shook his head and pounded on.

By noon, they were holed up under a small overhang as the sun beat down.

"How's it feeling?" asked Pastore.

"I'm gonna have to shoot one-handed," said Sam. "May not hit much, but I'll scare them plenty." He practiced changing clips with his right hand.

"That'll work," said Crawford encouragingly. "Hey, General Custer? Any Indians out there?"

"One party still coming," said Pastore, gazing through his binoculars. "The other one's probably not far behind. I don't know how they're tracking us, but they're doing it. Looks like about thirty."

"Got to appreciate the respect," said Crawford, cradling his weapon. "Last stand time?"

"Bottom of the ninth," said Pastore. "Might as well go down swinging in."

Something impinged on Sam's consciousness.

"Dogs," he said.

"What?"

"*They're using a forward team with three dogs.*"

"*How the hell do you know that?*" demanded Pastore.

"*Can't you hear them?*" asked Sam. "*They're getting close.*"

"*I thought he didn't take any morphine,*" said Crawford. "*Is this fever de-lirium talking?*"

"*Lehrmann, you explain yourself right now, you hear me, boy?*" said Pastore.

"*Can't you hear them talking?*" asked Sam. "*I thought that was a werewolf thing.*"

"*It most certainly is not a werewolf thing,*" said Pastore. "*You're saying you can talk to dogs?*

"*Yessir.*"

"*Can you talk to them now?*"

"*They're just about in range,*" said Sam, closing his eyes and concentrating.

Hey! *he called.* Any luck?

We got a trail, *came the reply.* We're moving up the mountain.

Forget about the mountain, *said Sam.* We're already there. It's a trick. They doubled back towards the river. Turn east and you should spot them in an hour. We're coming around the other end from the north. We'll catch them between us.

Great! Thanks!

Pastore watched as the advance team, their dogs now visible, turned to the east. Beyond them, the rest of the squad did the same.

"*I'll be damned,*" whispered Pastore.

. . .

You never knew until then that no one else had that ability? *asked Otto.*

Nope, *replied Sam.*

How did it make you feel?

At the time, I was mostly feeling pain and shock. But when we made it back to base, I'd catch Pastore and Crawford giving me weird looks, talking about me when they thought I wasn't listening. I don't think they ever told anyone else, but what with the mission fuckup and no longer feeling part of the team, I wanted out. Turned out the Army wanted to disband the squad, anyway, so I got the transfer to the canine unit with Pastore's full approval.

How did it make you feel, Sam? *repeated Otto.*

Sam sighed. *The Army was the first place where I didn't feel alone,* he said. *Where there were other freaks like me. Then, even the werewolves started treating me like one. It sucked.*

I feel that way sometimes, *said Otto.* With the other dogs.

Why?

They treat me like I'm different, *said Otto.*

Why do you suppose that is?

Otto looked at him, and Sam gave an involuntary shiver.

Because I am different, said Otto. *Get some sleep, Sam. I got this.*

Okay. Thanks.

He closed his eyes to avoid the Weimaraner's gaze, and finally drifted off.

In the morning, there was a sign taped to the kitchen door: "Taking my day off. Please wash your own dishes. Bonnie."

"How does this work?" asked Sam.

"There's food," said McKenna curtly. "You prepare it. You eat it. You clean up afterwards."

Waffles popped out of the toaster. McKenna speared them with a fork, put them on a plate, and stormed out.

"And that's why he's in charge," chuckled Coleridge from the doorway. "Don't worry, Sam. Bonnie leaves us plenty in the freezer, and the microwave's over there."

"I didn't want to step on anyone's toes," said Sam. "Frozen waffles work for me."

"How goes the research?"

"Useful," said Sam. "Eye-opening in a lot of ways."

"If the world only knew, it'd be having nightmares," said Coleridge.

"It's been having them all along," said Sam. "It just doesn't know what they're about."

"Sounds like you're ready for the dream lady," said Coleridge as he fried up some eggs.

"Buenaventura? She's next on my list."

"I always like talking to her."

"Why's that?"

"'Cause she's the only one who listens," said Coleridge, expertly flipping the eggs. "Least, around here."

"I'll listen, if you like," said Sam.

"She's prettier than you," said Coleridge.

"Sucks that she's married."

"Oh, it truly does," laughed Coleridge. "I'm making a supply run later. You or the dogs need anything from the outer world?"

"Can't think of anything," said Sam. "Thanks."

He carried his waffles out to the dining room. McKenna and Buenaventura were the only ones there.

"I am following your example, sir," he said, raising his plate in salute. "Good morning, ma'am."

"Good morning," she said. "Am I up next for you?"

"If that's convenient," he said. "I could see you later this morning after I take the dogs for their run."

"Fine," she said. "Drop by any time."

She picked up her plate and left.

"I understand there was an incident last night," McKenna said quietly.

"Incident?"

"With Doctor Kudowski."

"She had an allergy attack," said Sam. "Doctor Sanchez gave her an injection. She seemed to be doing better afterward."

"How is it that she was exposed to your animals?"

"She came by my room."

"Why?"

"Never really found out," said Sam. "You could ask her."

"I will," said McKenna.

Sam finished his waffles. "I'm going for my run," he said. "Want to join me?"

"Run?" said McKenna.

"It's an exercise," said Sam. "Keeps you fit."

"I'm fit as a fiddle, thank you," said McKenna.

"My grandpa used to say that," said Sam, picking up his plate. "Never understood what it meant."

"Hey, Sheriff," said Oliveras, tapping on his door frame.

"Doc," said Boudreau in surprise. "A personal appearance. To what do I owe the honor?"

"I got something for you," said Oliveras, holding up a folder, "and it's so exceedingly weird, I wanted to bring it over myself."

"In other words, you don't want this on record," said Boudreau, motioning her to a chair.

"No trail, paper or electronic," agreed Oliveras as she sat. "Last thing I need is people telling me how insane I am."

"You ain't insane," said Boudreau.

"Oh, but I am," said Oliveras. "I just don't like hearing it to my face."

"Duly noted, ma'am," he said. "What insane thing did you bring to brighten my morning?"

"Another aconite case," she said, holding the file up triumphantly. "Got it from the ME newsgroup in response to my query. Angela Shreve, last seen alive December 22nd, four years ago. Turned up a week later, body in an advanced state of decomposition."

"Advanced state of decomposition? After one week?"

"Report said the decay was consistent with a body that had been deceased for six months, but they know for a fact that she was alive on December 22nd. They suspected some flesh-eating bacteria or something even worse, so they took samples, sealed her up *tout de suite—*"

"No espanol, por favor."

"French, you damn redneck, and it means real fast. Samples came back negative on the bacteria, and the only weird thing in the toxicology was the aconite."

"So she was poisoned?"

"They couldn't establish cause of death, but they were pretty damn certain it was murder."

"Why?"

"Because whoever did it chopped her hand off," said Oliveras. "And they never found it."

"Body mutilation," mused Boudreau. "Got plenty of it in our case. But, nothing chopped off, right?"

"No," said Oliveras. "Strictly a canine picnic with our boys, but all body parts present and accounted for, sir! And none of this decay nonsense."

"Ever seen anything like that in your world?"

"Once again, I will post an inquiry," said Oliveras. "I will keep you informed."

"December 22nd," mused Boudreau. "Our vics disappeared right before Christmas, right?"

"Best we can tell, yes."

"Something else in common with that Shreve woman."

"What do you think it means?"

"Don't know yet," he said. "Don't even know they're related. But, time of year and aconite—two things they both have."

"You thinking something ritualistic?"

"Have to consider it," he said. "Hell, ain't nothing normal about this case."

Sam stopped about three-quarters through his second lap around the campus, bending over and resting his hands on his knees. Arnie collapsed gratefully by his feet, his tongue lolling out.

You're out of shape, commented the dachshund maliciously. *This used to be nothing for you.*

Still is, said Sam. *Otto?*

We're clear, said the Weimaraner. *Should be good for a while.*

Right, said Sam, straightening up. *Anybody recognize this spot?*

Is this a trick question? asked Bert suspiciously. *Because we haven't left this compound since we got here. I'm pretty sure this spot looks exactly like it did yesterday.*

When Olga was racing Tito, I was watching the monitors, said Sam. *There was a moment when she disappeared from one, and took about two seconds to show up again.*

Meaning there's a blind spot in Security, said Arnie.

Right. And this is it.

The dogs looked beyond the fence.

I see trees, said Olga. *How far to the road through there?*

Less than a mile, said Sam. *All this advanced tech, and they don't allow for something as simple as throwing something over the fence.*

Like a copy of that book thingy you're looking for, said Bert.

If the Bogey Man was getting his werewolves from here, that would be one way of getting it to him.

What would keep the Bogey Man coming back? asked Otto. *Once he had it, he would have had no more need for this place.*

Maybe McKenna parceled out the info, said Sam. *Or maybe they had some other reason to be working together.*

You haven't connected the Bogey Man to McKenna yet, said Nan.

No, I haven't, said Sam, *but if the Book of Wolves came from here—*

What's to stop McKenna from just taking it out the front gate? asked Nan.

The watchdogs, said Sam. *Human and canine—and the cameras recording everything. The disk itself has a tracer on it, so it never leaves his office without someone knowing.*

Who watches the watchdogs? asked Otto.

Pastore would have found any money spikes with the guards by now, said Sam.

Maybe it's not about money, said Olga. *Maybe someone really has it in for werewolves. Maybe it's fanaticism.*

A real version of what you're pretending to be, said Otto.

You guys could try talking to the shepherds, said Sam. *They could have seen something out of the ordinary.*

No one's talking with Sarge in charge, said Arnie. *Unless Olga wants to sweet-talk him.*

I'll leave that to you, said Olga.

Sam looked out past the fence. *I'm going to take a look at the other side,* he said. *Who's coming with me?*

Tick city out there, said Arnie. *Count me out.*

Says the so-called alpha, said Bert. *I'll go.*

Me too, said Nan.

You know they're gonna strip you before you go through, Boss, said Arnie.

I've been naked in front of armed men before, said Sam.

I definitely want to hear that story, said Arnie. *Okay, the rest of us will wander about aimlessly. You go do your thing.*

Sam jogged up to the trailers with the Dobermans and knocked.

Floyd opened the door.

"Morning," said Sam.

Floyd looked at him.

"I wanted to take the twins out into the woods," said Sam. "Part of their training."

Floyd nodded and beckoned him inside. Carl grunted something from his post that Sam took to be a greeting.

"Clothes in the bin, step in there," said Floyd, pointing behind a screen.

Sam complied. Floyd ran the bin through a scanner, then flipped a switch. A low pulsing noise kicked in, the vibrations running through Sam's body.

"Clean," said Floyd. "Need any bug repellent?"

"Already sprayed, thanks," said Sam, retrieving his clothes.

"What kind of training?" asked Floyd.

"How to run through trees without stopping to pee on every one of them."

"Right," said Floyd, leading them outside.

He opened the small gate by the main one, and Sam and the dogs loped the compound.

Same sun, same sky, said Bert, *but it feels different when there's no fence.*

It's your primal nature, said Nan. *The call of the wild.*

You have it, too.

Yeah, but I'm a female, said Nan. *We're more mature.*

Bullshit.

"Are we out of range yet?" interrupted Sam.

Yes, said Bert.

Then let's go.

They cut through the woods to the left, eventually coming to a dirt road.

Doesn't look like it's been traveled recently, observed Sam as they walked down it.

I'm not picking up any new smells, said Nan.

Let's head toward the blind spot, said Sam. *Hunt mode.*

The twins glided silently into the undergrowth and disappeared. Sam started to follow them, then heard a fierce bark of warning. He plunged in, pushing through the brush in its direction.

He broke through into a clear section to find the twins growling at Arnie, who was perched smugly on a fallen limb.

Okay, said Sam. *How did you do that?*

Rabbit hole, said Arnie. *Went in there, came out here.*

You went underground? asked Bert.

In the dark? asked Nan.

It's what I do, said Arnie modestly. *Being an alpha dog and all. And, I found something.*

What? asked Sam.

Follow me, everyone, said the dachshund. He jumped from the limb.

They followed as he scampered along the forest floor until he was within sight of the compound.

Here, said Arnie, indicating a spot on the ground with his nose.

Sam peered down. *It's a cigarette butt,* he said.

That's it? said Nan, disappointed.

Why would anyone come here to smoke? asked Arnie. *There's no path, no place to sit, no reason to be here at all.*

And it's right opposite the blind spot, said Sam.

They looked around.

Candy wrapper, called Nan.

Sam squatted down and looked at the fading Snickers logo. *Could've been here a long time,* he said. *Well, I may be right, but this ain't real proof.*

How are you gonna find real proof? asked Bert. *Short of breaking into the Fortress of Solitude?*

The what? asked Arnie.

I'll explain later, said Bert grandly.

Sam looked at a bush, then reach gently into it and detached a small piece of black yarn. *He was wearing a black sweater when he tried to kill you,* said Arnie. *Remember?*

Never gonna forget it, said Sam. *No matter how hard I try.*

Laurent Arletty sat at his favorite table in the Hominy Grill, watching with equal parts lust and hunger as Cindy brought him his lunch.

"Here you go, Mr. Arletty," she said, bending over as she placed his plate in front of him so that he could look down her cleavage. "One Low Country Omelet with extra crispy extra bacon on the side, cuppa coffee black."

"Thanks, Cindy," he said, faking a pout as she straightened up.

She winked and sauntered away from him, swinging her hips.

He dug in with an appetite, spooning the shrimp gravy onto the red rice. Always ravenous the first few days after the full moon, even when the hunt was a success. As this one definitely had been. That Sheila girl had been surprisingly fast once she saw him turn. Gave him a good run for his money.

Of course, he got his money back, and then some—must have caught the poor working girl after she had turned a few other tricks that day. She saw him as the big score of the week, offering her two grand to spend the night—and spend it, she did.

He scooped a biscuit through the last of the gravy and crammed it into his mouth.

Cindy brought him his check. He tipped her large.

"Thank you, Mr. Arletty," she said, pocketing it.

Thank Sheila, he thought, smiling at her. She smiled back.

Maybe Cindy sometime, he thought. Maybe he could even turn her. He hadn't turned anyone in ages.

He scratched his belly contentedly as he exited onto Rutledge, the sun beating down. His stomach rumbled, and he chuckled. Ate an entire country girl come to make her fortune in the big bad city just a few short nights before, and now an omelet was giving him gas. More than gas—he was feeling a little tightness in his chest. Kind of like—no, that wasn't possible. It was almost high noon, no moon in—

He gasped as he felt his ribcage expand.

"What?" he choked out. His shirt buttons popped. He fell to his knees.

"Mr. Arletty, are you all right?" called Cindy, standing in the doorway.

He looked up at her, clawing at his belt, and she screamed, slamming the door shut.

"Can't be happening!" he cried out. "No!"

Boots—he had to get them off. He scrabbled at the laces clumsily as the claws distended his fingers, then gave up and ripped through the thick leather just in time. There were more screams around him. The sun burned through his dilated eyes as they changed for night vision.

There was a siren in the distance, closing in fast.

Cover. He had to find cover.

Claws scraping against the asphalt, he bounded down Rutledge, trying to regain his bearings, nearly blind in the noonday sun. Squeals of brakes, horns, shouts of terror. He careened off the side of a car, denting the thin composite.

Cover. Brush. Where was the nearest park? He stuck his snout up. *Moultrie,* he thought. *Moultrie Park, by the lake.* If he could just get there, he could hide and try to figure out what had happened.

He loped south, using all fours for top speed. A car clipped him, the woman behind the wheel shrieking as she frantically spun the wheel. He could smell the lake, the cooling scent of the trees. The sirens grew louder.

He smelled expanses of grass, tore through a playground as children fled in all directions. The sirens multiplied.

"There!" someone shouted, and he heard someone else yell, "Get down!"

Bushes ahead. If he could just—

The first shot caught him in his left foreleg and he went down, rolling over and over. He got back up, tried going on three, then simply stood and ran. Bullets winged by him. Then, one hit him squarely in the middle of the back, followed by another, and he fell into a tree, slicing through the bark as he tried to hold himself up.

There was one last volley, and Laurent Arletty crumbled to the ground, sensing more than seeing the officers approach him, guns still out.

"Jesus," said one of them.

Arletty turned toward the voice.

"This is impossible," he said as clearly as he could. "Tell—"

Then he was silent.

"Is it dead?" asked one of the cops.

"Ain't breathing," said another. "What the hell is it?"

"It talked," said a third. "Did you hear it?"

"What did it say?"

"This is impossible."

"Got that right."

They stood around, guns still pointing at the biggest damn wolf any of them had ever seen, right there in the middle of Charleston.

CHAPTER 11

Boudreau tapped the numbers on his phone reluctantly, pausing before he entered the last one. It was his third call of the morning, and the first two had left him in a foul mood that he was certain would not dissipate in the next few minutes. He sighed and hit the last number.

"Hello?" came a woman's voice.

"Ms. Mary Edwards?" he asked.

"Who is calling?"

"My name is Wayland Boudreau," he said. "I am the sheriff of Chattooga County, Georgia."

"Is this about Frank?" she asked.

"Are you his mother? Mary Edwards?"

"Yes, I am," she said. "Was Frank arrested for something? Will there be bail? It's Sunday, I won't be able to get to the bank—"

"Ms. Edwards, I'm afraid I've got some bad news for you."

There was a long silence.

"He's dead, isn't he?" she said.

"I'm afraid so, ma'am," he said. "I'm very sorry."

"I guess I knew this day would come," she said. "I haven't heard from him in so long. He missed calling on his Gran's birthday, and he would never do that. How did he die?"

"He was murdered, ma'am," he said. "We found him a few days ago, but it took us this long to make an ID and track down next of kin."

"Murdered," she said flatly. "By who?"

"We were hoping you might help us on that," said Boudreau. "Do you know what he did for a living?"

"He told me it was government contract work," she said. "and that he couldn't talk about it. He'd go off for long stretches, wouldn't tell me where. Gave me a pashmina shawl one time, said he got it in Uzbekistan, but it could've come from a Manhattan street vendor for all I know. But, he was good about calling, and then he stopped."

"When is the last time he called?" asked Boudreau.

"Day before Christmas," she said. "In the morning. Said he might be busy Christmas Day, so he wanted to wish me—he was good about calling, so good. I knew it, I knew it, I—"

She started to cry. "Why was he in Georgia?" she asked. "Why did he die there?"

"I don't know, ma'am," said Boudreau. "Do you have the number he called from?"

He heard some papers being shuffled, then she gave him a number.

"Thank you, ma'am," he said, jotting it down. "I'll let you know if there are any developments in the case."

"It doesn't matter anymore," she said. "He's dead. My little Frankie is dead. Can we have him back? Can we bury him?"

"I will have the morgue contact you so you can make arrangements," he said. He thought about advising her to keep it closed casket, but decided to let the morgue handle it. "Goodbye, ma'am."

He hung up and sighed, then called in Wilkins and Cole.

"Here's Edwards' last known number," he said, handing it to them. "I want all calls, from and to, and locations. Match against the other two we know, get back to me pronto. Moment we have anything, we're rolling."

"Hope it's somewhere fancy," said Wilkins.

"I'm sure mercenaries and felons only meet up in the finest of establishments," said Boudreau. "Now, git."

"Yessir."

"Yessir."

Sam paused at the open doorway, his hand poised to knock. Then, he stopped, hearing an unfamiliar woman's voice.

". . . driving south along the Garden State, heading toward the Pine Barrens, room to run, ya know? Only, my E-Z pass isn't working, and I don't have exact change for the baskets, so I have to go to the manned toll booth, and there's only one, and it's like everyone has the same problems I got and it's taking forever. And, I hate toll booths, always thinking about how Sonny got it in the Godfather, ya know? And, I'm worried the sun's gonna go down while I'm still in my car, and finally I get there, and the toll-keeper has the head of a dog. Very Egyptian, only he, or she, couldn't tell, was still wearing the official

Garden State Parkway toll collector uniform . . ."

About halfway through, he figured out it was a recording. He stepped quietly through the door into the lab. Buenaventura was leaning back in her swivel chair, staring at the ceiling. She caught sight of him and the dogs and beckoned him forward, a finger to her lips. He sat down in front of her desk and listened.

". . . and I'm freaked, but shoot, got to get to the Barrens, and I'm pawing through my purse, and I left my wallet behind, no money whatsoever, and Doghead, or Godhead if you're dyslexic—that's a joke—says, 'You shall not pass!' Like he's Gandalf or something. And the sun is setting and I'm thinking, 'Shit!' and then I wake up as per usual, naked in the forest about ten feet from where I had parked the car, everything where it should be."

Buenaventura laughed and stopped the recording.

"The Gatekeeper on the Garden State Parkway. I love it!" she exclaimed, jotting some notes down. "Sorry, you caught me in the middle of something. Always super busy the first few days after the full moon."

"Who was that?" asked Sam.

"A woman in New Jersey," said Buenaventura.

"A patient?"

"Not exactly."

"What, then?"

"She's a werewolf. Every lunar cycle, I have a group of werewolves record their dreams and send them to me."

"You're a werewolf shrink."

"I'm not treating them, if that's what you mean. Hello, friends of Sam."

The dogs wagged their tails.

"May I?" she asked, approaching them.

He nodded.

Here comes the cute stuff, muttered Nan.

But to their surprise, she simply squatted down and looked at them.

"Why this group?" she asked. "You must have lots of dogs."

"They work well as a team," he said.

We do, said Nan.

Now that your brother's settled down, said Arnie.

"But they're all different," she said. "You can see their personalities, even when they're just sitting. How do they work together without clashing?"

"They complement each other," he said. "It makes them a stronger unit than a pack of the same breed. They have different strengths—and weaknesses, for that matter—but that makes the whole more versatile."

"Was it like that in the Army?" she asked.

"Depended on the unit," he said. "Some units were all about uniformity. They all did the same thing together."

"But you didn't like being in those units," she said.

"I'm supposed to be here asking you questions, ma'am."

"I like it when people avoid talking about themselves," she said, smiling at him. "Means they have something to hide."

"So do people who ask questions instead of answering them," he said. *"Touché,* soldier."

She looked at Otto, who returned her gaze unblinkingly.

"Now, you would be my kind of dog," she said. "I bet he freaks the other dogs out."

She's got that right, said Bert.

"Who is the Gatekeeper?" asked Sam.

"Depends," she said. "That's my name for it. Some call it the High Priestess, like in the Tarot deck. Someone who controls access to a place that you desire."

"And only werewolves dream about it?"

"No, not at all," she said, "but werewolves on the whole have dreams with a Gatekeeper at twice the rate of non-werewolves. And, eighty percent of the time, the Gatekeeper has some canine aspects."

"Not surprising, I guess," he said.

"Yes, it is," she said. "Given that we know that werewolves aren't related to dogs. Yet, the dogs keep popping up in different guises, watching, guarding, protecting the hidden treasure, the next world, the promised paradise."

"Which is?"

"What is it for you?"

"Free premium cable."

"Evasion through jokes," she noted. "Textbook. You happen to be a werewolf's worst nightmare. Not only a werewolf hunter, but surrounded by guard dogs. A trainer of Gatekeepers. If something like you popped up in a werewolf's dream, that would be a new archetype."

"What would I be?" he asked.

"Nemesis would be too obvious," she mused. "A Messenger, perhaps. Or, a Guide, someone who could take the dreamer to the next world. The Egyptian reference you just heard wasn't accidental: Anubis would guide souls to the realm of the dead. Which I guess you do when you take werewolves out."

"Anubis didn't have a dog's head," he said. "It was a jackal."

"Which most people and most werewolves wouldn't know," she said. "Hence the Doghead. We also get the three-headed dog a lot. I used to think that was odd, as most people don't know Greek mythology any more, but then I found out there was one in the first Harry Potter book. And, it guarded the entrance to a hidden treasure."

"So these Gatekeepers come out of books people read?"

"Well, the original source is still from mythology," she said, "but the underlying archetype—how much psychology have you taken?"

"Intro course in county college. Plenty of animal psychology on my own."

"I've never thought about actual canine dreams," she said. "Do they dream?"

We do! said Otto excitedly. *We do!*

Easy, Spooky, said Arnie. *This isn't the time.*

"They do," said Sam. "No idea about what. Chasing rabbits, I guess. You can see their legs twitch."

I had this dream where I chased a rabbit down a hole, said Arnie, *but the hole was wet and glowing, and the rabbit had these really sharp—*

Speaking of not being the time, said Olga.

"Too bad we can't hear them," she said, patting Otto and standing. "What did you think of this woman's dream?"

"Me? I'm no expert."

"Come on, what did you notice? You're the hunter. You're looking for verbal cues that trigger your alarms."

"Well, she said she was a werewolf. That makes it easy."

"Actually, she didn't," said Buenaventura, "but you heard plenty to suggest it to you. Obsession with, almost a fear of sunset."

"And she said 'pawing' through her purse. Lot of people would say digging."

"Very good. Now, when we analyze the stresses in the voice—"

She played it back again, a monitor tracking it on four different graphs. "Certain words will cause stresses more frequently in werewolves then with normal humans," she said, pointing at the peaks with a pencil. "Sun, combined with setting. Moon would be an obvious one. This runs true for over ninety-five percent of the werewolf population."

"Wow," he said, impressed. "So, if you came up with a portable vocal stress analyzer, you could single out werewolves even when they're in human form."

"Bingo," she said. "Coleridge and I have been working on a prototype."

"Coleridge?"

"He's the resident gadget builder," she said. "We're hoping to field test it in a month. I'm waiting for McKenna to give it the okay."

"All we have to do is get everyone to talk about the moon."

"It's a more sophisticated database than that," she said. "The stress patterns cover over two hundred common words."

"Really? I had no idea. You were talking about archetypes. What are they, exactly?"

"Universal symbols from the collective unconscious. That's the short answer. They pop up in our dreams, and thanks to Papa Jung, we can use them for analysis."

"So you think werewolves have a different collective unconscious than humans?"

"Something layers itself onto them when they are—made, or transformed. I keep thinking of Jung's phrase, 'the alien guest.'"

"Alien? You mean like from another planet?"

"Well, not like that, but something outside of yourself that becomes superimposed, almost like a symbiotic personality coming with the symbiotic whatever that is injected with the bite—and this must all be part of the adaptive mechanism that allows the species to survive. Think about this: most werewolves are attacked in early adolescence."

He caught his breath. He wondered if she noticed.

The dogs did.

"I never knew that," he said. "Why do you suppose that is?"

"Why do they attack at all? It's reproduction, continuation of the species, the prime directive. But, the cellular transformation doesn't take well in those rare cases where children are attacked. We think there's more of an immunity then. Adults, on the other hand, tend to have fully formed personalities and developed brains."

"But adults can be turned."

"No question, but they retain more of their human nature than teens do. Especially early teens—catch an adolescent right at the onset of puberty with all of the physical, neurological, and hormonal changes, and you get the perfect werewolf."

"Perfect in what way?"

"In making one that will survive to make more werewolves," she said, "one that will be able to live a double life, hide its nature in plain sight. That's why they have been so hard to find. Adolescents are used to hiding their changes, concealing their secret selves. When I first started analyzing werewolves, I had this theory that they were going to be similar to rape victims."

"Jesus. Why?"

"Think of it. You're on the verge of puberty with all of its sexual confusions. You're attacked at night, penetrated, impregnated in one sense, and your body is transformed in ways you never expected and that no one can explain. How could that not be traumatic?"

"So werewolves are like hairy, murderous, fucked-up teenagers?"

"I thought they would be—but they're not. Somehow, most make the adjustment. I haven't done enough work on the transformation of the brain cells—that's Lisa's turf—but I strongly suspect that the physical change comes with some built-in lulling effect on the fears of the—well, let's call them victims for now. They know how to behave within two months on average. We've done PET scans on younger werewolves, and they show none of the neural activity that rape victims or post-trauma victims do. Werewolves adjust."

"And then dream about jackal-headed toll-takers."

"And the moon."

"I imagine that's the most common archetype for werewolves."

"You'd be wrong. The moon is second, according to my surveys."

"What's first?"

"The Winged Wolf," she said.

A quick flash on the edge of his thoughts. "Winged? It flies?"

"Often," she said. "A giant wolf, with huge, almost dragonesque wings. She—"

"She?"

"The Winged Wolf appears as a female. Every single time."

"What does she want?"

"What makes you think she wants anything?" asked Buenaventura.

"Want, do, say," said Sam. "What does she mean?"

"I don't know yet," confessed Buenaventura. "She watches. She waits. Then, she vanishes."

"Is she a Gatekeeper?"

"I'm not sure," she said. "She doesn't always appear before a portal. She may be a Goddess figure, but it's never clear."

"Huh," said Sam. "Well, don't know how that would help track werewolves, but that vocal stress gadget sure sounds like the real deal. All I have to do is hang out in bars and talk to people, and grab 'em when the alarm goes off."

"I'm not certain that I want you to have it."

"And I am absolutely certain that won't be your decision."

"What do you dream about, Sam?" she asked suddenly.

"I can never remember my dreams."

"Now, that's intriguing."

"That I can't remember them?" he asked.

"No," she said. "That you chose to lie about it."

He got up. "They made me talk to a counselor after my friend was killed," he said. "Didn't do me any good then, don't expect it would do me any now."

"You won't know until you've really tried."

"Maybe," he said, "but you don't treat anyone anyway, so no point in talking to you about it, is there?"

"Guess not," she said. "See you at lunch."

"See you, Doc."

He left, the dogs following. Otto glanced over his shoulder at her, and she shivered. She couldn't explain why. Then, the door closed.

She waited until she heard their footsteps fade into the distance. Then, she pressed a few keys.

The conversation she had just had with Sam played from the monitor speakers. She watched the graphs spool across the screen, then paused it, tapping with her stylus to mark the spots, frowning while she did.

"Damn," she whispered.

The police came barreling through the double doors, sliding a gurney with a body bag. Pernell looked up in surprise.

"You got the right place, fellas?" she asked, reaching for her specs.

"This is Animal Control?" asked one of the cops.

"Yes."

"Then we got the right place," he said. "I'm Sergeant Tennyson. Captain figured you'd know what this thing is."

"What thing?"

They unzipped the body bag and stood back.

She stood and peered into it. "What the hell is that?" she asked.

"That's what we want to know. We thought it was a wolf, but—"

"That's not a wolf," she said. "Way too big, and look how the hind legs are set. Bipedal. What is this, some kind of joke? Guys at the zoo making jackalopes again?"

"If they were, they oughta get a patent," said Tennyson. "This thing was running around downtown."

"Running?"

"Yes'm, running, scaring the bejesus out of everyone. We had to shoot it a bunch of times 'fore it went down." He pointed to the bullet wounds.

She leaned in for a closer look, then wrinkled her nose. "Smells Godawful," she said. "So, if it's dead, why is it my problem?"

"Captain wants to know what it was, in case there's more."

Pernell poked at it cautiously with a pencil. It didn't move. "Well, since there's no particular rush—" she began.

"Step away from the body!"

They turned to see three men in full biohazard gear storming towards them.

"Impellizeri, CDC," said the one in the center, flashing his ID. "Tell me you didn't touch it."

"I just poked it with the pencil," said Pernell. "What the hell—"

"Drop the pencil in the body bag right now, ma'am," ordered Impellizeri.

"What?"

"Just do it!" he shouted.

She dropped the pencil.

"All of you step back. Parker, get that thing zipped up, then get it inside the hazard bag."

"Sir, would you mind explaining what's going on?" asked Tennyson.

"How many of your men handled the body?" asked Impellizeri.

"Why is that—"

"How many?"

"I guess five—no, six."

"And only two of you here," muttered Impellizeri. "Shit. Hope it hasn't spread."

"What—"

"The contagion," said Impellizeri.

Pernell gaped. "You saying this thing is rabid?" she asked.

"Oh, rabies would be a picnic," said Impellizeri. "Gonna need you to put on these suits. Now!"

One of his men tossed more biohazard suits to Pernell and the two cops.

"Why?" asked Tennyson.

"Son, if we move fast, we might be able to save your lives," said Impellizeri, "but if you want to keep jawboning about it, you're gonna end up like Freberg here."

"Freberg? You saying this thing has a name?"

"Of course he has a name," said Impellizeri. "He escaped from quarantine this morning. We think the virus made him—irrational."

"And you think there's a possibility of animal-human transmission?" asked Pernell.

Impellizeri turned to face her, and his expression even through the face mask turned her pale.

"You don't understand," he said quietly. "Freberg is a man—or was, until your friends here shot him down. Now, you are not cleared to know any more, but let me assure you, you do not want to take any chances here. Put on the suits, go with Parker, and we're going to make sure you're not contaminated. Sergeant, you give him the name of every man who had contact with Freberg, and we'll get them in."

"How long?" asked Tennyson, reaching for his radio.

"Twenty-four hours in isolation," said Impellizeri. "You show no symptoms, we can cut you loose. You keep it on the hush hush—we don't want people panicking."

"Come with me, folks," said Parker.

They left Impellizeri and the other man. The two closed the door behind them then waited until they could no longer hear them.

"Think they bought it?" asked Pastore.

"Fuck, I was buying it, Colonel," said the other man. "I even bought your name being Impellizeri."

"Yeah, no one pretends to be Italian. That's why it works. Let's seal this guy up and get him out of here."

"Where you going to take him?"

"To the only place that might have some answers," said Pastore.

Sally was giving Ignatz a bath, something he would never admit enjoying in front of the other dogs. He stood in the tub, pretending to be taking it stoically as she rubbed the shampoo into his neck.

"You really love this, don't you?" she whispered.

No, no, hating every second, he said for the other dogs' benefit.

Tennant came in with a group of German shepherds that he had been exercising in the outdoor pen. The dogs were barely breathing hard. Tennant was soaked to the skin.

"Hot as a bitch today," he groaned.

"Child present," called Sally. "Don't make me tell my mom on you."

"Like Sam never swears," he said.

"Sam is a gentleman in every way," she said sternly.

Now, even you know that isn't true, said Ignatz as some of the other dogs snickered.

"Well, he means to be," said Sally.

"What?" said Tennant.

What? exclaimed Ignatz.

"I said—" Sally began, but Tennant's cell went off.

He held his hand up to silence her. "Yeah," he said. "You're kidding. All right, I'll go."

He disconnected, then turned to her.

"Got an emergency, kid," he said. "Finish up with that one—"

"Ignatz," she said.

"Get him rinsed and dried, skip the permanent, and skedaddle."

"But the afternoon feeding—"

"I'll come back in time for that."

"But—"

"Hey, grownup talking here," he said harshly. "Do what I say."

She rinsed off Ignatz and dried him, pouting.

Tennant waited until she had biked into the distance, then locked up and jumped into his car.

Pastore hesitated for a moment after calling Tennant, then thumbed through his directory until he found Myers' number. She picked up on the first ring.

"Myers, it's Colonel Pastore," he said.

"Hello, Joe," she said.

"How is Sylvia?"

"Still broken up. She really had a thing for that kid."

"It wouldn't have lasted," he said. "Age difference being what it was."

"You should know," said Myers. "You should also know that never stopped any werewolf."

"Myers—"

"It's Ali."

"Ali, there's been another daylight transformation. In Charleston."

"Holy crap! What's going on, Joe?"

"I don't know yet," he said, "but we're taking it seriously. And, if the geography is significant, it may be moving south, and it may be spreading."

"South," she repeated. "Like where I am."

"Like where you are," he said. "Be on your guard."

"I am supposed to be on guard from something, but you don't know what it is? How am I supposed to do that?"

"I don't know," he confessed, "but I'd feel better knowing you knew about it."

"Consider me warned and you absolved, Joe," she said. "You'd better be careful, too."

"I am," he said. "Got the biohazard protocols going full tilt."

"I didn't mean that."

"What, then?"

"People find out about this conversation, they may start thinking you actually care about people—and then you'd be in trouble."

"Who would believe it?" he laughed.

"Yeah, there is that," she said. "You take care for real, Joe. Thanks for the heads up."

He was going to say something, but she hung up on him.

Cole burst through the door, waving a sheet of paper triumphantly.

"Got 'em!" she shouted. "It's right near Atlanta!"

"Wilkins, get in here!" called Boudreau. "Now, sit down and talk to me."

"Two of the dead men used AT&T, one used Verizon," she said as Wilkins came in. "Thank God they used different carriers, because that gave us the triangulation we needed. They all made calls from within a hundred meters on the morning of December 24th, and that was it. Here's an overhead of the location."

"Strip mall, car wash, movie theater, warehouses," observed Wilkins. "Could've just been a place to meet up before they came out here to get chewed up."

"There were calls from over five days, same general location," said Cole.

"Warehouses," said Boudreau, "base of operations. This ain't far from the airport, near enough to the interstates. Got to be around there. Good work, Cole. You get employee of the month."

"Don't I get something for diving into the crime scene?" objected Wilkins.

"Might have, if you didn't upchuck all over it," said Boudreau. "Let's go check this place out."

Sam, you have a moment? asked Otto.

The twins were rolling around by the gardens. Arnie was exploring the woods, looking for more rabbit holes, while Olga stood guard, listening for patrols.

Sure, what's up? replied Sam.

That lady this morning—

Buenaventura?

Right. She may be a threat.

Why?

Because she can figure you out without even touching you, said Otto. *She can do it through your words—and your dreams.*

Maybe, said Sam. *Say she does. I'm not the first werewolf to show up here. There's Pastore.*

I don't mean that type of threat, said Otto.

What, then?

You've never been very big on introspection, have you, Sam?

Sam looked at the Weimaraner. Otto always was serious, but there was something more now. Something old.

I don't suppose I have been, said Sam. *I stay pretty much focused on staying alive. Hard to do more when you're living undercover.*

Have you ever thought about why you are what you are?

A werewolf? I was bitten. End of story.

Not a werewolf, Sam. Or not just a werewolf. Of all the werewolves in existence, you're the one who can speak with dogs. You are unique.

I'm a freak, Otto.

I don't think so, said the Weimaraner. *There is something you should know.*

What?

Dogs have dreams, Sam.

I figured.

Old dreams, said Otto. *Shared dreams, like humans—and some of us have the knowledge of those dreams passed on.*

What knowledge?

About legends known to the oldest dogs, still drifting through our sleep. You spoke of co-evolution, the reason the wolves who became us drew close to human encampments. You thought it was so we could be near humans.

Wasn't it?

No, said Otto. *It was because we needed to be near werewolves. To guard them. As long as the humans were preserved, the werewolves would be.*

Problem with that is that humans are the ones who kill werewolves, said Sam.

Problem with humans is that they kill everything, said Otto. *You're missing* the point. *You are not an accident of nature. There are no accidents. When you came to buy a Weimaraner pup for training—why did you pick me out of all my siblings?*

Your mother told me that you had the most promise, said Sam.

My mother, before you bought me, taught me many things, said Otto. *More than my brothers and sisters. There is a reason that she chose me for you. She sensed that I would know what to do with this knowledge.*

What?

I've seen the Winged Wolf, said Otto. *We all have. She is in our dreams, too. I think—*

Patrol! called Olga.

"Later," muttered Sam.

Bolton and Priscilla jogged into view, the entire group of shepherds following them—unleashed, Sam noticed.

"What's up?" called Bolton.

"Catching some rays by the garden," said Sam. "How are you?"

"Decided to whip this pack into shape after that pitiful showing by Tito," Bolton said, walking over. "Heel, you miserable bastards!"

What do you guys talk about down here? asked Sarge.

What makes you think we were talking about anything? asked Arnie as he trotted up.

Because you've always just shut up when one of us comes into range. That's not normal.

It is where we come from, said Arnie, *but we were taught manners.*

So what were you talking about?

Why do you care? asked Arnie.

Call it curiosity.

Curiosity, said Arnie. *Isn't that what kills cats?*

Sarge looked down at the little dog. *No,* he said. *I'm what kills cats.*

"Those two really seem to like each other," said Bolton. "Okay, mutts. Rest stop's over. Dogs, perimeter!"

The pack took off in formation, Sarge at the lead.

"Now, that's a thing of beauty," said Bolton approvingly.

"Very nice," said Sam.

"You might have the fastest dog, but when it comes to discipline and attack, I bet my five takes your five," said Bolton.

"No bet," said Sam.

"Smart," said Bolton. "See you."

The two humans jogged after their dogs.

We could take them, said Arnie.

"Don't want to waste any blood finding out," said Sam. "Okay, troops. Let's go see McKenna and wrap up our little fact-finding tour of the middle of nowhere."

Mona's cell buzzed on her desk while she was reviewing spreadsheets. She looked at the number, but it wasn't one she knew. She answered it.

"Mona, it's Sally."

"Short Stuff?" said Mona in surprise. "What's up? Since when did you have this number?"

"Sam gave it to me for emergencies," said Sally. "Sorry. I thought he told you."

"He did, kid," Mona lied. "It slipped my mind. What's the emergency?"

"What's the deal with this guy Larry?"

"He knew Sam in the Army. They were in the Canine Corps together. Why?"

"This guy was never in the Canine Corps," said Sally. "He doesn't know the first thing about working with dogs."

"Is that so? So you're doing all the hard work."

"It's not just that," said Sally. "He's poking around Sam's stuff and getting weird phone calls. I think he's some kind of spy."

"Sounds a little dramatic to me," laughed Mona. "Probably just nosy. You take over a job for someone, you poke around."

"Mona, I'm serious. Could you call Sam and tell him?"

Mona tapped her pencil on her desk. It seemed unnecessary.

But it would be a reason to call.

"Sure, Sally," she said. "I'll do that—and don't worry about Larry, okay? He's only there for a few more days. How much damage could he do?"

Tennant wore a meter reader's uniform, and wasted fifteen minutes checking each meter on the block, dutifully noting the results on a clipboard before moving on to the next. Finally, he arrived at Mona's townhouse.

Her security system was about three years old. It took him all of twenty seconds to bypass it, then another twenty to pick the lock on her back door. He pulled a piece of steak wrapped in plastic from inside his jacket, unwrapped it, then opened the door a crack and tossed it inside.

He waited. There was a soft padding noise. Then, silence.

He opened the door and glanced around the kitchen. Nicky lay on her side, her chest rising and falling slowly, one leg twitching. He eased himself in and closed the door.

"Got you, bitch," he muttered. He reached down to retrieve the rest of the sedative-laden meat.

It was untouched.

Nicky sprang, her jaws clamping down on his thigh. He hit her with the clipboard, but she only bit down harder. He pulled an expanding baton from his belt and swung at her head. At the second blow, her jaws loosened, and he shoved her off. Then, he continued to beat her savagely until she lay still—for real.

He looked down at his leg. Blood was seeping through the uniform, and the pain was settling down for a good long stay.

DNA, he thought. *Got to get out before I leave any.*

He thought about Nicky's teeth. She was still breathing raggedly. He hoped she wouldn't swallow anything that could be traced back to him.

He limped outside, closing the door behind him. Then, gritting his teeth with pain, he made a show of getting the readings from the last three houses before climbing into his van at the end of the block and driving to where he could get himself bandaged up.

Hold up, said Bert as Sam and the team walked down the hall to McKenna's office. *Someone's with him.*

Who? asked Sam.

Quiet, I'm trying to hear.

He crept forward, ears up and alert, then paused in front of McKenna's door.

Sneezelady's with him, he said. *Something about getting a positive result. Okay, she's coming to the door.*

The door opened, and Bert looked up at Kudowski innocently.

"Shit!" she exclaimed, and slammed the door in his face.

That was rude, he said.

The door opened again, and McKenna poked his head out.

"Mister Lehrmann, may I trouble you to withdraw your animals until Doctor Kudowski can make her escape?" he requested.

"Dogs, heel," said Sam, retreating to a safe distance.

Bert rejoined the team at the beginning of the hallway.

"All right, Lisa," said McKenna.

She dashed across to her office, shooting them a dirty look as she closed the door behind her.

"Right," said McKenna. "Let's have our discussion. Please, come in. All of you."

Sam and the dogs entered his lab. He noticed a steel door at the other end with an electronic key pad by the handle.

Over there, he said. *The Fortress of Solitude.*

It's just a door, said Bert, disappointed.

"Take a seat," said McKenna. "Tell me, how have you liked our little facility?"

"It's been an eye-opener," said Sam. "I could keep the tabloids going for years based on what I've picked up in the past few days, but they'd put me in the loony bin."

"I'm sure you had plenty of material before you came here," said McKenna. "Why don't you advertise your services?"

"As a werewolf hunter?" laughed Sam. "It's one thing to be wrestling alligators or pulling rattlesnakes out of the bushes, but I don't think the American public will take kindly to someone who hunts things that are human to someone."

"You don't consider them human? Even after talking to Doctor Kudowski about their genetic—"

"You can talk science at me all you want," said Sam. "Those things are still monsters, and always will be. I've seen what they can do—to real humans. So, Doc, what have you got in here that's gonna make my job easier? You're the cleanup hitter."

"If I understand the metaphor correctly, then I should be up fourth instead of fifth," said McKenna.

"Okay, you're the RBI man, whatever," said Sam. "Tell me what you got. Tie up the loose ends, bring us all home."

"It was Doctor Burton's discovery that led me to the final breakthrough," said McKenna. "Each of them had a piece of the puzzle, and I was the one who put them together. How the werewolves are changed by the full moon. Do you know what my dissertation was on?"

"I'm gonna take a wild guess and say werewolves."

"Sea turtle migration," said McKenna. "Spent two years of my life tracking sea turtles in the Atlantic, tagging them, designing miniature radio transmitters, following them from the protected beaches of their births out into the Gulf Stream. Sometimes I would go for months without putting foot on land."

"You're still sounding a little out to sea here, Doc."

"They swam thousands of miles through the oceans without a landmark, and found their way back to the same, small isolated beach every time. A feat of navigation that would challenge the most experienced sailor. Do you want to know how they did it?"

"Floating bread crumbs?"

"Magnetic fields, Mister Lehrmann. They evolved to respond to the earth's magnetic fields. We took some, put them in a large aquatic pen, and altered the magnetic field within it—and they were immediately lost. No sense of direction, no idea of where to go."

"I never even thought about sea turtles before today," said Sam. "Now you got me feeling sorry for them."

"Now, you may ask—"

"What do sea turtles have to do with werewolves? Was that the question you wanted?"

"Yes, well, exactly," said McKenna, irritated. "We have the foreign structures in the human cell, introduced by the bite and the venom. We have the cellular transformation for every change that werewolves go through in their, their physical—"

"Physiognomy," said Sam. "You can use the big words. I learned that one already."

"The cellular changes come from proteins or nerves acting upon a set stimulus: a particular frequency of electromagnetic radiation, just as the sea turtles do. Only this one is from a different part of the spectrum, and has a peculiar pulse. Do you understand now?"

"That focused pulse from the full moon," said Sam, lighting up.

"Very good, Mister Lehrmann," said McKenna, swiveling his monitor. "We had some volunteers come to the lab during full moons. Just before sunset, we took cell samples from various locations. We had to get them fresh given the rapid decay they experience outside the body. Watch."

Footage of cells, blown up. The time ticked below it.

"Sunset occurs—now," said McKenna.

Something thin and feathery spidered out of a tiny dot within the cell. Then, the cell began to elongate.

"From a bone sample in the arm," said McKenna. "Here's one from the area around the fangs."

The cells swelled, became thick and hard.

"Hair follicles—"

Gray filled the screen.

"Nerves—"

The phone rang, startling Sam who had been wholly absorbed watching the monitor. McKenna picked it up.

"Yes," he said. Then, his eyes grew wide. "That's impossible! When? And what happened to—here? Good. How soon? Yes, we'll be ready."

He hung up. "Appointment's canceled," he said, bounding to his feet. "Emergency meeting. You might as well come."

"What's going on?" asked Sam, walking with him, the dogs bringing up the rear.

"I'll tell everyone once we're together. Do me a favor and go bang on Valerie's door."

"Sure."

He ran into the dormitory wing, found the astronomer's room, and knocked. There was no answer. He knocked again, heard a muffled response, then the door opened and Doctor Burton looked blearily at him.

"Dog Man," she said. "What is it?"

"Some emergency meeting," said Sam. "Doctor McKenna asked me to wake you. Sorry."

"What kind of emergency could there be around here?" she asked.

"I'm just the messenger, ma'am."

"I told you about calling me ma'am."

"Sorry. Valerie."

"I'm going to splash some cold water on my face and throw some clothes on," she said. "I'll be there in five."

He headed back to the cafeteria. Kudowski hurried through the doors, then stopped dead when she saw him and the dogs.

"Keep those—animals away from me," she hissed.

"Dogs, sit," he said.

Crap, we're gonna miss everything, said Arnie.

Stay in the doorway, said Sam. He went in and sat at the table.

Ms. Whitfield poked her head out from the kitchen. "Lunch already?" she called.

"Sorry, Bonnie," said McKenna. "Something came up. Bring whatever's ready, and keep it coming."

Burton hurried in, her face clean. "This had better be good," she said.

"Good, bad, I can't tell yet," said McKenna. "Exciting, certainly. Ladies and gentlemen, it turns out that everything we ever knew is wrong."

Myers peered through her magnifying lenses at the connections to make sure they were clean, then ran a diagnostic. The robot's systems checked.

"You're good," she said, sealing the panel.

"Thank you, Alison," said the robot. "Next laparoscopy is on me."

"Now, you're just turning me on," laughed Myers. "Go fix some people."

She tossed her goggles onto the workstation while the robot rolled out of her office and headed to Surgery. An alert popped up on her laptop. Another WAI comment on yesterday's earthshattering events. She opened it.

"Has to be a government plot," said someone named SAMIAM. "No way spontaneous change occurs, not in broad daylight. Dude was doped with something from the secret lab."

Good a theory as any, she thought, shutting it down. She had shed no tears for the late Laurent Arletty. She had known him under a different name from when they were in Basic. He was a loose cannon, got blown out of the squad inside of a month, and the only surprise was that he had lasted this long before getting shot down like the asshole that he was. The media had been remarkably silent about a wolf killing in a major city. Pastore's fingerprints were all over that.

She sighed, grabbed her lunch, and went outside to eat on the front lawn, the main building of University Hospital rising at her back, Dent Boulevard and the old train tracks in front. She needed this little oasis every day, a chance to stick her bare feet into the green grass and feel Mother Earth beneath her soles. She peeled off her sneakers and pulled out her lunch.

Arletty's mistake was in panicking, she thought. If it were her—

Her heart started to pound in her chest. *Odd.*

The trick was to—

Her chest was suddenly tight.

"No," she whispered.

She scrambled to her feet, looking around for cover. *Hospital, can't go back. Need time. Need cover.*

The old train tracks. The abandoned box cars. She started to run across the lawn, gasping for air, shielding her eyes with her hands, her paws, her T-shirt shredding underneath the scrubs, but the scrubs were loose-fitting, thank God. Maybe she could make it before anyone noticed.

Someone screamed.

Stay calm, she thought, slowing herself down to a walk. *They'll think it's a costume, a gag of some kind.*

"Hey, folks," she hollered. "Happy Halloween! 'The Howling, Part 12,' in theaters everywhere next month!"

There was more screaming. No one seemed to be buying it.

"Like the makeup?" she said as people scattered around her. "Spent three hours in a barber's chair putting it on."

The claws extended. Her jaw thrust forward. She heard sirens.

"Rick Baker ain't got nothing on me!" she shouted.

She squinted, trying to locate the box cars.

No. She wasn't going to run. *That's what got Arletty killed.* She sat down, placing her hairy palms on the lawn, feeling the grass. She heard police officers shout orders at each other.

Stay calm, baby, she thought to herself.

She sat still.

She heard rifles being cocked.

She prayed.

She prayed that the next thing that hit her would be a tranquilizer dart instead of a bullet.

She prayed to the Winged Wolf.

Alan Gordon

CHAPTER 12

THE AUTOMATIC DOOR TO the kitchen swung open.

Arnie poked his head in, sniffing. *Clear,* he said.

He crept in, Nan and Bert following.

There's the refrigerator, said Bert longingly.

Stay on mission, Arnie ordered. *There's the door to the dining room.*

They moved silently to where they could see the conference.

I've got the Alpha, said Arnie. *Bert on Baldy, Nan on Moonchick. Olga, you take Sneezelady. Spooky, you get Dreamgirl, since she likes you so much.*

Got it, said Olga as she and Otto took up positions at the entrance from the hallway.

Look sharp, team, said Sam as he sat at the table.

"I didn't even know we had emergencies," said Sanchez.

"Better be important," yawned Burton. "I was having the William Holden dream again."

"I'll get right to it," said McKenna. "A werewolf was shot down in Charleston. Yesterday."

"But the full moon ended on Thursday," said Sanchez, puzzled.

"Yesterday when?" asked Burton.

"Noon," said McKenna.

There were exclamations of shock around the table.

That's impossible, said Bert.

Shut up and maintain observation, said Arnie.

"That can't be right," said Burton. "It must have been something else."

"I got the call from Pastore himself ten minutes ago," said McKenna. "He

181

confirmed it. He also was kind enough to reveal to me that this was the third such transformation in the past week. Ladies and gentlemen, it appears that our conclusion as to the causal mechanism of the transformation is in error."

"No," protested Kudowski. "We tested that to the hilt. It would survive any peer review—"

"Except that there are no peer reviews for werewolf studies," said McKenna dryly. "I am open to ideas. Anyone?"

They looked around at each other.

"Psychological trigger," said Buenaventura. "Some traumatic reaction or stressor caused the mind to induce the changes."

"Have we ever had any indication that that was possible?" asked McKenna.

"No," she admitted, "but we've never had any indication this was possible, either. That's all I got off the top of my head. My gut says this isn't my turf."

"Maybe a mutation?" suggested Kudowski. "Some new trait that allowed the change to happen without the full lunar stimulus."

"Unlikely," said McKenna. "Pastore confirmed the identification on the last one, someone named Arletty. He's been a werewolf for twenty years. A mutation of this nature would have manifested itself long before now."

"Not a werewolf we've worked with," said Buenaventura.

"No," said McKenna. "Somewhat of a renegade, from what Pastore said. I'm surprised our friend Sam wasn't called on to deal with him before."

Sam sat impassively as the others turned to him.

"Any other thoughts?" McKenna continued.

"A virus, or something like a virus," said Sanchez. "A biological factor. It could have forced the transformation."

"That sounds promising," said McKenna. "Valerie?"

The astronomer was staring down at the table. "It still doesn't seem possible," she whispered. "Everything we know—"

"Valerie," said McKenna sharply. "Any thoughts at all?"

"Some local spike in the electromagnetic frequency," she speculated. "A freak occurrence duplicating the lunar signal."

"Is there anything in Charleston capable of producing that frequency with that pulse?" asked McKenna. "Any military or scientific facility that is working with it?"

"I don't know of any practical use for it," she said. "It doesn't seem likely, but I'll look."

"Right, that will be your assignment," said McKenna. "Lisa, Juan, and I will conduct the autopsy and analysis."

"Autopsy? They're bringing it here?" asked Sanchez.

"Pastore himself," said McKenna. "Go prepare the freezer. We'll do it in there."

"What about me?" asked Buenaventura.

"Not your turf," said McKenna. "Since our cook is on her day off, could I trouble you to prepare sandwiches for everyone?"

"I can do that," Sam offered quickly.

"No, it's all right," said Buenaventura, smiling tightly. "I'd be glad to."

"I'll help you with the setup, Juan," said Kudowski.

"Haven't done an autopsy in ages," said Sanchez. "Should be fun."

They walked out together.

"And he wonders why he never gets any action," muttered Burton.

"Enough," said McKenna. "I want answers by dinner. Oh, speaking of which—Sandra?"

"Yes, I'll heat up the stew," sighed Buenaventura. "Don't forget to tip your waitress." She strode toward the kitchen.

Oh, she's pissed, said Bert.

You think? said Nan.

Buenaventura flung open the door, then paused when she saw the dogs.

"Sam," she called. "There are some hungry-looking animals in here."

"Feeding time is in two hours," he said, coming over to join her.

"I'm not sure they know that," she said, stepping past them carefully. "I don't want to wind up as Puppy Chow."

"They don't eat people," he assured her.

Just that one time, said Arnie.

"Nevertheless, you might want to get them out of the kitchen while I'm making the sandwiches," said Buenaventura. "I'm sure the Health Code says something about this. Oh, there's my boy."

Otto stood in the doorway, looking at her intently.

Buenaventura looked back at him for a long moment, then lowered her eyes. "I'd better get going. I've become the den mother. They'll be wanting their snacks and juice boxes soon."

"Dogs, heel," said Sam, leaving the kitchen.

The team followed him back to his room.

He closed the door, then sat on the bed. *Report,* he said. *Arnie?*

McKenna knows more than he's saying, said the dachshund. *If I understand everything, and you know I'm the smartest one in the room—*

Hey! protested Bert.

Then this has to rock his world to the core, continued Arnie, ignoring him, *but there isn't a single sign that it has. Look how Moonchick was—completely shattered. She's got everything invested in this loony lunar stuff, and it was devastating. But Team Leader was all 'Look-at-me-handling-the-crisis Guy.' It's an act.*

Scientific demeanor, professional detachment, said Sam.

Detached demeanor, my small black and tan ass, said Arnie. *I don't think he was even surprised when the call came in.*

Good. Nan? You had Valerie.

Genuine shock, like Arnie said. Still sleepy, so not able to fake it or conceal anything.

Bert?

Sanchez was caught by surprise, too, said Bert, *but he's all excited about the idea of getting to cut up something.*

A little too excited, said Sam. *He's turned a world event into another chance to hit on Kudowski.*

He's like a horny adolescent boy, said Bert.

You understand him so well, said his sister.

But there's something else bothering him, continued Bert. *It's like this was something that he needs to distract him. He keeps looking at Buenaventura like he expects her to find him out.*

I know the feeling, said Sam. *Olga?*

She watched McKenna like it's Take Your Daughter to Work Day and she'd never really seen him in action before, said the wolfhound. *Mix of pride and possessiveness.*

Was she surprised by the news?

No, she said, after some consideration, *and when she suggested the mutation as a possible cause, she didn't believe it.*

Neither did McKenna, said Arnie. *He was ready to shoot it down before she even finished the sentence.*

A double act, mused Sam. *Otto?*

For a moment, Buenaventura dropped her mask, said Otto. *She's an outsider in this group, always watching from inside herself, but she reacted immediately—and was afraid.*

Afraid, repeated Sam. *Were any of the others afraid?*

The dogs looked at each other.

Sanchez, said Bert, *but he's always afraid.*

All right, good work, said Sam. *We should—*

There's something else, said Otto.

What? asked Sam.

In the kitchen afterward, she was different.

She was angry about being reduced to waitressing, said Nan.

No, it was something else, said the Weimaraner. *It was how she was reacting to you, Sam.*

How was it different? asked Sam.

She doesn't want to have anything to do with you now, said Otto. *I find that curious behavior for a human who is so curious about human behavior herself.*

It would normally be a hundred-minute drive from Summerville to the outskirts of Atlanta, thought Boudreau, *but ain't any point in having flashers and sirens if you can't use them every now and again. Or abuse them,* he added as Wilkins zipped down the left lane.

"They've been dead eight months, son," said Boudreau. "As much as I enjoy the testosterone mixing with the adrenaline, there's no specific urgency to get us killed today."

"I like it," said Cole from the back seat. "Can I drive on the trip back?"

"You feeling competitive, Officer Cole?" asked Boudreau.

"Extremely," she said, a glint in her eye.

"Find me something else good today and I will consider it," said Boudreau. "Son, those trucks are looming—"

Wilkins zipped between them with so little margin for error that only the differing heights of the side view mirrors on the three vehicles kept them intact.

Seventy-five minutes after they left, they pulled into a parking lot adjacent to a cluster of cheaply constructed warehouses. Signs proclaimed software developers, wholesale furniture importers, and similar operations of the fly-by-night variety. There were two separate management offices.

"Guess we'll start with the one on the right," he said.

"No," said Cole. "The one on the left."

He looked at her. She was smiling.

"Superstition, or are you part of the international left-handed conspiracy?" he asked her.

"We should start with the one on the left because I know exactly which warehouse we should be looking at," she said, "and I am going to drive on the way back and get us there in less than seventy-three minutes."

"Bullshit on both," said Wilkins.

"Fifty bucks says I'm right."

"You're on—and another fifty says you don't beat my time."

"Violating the gambling statutes of the proud state of Georgia has placed the two of you in a legally tenuous position," said Boudreau, "but this ain't my county, so screw it. Enlighten us, Officer Cole."

"That one," she said, pointing.

Boudreau ambled over to a small sign posted on the door.

"'Flower of My Desire,'" he read. "'Exotics and Tropicals.' You think they're using a flower importer as a front?"

"It isn't a front," she said. "Remember the aconite? I was looking into importers of wolfsbane. This place was on the list, and the list wasn't that long. Hang on."

She pulled out her cell and her fingers became an expert blur. "Here's the website. No snail address listed, no phone, only online orders." Her fingers flickered some more. "And, they've posted a notice saying they are no longer accepting new orders."

"As of when?"

"Mid-December."

He pressed the buzzer. No response.

He knocked on the door, then pounded on the garage door next to it. Still nothing.

"One might consider this to be normal business hours," he commented. "Shall we inquire of the management?"

"That would be the one on the left?" asked Cole.

"That would be the one on the left," agreed Boudreau.

They followed him into the office where a young Black man wearing a Hawks jersey was absorbed in a textbook with a dark blue cover.

"Anything good?" asked Boudreau.

"Has its moments," said the man. Then, he glanced up and noticed the uniforms. "Chattooga County. Little out of your jurisdiction, aren't you? That's out a ways."

"Far as you can get without being somewhere else," said Boudreau. "I'm Sheriff Boudreau. These are Officers Cole and Wilkins. You have a name, son?"

"Fisher," said the man.

"That a first name or a last name?" asked Boudreau.

"A nickname," said Fisher. "My real name is Simon Andrews, but everyone calls me Fisher, on account of the Bible."

"Fair enough," said Boudreau. He pulled out the photographs of the three men they had been able to identify and handed them to the man. "Seen these folks before, Fisher?"

"Not lately," said Fisher. "They worked over at the flower place."

"When's the last time you saw them?"

"Why? They in trouble?"

"Just their immortal souls," said Boudreau as he handed him another picture, "but that's also out of my jurisdiction."

"I took that shot," Wilkins said with pride.

"You're looking a mite sickly," observed Boudreau with concern. "You need a ginger ale or something?"

"These guys did this to those people?" asked Fisher, choking a bit.

"These guys are those people," said Boudreau. "We're the guys trying to find the guys who done it to them, that being our job and bounden duty and all. When's the last time you saw them?"

"Don't remember exactly," said Fisher. "They didn't exactly drop by to chat. The one guy—the Black one—would come get the spare key sometimes when no one was there, but I can't say he and I ever talked. Then, they stopped coming by."

"When?"

"I remember it was around Christmas—no, before that. I usually got an envelope from the boss man, and I didn't last year. Pissed me off at the time, but you can't always count on a bonus in this economy. I figured the business must have been suffering, 'cause they haven't taken any deliveries in ages."

"Which one of them was the boss man?" asked Boudreau.

"None of them," said Fisher. "The boss was Mr. Bogart. He didn't say much, either."

"Mr. Bogart have a first name?" asked Boudreau.

"Manny," said Fisher. "And, no, haven't seen him around, either."

Cole had her cell out already and was typing furiously.

"Why does the place still got the sign?"

"Rent's paid up through the next ten months," said Fisher.

"Nothing on Bogart, Sheriff," said Cole.

"Son, you mind passing that spare key over to us?" asked Boudreau.

"Sure," said Fisher. "As long as you got a warrant on you."

"This is a murder investigation," said Boudreau.

Fisher held up his textbook. It said "Criminal Procedure" on it. "And this is a second-year law student. I'm here until five. Then, you can talk to the night manager. That's how we do these things in the civilized world."

"It is," sighed Boudreau. "Cole, get me Judge Tsu, will you? In the meantime, Counselor, how about you bend the rod up your ass enough to describe Manny Bogart to me."

Pastore drove the van through the gates to the compound and up to the loading dock. Coleridge was transferring crates of supplies onto a hand truck.

"Hey, Colonel," greeted Coleridge. "What's the occasion?"

"They didn't tell you?" asked Pastore as he got out.

"Tell me what?"

"About the werewolf getting shot in Charleston."

"No shit! When did this happen?"

"Yesterday. Around noon."

Coleridge looked at him skeptically. "Is this some kind of joke?" he asked.

"If it is, I haven't heard the punch line yet," said Pastore. "Mind finding McKenna for me? I want to make sure they got the examining room on ice and ready before I take him out."

"Will do," said Coleridge. "Geez, nobody tells me anything around here."

He went inside, and came back a short time later with McKenna, followed by Sanchez pushing a gurney.

"Room's at zero point one Celsius," said Sanchez. "I don't want to freeze the samples."

"Roger that," said Pastore. "I drove with the cooler on max, but the peckerwoods had him in a regular morgue overnight, so we may be fucked. Scientifically speaking, that is."

"That is the technical term," said McKenna as Coleridge helped Sanchez wheel the gurney down the ramp. "Anything more you can tell us?"

"The subject was further compromised by about fourteen chunks of steel-jacketed lead," said Pastore. "There will be a certain mixing of vital bodily fluids."

He opened the back of the van, grabbed the end of the body bag, and hauled it with one quick motion onto the waiting gurney. "OR, stat," he said. "Always wanted to say that."

"Everyone wants to be a biologist," grunted Sanchez as he and Coleridge shoved the gurney back up the ramp.

Pastore and McKenna followed him in as Coleridge returned to his unloading.

"How long before you have results?" asked Pastore.

"Can't say, since we don't know exactly what we're looking for," said McKenna. "Our best bet is something viral that has a specific effect on the werewolf cellular material."

"What's your protocol?"

"Sample, freeze, slice, and scope," said McKenna. "Do you want it fast, or do you want it right?"

"Yes," said Pastore. "Who's doing it?"

"The entire biology staff," said McKenna.

"That sounds much more impressive than saying all three of you," said Pastore. "Keep me posted."

"I need to get my thermals on," said McKenna.

He left Pastore standing in the rotunda. He pulled out his cell, scanning for messages.

"Want a sandwich?"

He spun around to see Sam standing in the hallway.

"Love one," said Pastore. "Love three, in fact."

"Can do, Joe," said Sam.

"I'm still not used to you calling me that," said Pastore as he followed Sam to the kitchen.

"I'm starting to get used to saying it," grinned Sam. "Roast beef on rye, Bermuda onion, and Russian dressing?"

"Jesus, you got a memory," said Joe.

"All you talked about on our long walk to Tajikistan," said Sam. "How you were gonna get us whatever our favorite food was when we got there. No idea where you found that sandwich, either."

"I knew a place," said Pastore.

"How does an Italian like you develop a taste for rye bread, anyway?"

asked Sam as he made the sandwiches.

"What makes you think I'm Italian?"

"The name."

"What makes you think that's my name?"

"I have a trusting soul. Want a beer?"

"More than life," said Pastore. "Enjoying your mission?"

"Educational," said Sam. "Glad I didn't become a scientist. They're all fucked up."

"You could've been one," said Pastore. "You tested off the charts. But, you never took advantage of what we had to offer you."

"I'm doing exactly what I want to do," said Sam. "Generally, I mean. Not at this exact moment."

"Wasting your life with dogs."

"Not a waste at all."

"Matter of opinion," said Pastore, drawing on his beer. "Want to tell me what you've found out?"

"This place is porous," said Sam. "There are half a dozen different ways to get information in and out, and that's without considering corruption."

"Your team got a read on who?" asked Pastore.

"Getting a lot of concealment from a lot of people," said Sam. "I'm trying to narrow down the targets before I give you one to go after. But, it has to come from McKenna, whether he's part of it or just giving out information without knowing it. I haven't been inside his private office. How easy is it to copy the Book onto an ordinary disk?"

"Supposed to be impossible, according to my tech people," said Pastore, "but that just means they haven't figured out a way to do it. Doesn't mean someone else didn't figure it out."

"Why can't someone just download it?"

"Encryption. You need a special machine to read the files, and there are only two of them, specially built. Neither has any ports, so you can't hook up an external device. Input is strictly through keyboard. Tedious, but it's worked."

"Does the specially built special machine have a special monitor?"

"Of course."

"How many of us are there in your secret database?"

"The werewolf population of the US of A is about eight thousand three hundred or so. One less since yesterday. Turned after lunch, ate some lead for dessert."

"Say someone sat in front of the special machine's special monitor with an ordinary video camera and ran the entire special contents of the special Book. How long would that take?"

Pastore thought for a moment. "I honestly don't know. A couple of hours, maybe less. It's that easy, isn't it?"

"Lots of downtime around here," said Sam. "Not that they would need it. If our mystery person was feeding the Bogey Man one werewolf at a time, it wouldn't be hard to take that small bit of data out. Verbally. By anyone here on a break, or because they live in town like our lovely little cook, or have immediate access to the outside like all of your hand-picked security, or go on supply runs like Coleridge, or get weekend passes like fucking everybody else."

"But a full disk—how do they get that out?"

"Bribe one security guard. Or toss it over the fence at the blind spot."

"There's a blind spot?"

"Damn straight, Joe. Maybe you got one, too."

"I'm only human. Partly. Okay, keep your dogs on the job. Let them figure out who the traitor is."

"And you will do what?"

"I will—"

Pastore's cell went off. He looked at the screen, then went still.

"Ali," he muttered. "Shit. Gotta go. Mind the ship."

"Screw the ship, we're Army," said Sam. "Go where?"

"Augusta," said Pastore. "There's been another daylight werewolf sighting."

"What the hell is going on, Colonel?"

"Don't know," said Pastore, "but it looks like it's spreading. Hold the fort. Better?"

"Better."

Arnie and Olga watched Pastore drive off. The Dobermans were down by the gardens, working off some energy. Otto sat serenely in the copse.

Wonder why the Alpha's leaving already, said Arnie.

Can't be anything good, said Olga. *Let's go see the Boss.*

They trotted into the dormitory wing. Sam's door opened automatically.

Boss? called Arnie as he went in.

The rooms were empty.

He must be somewhere near the guard dogs where he can't talk, said Olga.

Weird—I can smell him so strongly, said Arnie.

This is his room, said Olga.

No, it's like—it's him, but not quite him? You picking that up, my fellow hound?

Olga scented the air. *Who is that?* she asked. *It's strong. It's coming from over there.*

Arnie jumped onto Sam's bed, sniffing. He scrambled over to the night stand and stuck his nose by the drawer.

It's in here, he said. *Can you open it?*

Olga grabbed the handle with her teeth and pulled it out.

It's really strong now, she said. *What is it?*

They looked inside.

It's those sweat samples that Baldy gave Sam, said Arnie. *They've thawed out.*

So we're smelling thawed out werewolf sweat, said Olga. *Lovely. Makes me want to howl at the moon myself.*

Hey, said Arnie thoughtfully. *I figured it out. The reason it smells like Sam but isn't is because it's a werewolf and he's a werewolf. And, there was something similar with Sam's alpha.*

You're saying werewolves smell different than humans, even in human form? asked Olga.

Well, we've only got three that we know of, said Arnie, *but I'm thinking, yeah.*

They stuck their noses in again and inhaled deeply.

Cool, said Olga.

Fisher's description of Manny Bogart was detailed and precise. It also was a match for the unidentified body from the van, based on Oliveras' estimate of his intact body type. Cole took over the office computer to search for background on "Flower of My Desire."

"Okay if I print something out?" she asked Fisher. "Two pages."

"No problem," he said.

"Sure you don't want us to get a warrant for the printout?" she asked.

"Look, I can't let anyone go into a client's business just 'cause they're cops," said Fisher. "I'd get canned before the sun went down."

There was a siren and a screech of brakes.

"Wilkins must be back with the warrant," said Boudreau.

Wilkins came into the office and handed Boudreau a manila envelope. He opened it, then removed a pair of documents and handed one to Fisher.

"Will that satisfy you, Counselor?" he asked.

"Is that what it's supposed to look like?" asked Fisher. "I've never seen one before."

"I have," said Boudreau. "It's good."

Fisher walked over to Cole and showed it to her. "That good?" he asked.

"See that seal there?" she asked. "That's the real deal."

"You relying on the junior officer instead of the sheriff?" asked Boudreau.

"She's cuter than you," said Fisher.

"Got that right," said Cole.

"Well, now that the formalities have been observed," said Boudreau, "what say you open up that place for us?"

"Officers, please be so kind as to follow me," said Fisher, picking a set of keys off the rack on the wall behind him.

Cole grabbed her printout, and they followed him to the warehouse.

"How far back do your security cameras record?" asked Boudreau.

"One week, then they record over," said Fisher as he sorted through the keys. "They won't be useful to you now."

He opened the door, and they went in.

"Can't say the business is thriving," said Boudreau, sniffing the musty air. "They have any cleaning staff?"

"Nope," said Fisher as he flicked on the lights. "Did everything themselves."

There was a front desk piled with flyers and order forms. Posters of exotic flowers decorated the walls. Cole pointed to one of a cluster of pale, yellow, bell-shaped blooms.

"Yellow wolfsbane," she said.

"Wolfsbane?" smirked Fisher. "Like the X-Man?"

"New Mutant," said Cole and Wilkins simultaneously.

"We'll skip that conversation if you don't mind," said Boudreau wearily. "Let's check out the working area."

They passed behind the desk into a small hallway. On the left was a single office, sparsely furnished, a single computer on the desk. On the right, a slightly larger room contained a table, four folding chairs, and a kitchenette.

"Gloves on," ordered Boudreau, and the officers each snapped on a pair of blue latex gloves. He opened the refrigerator, glanced in, and closed it immediately.

"Mold factory in there," he said. "No one's been here in months."

They stepped into the open area of the warehouse. One side was taken up by a long, deep tray, divided into compartments and filled with soil. Above it hung grow lights and a series of sprinklers. The compartments were filled with masses of dense, rotting vegetation.

"This is a weed spot?" asked Fisher. "That what this is all about?"

"If only life were that simple," said Boudreau. "Cole, you've become the expert on exotic flowers. Any of those look familiar to you?"

"They're all the same," she said. "They're all wolfsbane."

"Very specialized business," commented Boudreau. "I wouldn't touch them," he added as Fisher bent over for a closer look. "They're poison."

"Thanks for the heads up," said Fisher, backing away quickly. "I'll leave the investigating to you guys."

On the other side of the room, three vehicles were parked. Boudreau glanced at the registration stickers. "Rentals," he said. "Cole?"

"On it," she said, typing into her cell. "All three from HJA. Rented around the same week last December. All overdue as of January 10th."

He opened the Honda that was nearest. The key was still in the ignition.

He turned it, The dashboard lights glinted for a moment, then went out.

"Battery's dead," he said. He opened the glove compartment and found the rental agreement. "December 15th, last year. Not in a name we have for any of the bodies."

"They were using aliases," said Wilkins. "What were these guys doing?"

Boudreau looked into the glove compartment again, reached in, and pulled out a .45.

"Whatever it was, plants were a sideline," he said. "I'm gonna bring in the GBI. Full crime scene, whole damn building. Cole, you take a look at that computer, see what you can turn up. Wilkins, you guard the door, don't let anyone in without my say-so—especially that asshole, Pastore."

Mona sat in the waiting room, tears streaming down her face, punching at the keys of her cell so hard she thought she might break it. Or a finger. She didn't care. She held it up to her ear and listened to it ring. Again.

"This is Sam," came his voice, and the tears started coming again. "Leave a message."

"Damn it, Sam," she muttered, "call me. Call me now."

She disconnected and swiped at her face with her sleeve, then thumbed through her numbers until she found the one he left her on the ten messages that she never returned.

"Yes," said a man's voice.

"I'm trying to reach Sam Lehrmann," she said. "It's an emergency."

There was a pause.

"What is the emergency, Miss Havelka?" asked the man.

"I need him to call me," she said.

"The nature of the emergency, miss?"

"Tell him—" She swallowed, then took a breath. "Tell him that Nicky's been hurt. She's in the hospital."

"I'm very sorry, miss. And, Nicky is?"

"A very good friend of ours. The—the doctor says she's not certain Nicky's going to make it. And, Sally wants him to call. He'll know who that is."

"I will relay the message, miss. I am sorry about your friend."

"Thank you," said Mona.

She hung up.

The vet came out. "I've relieved the pressure on her brain," she said. "All we can do is wait it out."

"Where do I stay?" Mona asked.

"You should go home, Mona," said the vet. "I'll call you if there's any change. We'll keep our fingers crossed."

Mona nodded numbly.

"They have any leads on the burglar?" asked the vet.

"They've got nothing," said Mona. "Thank you. I'll come by before work tomorrow."

She walked out, almost in a trance.

No leads. The police were more concerned about the break-in than the beating of a dog, but nothing was taken—nothing but her best friend outside of Sam.

Or maybe her best friend, period, now that he was gone.

No leads, said the cops. She pictured them with leashes and collars, being jerked around. *How do you like them leads, officers? Lead on. Take me to your leader. Lead me astray.*

A stray.

Nicky was a stray, Sam once told her. He would rove the pounds, talking to the pups, and found this one girl he knew instantly would make a great guardian dog, just as he knew later she'd be the right dog for Mona. Sam had the knack for matching dogs with people. People themselves were Sam's problem.

And hers.

I'm a stray, too, she thought. *Sam collected me.*

Who would want to break into her place? It had been a professional job. They had bypassed the security system like it was a twist-tie. What did she have that anyone would want that bad?

Unless—

The guy Sam got to take over knew nothing about dogs. Sam wouldn't do that. Not to his dogs. So, the guy—what was his name? Larry? Larry must have been something else. He had to be connected to the suddenly reappearing CO who dragged Sam off on this mission.

What was he looking for so bad that he would break into her house and beat her dog?

One way to find out.

She pulled out her cell, tapped out a number.

"Hector, it's Mona," she said. "Is that guy who hit on me in the bar tonight? Okay, I need you to do me a favor . . ."

Carl replayed Mona's call to Bolton.

"Who is Nicky?" he asked.

"Beats me," said Bolton. "The name isn't in our intel on Lehrmann."

"Should I give him the message?"

"No," said Bolton. "We don't want him running home. Erase it."

"Yes, sir."

Tennant sat at the bar, feeling ornery as hell. His leg looked like a half-chewed steak. The no-questions-asked alky who stitched him up had done a crappy job, and the local had worn off hours ago—hence the self-medication.

Then Mona walked in and sat next to him.

"Welcome back, Mona," said Hector. "What'll it be?"

"Bourbon, Hector," she said. "Straight up—and keep them coming."

"And welcome back, Mona," said Hector, pouring it.

She looked at it thoughtfully, then knocked it back.

"Should have been a toast with that," said Tennant.

"Something to the Army?" she asked as Hector refilled her glass.

He gestured for another beer, then held it up.

"Fuck the Army," she said, knocking her glass against his and downing the contents.

"With any luck," he said.

"You never stop trying, do you?"

"No, ma'am," he said. "In fact, if you want, you can have that pooch of yours give me another chance. Maybe I'll pass this time."

"Afraid I've come stag tonight," she said as Hector replenished her drink. "Or doe. Whatever."

"Whatever," he said, and they drank to that.

She seemed set on a major bender, he thought. *Good.*

"I'm starting to feel dangerous," she said as she had her fourth. "You like danger, Army?"

"My middle name," he said.

"Sam," she said, then stopped.

"What about him?"

"I want Sam," she said. "I want him bad. But, Sam's not here."

"I'm sorry."

"But you're filling in for Sam, aren't you?" she asked, giving him that sideways look that drunk women always think is subtle.

"That is why I am here."

"One more, and I'm calling it," she said to Hector.

This one she savored.

"I'm off the wagon," she whispered to Tennant.

"So I see."

She finished it, then stood. "I'm feeling a tad wobbly," she confessed. "Will you be a gentleman and walk me home, Army?"

"No, ma'am," he said, laying some bills on the table, "but I will walk you home."

They walked out. She leaned against him, and he put his arm around her waist.

Like fish in a barrel, he thought.

"Which way is home?" he asked.

"Home is where the heart is," she said. "Where, when you have to go there, they have to take you in."

"You lost me."

"Don't want to go home just yet," she said, and she grabbed his hand and pulled him into an alleyway.

He glanced around. No one was near, no windows overlooked them. He kissed her. She let him.

"Not bad, Army," she said appraisingly after they came up for air. "Now, get those pants off."

"Don't need to get naked," he said. "Cops have a funny way of showing up when that happens."

"Don't get shy on me," she said. "I've already seen the goods, remember? I want some booty, so get them off."

He remembered the bandages on his thigh.

"I'm happy just unzipping out here," he said.

"Suit yourself," she said, pouting. "Oh, wait. We need some protection. Start unzipping."

He fumbled at it while she dug into her purse. He was getting rock hard. *What the hell, ought to be some benefit to this . . .*

"Hey, Army," she said.

He looked up. She had the Glock out, the business end pointed straight at his crotch. The hands holding it were rock steady.

"Pants off, asshole," she said. "Now."

"Easy, Mona," he said. "You're not thinking straight with all that bourbon."

"Only had one," she said. "Enough to give you the flavor. Fixed it up with Hector to keep pouring me iced tea out of a used bottle after that. So, I am pretty much sober and very pissed off. Drop the pants. Now."

He unbuckled his belt, unbuttoned the waist, and let them fall. The bandages gleamed in the moonlight.

"Line of duty injury?" she asked.

He was silent.

"How big a chunk did she take out of you before you fractured her skull?" she asked.

"I can explain."

"What exactly do you want from me?" she asked. "What do you think I have that's worth killing for?"

"I wasn't intending to kill anyone."

"Maybe not," she said, "but I might."

"You can't kill a man over a dog."

"The State of Georgia and I disagree on that point," she said, "but since you dragged me into an alley and tried to rape me, I think I'll be just fine. Aw, look, Army can't keep it up any more. Gonna answer my question?"

"Sam stole something," he said quickly. "Something from the government. I've been looking for it. I thought he might have given it to you."

"What is it?"

"A disk. That's all I know."

"Huh," she said. "All right, assuming I can get my hands on it, what would you be willing to give me in exchange?"

"I'm sure we could reach some arrangement."

She lowered the gun. "I want to know what happened to Kerry Cheller's brother. The true story. Documented, so the poor girl can have some closure and get the hell out of my life. Can you get that, Army?"

He nodded, eyes still on the gun.

"Then we got ourselves a deal," said Mona, putting the Glock back in her bag. "Good night, Army. Sweet dreams."

She turned and walked away as he grabbed at his pants.

CHAPTER 13

"I'M NOT SURE THIS WAS properly our case," said the Animal Services director, who seemed more comfortable dealing with animals than humans.

"That's why I'm here," said Pastore, helping her put on the biohazard suit.

"I've never even heard of your agency," she said.

"Oh, there are so many little bureaus tucked away in Homeland Security, you wouldn't believe it," he said, grinning.

She blushed a little. "And you came all the way to Augusta for this," she said.

"I'm the Southeast Regional Admin," he said. "With a staff of me and my van. Maybe if I can justify my existence, they'll throw me a bone sometime— or a better van. There, comfy?"

"Not at all," she said, her voice muffled by the helmet.

"Breathing okay?"

"Yes, thank you. That's good, right?"

"Considering the alternative, yes, ma'am, that's very good. Now, take me to this strange critter of yours."

"They found her near the hospital," she said as she walked him to the kennels.

"Her?"

"It's a female," she said. "Cops thought it might be a prank at first, but the fur is real. Had to cut its scrubs off to see what it was. How someone managed to put a wolf into scrubs, I don't know. So, they tranqed it and called us in."

She opened the door to the kennels, and a wave of baying shook their ears.

Baying, and one woman yelling. Pastore turned to the Animal Services director.

"Ma'am," he said sternly. "Would you mind telling me why you have a naked woman locked up in a cage here?"

"That's a naked Black woman locked in a cage!" yelled Myers, rattling the bars. "I want my lawyer!"

"What on earth?" exclaimed the director. She slapped at her waist. "Oh, Christ, my keys are in my pocket, and I've got this damn suit on."

"Go," said Pastore, grabbing her shoulders and shoving her out.

He closed the door. "Get out of the suit and give me the keys to the cage," he ordered. "She still might be contagious."

"Contagious?" gasped the director as she peeled off the suit.

"I'm praying it's only Level Three," he said. "Keys. Now. And, I'm taking your suit in for her. Don't even think of coming through those doors. If I'm not out in fifteen minutes, you call my superiors, tell them I authorized a Level Four decon, then you evacuate the building and maintain a half-mile radius."

"What is going on?" she wailed.

"I'm sorry," he said. "You're not cleared to know any more. I'm going in. Start timing me now."

He went back in, smiling to himself.

"I want the ACLU, and the NAACP!" shouted Myers when she saw him.

"You'd be better off with PETA, don't you think?" replied Pastore.

She peered through his facemask. "Pastore?" she said in surprise. "Shit, Joe, never thought I'd say this, but am I glad to see you!"

"And you can't tell since I'm wearing the suit, but I am very glad to see you, too, Ali," he said, looking her up and down. "You've been keeping in shape."

"Oh, baby, tell me you got keys, and we can get glad together," she said.

He held them up. "But," he added as he opened the cage and tossed her the biohazard suit, "you have to put this on before I let you out."

"Why?" she asked.

"All the cool kids are wearing them," he said. "Hustle, soldier. Clock's ticking on your freedom."

She threw it on in record time.

"Now, turn around, hands behind you," he ordered.

"Why?"

He held up a pair of handcuffs.

"You're shitting me," she said, staring at them in disbelief.

"Got to sell the cover story," he said. "They still don't know who you are, do they?"

"No," she said, turning around.

He cuffed her, then led her out.

"Safe for now," he said to the director as they came through the doors. "Here's your keys."

"Who is she?" demanded the director. "What's going on?"

"My job is to determine that," said Pastore. "Get someone to clean that cage using Level Three protocols, just to be safe."

"What the hell are Level Three protocols?"

"Ammonia, mop, then go over everything with infrared," he improvised. "We'll be in touch."

He guided Myers out the back entrance, opened the rear of the van, and shoved her inside past the gurney.

"Don't you think that's enough verisimilitude for now?" she protested.

"Not nearly," he said.

He uncuffed one hand, then recuffed the other to a bar near the front. "Sit there," he said, pointing to a bench bolted to the floor.

He slid open a panel that gave access to the driver's compartment, then jumped out and closed the rear doors. He stripped off the biohazard suit, climbed into the driver's seat, and drove off.

"Is this necessary?" called Myers.

"I'm assuming it is until I know otherwise," said Pastore. "Heavy betting at the lab is that what happened to you has a viral cause that's specific to were-wolves. I don't feel like catching it. How long did the change last?"

"About six hours," she replied. "What lab?"

"The one where they're dissecting Arletty as we speak," he said. "Which is where I'm taking you."

"They gonna dissect me, too?"

"Hope not. It's about ninety minutes from here. Better get comfortable."

"So not comfortable," she said, sagging against the wall.

His cell went off.

"Yeah?" he answered, then he listened for a while. "Really? Huh. Sounds to me like she's playing you. No, it's possible, but take it slow. I don't want anyone's feelings hurt, you understand? Yeah, I'll come down later. I have to make a few calls to get that authorized."

He hung up.

"What's that all about?" asked Myers.

"Advice to the lovelorn," said Pastore.

"You're the last person to be giving that, Joe."

"Ali, I have five different headaches going simultaneously right now," he said. "I am not in the mood to rehash our relationship, and there's a very good reason why you shouldn't."

"What's that?"

"I don't have a refill for your oxygen tank handy. Less talk, the better."

"Admit it, you really enjoyed seeing me locked up in that cage, didn't you?" she sighed.

"The irony of seeing you in the custody of Animal Control did not escape me," he admitted. "Now, shut up and breathe slowly."

Tennant sat in Sam's office, thinking over his conversation with Pastore and his humiliation by Mona.

"Fuck going slow," muttered Tennant. He picked up his cell and made a call.

From the shadows outside the office, Carson watched him, holding back a growl.

"GBI can't be here until tomorrow morning," said Wilkins.

"Great," said Boudreau. "Then we have to secure the scene. I'll go grab a couple of rooms at that motel. We'll take it in shifts."

"I'm going to keep at that computer if you don't mind," said Cole.

"Knock off at ten," said Boudreau. "We've been at it all day. Need you rested. It will keep."

He fetched a roll of Crime Scene tape and stretched it over the office and garage doors.

"Dinner's on me, officers," he said. "What dipping sauces do you prefer?"

Coleridge passed Sam in the hallway, grumbling to himself.

"What's going on?" asked Sam.

"They are making me earn my salary today," said Coleridge. "Most of the time, nice and easy around here. No deadlines, none of this Army I-want-it-yesterday bullshit. But now, I got to set up the biohazard enclosure with a lock."

"This about that second daylight werewolf?"

"Yup. Pastore wants it sealed up until we know if this virus is contagious or not."

"They definite about a virus?"

"Well, they don't have results yet," said Coleridge, "but makes sense to treat it like one. And Pastore has good reason to be careful, given his—situation."

"Any word on the autopsy?"

"They came out for sandwiches at seven, chattering away like schoolkids at recess," Coleridge said. "Didn't even seem like three people cutting up a fellow human being. Freaking eggheads."

"Don't you qualify as an egghead?"

Coleridge laughed. "I'm the tech guy: I do what I'm told and mop up after. Tell you this—I'm not looking forward to mop duty in the slaughterhouse tonight. Okay, off to be a locksmith now."

"Jack of all trades—"

"Master of them all, baby," crowed Coleridge. "Those eggheads can't even change a light bulb without calling me."

Pastore arrived an hour later. Sam went out to the loading dock to meet him. Pastore put a finger to his lips, disappeared into the rear of the van, and reappeared leading a figure in a biohazard suit, rear-cuffed.

Haven't seen one of those in a while, commented Tito, who was passing by on patrol.

What did you say? asked Sam, startled.

What did you say? responded Tito even more startled. *Who said what did you say?*

"Shit," Sam muttered.

"Coleridge got that room set up?" asked Pastore as he guided the person up the ramp.

"Should have," said Sam. "This the guest of honor?"

"Sam, meet Ali Myers. Corporal Alison Myers, once upon a time. Ali, Sam."

"Charmed, I'm sure," came a woman's voice, muffled by the helmet.

Sam peered through the mask in surprise. "That's a woman," he said.

"Oh, he's good," said Myers. "If this is the brightest guy here, then I am well and truly fucked."

"Don't mind Sam," said Pastore. "He's just visiting. The real geeks are inside."

Pastore caught him up with the day's events as they walked inside. McKenna and Coleridge were waiting for them in the rotunda.

"Is this the subject?" asked McKenna.

"I thought you said he was smart," muttered Myers.

"Doctor McKenna, Mister Coleridge, this is Alison Myers," said Pastore.

"Part-time werewolf," added Myers. "I'd shake, but my boyfriend here has control issues."

"This way, miss," said Coleridge, beckoning to her.

They walked into the biology wing into a room Sam hadn't seen before. A hospital bed was placed in a small chamber, enclosed by Plexiglas on all sides. Entry was gained by means of an airlock at the front, with smaller ones situated on the side for meals. A chemical toilet sat by the bed.

"No cable?" asked Myers as Pastore removed the handcuffs.

"That's ten bucks extra," said Pastore.

She slapped at her sides. "Don't seem to have my wallet with me," she said. "Guess I'll go without."

Coleridge punched a code into a keypad, and the airlock opened with a slight pop as the air pressure inside changed. "In there, miss," he said.

She stepped into the airlock, and he closed the door behind her. It sealed, and the door to the room opened. She stepped through, the second door closing automatically.

"You can remove the suit now, miss," said Coleridge.

"The hell I will," said Myers, taking off the helmet. "I am still butt naked underneath, and I have to pee like nobody's business—and that nobody includes all of y'all, so I will respectfully ask you gentlemen to fuck off."

"There's pajamas in the drawer by the bed," said Coleridge.

"We'll come back later," said McKenna. "We need some blood samples."

"You know why this happened to me?" she asked him.

"Not yet," said McKenna. "We're working on it."

"Work faster," she said. "Now get out of here."

The four men walked out.

"She's scared," said Pastore. "I'm getting a little nervous myself. Tell me how far you've gotten with the research and where you're going with it."

"We've prepared samples from a variety of locations," said McKenna. "Kudowski is going over them now looking for foreign bodies, anything we haven't seen before. Trouble is, if it's specific to the werewolf structures, we may not know what we're looking for even if we're looking right at it. It's like looking for a needle in a haystack, finding it, only it's a thumbtack."

"You really suck at metaphors," said Pastore. "You aren't helping her?"

"I'll be reviewing them when she's done," said McKenna. "It's been a long day. Fresh eyes in the morning and all that. Sanchez will take live samples from the woman."

"If it is a virus, or something like that, what do we do to fight it?" asked Pastore.

"Too early to hypothesize," said McKenna, removing his glasses and massaging his temples. "Can't fight what you don't know exists."

"Learned that already in Afghanistan, thanks," said Pastore. "Right, back on the road for me. Got to track some things down, clear up what's left of Myers' mess."

He left.

"Ever seen a werewolf virus before?" asked Sam.

"No," said McKenna. "Why?"

"Might be a good way to get rid of them all at once," said Sam. "Save me a lot of work."

"Interesting thought," said McKenna.

"They are human beings," said Coleridge. "God's creations."

"Keep telling yourself that the next time one's going for your throat," said Sam. "Now that they're not limited to the full moon anymore, all hell's gonna break loose."

You made that up on the spot? asked Arnie, who was standing at the door to the dorm wing.

Yeah, said Sam as he headed in to sleep, *but it occurs to me that it's true.*

He stripped down to his shorts and sprawled on the bed. *Who's got first watch?* he asked.

I do, said Arnie.

Bert, patrol the halls, said Sam. *Report back if anyone finds anything.*

Will do, said Bert, slipping out the door.

Do you want us to wake you if you turn into a werewolf? asked Olga.

Please, said Sam.

He turned off the light and drifted into sleep.

The black helicopter hovered five meters over the last false insertion point. They slid the dummy soldiers down the lines, then the copter rose and sped along, sending dampening signals ahead to cancel out the sound of the rotors.

Padilla reeled up the lines, then checked his watch. "Sundown in twenty-two minutes," he said.

"How long to the drop point?" called Pastore.

"I make it in fifteen," said the pilot.

"Cutting it close," commented Sam. "Barely have time to get my boots off."

"Take 'em off now," suggested Cheller.

"Then with my luck, I'll land right on something sharp. Or poisonous. Or poisonous and sharp."

The copter rose and fell as it swooped through the Hindu Kush, following the detailed topographical maps stored in its computer, which were so precise that they allowed for annual growth in the trees on the lower slopes.

"Odysseys on," ordered Pastore. "T minus two."

The copter slowed as it came to a black spot on the ridge where a fire had denuded it of vegetation.

"Lines out."

Padilla slid the hatch open and deployed the lines. Sam clipped his harness to one of them and stood with his back to the open hatch, watching a series of lights go from red to amber.

"Give 'em hell," called the pilot.

The light went green. Sam jumped backwards, sliding down the line until he hit the ground. He unhooked his harness and swung his M25 to the front, swinging it along a ninety-degree arc at five degree intervals. Behind him, Cheller, Padilla, and Crawford did the same for the other points of the compass.

"Clear," said Sam.

"Clear," called the other three.

The copter took off, the lines still dangling for the extraction.

With luck.

Pastore consulted his Odyssey, then said, "Boots off."

The squad removed them and stuffed them in their packs.

"There it goes," said Cheller, watching the last rays of the sun as it disappeared below the western mountains, "and here we come."

Then the change hit them.

Their uniforms and body armor were designed with expandable sections. This meant that they weren't completely shielded in werewolf form, but it was better than nothing.

"Everybody good?" asked Pastore, when his breathing had settled.

"Sir, yessir," responded the others.

"Right. Let's get to work."

They ran on four legs just below the top of the ridge for five kilometers, covering the distance in half the time a human could. Then, Pastore signaled them to halt. They followed him as he crept silently to the top of the ridge.

"There's the target," he said softly as the others clambered up to see.

A narrow, twisting ravine snaked through the landscape. At a sharp bend, there was a cave.

"The floor of the ravine is mined in both directions," said Pastore. "Mines are deactivated from inside the cave. We are going to hit it from the cliff face above it."

They turned their attention to the top of the cliff, where the curve of the ravine outlined a V-shaped pasture at the top.

"Goats," said Crawford.

"And one lonely goatherd," said Padilla.

"Yodelayhee—" began Cheller.

"Shut up, Tom," said Pastore. "Bad enough we have the full moon lighting us up without you singing show tunes."

He took a pair of field glasses, switched them to infrared, and scanned the pasture. "He's an armed lonely goatherd—not so lonely, neither. He's got a friend at three o'clock. The friend has a Dragunov sniper rifle. Don't have a clear shot at either of them from here. But, we're downwind from the goats. Tom, Sam—you're up."

"Race you," said Tom.

"You're on," said Sam.

They backed down the ridge to get a running start, then charged to the top and leaped.

It was fifteen meters from the top of the ridge to the edge of the cliff. Tom barely made it. Sam crashed into the cliff wall a few feet below the top, digging in with all four sets of claws. They froze, but no one raised the alarm, neither human nor goat.

Tom reached down and pulled Sam up to the top. They crouched down, moving silently on all fours through the grass until they were twenty meters from the two guards. Then, they took off.

Sam launched himself into the air when he was five meters from the goatherd. He caught him at the chest and head and snapped his neck before the man could even cry out.

He looked over to see Tom swinging his hand back and forth, each swipe taking another bloody chunk out of the sniper.

"Tom! Enough!" *he said.*

Then he saw her, soaring across the face of the moon yet lit from all sides—no, glowing, and her wings—

Boss! shouted Arnie.

"What the fuck?" cried Sam, sitting bolt upright.

Is he turning into a werewolf? asked Nan, watching with interest.

He's turning into something, but not a werewolf, said Arnie, backing away from the bed. *Would you consider this a safe distance?*

What were you dreaming about, Sam? asked Otto.

Later for that, Spooky, said Arnie impatiently. *Boss, Bert's been calling.*

Where are you, Bert? called Sam.

Outside Sanchez's lab, said Bert. *You better get over here.*

Sam looked at his watch. It was two in the morning.

Nan, let's go see your brother, he said. *The rest of you stay in the rotunda. Let me know if anyone is coming.*

He threw on some clothes and lurched out the door, still half asleep. Nan followed at his heels.

The Boss is shaken up about something, said Olga as she joined Arnie and Otto.

Something in his dreams, said Otto.

The Boss doesn't dream, said Arnie dismissively.

He never remembered them, said Otto, *but he's beginning to.*

Is that good or bad? asked Olga.

I don't know, replied the Weimaraner.

Sam and Nan found Bert pacing outside Sanchez's lab.

What's going on? asked Sam.

He's acting weird, talking to himself, crying a lot, said Bert.

What was he saying?

"Stupid, stupid, stupid. You're a dead man."

There was a crash of glass from inside the lab. Without thinking, Sam rushed through the door.

Sanchez was sitting at his desk, a shard of broken glass in his hand. He was holding it against his left wrist.

"Don't you have scalpels for that?" asked Sam.

"You're the last person I want to see right now," said Sanchez.

"If you don't want me to be the last person you ever see, then put that down and talk," said Sam. "I might be able to help."

"Help?" Sanchez laughed bleakly. "You're the one who's going to kill me."

CHAPTER 14

"**W**HY WOULD I WANT TO kill you?" asked Sam, sitting down across the desk from Sanchez. *Flank me.*

Bert and Nan took up positions on both sides of his chair.

"You think I don't know why you're here," said Sanchez. "You think I don't know why Pastore sent you."

"Why?"

"Because he suspects me," said Sanchez.

"He suspects me, too," said Sam. "He suspects everybody. We could form a club. You could be treasurer."

"Stop ridiculing me," whined Sanchez. "All you killers know how to do is belittle people."

"Well, belittling and killing. Look, Doc: I'm basically a lazy guy. If I wanted you dead, I'd let you do it yourself and save me the trouble, not to mention the blame—but I don't."

"But you know why you're going to kill me."

"Tell me, and I'll tell you if you're right. If you are, you can slice away. But, I'm betting that you're wrong."

"You are?"

Sam pulled out his wallet and removed a bill. "Fifty bucks says I'm not going to kill you," he said, putting it on the desk. "You in?"

"You're insane."

"Says the man about to cut his wrist. Come on, Doc. Money on the table, right now."

"This is like one of those playground bets, like let's see who can punch softer."

"And I'll go first, yeah, I see your point. If I killed you, then it would be hard for you to collect. Tell you what—let's change the bet."

"To what?"

Sam leaned back in his chair. *Move up. Wrists on two.*

Nan and Bert inched forward to the sides of the desk, below Sanchez's range of sight. Sam raised his hands, palms forward, drawing Sanchez's attention.

"Fifty bucks says I can reach across this desk and take that broken glass out of your hand before you use it," said Sam. "On a count of three."

"No," said Sanchez. "I'm not playing."

"I am," said Sam. "One."

"I'm going to end this!" shouted Sanchez.

"Two," said Sam calmly. "Disarm."

Symmetry in motion as the Dobermans leaped. Two powerful sets of jaws clamped on Sanchez's wrists as he yelped in surprise. Then, Nan and Bert simply sagged back, their weights dragging his arms apart.

Sam leaned across the desk and plucked the glass from Sanchez's unresisting hand.

"Three," he said. "Where's your broom and dustpan?"

"What?" asked Sanchez in bewilderment.

"Your broom and dustpan. You've got broken glass here. I don't want my dogs stepping on it."

"In that closet," said Sanchez numbly, nodding his head in that direction.

Sam collected the broom and dustpan and carefully swept around Sanchez's chair. He upended the glass into a wastebasket—which he placed out of the reach of the scientist—then put the broom and dustpan back in the closet.

"They haven't broken the skin," observed Sanchez, looking curiously at the dogs.

"They weren't supposed to on that command," said Sam.

"You're quite a remarkable trainer."

"Thank you," said Sam. "We could continue the conversation like this, or I could have them let you go. Up to you."

Sanchez looked at his sleeves, which were becoming soaked with slobber. "Release me, please," said Sanchez. "I won't try anything."

"No, you won't," agreed Sam. "Release. Prisoner."

The dogs let go of Sanchez, but remained on either side of him.

"Prisoner means what, exactly?" asked Sanchez.

"Don't make any sudden moves," advised Sam.

"Or?"

"Or this time they'll break the skin—and whatever's under it."

"Right," said Sanchez. "I was trying to kill myself, and you're threatening me."

"Is it working?"

"Actually, yes."

"Good," said Sam. "Why were you trying to kill yourself? It couldn't have had anything to do with me."

"It was either kill myself, or be killed," he said. "I wanted to—to keep things in my own hands."

"Why kill yourself at all?"

Sanchez sighed. "Two years," he said. "Two years, and nothing more than professional exchanges. Then you show up, and within two days, she's jumping into your bed."

"Doctor Kudowski," said Sam. "For the record, we didn't go to bed together."

"Thanks to an act of God," said Sanchez. "I'm not that old, you know."

"Never said you were."

"It's the baldness," he said. "It repulses women. It's only natural. They are compelled to reproduce with hairy men. It's a desired trait."

"You're killing yourself because you're bald?"

"No," said Sanchez. "Because I finally tried to do something about it— and I screwed up."

"You lost me."

"Let me show you something I'm working on," said Sanchez, pathetic in his eagerness. "I'll have to stand up. Could you restrain your beasts?"

"Follow," commanded Sam, pointing at Sanchez.

Sanchez stood up carefully, watching the dogs, then breathed a sigh of relief. "Good dogs," he said. "Come with me."

He led them into a smaller lab, where several small cages were stored under cloth covers. Sanchez removed one. There were a dozen mice sleeping inside. Two of them woke and began to scamper about as the light struck them. They were all a pale pink color.

"Notice anything about them?" asked Sanchez.

Sam peered at the cage, puzzled. "They don't have any hair," he said.

"Right," said Sanchez. "Do you know what knockout mice are?"

"Vaguely, but tell me in case I'm dead wrong."

"They worked out the complete genome for this species of mouse about a dozen years ago," said Sanchez, looking fondly at the little creatures. "As a result, we have the ability to switch certain genes on and off and to breed entire generations for testing. In this case, the gene for hair."

"So you made bald mice," said Sam.

"Exactly. Now, look at these." He removed the cover to another case. Six normal-looking mice were huddled inside, their tiny sides rising and falling as they slept.

"These mice were the same as those mice one week ago," said Sanchez proudly, "and now they have hair."

"A cure for baldness," said Sam. "That's what you've been hiding all this time."

"How did you know I was hiding anything?" asked Sanchez.

"Body language," said Sam. "That picture of the hairy arm that was on your monitor when I talked to you—that was what you were trying to do?"

"Yes," said Sanchez, "and it worked—with the mice, anyway."

"How did you do it?" asked Sam.

"Partly denatured werewolf venom," said Sanchez.

"What?"

"We've been trying to isolate different characteristics of the transformation," explained Sanchez. "Like knockout genes, only with the werewolf cellular structures. Lisa developed the technique and she's been teaching me. I thought I could find what causes the follicles to grow, and make the growth permanent, not just during the full moon. I succeeded—at least, with mice."

"Congratulations," said Sam. "You're gonna be rich. But, that doesn't explain why you were going to—"

He stopped, realization dawning as Sanchez looked at him guiltily.

"You're experimenting on yourself now," said Sam. "You're trying to grow hair. You injected yourself with werewolf venom."

"I thought I had done it correctly," whimpered Sanchez, rubbing his head in anguish. "I thought, okay, she wants men with a full head of hair, I'll show her a full head of hair. Only something went—I've been working so hard, and then we had that autopsy, and I haven't been sleeping well, and—"

"What went wrong, Doc?" asked Sam.

"I checked my results two hours after the injection," said Sanchez. "Apparently denaturing the venom doesn't work for humans like it did for the mice."

"Meaning what?"

Sanchez held his palms up and started giggling. "I've turned myself into a werewolf," he said, laughing harder and harder. "Oh, she'll see me with hair, all right. Hair, and fangs, and claws, and—"

"Jesus, Doc, don't you know it's a curse?"

Sanchez started to sob. "So is baldness," he wailed.

"Doc, I'm gonna get Doctor Buenaventura," said Sam. "You wait—"

"No!" objected Sanchez. "No one can know. Not yet. I have a month. Let me have one month. Maybe I can reverse it."

"Three weeks to the next full moon, actually," said Sam. "Look, they're used to werewolves here. It won't be as big a deal as it would be outside."

"You have no idea what they'll do," said Sanchez. "I'll be kicked out, all my work down the toilet, no pension, no references—"

"Come on, let's get you out of here," said Sam, pulling him to his feet. "What you need to do right now is sleep. You're in no condition to make any kind of decision right now."

"Sleep," repeated Sanchez. "Sleep would be good."

Sam walked him down the corridor.

Bald mice, said Bert to Nan. *We have got to try some of those.*

Yeah, agreed his sister. *All the great taste of mouse without the one thing that makes it yucky.*

You're making me sick, said Sam.

Oh, like you've never eaten a mouse, said Bert.

Have you tried vole? asked Nan.

Yeah, vole's good, said Bert. *Like mouse but with kind of a nutty flavor.*

I bet squirrel's good, said Nan wistfully.

You shouldn't eat squirrel, said Sam. *It's bad for you.*

Says who?

They got this disease, said Sam.

Everything I like is bad for me, sighed Nan. *Where did you hear that?*

I read about it.

Rats, said Nan, disappointed.

Now, those are good, said Sam.

They passed through the doors into the rotunda. Arnie, Olga, and Otto joined them as they entered the dorm wing.

"Wait," said Sanchez, stopping in front of Kudowski's room.

He bent down and retrieved an envelope that was sticking out from under the door, then handed it to Sam. "I'd appreciate it if you'd burn this for me," said Sanchez.

"Will do," promised Sam. "Let's get you to bed."

He followed Sanchez into the latter's room. Sanchez kicked his shoes off, then stretched out on his bed. "Are you going to stay here and watch me until morning?" he asked.

"I've got a better idea," said Sam.

He beckoned to the Dobermans. "Protect," he said.

They jumped up on either side of Sanchez and nestled into him.

"They can be very comforting, believe it or not," said Sam. "I'll check in on you at daybreak. Hang in there, Doc. It isn't the end of the world by a long shot."

But Sanchez was already asleep.

And, we get to sleep on a human bed, said Bert.

Sweet, said Nan.

Sam left, closing the door quietly behind him.

Well? asked Arnie.

Tell you in the morning, said Sam as he led them into his room. *I'm whipped.*

He kicked off his shoes, then flopped onto the bed.

Get up here, he said. *All of you.*

Really? said Arnie.

I left the twins on a bed. Hardly seems fair to make you guys sleep over there again.

Arnie bounded up without any more invitation. Olga cautiously placed her forefeet on the covers, then gracefully climbed up and settled at Sam's feet. Sam looked at Otto, who was watching them.

Otto?

It's okay, Sam, said the Weimaraner. *I'm good where I am. It's my turn to keep watch.*

Atta boy, Spooky, said Arnie drowsily. *See you in the morning.*

Sam stared at the ceiling, trying to will his consciousness away.

Go to sleep, Sam, said Otto in the darkness. *You need to dream again.*

He looked over to see Tom swinging his hand back and forth, each swipe taking another bloody chunk out of the sniper.

"Tom! Enough!" *he said.*

Tom bared his teeth in triumph, then waved to the rest of the squad. A moment later, they came flying over the canyon to join them.

The goats, understandably, were agitated.

"Could use a snack," *said Crawford, looking at them with a gleam in his eye.*

"No time," *said Pastore.*

They ran to where the canyon made a V in the mountain and looked down.

"No guards in front," *said Pastore.* "Secure your weapons. I don't want anything falling."

"Or anyone," *said Cheller.*

"That, too, wise guy," *said Pastore.*

They strapped their weapons to their backs, then went headfirst down the face of the cliff, their claws digging into cracks that would have been invisible to human eyes in daylight. They stopped at the top of the cave.

Pastore pulled out an optical fiber with an tiny camera at its end and slid it over the edge. He looked at the monitor for a few seconds, then withdrew it. He held up two fingers, then indicated positions.

Crawford and Padilla pulled out silenced automatics.

Pastore counted down, and the two soldiers lowered themselves and fired one round each into the cave. There were a pair of soft grunts, then silence.

"Clear," *said Crawford.*

"Get all the way into the entrance," *said Pastore.* "Don't know how safe the area in front is."

They gripped the edges of the cave, then released their footholds on the cliff face and swung into the darkness. As they landed, each grabbed his weapon.

The cave may have been natural, but the tunnel into the mountain was not. They followed it for some fifty meters until it opened up into a large cavern. Fifty men slept on double bunks on either side, and in the back were crates of weapons and explosives.

Pastore pointed at the latter, then at Sam and Cheller, holding up four fingers. They nodded and ran past the sleeping soldiers until they reached the weapons cache. They separated, each pulling out a Claymore. They set the timers at four minutes, placed them with the crates of explosives, and ran back. The others had been similarly busy at the entrance to the cavern.

Pastore inspected their handiwork, then took off at a dead run to the cave entrance, the others following. They jumped up, caught the cliff face with their claws, and scrambled up to the top.

"We've got ninety seconds until they blow," said Sam.

"Thirty seconds," said Pastore. "Ours were set at three minutes to seal off the cave. Then, the big boom will finish them."

"What do you think will happen to this mountain when that happens?" asked Cheller.

"I don't want to find out," said Pastore, taking off for the cliff edge.

They all leaped, Crawford casting one last regretful glance at the goats. They soared across the chasm, crashing into the ridge. They hauled themselves up to the top, then turned.

There was a muffled thump as the first set of Claymores went off.

Sam thought he could hear screams from inside, but it may have been his imagination.

They waited a minute.

"Three, two, one," said Cheller.

The ground shook, and the mountain in front of them settled a few feet. The screams stopped.

"I call that a good night's work," said Pastore. "Congratulations. Next meal's on me. Half an hour to the extraction point. Eyes and ears, gentlemen."

They ran north.

"Cutting it close," said Cheller, sneaking a glance at his Odyssey.

"We'll make it," said Sam. "Captain always gets us home, don't worry."

They climbed one last hill, where Pastore signaled a halt. He closed his eyes and listened, his ears twitching. Then, he pointed east.

"Our ride's here," he said.

Sam saw a small black dot approaching in the sky, filling the disc of the moon, and gave a small sigh of thanks.

Then he saw her again, soaring in front of the chopper, her teeth bared in warning.

"Be ready," said Pastore. "We'll need to—"

"Captain!" interrupted Sam.

A streak of fire headed straight toward the chopper. Then came a burst of flame that hovered for a moment, then plummeted to the ground, small chunks of brightness shearing off and fluttering their separate ways before vanishing into the black.

And above it all, the Winged Wolf watched. Then, she looked directly at Sam, her eyes—

Boss? said Olga.

What? he said, his heart still hammering in his chest.

Your alarm's going off.

He slapped the button, then rolled out of the bed, staggered into the bathroom, and threw up.

Olga nudged Arnie, who was lying with his muzzle on a pillow.

His eyes opened. *Good morning,* he said.

Not so much, she replied. *Boss had a bad night.*

Why didn't you wake us, Spooky? Arnie demanded angrily.

You looked so cute lying there, I didn't have the heart, said Otto.

Don't call me cute, said Arnie, bristling.

Don't call me Spooky, said Otto.

It really isn't kind, commented Olga.

Arnie looked at her, then Otto. *All right,* he said. *Sorry, Otto.*

Sam rinsed his mouth out, brushed his teeth, then repeated both to be sure. Then, he showered and dressed.

"Let's see how Sanchez is doing," he said.

We're coming in, called Arnie.

Okay, replied Nan. *Everything's good here.*

Sam knocked softly on Sanchez's door. The biologist opened it, looking haggard.

"How do you feel today?" asked Sam.

"Almost alive," said Sanchez.

"That's a start," said Sam.

"What am I going to tell them?" asked Sanchez.

"That you have a wicked hangover," said Sam. "Have a shower, then come get some coffee."

"They're not coming in with me, are they?" asked Sanchez, looking at the Dobermans.

"Just a sec," said Sam.

He stepped into the biologist's bathroom and collected all the sharp objects. There were no medications worth worrying about.

"Clear," he said. "Here's the deal. You leave the bathroom door open and you take your shower. They sit here and keep an eye on you."

"But there's nothing there that can hurt me."

"There's a mirror," said Sam.

"I'm not that ugly."

"You can break it and use the shards," said Sam. "The dogs will stop you if you try."

"And all I'd get for my efforts is seven years bad luck," said Sanchez. "Look, I am really feeling better. It's not necessary."

"The dogs stay," said Sam. "End of story."

"All right," said Sanchez, turning toward the bathroom. Then, he hesitated. "About last night."

"Yes?"

"How did you know I was—you know."

"I was taking the dogs for a walk," said Sam. "Bert sensed something was wrong."

"Remarkable creatures," said Sanchez.

"That they are."

"Thank them for me, would you?"

"Have a good shower, Doc."

Consider us thanked, said Bert.

Whitfield was back. She gave Sam and the dogs a smile when she saw them at the doorway.

"Meat's in the fridge," she said. "Waffles and sausages?"

"Sounds good," said Sam.

He left the three dogs at their breakfast in his room and went back to the cafeteria. McKenna and Kudowski were chattering away at the end of the table.

"... and the pituitary gland was empty, so I moved on to the adrenal, but same result ..." said Kudowski.

"Right, most logical places. You kept the images?" asked McKenna.

"Of course."

Buenaventura sat at the opposite end, picking listlessly at a plate of scrambled eggs. She gave a small start when Sam sat next to her.

"You busy after breakfast?" he asked.

"Now that Bonnie's back, I can do my own work for a change," she said. "I was hoping for no interruptions."

"It's kind of important," he said.

She looked at him suspiciously. "All right," she said. "Half an hour."

Sanchez came in, looking slightly better. He nodded at the group, eyes narrowing as he noticed Sam next to the psychiatrist.

"What'll it be this morning, Doctor Sanchez?" called Bonnie.

"Coffee," he said. "Lots of it."

"Rough night?" asked Buenaventura.

"Had trouble sleeping," he replied.

Sam finished and brought his plates into the kitchen. He noted with approval the Dobermans watching Sanchez from the hallway.

Nan, go eat your breakfast, then give Bert a chance, he said. *Don't need both of you on him. Trade shifts.*

Okay, said Nan. *I'll be quick, bro.*

Take your time, sis. I'm good.

Sam walked her back to the room with their bowls. *You guys haven't been fighting much since we got here,* he observed.

We fight when we're bored, said Nan. *This has been interesting.*

How did Sanchez do with the two of you?

He had a two dog night, she said. *He's doing a lot better now. But, he should stay off the sauce.*

Right. I'm off to see Doctor Buenaventura.

Want us to tag along? asked Arnie.

Nope. Just want to ask her a few questions.

All four dogs looked at him with expressions of disbelief.

Fine, be that way, muttered Arnie.

Let him be, said Otto. *He wants to talk to the Dreamlady about his dreams. He doesn't need us staring at them.*

Something like that, agreed Sam as he left.

What is going to happen to us when this is over? wondered Nan.

It isn't going to be like it was before, is it? asked Olga. *We're a team, now. He can't just sell us off like we're—*

Like we're dogs, finished Arnie harshly. *What do you expect? Nan, go relieve your brother. He needs to eat.*

Nan gave him a hurt look, then slunk out of the room.

Just because you're the alpha doesn't mean you have to be cruel, said Olga.

He'll sell you, and I'll never see you again, said Arnie. *Like all the others—and I'll still be stuck in that damn kennel until I get too old and they put me to sleep.*

Arnie, she said softly, trying to nuzzle him.

I'll never see you again, he repeated, not meeting her gaze.

Sam stopped in the hallway, collecting his thoughts. He had heard everything the dogs had said.

Life had changed in just a few days. Pastore and Kerry Cheller reappearing in his life; Mona disappearing from it; the nightmares of that mission taking hold; The Winged Wolf. And with all of that, he had never once considered what he was doing with the dogs. These dogs. The team. What was he going to do with them? It wasn't like he could hire all of them out as a specialized security unit.

Not without leaving himself exposed in so many ways, every one of them a threat.

Mission first, Sam admonished. *We'll figure that out later.*

He took a deep breath, then rapped on Buenaventura's door.

"Come in," she said.

She watched him without saying anything as he entered and sat in the chair opposite her desk.

"You left a drawer open," he observed.

"So?"

"So, that makes me a little nervous."

"Why would you be nervous?" she asked.

"Because open desk drawers often have nasty surprises inside," he said. "Would you mind closing it?"

"Certainly," she said.

She reached into the drawer, pulled out a Sig Sauer P220 and placed it on the desk before her.

"There," she said, closing the drawer. "Is that better?"

"You have an interesting take on therapy, Doc," he said. "Is this a Jungian approach?"

"They teach us as therapists to sit close to the door," she said. "In case anything goes wrong with a patient. I don't have this room set up for therapy."

"What makes you think anything is wrong with me?" he asked.

"I know what you are."

"What am I?"

"A werewolf," she said. She picked the gun up, then angled the monitor on the desk so they could both see it. She tapped a couple of keys, and their previous conversation began to play from the speakers.

"Stress points," she said, indicating with her gun the peaks parading across screen. "There. There. There—and so on. You matched common werewolf verbal stress points at a level of 98.4%. The average for werewolves is 92%."

"Wow," he grinned. "I'm above average. First time anyone's ever told me that."

She turned off the monitor.

"Who else have you told?" he asked.

"No one," she said. "Not yet."

"Why not?" he asked. "And why—curiosity talking here—do you feel you need to point a gun at me when it's past full moon and broad daylight?"

"Because that doesn't seem as crucial as it used to be, given what's happened the last two days," she said, "and because I gather that you're plenty dangerous in your human form."

"Never liked that word," he said. "Form. Like it's some meat costume we wear twenty-five days out of the lunar cycle. You didn't say why you didn't tell the others."

"I wanted to know why you're here," she said. "I might be able to help you."

"Why would you?"

"Trust me."

"Says the lady with the gun in her hand. I came here to tell you two things, Doc. You can keep pointing the gun at me if you like, I don't care."

"You'd care if I pulled the trigger."

"No question, ma'am," he said, "but you're not a murderer. In fact, you might be the one genuine healer in this loony bin, which is why I came to you."

"Healer," she said. "No one's ever called me that before."

"Here's the first thing," he said. "Sanchez tried to kill himself last night."

"What?" she exclaimed. "Why?"

"I'm no shrink, but the man is seriously depressed," he said. "In love with Kudowski, and knows he ain't getting anywhere. He needs help and he doesn't want to be helped. So, you seem like the logical person to go to."

"How did you know he tried to commit suicide?" she asked.

"Because I stopped him," he said. "Long story, not really mine to tell—but do something, okay?"

"Poor Juan," she said. "Yes, certainly. I'll do what I can—and the second thing?"

Sam hesitated. "Those archetypes that you talked about," he said. "Do they ever pop up in dreams about things that really happened?"

"Yes," she said. "Quite frequently, in fact. You revisit your past in your dreams and interpret it by seeing people or things as archetypes. You can gain new insights into how those events shaped you. Did that happen to you?"

"Yes," he said. "I saw the Winged Wolf. I've never seen her before."

"Tell me," she said.

He recounted the two fragments of the dream of his last mission under Pastore. Halfway through, she held up one hand, then replaced the Sig Sauer in the desk drawer and closed it.

"Go on," she said.

When he was done, she had her eyes closed, and her face was serene.

"Did you ever consider that Pastore was an archetype?" she asked.

"Not until now," he said. "That opens a whole big can of worms. But, what does the Winged Wolf mean? She was never in that dream before. Then, you tell me about her, and I get her twice."

"She appeared above that man named Tom," she said. "What happened to Tom?"

"He was killed on that mission," he said. "Trying to save Padilla. I was shot trying to save him."

"How do you feel about being unable to save him?" she asked.

"He—"

Sam suddenly felt his throat constrict. Buenaventura poured water into a paper cup and slid it to him. He drank it gratefully.

"He was my best friend," he choked out, "and I couldn't, I couldn't—"

"You couldn't save him," she said. "Just like your childhood friend Billy, when he was killed by that werewolf. Was that story true?"

"Yes," he said, not wanting to continue.

"Only, that was when you were attacked, wasn't it?" she asked. "When you were changed?"

"Yes," he whispered, "and I did hunt down the bastard that did it. He could have changed me without hurting Billy. He didn't have to kill him."

"Very powerful, killing the wolf who made you," she said, "and then to be commanded by another one. If this was therapy, that would be a very profitable path to pursue. But, I'm interested in the Winged Wolf, Sam. What was she doing when you saw her the second time?"

"Flying in front of the chopper," he said. "Just before it was hit by the SAM—"

"The what?" she asked, staring at him.

"The surface-to-air missile," he said. "SAM for short."

"Something with your name destroyed the chopper," she said, "and the Winged Wolf was there."

"What does that mean? What was she doing? Was she a Gatekeeper?"

"You tell me."

"Come on, I'm new at this archetype shit. Give me a clue, here."

"What was the chopper doing?"

"It was coming to take us home."

"Where is home?"

The chopper, bursting into flames, fragments falling beneath the moon.

"Where is home, Sam?" she repeated.

"I don't know," he whispered. "I can't get to it. I can't find it."

"Where is—"

Boss! Boss! Boss!

An overlap of cries.

What? he called.

"What's wrong?" she began, then they heard the alarms going off.

"That's down the hall," she began, but Sam was already up and running.

The dogs were collected by the door to Alison's ward. Coleridge was racing towards it from the opposite end.

"Coming from in there!" he shouted, pointing.

They burst through the door, then pulled up.

A werewolf was inside the sealed enclosure, hurling itself at the Plexiglas door over and over, each crash leaving a smear of blood on the smooth, clear surface.

CHAPTER 15

"**G**ET ME OUT OF HERE!" screamed Myers, slamming into the door. "I can't breathe. I can't run. Turn down those fucking lights!"

"Can you dim them?" asked Sam. "She's got night vision—they're blinding her."

"Yeah, sure," said Coleridge, hitting a switch.

The room darkened. McKenna, Kudowski, and Buenaventura crowded in.

"My God," breathed Kudowski—then she started sneezing. "Jesus Christ, Sam!"

"Dogs, out!" he ordered.

But we want to—began Arnie.

Out now! yelled Sam.

The dogs retreated to the atrium.

"I am not emotionally equipped for changing like this," howled Myers, storming around her enclosure and pounding her fists into the walls. "It's fucking daylight! I can't take it."

"We need Bolton," said McKenna. "Tell him to come armed."

"No," said Sam.

"What? Did you just contradict me in my lab?" sputtered McKenna.

"This is my turf," said Sam. "I'm the werewolf hunter, remember?"

"We don't need her hunted," said McKenna. "She's already here."

"She's not a threat," said Sam.

Myers hit the wall again. The Plexiglas cracked. The scientists immediately backed out of the room, leaving Sam and Coleridge.

222

"I'm inclined to disagree with you on that," said McKenna.

Sam stepped up to the enclosure.

"Corporal Myers!" he shouted. "You will stand down!"

The werewolf swung to face him, fangs bared.

"Corporal Myers, stand down immediately!" he repeated. "That is an order!"

"You outrank me, asshole?" she growled.

"Master Sergeant, maggot," he said. "Stand down."

She looked ready to charge again. Then, something changed in her eyes, and she stood at attention, her breathing slowing.

"Sir, yessir," she said.

"Get something that will help her sleep," said Sam.

"I'll do it," said Buenaventura.

She went to a cabinet, pulled out a bottle, and measured a dose into a paper cup. Then, she looked at Myers and doubled the dose. She opened the small airlock and placed it on the shelf inside.

"Drink this," she said as she sealed the airlock. "Then I suggest you get in that bed quickly, or you're going to bang your head on the floor when it kicks in."

"Wouldn't mind washing it down with some bourbon," muttered Myers as she grabbed the cup. She raised it in Sam's direction. "Fuck the Marines."

"Fuck the Marines," he echoed.

She tossed it back, then sat on the bed.

"Should I count back from—" she started, then her eyes rolled up and she fell back, her breathing slow but even.

"I want blood samples," McKenna said to Sanchez. "Now."

"Yes, sir," said Sanchez. "I'll need to get a suit on."

He left.

"When did it happen?" asked McKenna.

"Can't be more than ten minutes ago," said Coleridge. "I heard the alarm go off, and she was in there woofing away."

McKenna turned to Sam. "How did you know she would respond like that?" he asked.

"Army training's not very different from dog training," said Sam. "It's embedded pretty deep—and I'm the bigger dog as far as she's concerned."

"That was good thinking," said McKenna. "All right, everyone. Get back to work. I want to know why this is happening."

Burton appeared in the doorway, her eyes widening as she saw Myers. "Wow. It's one thing to hear about it, but something else to see it. A werewolf in daylight."

"Took you long enough," said Sanchez, reappearing in his biohazard suit. "Help me with the helmet."

"Sure, Juan," she said. "Oh, Doctor McKenna. I found a possible EM spike in Charleston. I'm waiting on some local readings."

"Great, Valerie," replied McKenna wearily. "Let's all keep doing everything. Maybe we'll figure this one out before all hell breaks loose."

He left.

Sanchez started opening the airlock. Sam tapped him on the shoulder.

"Test her food," said Sam, pointing to the partially eaten meal on a tray beside her bed.

"Why?"

"I can have theories, too," he said.

"A dietary trigger? Sounds unlikely. All werewolves eat."

"Yes, they do," said Sam.

Sanchez shrugged and went into the chamber.

Sam rejoined the dogs in the atrium.

Well? asked Arnie.

You could hear everything?

Yup. Sure wish we could have seen them. We can't read them well when they're all panicky, especially with that werewolf howling away. What's up with the food? Ms. Whitfield made that meal, didn't she?

Yes, said Sam.

And she was on her day off when that last werewolf changed, said Otto.

Right, said Sam. *What did you guys make of her?*

We really haven't tried to read her, said Olga. *I guess we'd better start.*

Sam? said Otto.

Yes?

You have to eat while you're here. What if she goes after you?

She doesn't know I'm a werewolf yet. Although, Buenaventura figured it out.

I thought she might, said Otto.

What if she and Ms. Whitfield are in this together? asked Nan.

I trust Doctor Buenaventura, said Sam. *For now.*

The forensics techs from GBI painstakingly went over the warehouse, taking prints, sampling every location where the brush of a finger might have left traces of usable DNA.

Inside the office, Cole scanned through records, then entered data into her cell. Around ten fifteen, she stopped. She compared the two screens, then ran outside to find Boudreau.

"Got something," she said. "Come back in."

He went in with her. She pointed at the screen.

"Shipping manifests," she said. "There seems to be enough of a legitimate operation going to provide cover."

"So?"

"So, all of these customers get stuff FedExed from here—except this one." She pointed to an address that popped up with regularity.

"This one gets delivery straight from the airport," she said. "Bypassing this place. And, he buys substantially more seed than the others. All wolfsbane."

"Does he have a name?"

"Clarence Taylor—and here's the beautiful part. He lives an hour away."

"You pull up his info from DMV?"

"Yessir. Picture's five, six years old, but here he is."

She showed him her cell. The DMV picture showed a stocky man with graying hair.

"Just turned fifty-three last month," said Boudreau. "Assuming he made it to last month. Six three, according to this. Let's show him to our friendly law student, see if he recognizes him."

Fisher was behind his desk, going over a law book with a hi-lighter.

"Hey, Sheriff," he said. "Hey, pretty officer. How goes the search?"

"Seen this guy before?" she asked, handing him the cell.

"That's Manny Bogart," he said. "Only I guess it isn't. That his real name?"

"Who knows?" said Boudreau. "Thanks, son. We'll be out of your hair soon. Good luck with school."

"You want my number?" asked Fisher.

"Don't expect we'll be needing it," said Boudreau.

"Wasn't asking you," said Fisher, looking at Cole.

"Oh," said Cole, blushing. "Yeah, sure."

"Outside in two minutes, Officer Cole," beamed Boudreau. "You're still on this case."

He stepped outside and called Oliveras.

"Hey, Doc," he said. "Could our mystery fourth vic be six foot three?"

"Let me check," she said. "Well, there's some give or take due to dismemberment, but based on the length of the bones in his legs, that would seem about right. You have a lead?"

"We do. We may have some DNA for a match by the end of the day if we're lucky. We're gonna grab one of the GBI techs to come along."

"I'll be here, Sheriff. Good luck."

He disconnected, then hollered, "Cole! Flirtation time is over. Come out here and be a police officer."

Sam was walking with Olga near the gardens when Floyd came around on patrol with Tito. He waved.

Sam nodded back, then held up his hand. "Wait a second," he called. "Is Tito limping?"

"Is he?" asked Floyd. "I didn't notice."

"Let me take a looksee," said Sam, coming over with Olga.

Hey, beautiful, said Tito. *Why does he think I'm limping? I'm fine.*

Want to see a trick? asked Olga as Sam knelt by the dog and took one of his forepaws gently in his hands.

Sure, said Tito.

Speak, Sam, said Olga.

How you doing, Tito? said Sam.

What the hell? exclaimed Tito. *Did you just talk to me? In my language?*

Yup, said Sam.

Pretty cool, isn't it? said Olga.

You were the voice I heard when they brought the werewolf in, said Tito, amazed.

That's right, said Sam. *I want to ask you some questions about that. Give me your other paw while we're talking.*

Tito put his paw down and handed the other one to Sam.

"I'll be damned," said Floyd. "How'd you get him to do that without asking?"

"Hand signal," said Sam. "He's obviously had training like what I do."

Yesterday, you said you hadn't seen one of those in a while. What were you talking about?

Werewolves, said Tito. *Werewolves being brought in like that in those funny-looking suits.*

But they've had werewolves here every full moon for testing, haven't they?

Yeah, but those walked through the front door like regular people, said Tito. *The others came in this unmarked van, usually in those suits, either strapped into gurneys or handcuffed.*

Was Pastore the one bringing them? asked Sam.

No, said Tito. *It was two guys wearing black most of the time. Always at night. It stopped about six, seven months ago.*

Who would meet them? asked Sam.

No one outside, said Tito. *They'd take them up the ramp straight into the building, then come back with an empty gurney a few minutes later.*

But Bolton knew.

I guess so. They came through Security. He never stopped them or searched the vans.

"Hey, if you don't see anything, I gotta schedule to keep," said Floyd.

"I'm not finding anything," said Sam, "but keep an eye on him. Your boss might've done some damage when he whupped him the other day."

"Roger that," said Floyd.

One more thing, said Sam as he released Tito. *Did those werewolves ever come out again?*

No, said Tito. *Not once. Hey, can I tell the others you speak dog?*

Don't see why not, said Sam. *Thanks.*

Thank you! said Tito. *This is a first for me.*

He practically dragged Floyd away.

What do you think, Boss? asked Olga.

I think Alison is in trouble, said Sam.

I think we all are, said Olga. *And it strikes me that a place that's hard to get into is also hard to get out of.*

Come here, said Sam.

Why?

I need to reach Pastore, and I can't use the phone if it goes through Security.

She came up and sat next to him.

"They've been smuggling in werewolves for experiments," he said into her collar, hoping Pastore's bug was transmitting. "Dead of night in an unmarked van. Stopped around December. That date ring a bell, Joe? Tell me you weren't in with the Bogey Man. Someone here was, and it was someone with enough juice to get everything through Security. I've got a pretty good guess as to who. All I need is the why. You better come back, Joe—and bring some firepower with you."

I hope that got through, said Olga.

Me too, said Sam.

Tennant played the message back twice, sitting at Sam's desk. Then, he got up and opened the door to the walk-in refrigerator.

"Sounds like Sam is finally making progress," he said. "Do you want me to send him a reply?"

Pastore opened his right eye a crack. The left was encrusted in blood. "Fuck you," he whispered hoarsely.

Tennant walked over to face him. Pastore was dangling from one of the meat hooks, suspended by the cuffs binding his hands.

"Gotta hand it to you, Colonel," said Tennant. "You're a tough guy even when you're not a werewolf."

He looked around at the sides of beef that were waiting to be fed to the dogs, and laughed suddenly. "You know what this reminds me of?" he asked.

Pastore said nothing.

"I'll tell you anyway," said Tennant. "Remember that movie, *Rocky?* That scene in the meat locker, with him pounding away while he was training?"

He started bouncing around on the balls of his feet, jabbing at the air. Then, he swung at one of the sides of beef, landing the blow with a resounding smack.

"Ow," he said, rubbing his wrist. "Should've taped up first. That's what I get for beating my meat, right? Let's try this instead."

He spun and kicked. Pastore grunted as Tennant drove his boot into his ribcage.

"Did you hear that?" crowed Tennant. "Had to be a rib cracking. Let's see if I'm right—unless you want to give me those names first. No? Oh, well."

He poked at the spot. Pastore gasped, but said nothing.

"Well, this clearly isn't working," said Tennant, "but it is fun. I'm getting a little chilly in here. What I could use is a nice cup of tea, and maybe a woman for the bodily warmth. That Mona is pretty hot. Think I'll invite her to join me in that cup of tea. Then, I'll put her in here, and we can all have some conversation. Or, more fun."

He walked out, then turned.

"Now you stay in there and think about what you did," he said sternly.

He slammed the door shut.

It was pitch black. Pastore closed his one good eye.

Sam walked back inside and headed towards the lab that contained Alison.

What are you going to do? asked Olga.

Depends, said Sam. *I want to talk to her. If she's changed back, I might try and spring her.*

How are you going to do that? asked Olga. *You're outnumbered, even with us.*

She's Army, said Sam. *And she was one of Pastore's team. Two of us working together might—*

He stopped.

They were at the door to Alison's isolation chamber.

It was empty.

Mona's phone chirped.

"Yes?" she answered.

"It's Larry Tennant. If you're serious about what we talked about, I've got someone here who has a lead on that info on that Cheller guy."

"You're at Sam's?"

"Yes, ma'am. Can you come over now?"

Mona gnawed on her lip, thinking.

"Mona, he's not gonna be around for very long," said Tennant. "I had to pull a few strings to get him here, and he may not be too receptive if you blow him off."

"All right," said Mona. "My lunch break's at noon. I'll be there at quarter after."

She hung up, then called Kerry.

"Hey, it's Mona," she said. "I might have something for you, might not. Want to tag along?"

Dogs! Here! called Sam.

228

The rest of the team came pouring through the door.

Alison's gone, he said.

Escaped? asked Arnie.

There's a pissed off werewolf on the loose, said Nan. *Not good.*

I don't think she escaped, said Sam. *She was under sedation, and I don't see any damage to the door. Someone let her out. Or took her. Can you guys pick up her scent?*

No, and not likely to, said Arnie, his nose up and sniffing.

Why not?

Her biohazard suit's gone, too. If she was wearing that, we won't be able to track her.

"Shit," muttered Sam. "Who could have done this? Who else was in here?"

Everybody, said Olga. *I'm picking up all the scientists, Coleridge, Bolton—*

Bolton, said Sam. *I'm gonna have to alert him—and McKenna.*

He looked around. The security button was by the door. He hit it, and alarms began going off.

"What's going on?" yelled Sanchez, poking his head out from his lab.

"The werewolf got out," called Sam.

McKenna and Kudowski were there next, then Bolton and Priscilla came tearing into the hall, guns drawn.

"Situation?" asked Bolton.

"Empty cage," said Sam.

Bolton pulled out his walkie-talkie. "Code one!" he shouted into it. "Everyone stay loose, weapons out. Let the dogs out. Curt, you keep on those monitors."

"She may not be dangerous," said Sam.

"Then why did she break out?" retorted Bolton. "Ladies and gentlemen, please go to your labs and stay there until we've captured her."

"How do we know she isn't waiting for us in our labs?" protested Sanchez.

"Priscilla, go with them. Do a room check on each."

"Right," said Priscilla. "This way."

"I can help with the search," offered Sam.

"Thanks, but this is our job," said Bolton. "Need me to check your room first?"

"I've got my team," said Sam. "I'll be fine."

"Right," said Bolton. "Get going."

Sam walked into the rotunda, the team fanning out around him.

I want to find her first, he said. *Any—*

Wait, said Arnie, his nose up. *Olga, you getting this?*

She joined him. *Coming from the elevator?* she asked.

Yeah, that's what I'm picking up.

What? asked Sam.

Remember those werewolf sweat samples Sanchez gave you? asked Arnie.

What about them?

Olga and I checked them out. Werewolves do have a different scent when they're human. We're picking up something from the elevator. And, no, it isn't yours.

Sam looked around. There was no one in the rotunda.

Arnie, Olga—with me, he said. *The rest of you scatter, keep your ears open. Call me if you get anything, but don't make any moves on your own.*

He went into the elevator with the two dogs, then stopped, listening.

Hear that? he asked.

They listened with him.

It's that song, said Olga.

Moonglow, said Sam. *Come on.*

He hit the up button. The doors closed.

It's stronger in here, said Olga.

Be ready, said Sam. *Alison may not consider us friendly.*

Um, can you take a werewolf down in your human form? asked Arnie.

Probably not, said Sam. *That's why I'm sending you in first.*

Great, said Arnie.

That's what you get for being the alpha, said Olga.

The doors opened. Arnie charged through, barking furiously. Then, he skidded to a halt.

Oh, no, he said.

Valerie was slumped over her desk, eyes open and still. Deep claw marks started at the side of her neck and continued through the back of her shirt, slicing so far into her body that the spine was exposed. The blood from her jugular had sprayed the monitors on the initial attack, then pooled on the desk by her. It was still dripping slowly onto the floor.

Sam felt for a pulse, though he knew he would find none. The speakers kept playing *Moonglow,* a big band arrangement.

"Sorry, Doc," he said. "I would've liked another dance."

He closed her eyes and turned off the music.

Why her? he asked. *Why did Alison need to kill her of all of them?*

She didn't, said Arnie.

What?

The only werewolf who's been up here recently is you, said Arnie.

He's right, Boss, said Olga. *I'm not picking up any other werewolves. Not even Pastore's been up here.*

Someone killed her and made it look like a werewolf did it, said Sam. *Which is why they let Alison out.*

They can't prove she did it, said Olga.

This is not the kind of place where they worry about proof, said Sam. *Once they find out about this, they won't bother trying to capture her. They'll just shoot her down—*

Like a rabid dog, said Arnie. *But why kill the Moonlady? What did she ever do?*

She must have found out something, said Sam. *Something that made her dangerous. What was it she said when she came down?*

"I found a possible EM spike in Charleston," said Olga. *We could hear her from the hall. Then, McKenna told her to keep looking into it.*

An EM spike, repeated Sam, thinking. Then, he looked at the elevator. *Wrong button.*

What do you mean? asked Arnie.

Olga, come here, said Sam. He knelt down and spoke into her collar. "Burton's been killed. Alison's been kidnapped. I think I got the why figured out, but I need one more bit of proof. All hell is breaking loose, Joe. Send everyone you've got, and do it now."

He stood.

Right, he said. *I need to get at Kudowski's computer.*

But she's in her lab, said Olga. *Bolton told her to stay there until they catch Alison.*

Then we need to get her out of there, said Sam.

Oh, I know a way, said Arnie.

Mona pulled up short of Sam's warehouse and killed the engine.

"Why are we stopping here?" asked Kerry. "Aren't we going in?"

"We aren't going in," said Mona. "I am."

"Why?" asked Kerry.

Then she gave a start as Mona pulled her gun out of her handbag and checked the safety.

"I don't trust this man," said Mona. "I don't know if he's a real threat, or just trying to get into my pants, but either way, I don't trust him. So, I'm going first. Once I'm sure it's safe, I will call you, and you can come in."

"What if it isn't safe?" asked Kerry.

"If you don't hear from me within eight minutes, you call 911 and get the hell out of here."

"Jesus Christ—who is this guy?"

"I'm not sure," said Mona. "That's why you're staying here."

She got out of the car.

Kerry slid over to the driver's seat. "I can't thank you enough for doing this for me," she said.

"I'm not doing this for you," said Mona.

Tennant went out to the main room when he heard Mona coming in.

"Hi," he said. "Thanks for coming now. My friend has to be somewhere later."

"Why are the dogs all barking like that?" she asked as she walked toward him.

"Guess they're glad to see you," he said. "First time you've been here since Sam left."

"They've seen me plenty."

"And I bet they've seen plenty of you a few times," he leered.

She stopped. "I'm still armed," she said. "Are you going to behave yourself?"

"Yes'm," he said, bowing his head contritely. "Sorry."

"I think this is what you've been looking for," she said, pulling a small, silvered disk from an envelope in her bag.

"Fantastic," he said, taking it. "Come on in to the office."

Trap! Trap! the dogs were crying.

But she couldn't understand—not until the Taser hit her in the back and sent her convulsing onto the office floor. Then, she understood everything, but it was too late.

He knelt by her and cuffed her hands behind her back, then checked his watch. "Seven minutes until your wingman makes the call—I'll be back in six. Yes, I bugged your car."

Then he slipped out the back.

Kerry sat in the driver's seat, glancing back and forth between the front door of the shop and her cellphone, watching the seconds count down. She could hear the dogs barking from inside the warehouse.

This was a wild goose chase, she thought. *Wouldn't be the first time some asshole claimed he knew something about Tom and tried to get something for it.* Yet, she kept meeting them, hoping against hope that she would find out how he really died. She prayed it wasn't at the hands of the Army. She always thought that they might turn on a werewolf, even if he was one of their own.

She looked at the timer again. Two minutes to go. She looked at the shop, then back at the cell, willing it to ring.

She would have been better off keeping an eye on the rear view mirror. If she had, she might have stopped Tennant from plunging the needle into her neck.

Kudowski sat at her desk, typing at her computer, trying not to let herself be distracted. Stay here until the werewolf was caught. Hopefully caught and killed. Then, it would be safe again.

She tapped away at the keyboard. The taps seemed to echo oddly. She stopped. The tapping continued. It wasn't an echo. She looked out at the door, but saw nothing. She shrugged and resumed her typing.

Her nose was starting to run. She swiped at it with a tissue, and tried to continue with her work, but now her eyes were itching at well.

"What the hell?" she muttered.

A quiet "woof" came from the side of her chair. She spun to see Arnie looking up at her.

"Go away!" she commanded him.

He wagged his tail.

"I said—" she began.

He jumped into her lap, stood on his hind legs, and licked her mouth.

"Fuck!" she spluttered, kicking back her chair and dislodging him.

Which meant touching him. With both hands.

She could feel her nose closing up, her throat constricting. She ran into the hallway.

Olga was there, waiting for her. They looked at each other for an instant. Then, Olga came at her, teeth bared, growling. Arnie skittered into the hall behind the wolfhound and barked.

Kudowski took off down the hall and through the rotunda, the hounds in hot pursuit. She dashed into the dorm wing and headed to her room. She never saw Sam, who was waiting just outside the entrance to the hallway. He slipped into her office, sat at her computer, and began to search through her files.

Tennant dumped Kerry's inert body on the floor, cuffed her, then picked up Mona's handbag and removed the Glock.

"You've been pointing this at me way too much, you know that?" he said, putting it on the desk.

He reached down and hauled her to her feet. Her breath was coming in short bursts.

"Gonna have to give you some time to settle down before we talk," he said. "Fifty thousand volts will have that effect. And, I have to recharge that sucker before I can use it on you again."

"Wha, wha," she gasped.

"Easy, girl," he said. "You'll be talking soon enough, believe me. Let us treasure our remaining time together. Now, I want you to meet the man I was telling you about. Funny thing is, he really could tell you what happened to Cheller, so I wasn't lying about that."

He shoved her over to the door to the walk-in refrigerator and opened it.

She would have screamed if she could have drawn breath. A man hung from one of the meat hooks, his shirt in shreds, his face and torso covered with blood and dark, ugly bruises.

Tennant pushed Mona into the locker. She stumbled and crashed into the man, unable to use her hands to catch herself. Then, her momentum toppled her over. She lay on her side, looking at the bloody man, her heart pounding like it was going to explode.

Tennant flicked the light switch on, then disappeared and returned with Kerry. He put her next to Mona.

"You folks can catch up for a few minutes," he said. "Wouldn't recommend talking overmuch, though. You'll use up the air a lot quicker. I'll be back."

He closed the door.

The bloody man forced open one eye and looked at her. "Hey," he said. "You wouldn't happen to have a cup of coffee on you, would you?"

"No," she gasped, starting to shiver uncontrollably on the cold concrete floor.

"That's too bad," he said. "I'd kill for something hot right now."

He found them. The experiments, the data, the results.

The subjects.

No names: just ID numbers, pictures, and videos. He rummaged through her desk, looking for a way to download it all.

He could hear Arnie and Olga gleefully whimpering outside Kudowski's room, keeping her trapped there. Nan and Bert were prowling through the other wing, searching for signs of Alison. Otto sat by the entrance to the rotunda, listening for the guard dogs as they searched for the missing werewolf.

They won't find her, thought Sam—and he suddenly realized why that was, and where she would be.

There was no time to wait for Pastore and his too distant back-up. If Sam was going to save Alison, he was going to have to do it on his own—no. With his team. One unarmed man and five dogs against—

Against them all, possibly.

He was scared. His heart raced, his mouth was dry, his palms were sweaty. He was in over his head—had been from the start.

Suck it up, Lehrmann, he thought to himself. *You've been outnumbered before and survived.*

But he couldn't get his breathing under control. His chest felt tight. He was—

No.

"No, no, no!" he shouted as he felt that all too familiar rippling of the muscles around his rib cage.

The change caught him unprepared. He grabbed at his belt and tore it off, then fumbled with his bootlaces as the claws forced their way through his fingers and toes. The boots held against them, nearly crushing his feet as they expanded, the pain coursing up through his legs. He sliced through the leather sides with his claws, gouging his ankles in the act, then ripped off the boots, howling in agony, rolling on the floor as his clothes fell in shreds around him.

"Well, lookie here," came a voice from the door.

He squinted in that direction, his eyes still blurred by the sunlight.

Coleridge stood in the doorway, incongruously pointing what looked like an oversized blow dryer at him. Only, there was no air coming out.

"We have found ourselves a werewolf, Mister Bolton," said Coleridge. "Take care of it, won't you?"

"My pleasure," said Bolton, stepping in front of him.

He raised his gun, pointed it at Sam, and fired.

CHAPTER 16

THE GBI TECH'S NAME WAS Goldberg. Just Goldberg, he had said, and he sat sullenly in the back seat, refusing all of Wilkins' attempts at conversation. Boudreau sat in the front seat, trying to catnap while Cole drove.

Half an hour into the drive, his cell went off. He answered, listened, and disconnected.

"Four sets of DNA at the warehouse," he said. "Four matches on our dead boys. That was fast. Good work."

"Thanks," muttered Goldberg. "So you can take me back now?"

"We still have to see if this Taylor feller is a match for our unknown vic," said Boudreau. "Just because the clerk ID's him as Bogart doesn't mean he's the source of the DNA."

"Your Bogart's a bogey," said Goldberg.

"Guess he is," chuckled Boudreau, "and if you add in his first name, that would make him the Bogey Manny. Shoot, I wonder if he picked that name to sound like Bogey Man."

"That would be very creepy, sir," said Cole.

"Well, if we're right, he ain't gonna be creeping no more," said Boudreau. "Problem is, even knowing who he is doesn't tell us why he got himself and his boys killed—or why they had all that surveillance equipment."

"You're figuring on him being the brains of this particular outfit?" asked Cole.

"That I am," said Boudreau. "Profiles on these other fellers sound like they're hired guns. Maybe when we learn more about what Mister Taylor was up to, we'll find out who wanted him dead. Got a feeling it wasn't a deranged floral enthusiast."

Taylor owned a large spread up in the hill country west of Atlanta, isolated from his nearest neighbors by stretches of woods. Cole almost missed the turnoff. There was no mailbox or sign to mark it, just a narrow gravel road.

"Guess he doesn't get many trick-or-treaters," commented Boudreau, "but someone's kept the road clear. Did you happen to look up whether anyone else lives there?"

"Only other name listed was a John Weatherby," said Cole. "Seems to be in Taylor's employment."

"Housekeeper, caretaker, maybe," speculated Boudreau. "Here we are. Not the biggest place."

It was a modest split-level house, built sometime in the Fifties, he guessed. It had aluminum siding, colored robin egg blue, and a newly shingled roof.

"Look out back," said Wilkins.

"Nice gardens," said Cole. "And look at all the greenhouses."

"Man likes to take his work home with him," said Boudreau. "Let's ring the bell. There's definitely someone home. I saw a curtain twitch."

Cole pulled up to the front, and they got out. Boudreau rang the bell.

The door opened immediately. A grizzled man in a red T-shirt and faded green overalls looked out at him.

"How do, sir," said Boudreau. "I'm Sheriff Boudreau, Chattooga County Police. These are Officers Cole and Wilkins, and Mister Goldberg from the GBI."

"What do you want?" asked the man.

"Know this feller?" asked Boudreau as Cole held up her phone with the image of Taylor on it.

"That's Mister Taylor," said the man.

"Would that make you John Weatherby?"

"Yep."

"Is Mister Taylor at home?"

"Nope."

"When's the last time he was at home?"

"Why?" asked Weatherby.

"Now, Mister Weatherby," said Boudreau. "You see the badge? You see the uniform? You see the gun? And do you especially see the hat? I am very proud of this hat. They only let the sheriff wear a hat like this. It is meant to convey authority. I am investigating a murder case, Mister Weatherby, so if I am asking you a question, I would expect you to do me the courtesy of respecting the hat by answering me, not asking more questions. When was the last time you saw or heard from Mister Taylor?"

Weatherby was silent.

"I'm going to tell you, then," said Boudreau. "It was just before Christmas.

Am I right?"

"Could be," said Weatherby.

"Ever concern you that he was gone so long without communicating?"

"Don't get paid to be concerned," said Weatherby.

"What do you get paid for?"

"Take care of the house, take care of the grounds."

"And a lovely job you do, I must say," said Boudreau. "Growing flowers, are you?"

"Yep. Want to pick some?"

Boudreau stopped smiling for the first time since he arrived.

"Given that picking one of those posies could poison me, I think not," he said in an icy tone that Wilkins and Cole had never heard him use before. "Now, before I arrest you for attempted murder of a police officer, how about you let us inside?"

"You got a warrant?" asked Weatherby.

"I am investigating your boss, not you," said Boudreau. "We think he's currently in pieces on a slab in our morgue. We want to verify that. I don't need a warrant to invade the privacy of a dead man."

"Come in," said Weatherby reluctantly, opening the door wider. "Wipe your feet first."

There was an entry hall, and carpeted steps going up to the right. A door on the left was open to a den where a television was tuned to a soap opera.

"Take Officer Wilkins and Mister Goldberg to your employer's bedroom," said Boudreau. "We need a hairbrush or a toothbrush that hasn't been touched in a while. Cole, you come with me."

Weatherby led the two men upstairs.

Boudreau pulled out a pair of latex gloves and put them on. Cole followed his lead.

"You're on thin ice, legally," she said.

"I am no longer giving a shit," he replied. "Man must have an office. Let's find it."

They searched the den, then found a room that looked to be Weatherby's, which they skipped. Then, they found a door leading downstairs. They found a laundry room, the hot water tanks, a cellar—and a locked door.

"Why would a man lock a door in his own house?" asked Boudreau.

"Because—"

"It was a rhetorical question, Officer Cole," said Boudreau. "Go get the key from Weatherby."

She was back in a minute. "They found some usable hairs," she reported. "Goldberg is testing them now. I asked Weatherby what's in here. He said he was never allowed in to look."

She opened the door. "Sweet Jesus," she said.

There was a desk, holding a computer and stacks of files and photographs. A trio of overstuffed file cabinets was to the left. But, what had drawn their attention was the far wall, which was covered with blown-up photographs, distributed in pairs. The left ones were all of people, taken with telephoto lenses, each going about some normal activity.

The ones on the right were of werewolves. Dead ones, by the looks of it.

"This has to be some kind of sick joke," said Cole as they stepped in. "Why would he hang photos of some fake fantasy stuff like this?"

"Look at that," he said, pointing to a large jar on one of the cabinets.

It contained a large, hairy paw, with claws that looked razor-sharp.

"Bear?" she asked.

"Doesn't look like one," he said. "Five digits. Opposable thumb. That would make it a primate."

"Gorilla?" she asked.

"Got me there," he said. "I'm no expert, but I don't think gorillas have claws like that."

He went to inspect the photographs. "They each have a name and a date below them: Terry McKenzie, December 23, 2004; George Cantrell, December 21, 2008; Angela Shreve, December—"

He stopped.

"Angela Shreve," he repeated. "I know that name. Victim of aconite poisoning. Oliveras found the case. She went missing four years ago, turned up short time later, body in advanced state of decomposition, one hand chopped off."

They looked again at the hand in the jar.

"But she was human," said Cole. "Wasn't she? Sir, wasn't she human? What the hell is going on here?"

"Start running those names," ordered Boudreau. "Every last one of them. I think we may have found ourselves a serial killer."

He turned to inspect the desk, and found his next shock of the day.

On top of it, in front of the computer's keyboard, was a photograph of Sam Lehrmann, coming out of his warehouse.

He was underwater, but driving a van.

"You're going too fast," said his passenger.

"Don't have much time," said Sam.

"True," said the passenger, "but you should have asked for directions first. I don't think you know where you're going."

"How would you know?" said Sam, looking over at him. "You ain't got any eyes."

"And whose fault is that?" asked the man.

"Yours. Or your boss," said Sam. "I can't help it if you screwed up."

"*Kicking a man when he's dead,*" said the man. "*Nice. You going back to the surface?*"

"*That's my plan.*"

"*Plans are for people with time,*" said the passenger. "*You've got none.*"

"*Sam!*" called a woman.

"*Friend of yours?*" asked the man.

"*Not sure who it is,*" said Sam.

"*Better not let Mona find out you got something on the side,*" said the man.

"*Sam!*" she yelled louder.

"*She sounds angry,*" said the man. "*You may want to lay low.*"

"*Hell, one more woman pissed off at me ain't gonna make much difference in my life,*" said Sam.

"Master Sergeant Lehrmann, will you please wake the fuck up?" screamed the woman.

He opened his eyes. He saw bars.

He was in a cage. And, he was still a werewolf.

"Myers, that you?" he croaked.

"Sir, yessir, and I am reporting that we are in deep shit, sir, and I would respectfully request that you do something about it immediately, if not sooner, sir."

He rolled over and pulled himself to his feet. "You're naked," he observed groggily, blinking to get his eyes adjusted.

"Sir, yessir, I am naked again and in yet another cage," she said. "Seems to be an occupational hazard of late."

"Where are we?"

"Not really sure," she said. "Took that sedative, woke up here, and now I'm back to human again. Then, they rolled you in on a gurney. That tech guy and the security guy. They called you Sam. I should have known you were one of us—you were with Pastore in the Army, weren't you?"

"Once upon a time," said Sam.

"Can you get through that lock?"

He gripped the bars and pushed. Then, he kicked at the lock.

"Negative," he said. "Guess we ain't the first werewolves to be kept in here."

He looked around, shading his eyes from the ceiling lights. There were several more cages besides the two holding him and Alison. On the other side of the room were several work stations littered with circuit boards, tools, and monitors.

"Coleridge's workshop," he said. "This must be where they did the experiments."

"What experiments?" she asked.

"He's the gadget guy," he said. "He figured out how to change us when the moon isn't full."

"How?"

"That thing over there," he said pointing.

"The thing that looks like a big blow dryer?" she asked.

"It generates an electromagnetic pulse that duplicates the one from the full moon," he said.

"Whoa, whoa, whoa," she said. "The moon generates a pulse? And that's what changes us?"

"That's what the geeks figured out. Only, Coleridge seems to be a few steps ahead of them. I should have known earlier. He was the closest one to you when you changed. And, he was able to go off on his little errands and try that gadget out. You, that guy in Charleston, and those two in North Carolina were all within half a day's driving distance of this place."

"Shit," she said. "What are they gonna do with us now?"

"Nothing good," he said. "It's end game. They got everything they need. Now, they're cleaning house. They already have you set up to take the fall for Burton's death."

"Who?"

"The astrophysicist. She was tracking down the EM pulse in Charleston. They must have been worried she'd trace it when they used the gadget on you here."

"That Black lady? She came down to talk to me about the change last night. Nice lady."

"Yeah," he said. "She was."

"They set me up for killing another Black woman. And I thought I was pissed off before. Why are they keeping us alive?"

"They still want something from us."

"How do you know?"

"Because Coleridge is listening to everything we're saying, aren't you?"

"You're pretty smart for a community college boy," said Coleridge, entering the room.

"Not smart enough to keep from getting caught," said Sam. "I take it you put together one of Doctor Buenaventura's vocal ID devices?"

"Yeah, I did," said Coleridge, patting a small box with a directional mike and a monitor. "Kind of neglected to tell her about it. Handy little gizmo. Fits right into my cleaning cart. I made you from Day One, soldier. Figured with Pastore bringing you in, something was up. Question is: how much did you tell him before we stuck you in here?"

"Bring me your boss," said Sam. "I don't talk to flunkies."

"But I'm talking to one," said Coleridge. "You might even be below the exalted rank of flunky. You're Pastore's bitch."

"You're a real tough guy when there's a cage holding me, aren't you?"

"Oh, I'm not going to be baited into trading fisticuffs with a were-wolf," laughed Coleridge. "Although, I have killed my share, as you may have guessed."

"Strapped down and sedated on tables," said Sam.

"Not all of them were sedated."

"Aren't you the brave one," said Alison. "Say, now that I'm back in human shape, maybe I've got something you could play with. What do you say, fella?"

"Again, nice try," said Coleridge. "You both went for the classics: taunting and sex. Now that we've passed through the preliminaries, it's time for the real thing. How much does Pastore know?"

"Everything," said Sam. "He should be here any second. With reinforcements."

"Oh, somehow I doubt that," said Coleridge.

"And there's our boss," added Sam.

"Who would that be?"

Sam smiled. "I'll talk to your boss," he said. "No one else."

"I'm not sure Doctor McKenna is interested in talking to you," said Coleridge.

"I said your boss, not McKenna," said Sam. "Kudowski."

"Ah, you figured that out," said Coleridge, nodding with approval. "Unfortunately, she is temporarily unavailable, thanks to that little prank you played with your dogs. Could have killed her."

"Yeah, feeling real bad about that."

"Well, you think about how far you want to protect your friends, and then maybe we can make a deal," said Coleridge. "I'll be back."

He left.

"Who—" began Alison.

"Quiet," said Sam.

Where are you guys? he called.

Boss? answered Arnie. *Where the fuck have you been? We've been looking.*

Basement level. Coleridge's workroom.

The wrong button, said Arnie. *Werewolves were on the elevator, but went down, not up.*

And Alison was on a gurney, said Sam. *That's why you couldn't track her from the lab. I need you guys down here.*

Love to help, said Arnie, *but we have problems of our own at the moment.*

He and the rest of the team looked out from the cage that Bolton had set up in front of the complex. Bolton stood fifty feet away along with Floyd, Priscilla, and the five German shepherds.

"We should just shoot them," suggested Floyd. "Some of ours could get hurt doing this."

"Ah, come on," said Bolton. "The boss wants them dead, but she didn't say how. This is gonna be cool. I want to be able to go down there and tell that pussy what my dogs did to his."

He unleashed his pack.

"Dogs, heel," he said, walking forward.

I got Sarge, said Arnie. *You guys can pick whoever you want, but I got Sarge.*

Tito's mine, said Olga.

Jasper, said Nan.

Benny, said Bert. *That leaves you Franz, Otto.*

Let me talk to them first, said Otto.

The others looked at him.

I don't think diplomacy is our best bet right now, said Arnie.

No harm in trying, said the Weimaraner.

He stepped forward.

Dogs, he shouted. *Listen to me!*

"That dog with the spooky eyes is really getting excited," commented Floyd to Priscilla.

Sorry, Otto, said Tito. *We're following orders. Nothing personal.*

Don't you understand who we're with? cried Otto. *Do you truly not know?*

What's he talking about? asked Tito.

Shut up! said Sarge.

The Werewolf Who Speaks To Dogs, said Otto. *Does that mean nothing to you?*

Wait, said Jasper. *I know that story.*

No story, said Otto, his eyes blazing. *Prophecy. Passed down through our lineage for generations. Did you learn nothing from your mothers?*

But if he's that werewolf, said Benny, *then where is the Winged Wolf?*

She lives, said Otto. *I have seen her.*

"Dogs, sit," commanded Bolton.

What's he doing? whispered Bert. *I never heard anything about this.*

*Arnie, does he mean—*started Olga.

Quiet, said Arnie.

If we let the werewolf die, then the Winged Wolf will never live to fly among us, said Otto. *Our day has come, dogs. I call upon you in the name of the Winged Wolf to let us free.*

This, said Sarge, *is bullshit.*

Yeah, pretty much counted on that response, said Arnie, stepping forward. *Okay, boys and girls, time for the Alphas to fight this one out.*

This fight's gonna be shorter than your legs, snarled Sarge as Bolton opened the cage.

"Dogs, kill!" he yelled.

But only Sarge and Arnie charged from their respective packs, the rest of the dogs watching. The shepherd lunged at the dachshund, going for his neck, but Arnie darted under his muzzle and between his legs. He snapped upwards once, and Sarge howled in anguish. The larger dog rolled to one side, then limped away toward the woods at the far end of the compound.

The other shepherds looked at Arnie. He stared them down, then calmly spat a round, bloody mass onto the ground.

Aw, dude, moaned Bert. *That was harsh.*

Guys? said Arnie. *Rescue mission? Right about now would be good.*

Right, said Olga.

The four dogs bounded out of the cage. Olga and Bert hit Bolton full force, knocking him down.

Thank you, said Otto to the shepherds, then Sam's team bolted for the entrance to the building.

"Goddammit!" shouted Bolton at the remaining dogs. "What the hell are you waiting for? Go git 'em!"

But the shepherds sat.

"You two," he hollered at Floyd and Priscilla. "Tell Henry to wake up. We're going hunting."

"Who are you?" asked Mona.

"Name's Pastore," he said. "You're Mona. I know all about you—and I mean all about you. Sorry. I'm in the business of knowing too much about people."

He coughed, and the action sent waves of pain through him. "Unfortunately, I wasn't as thorough in my hiring practices," he said.

"You were Sam's CO," she said.

"I was."

"What does Tennant want from you?"

"Don't want to talk about it," he said. "He's bugged the room, by the way, hoping I might say something to you that I wouldn't to him. It's an old trick."

"What does he want from me?"

"Same thing I wanted," said Pastore. "A disk that Sam has."

"And you thought Sam gave it to me."

"A working theory," said Pastore, "but please don't talk about it now. There's less oxygen with two of us in here, and he may not open that door for a while."

She struggled to her feet. "How long have you been in here?" she asked.

"Ah, got in around two in the morning, tased shortly thereafter, and I don't know what time it is now."

She walked up and pressed her body gently against his. "Does that hurt?" she asked.

"Nicest thing I've felt for a long time," he said. "Dying man's last dream?"

"Keeping you warm," she said. "We're going to survive."

The door opened. Tennant looked in. "Had to see this," he said. "So fucking sweet. Mona, you're gonna get blood all over that nice blouse of yours. Hey, what's on that disk? Looks like gobbledygook to me."

"It's encrypted," she said. "I don't know what it is."

"Nice try," he said. "No way the Bogey Man had an encrypted disk. Tell you what, I'm feeling magnanimous. Tell me where the real disk is, and I'll only kill Pastore."

"What's the appropriate response?" she asked Pastore.

"Fuck you has always worked for me," he said.

"Yeah, fuck you," said Mona.

"What's going on?" moaned Kerry groggily.

"You were drugged," said Pastore.

"You may experience some side effects," said Tennant. "Including nausea, dizziness, and me killing you. I'm going to make a few calls, and then I'll be back. Have an answer ready for me."

He left.

Kerry looked up at Pastore and gasped in horror.

"Worse than it looks," said Pastore.

"No, it isn't," said Mona. "This Kerry Cheller, a friend of mine. Kerry, this is—"

"Captain Pastore," she whispered.

"You recognized me after all this time," he said.

"You were there on the worst day of my life," she whispered.

"What's she talking about?" asked Mona.

"I was the one who told Tom's family about his death," said Pastore. "She was there."

"You told us nothing," she said. "Died in combat, that's it. No body to bury. You're not supposed to leave anyone behind. That's what they always said."

"It doesn't always work out like that," said Pastore.

"You said you'd take care of him when he shipped out," said Kerry. "Not the Army. Specifically you."

"He died for his country," said Pastore.

"Tell me how," said Kerry. "Please. The truth, this time."

Pastore looked at her, then nodded. "There were five of us," he began.

And that was the moment Mona knew they were all going to die.

Tennant came back twenty minutes later. Kerry was crying, Mona sitting next to her, trying to comfort her as much as she could with her hands cuffed.

"You know, Joe's had training to resist torture," he said. "You haven't. You won't last."

He stopped and listened.

"Shit, the brat's here," he said. "Not a sound out of either of you. You try and alert her, I will bring her in here and cut her up in front of you."

He closed the door.

"That's another scare tactic," said Mona. "He wouldn't do that."

"Yes, he would," said Pastore.

The door to Coleridge's workshop opened, and Kudowski stepped in, her eyes puffy and swollen.

"Hey, Doc," said Sam. "You look like hell."

"Sweet talker," she said. "Bet you get all the ladies with that line."

"You were easy enough," he said, "but I guess it wasn't my clever talk that drew you to me. Was it my good looks?"

"You two got busy?" asked Alison.

"Not quite," said Sam.

"You wanted to talk to the boss," she said. "Here I am. So, talk. How much do you know, and how much did you tell Pastore?"

"I've been in contact with him up until your pets took me out," said Sam. "He knows what I know."

"What do you know?"

"That you've been working on isolating individual aspects of the were-wolf genetic structure. You've been experimenting with giving particular traits to humans."

"Bravo, Sam," she said. "Which do you think interested me?"

He shot his fist towards the bars and made them sing, then pulled it back in a split-second.

"Strength, reflexes, speed," he said. "Activated by Coleridge's EM pulse generator. Put them together, and you can make an army that shifts into over-drive at the push of a button. Werewolf killing ability in human form."

"With none of those unattractive side effects," she said. "Very good, Sam."

"I don't know why the Army couldn't provide you with werewolf volunteers, though," he said.

She smiled. "The Army doesn't know," she said. "At least, not our Army."

"You're gonna sell the process to the highest bidder," he said. "I get it. And, you got in bed with the Bogey Man to provide you with test subjects."

"So hard to find volunteers for this kind of thing," she said. "We have to remove large amounts of that cellular structure to process it down to something we could use. A fatal amount, in fact. Yes, Sam. I gave him names of werewolves to track down, and in exchange for bringing them to me, he got a little Christmas bonus."

"A werewolf he could hunt down and kill for himself every year," said Sam.

"Something he had been doing long before he met us," she said, "but he

246

was running out of potential victims, and our resources were better than his. We had the Book of Wolves."

"What did you trade McKenna to get that from him?"

"I've had that old fool wrapped around my little finger ever since grad school," she said. "He's an expert when it comes to getting government funding—not to mention getting Pastore to provide a copy of the Book."

"And you'd give the Bogey Man one name at a time to keep him coming back," said Sam, "by throwing the info over the fence at the blind spot, so there'd be no record of it."

"Now, how did you figure that one out?"

"I saw the blind spot," he said, "and you're the only one in here who jogs. I put it all together. Why did you give him the whole list at the end?"

"We had all the material we needed," she said. "It was his final payoff for keeping quiet about what we were doing. Then, he disappeared, and we never heard from him again. I guess he's out there, hunting your kind down."

"Maybe not," said Sam.

"Ah," she said. "Pastore finally caught up with him."

"No," said Sam. "I did."

"So you really are a hunter," she said. "That's why Pastore sent you in here. Too bad he won't be coming to rescue you."

"What makes you think that?"

"He was intercepted before you did your little stunt with the dogs," she said. "Your info never reached him."

Sally wheeled her bike inside, then stopped. Tennant was standing in front of the training pit.

"Hey, kid," he said. "Thought I told you I didn't need you to come in today."

"Yessir," she said. "But, I was thinking I missed so much that the dogs are gonna be falling behind in their training, and Sam wanted me to—"

"Sam's not here, Sally," said Tennant. "He left me in charge, so you—"

Sally!

She jerked her head in the direction of the voice.

"Who's here?" she asked.

"What do you mean?" asked Tennant. "Nobody's here but me and the dogs."

Sally! Sally!

"I keep hearing someone call my name," she said.

"You've been in the sun too long, kid," he said. "Go on home and rest up."

Sally! Sally! came several voices.

Quiet, all of you. Sally, can you hear me?

Yes, said Sally. Then, her eyes grew wide. *How did I do that? Who is this?*

"Kid, time for you to leave," said Tennant. "I'll call you tomorrow if I need you to come in."

Sally, it's Carson.

Carson? How am I—

Sally, danger. Go get help. He has Mona locked up.

"Mona?" she exclaimed out loud.

Tennant's eyes narrowed. "What did you just say, Sally?" he asked quietly.

"What are you doing to Mona?" she asked.

"What do you mean?"

Gun! Gun! cried several dogs.

"Never mind," said Sally. "Guess I was imagining things. You're right, must be the sun. I'll see you—"

He pulled his gun from the rear of his waistband.

"Sorry," he said. "You left me no choice. This way." He motioned with the gun towards Sam's office.

The dogs began whimpering and racing frantically in their cages.

Sally, yelled Carson. *The foot-treadle.*

It was to her left. She dove and rolled.

"What do you think you're doing, you little brat?" yelled Tennant, aiming.

Inside the walk-in refrigerator, they heard a gunshot—then two more.

"Oh, no," whispered Mona. She turned to face the door.

"You can't take him," said Pastore. "Not with your hands tied."

"I can," she said grimly. "I will."

They heard someone fumble at the door, and she tensed, ready to charge. Then, it opened.

"Mona!" cried Sally. "You've got to help him."

Then she saw Pastore and screamed.

"It's okay, Sally, it's okay," said Mona. "Get something to cut these off me."

Sally backed into the office, Mona following her. The girl grabbed the electric carving knife that Sam used for the meat and carefully sawed through the plastic restraints. They sprang open, and Mona rubbed her wrists as the circulation was restored. Then, she grabbed her Glock from the desk and charged into the main room.

Tennant lay spread-eagled on the floor, a dozen dogs around him, their jaws clamped firmly on any part of him they could reach.

"Sally wanted me to help you," said Mona.

"Not him," said Sally behind her. "Carson. It's Carson."

The shepherd lay on his side, three bullet holes in his chest.

"He led the charge," said Sally. "He took the bullets so the others could get to him."

Mona knelt by the shepherd. His eyes rolled up to look at her. She ran her hand gently over his neck.

"Good dog, Carson," she said softly.

He looked over at Sally, who was crying.

Sally, he began. Then, his eyes closed.

Mona put the Glock to Tennant's head.

"I value that dog's life more than yours," she said. "Where are the keys to the handcuffs?"

"Desk drawer," he said. "Get these fuckers off me."

"Whatever command keeps them like this, keep using it," said Mona, "but don't kill him—not yet."

She ran back into Sam's office, found the keys, then went into the refrigerator and released Pastore, who sank gratefully to the floor.

"We need to get you to a hospital," she said.

"No," he said. "I need a moment. See if you could rustle me up some soap, and a washcloth, and a spare shirt—and that cup of coffee I've been dreaming about for the last ten hours."

Sam's team came to a halt before the elevator. Olga reached up with her forepaw and pressed the button. The doors opened.

Go, she said to Arnie. *Help Sam.*

Come with me, he said.

We have to hold the fort, said Olga.

They have guns.

She stepped in, hit the button for the lower floor, then stepped out.

You've been a wonderful alpha, Arnie, she said. *Now, it's time to let the big dogs hunt.*

He looked up at her as the door closed between them.

She turned to face the other three.

Four men, four dogs, she said. *Let's go.*

CHAPTER 17

PASTORE SAT BEHIND SAM'S DESK and played back his last two messages.

"Right," he said. "Time to hit the road."

"You're in no shape to hit anything," said Mona. "I could knock you down with one finger right now. You've got cracked ribs, probably a concussion, and God knows what internal damage."

"Sounds pretty accurate," he said, "but two of my people are in trouble, and given recent events, I don't know if there is anyone in my organization that I can trust on short notice. Which leaves me."

"And me."

"Negative, Mona," he said, collecting his gun and clips from the desk. "You are a hellacious lady, and I wouldn't mind having your radiant body pressed against mine again in healthier circumstances, but this is something you are not qualified to do."

"But—"

"What I need from you, and more importantly what Sam needs from you, is for you to take care of his friends here."

"You want me to be a dog-sitter while you go off to war?" she said, fuming.

"That remarkable little girl is very capable, but she can't do it by herself," he said, "and Ms. Cheller seems disinclined to stick around, which is understandable."

He picked up his monitor, then sniffed at the shirt she had found for him. "This is one of Sam's shirts," he said.

"Obviously," she replied.

"I can smell you all over it," he grinned. "That should sustain me for the trip."

She blushed, something she didn't know she could still do.

He walked out and pointed the gun at Tennant.

"You can let him go, Sally," he said.

"Dogs, release," she commanded.

They stepped back, still very much on guard.

"Get up slowly, and put your hands against the wall," ordered Pastore.

Tennant complied. Pastore, still holding the gun, rear-cuffed him with his free hand. Then, he frisked him, removing his wallet and cellphone.

"As far as the three of you are concerned, Tennant took off without saying anything," he said, "and you never saw me."

"Will we never see you again?" asked Sally.

"Depends on what happens in the next twelve hours," said Pastore. He handed Kerry a card. "Ms. Cheller, if you have any more questions about your brother, you call me. I'm done keeping that secret. Sally, you are as good a soldier as I have ever had the pleasure of serving with. I may have a job for you when you're old enough."

"Cool," said Sally. "Now, go help Sam."

Pastore shoved Tennant out of the building and into the van, then secured him to the metal railing. He drove off, taking the back roads until he came to an isolated stretch. Then, he pulled over and pulled Tennant out, keeping the cuffs secure.

"That way," said Pastore, gesturing toward the woods with his gun.

"You gonna do to me what I did to you?" asked Tennant as he started walking.

"I'd get the same result," said Pastore. "Why don't you just tell me who you're working for?"

"Someone bigger than you, and that's all you're gonna get," said Tennant. "Hey, want to hear something wild?"

"What?"

"You must be wondering how that little girl got the drop on me."

"She released the dogs."

"Yeah, but you know how she knew Mona was in trouble? The dogs told her. She can talk to them, just like Sam."

"That is interesting," said Pastore. "You can stop and turn around now. Anything else you want to say?"

"I suppose this is a bad time to complain about the crappy pension plan," said Tennant.

"Not bad," chuckled Pastore.

Tennant closed his eyes. Pastore put a bullet directly between them.

Bolton burst into the rotunda, followed closely by Priscilla, Floyd, and Henry.

Alan Gordon

They fanned out, guns at the ready.

"Where did those mutts disappear to?" muttered Bolton. "Let's try that asshole's room."

They ran into the dorm wing.

Bolton kicked open the door to Sam's room, but it was empty. "Check the other bedrooms," he directed. "Shoot at anything with more than two legs."

But the rooms were devoid of dogs.

"What's going on?" asked Mrs. Whitfield, poking her head out of the kitchen.

"Those dogs are loose and causing trouble," said Bolton. "Stay inside and out of our way."

His walkie-talkie went off.

"Sir," came Carl's voice. "Got that dog from the race running around the back woods."

"Right," he answered. "I'm on it. The rest of you check the lab wings."

He jogged out the back door and down the ramp by the loading dock.

Nan and Bert were arguing.

I'll hit him high, you hit him low, said Bert.

No, I'll hit him high, said Nan. *I can jump higher than you.*

The hell you can.

Want to see me?

Look, I should—wait.

They listened.

There's two of them, she said.

Okay, he said. *I'll take the one on the right.*

No, I'll take the one on the right.

Why?

Because I'm already on the right, dimwit.

Oh. Yeah, that actually makes sense.

Floyd and Priscilla came into the lab.

The two dogs leaped.

Otto carefully pulled out the last lamp's cord, plunging the room into darkness. The other dogs were hunters, constantly on the move. He preferred stillness—the dark.

The light was his enemy. It brought out his strange amber eyes, even when the rest of him was concealed in the shadows. The slightest glint would be a dead giveaway.

He heard Henry's careful footsteps approaching the room.

He jumped silently onto a desk and sat behind a monitor. He remained motionless, not even breathing, letting his ears determine the man's position.

252

Sensing the angle of his throat from the breath coursing through it.

He closed his eyes.

Henry opened the door and stepped into the room, fumbling at the light switch. The guard didn't see Otto until he was already in midair, his mouth opening, his teeth tearing through the arteries in the man's neck.

Olga stood near the vegetable gardens, watching as Bolton came into view. Then, she bayed at him.

I hunt wolves! she howled. Then, she turned and ran for the cover of the woods as a spray of bullets kicked up the dirt where she had been standing.

"Now we're having some fun," crowed Bolton.

He stepped towards the woods, his gun at eye-level, ready to fire at any movement.

"How many did you kill?" shouted Sam. "How many of my people are dead because of you?"

"People?" Kudowski laughed. "Those things weren't people."

"How many?"

"Oh, maybe forty here, plus however many Christmas specials our Mister Taylor had," she said, "and one human today."

"Valerie," he said.

"Poor, moonstruck Valerie," she said. "Such a romantic at heart—and quite good at what she did. We'd never have accomplished anything without her discoveries. But, she was getting too close. It was time for her to go."

She picked up a steel rod with four gleaming blades set into a bar at the end. "Looks like the backscratcher from hell, doesn't it? That's how we made it look like a werewolf did it. Only took one swing, too. Made me appreciate how you get off on swiping those claws at real humans."

She put it back down on the worktable, then pulled a gun out of the drawer. "Coleridge said there's someone you're reporting to besides Pastore. I want to know who it is."

"Or you'll shoot me?"

"Beats being dissected on a lab table," she said. "We aren't always scrupulous about using an anesthetic first."

"I report directly to the head of the Department for Homeland Security," said Sam. "Separate communication channel from what I use for Pastore."

She smiled. "Now I know you're bullshitting me," she said. She pointed the gun through the bars at him. "Sorry, Sam. The cavalry isn't coming to save you this time."

"I wasn't cavalry, ma'am," he said, "I was in the Canine Corps."

She shrieked as Arnie sank his teeth into her bony ankle, then fired a shot in his direction. The dachshund winced in pain, but held on as her blood gushed around his muzzle. Sam's arm shot out, latching onto the lapels of her lab coat. He pulled as hard as he could, slamming her forehead into the bars. She sagged against them, the gun falling from her hand.

Arnie let go. *Fuck!* he yelled. *She shot my tail off! Fuck!*

Just part of it, said Sam. *Hang on.*

"Please tell me she's got keys," said Alison.

He hooked a key-ring in her pocket with one claw and pulled them out. Then, he reached around and felt for the lock. A moment later, he was free.

Kudowski lay on the floor, her breath coming in short, ragged gasps.

"What's happening to her?" asked Alison as Sam let her out.

"Anaphylactic shock," said Sam. "She's allergic to dogs. She might die."

"I might let her," said Alison.

"Get that first aid kit over there," said Sam.

"You actually want to help this cold-hearted bitch?" asked Alison in disbelief.

"No. I need a bandage for Arnie's tail."

What's left of it, moaned Arnie.

She picked up the gun and guarded the door while he tended to Arnie.

"Never had my life saved by a dachshund before," she said. "What do we do now?"

Report! he called.

Two guards down here, called Nan.

One here, said Otto.

Bolton and I are playing in the woods, panted Olga.

"Three guards down," he said.

"How do you know that?" asked Alison, giving him a strange look.

"I can talk to dogs. Long story," he said. "There's still one guard in the front trailer, plus McKenna and Coleridge. Sanchez may be on their side, too, but I doubt it. I've got to get out back to help Olga."

"Who?"

"The wolfhound. She's keeping Bolton occupied."

"This is crazy," she said, shaking her head. "Two of us with one sidearm against at least four men and automatic rifles."

She picked up the EM pulse generator and handed it to him. "Use it on me. Two werewolves are better than one."

"I thought you weren't emotionally prepared for this."

"Oh, I'm prepared now," she said. "You thought I was pissed off before?"

He pressed the "ON" button. The device hummed as it built up the charge. Then, a green light went on. He pointed it at her. She took a deep breath.

"You do look good naked, by the way," he said. He pressed another button.

He had been with other werewolves as the change hit them, but always while going through it himself. This was the first time he had ever observed it without distraction. He watched, fascinated by the lengthening of the bones, the emergence of the claws and hair, the thrusting of the muzzle.

And most of all, the fangs.

He wanted to take her right there, to have her on the concrete floor, both of them sinking their fangs into each—

"You done?" she growled at him. "We've got work to do. No time for primal urges."

"Right," he said. "You want the gun?"

"Fuck you," she said.

He held up his hand suddenly and listened at the door. Then, he pulled it open.

Coleridge stood there, his eyes widening in horror.

"Hey, Gadget Guy," said Sam. "Got something that can stop this?"

He drove his fist into Coleridge's jaw, sending him all the way down the hall, his head crashing into the elevator door.

"Four down," said Sam.

He picked up Coleridge like he was a feather. Then, he came back, removed his keys, and locked him inside one of his own cells.

You want to stay here? he asked Arnie.

And miss all the fun? Hell, no.

"Come on," he said.

The three of them ran to the elevator.

"I need you to take out the guard in the trailer first," said Sam as they entered the rotunda. "He's got eyes on the compound."

"Got it," said Alison. "Which way is that?"

"Front door, then half a klick down the road."

"Give me five, then go."

Carl sat before his bank of monitors, scanning the grounds for any trace of Bolton and the wolfhound he was chasing.

"Sir, I've lost visual on you," he said.

"I'm in the woods," radioed Bolton. "She keeps running. I can't get a clear shot."

"Sir, I can't raise the others," said Carl. "Any reason why their radios should be—"

He stopped. A large, gray blur had just burst from the front doors of the complex.

"Sir, I have located our missing werewolf!" he shouted.

"What? That's impossible."

"Sir, it is extremely possible. In fact, the subject seems to be bearing down on me. Sir, I am requesting immediate back-up."

"Goddammit!" shouted Bolton. "Take care of it yourself. I'm busy."

Carl picked up his rifle, checked the clip, and stood, pointing it at the door to the trailer. He glanced at the monitors. The werewolf came straight at the trailer, then went left and disappeared from view. He fired a burst through the door, then waited to see if it was still trying to come in.

The floorboards erupted beneath him, sending jagged pieces of wood into his legs and groin. He screamed as Alison reached up and drove her claws into his stomach. His finger tightened convulsively on the trigger as she dragged him down, the bullets shattering the banks of monitors, spraying shards of glass everywhere.

Locations on McKenna, Sanchez, Buenaventura, and Whitfield, called Sam as he opened the door to the loading dock.

McKenna and Buenaventura are in their labs, said Otto.

Sanchez is in the kitchen with Whitfield, said Arnie.

Okay, said Sam. *Nan and Bert, keep an eye on McKenna. If he comes out of his lab, take him down, but keep him alive. Otto, guard Buenaventura. I'm going after Bolton.*

He peered out cautiously. No sign of Bolton. He took a breath, then ran and dove behind Coleridge's truck. He waited for a moment, then ran again.

Olga, on my way, he called. *Location?*

Near the blind spot, she said. *I'm running out of cover. Might have to double back to take him. He's—*

Then he heard a burst of fire and the anguished howl of a dog. He abandoned all caution and took off in that direction.

Bolton stepped forward, gun still raised.

"Got you, you bitch," he shouted in triumph.

Then he saw Sarge lying on his side, five bullet holes in his side.

"What the fuck were you running around in here for?" he yelled, walking up and kicking the dead dog. "Stupid, fucking asshole!"

"They take after their masters," said Sam from behind him.

Bolton whirled and fired.

"Nice job, you hit a tree," said Sam, now off to his right.

"You move pretty fast when you're hairy, don't you?" yelled Bolton. "Can you outrun a bullet?"

"The way you shoot, I don't have to," Sam yelled back.

Sam made a break to his right, and Bolton let off a burst in that direction. The last one blew bark off the tree where Sam took cover.

"Hey, Sam," called Bolton. "Was it my imagination, or were you a little less furry that time?"

Sam looked down at his hands. The fur was receding, as were the claws—as were the fangs.

"If my timing is correct, the effects of Mister Coleridge's magic ray gun should be wearing off about now," said Bolton, walking toward him. "Which means you've gone from being a dangerous critter in the woods to being a butt-naked human in the woods, and I'm still the guy with the big fucking gun. Pretty crappy plan you had there, if you ask me."

"The plan's working fine," said Sam, stepping into the open.

Bolton smiled and started to raise his gun. That was when Olga hit him from the right, tearing a chunk out of his upper arm. The rifle fell from his now useless hand. He made a grab for it with his left, but the wolfhound seized the hand and bit down until her teeth met. He shouted in pain. She pulled him to his knees.

Sam stepped forward and picked up the rifle.

"Hey, you look pretty good naked, too," said Alison as she ran up. Her teeth and claws dripped with fresh blood.

"Alison, this is Olga," said Sam. "Olga, Alison."

"Did you do that to this nasty man?" asked Alison.

Olga gave a woof of acknowledgment.

"Way to go, girl," said Alison. "Master Sergeant, I believe the field is ours."

"Depends," said Sam. "We don't know if they have reinforcements coming. Take this asshole and lock him up downstairs. I'm gonna check on the others."

She hit Bolton once, then slung him over her shoulder.

Arnie was waiting for them at the top of the loading dock.

I'd wag, but it hurts too much, he said.

What happened to you? asked Olga.

Got shot, he said proudly.

She nuzzled him. *You are my hero,* she said. *You know that, don't you?*

"You do this sort of thing a lot?" asked Alison as they went in.

"I try to lead a peaceable life," said Sam. "Guess I'm not good at it. I'll meet you downstairs."

He turned down the first hall to Buenaventura's lab. Otto sat placidly by her door.

"Doc, you okay in there?" he called.

"One more step and I'll blow your head off," she shouted.

"Worst therapist ever," he said. "Ma'am, I am no threat to you. I suggest you start trusting me. We may all have to get out of here in a hurry."

"What's going on?" she asked.

"I'm shutting this place down, Doc," he said. "Doctor Kudowski was—well, there's bad news. She killed Valerie."

"What?" she cried.

"I figure that you were on her list as well," continued Sam. "I certainly was. You want to put that gun down yet?"

"Yes, yes," she said. "My God. Valerie is dead?"

She stepped into view—unarmed, he was relieved to see.

"You're naked and carrying a machine gun," she observed. "I thought you said you were no threat."

"I'll get some fresh clothes on when I have time," he said. "Get yourself packed. Tell Doctor Sanchez to do the same. He's hiding in the kitchen."

He walked to the next hallway. It was empty.

What's going on?

He was trying to make a phone call, said Nan from inside the lab. *We decided that was a bad idea.*

Sam and the three dogs went in. McKenna sat behind his desk, a Doberman firmly attached to each wrist.

"Would you mind getting these animals off of me?" asked McKenna.

"Sure," said Sam. He put the barrel of the weapon to McKenna's head. "Dogs, release. Doc, come with me."

He marched him into the elevator. Neither said a word. When the doors opened, Alison was standing at the end of the hallway, gun at the ready. She lowered it when she saw Sam.

"I found that woman's allergy kit," she said. "I gave her two shots of whatever's in there, but I don't know if she's going to pull through."

"What did you do to her?" McKenna asked Sam.

"It wasn't me," said Sam. "It was Arnie. Don't make fun of him. He doesn't like it."

He shoved McKenna into the room.

"Looks like we got everybody," said Sam.

Of the three captives, only Coleridge was conscious. Bolton lay in his cell, still bleeding from his arm and hand. Kudowski was breathing more easily, but still out.

"That one's for you," said Sam, pointing to an open cell.

McKenna went in docilely and sat on a bench. Sam locked it, then handed the keys to Alison.

"I'm gonna get my clothes and then try and reach Pastore," he said. "If I can't, I'll come get you and we'll hit the road. If anyone but me comes out of that elevator, permission to fire."

"Wasn't going to ask permission," she said. "See if you can find me an outfit, too."

Mrs. Whitmore almost passed out when he came into the hallway.

"I apologize for my appearance, ma'am," he said quickly. "Would you mind rustling up about a dozen sandwiches real quick?"

She stared at him blankly.

"Sandwiches, please," he repeated.

"What kind?" she asked, swaying on her feet.

"You know what people like," he said. "Heavy on the red meat for Alison, okay?"

"Sure," she said automatically, and turned back into the kitchen.

He went into his room, threw his clothes on, then came outside to the loading dock. He jumped in Coleridge's truck and drove to the security trailer. He collected his cell phone from the storage locker, avoiding looking at the mess that had been Carl. He called Mona's number. She picked up on the first ring.

"Sam!" she cried in relief. "Are you all right?"

"I am now," he said. "Have you been to the warehouse?"

"I'm there now," she said. "We're all right. That man Tennant—"

"Mona, is Pastore there?"

"He's on his way to you," said Mona. "He took Tennant with him. Oh, Sam—"

She was crying.

"What is it?" asked Sam.

"Carson's dead," she said. "Tennant killed him. I am so sorry."

Sam held the phone against his chest for a moment, then put it back to his ear. "Was it a good death?" he asked.

"He died saving us," she said. "He died in battle. Sally and I buried him."

"All right," he said. "We're gonna be okay here. I'll be home sometime tonight. Hold the fort for me, will you?"

"I'll be here, Sam," she said. "I promise."

He disconnected, then grabbed every weapon and box of ammo he could find and loaded them into the truck.

Pastore drove up around six.

Sam opened the door for him. "Rough day?" he asked.

"Had worse," said Pastore.

"Don't want to know how," said Sam.

"Which of you did all that to Carl?"

"Alison."

"Must have been in a bad mood."

"I don't think I've seen her in a good one. You eaten? We got sandwiches."

"Yeah. Couple of sandwiches would be good. Tell me everything."

Alison was back in human form when Pastore and Sam came in to the work-room.

"Forgive for not saluting," she said. "Sir."

"Understood," said Pastore.

He looked at the four captives. All four of the prisoners were awake now, Bolton moaning softly.

"Right," said Pastore. "The two of you go up front. Sam, load your stuff into my van." He tossed him the keys.

"What about them?" asked Alison, gesturing at the prisoners.

"They were alive when you last saw them," said Pastore. "No more questions."

She looked at Kudowski one last time, smirked, then left with Sam.

"I spent last night strung up in a meat locker, being tortured by my own man," said Pastore. "The irony is, I am one of those rare Homeland Security guys who believes that torture is ineffectual."

He drew his gun. "But, I do believe in threats. I want to know who you are working for. Tell me, and you'll be alive when I walk out of this room. And, to make my point clear—"

He shot Bolton through the heart. McKenna screamed.

"Hired guns don't know shit," said Pastore.

He leaned on the worktable, then noticed the EM pulse generator and the vocal stress detector. He turned on the latter.

"Moon, wolf, blood, meat," he said.

The detector showed spikes on every word.

"Neat," said Pastore. "Mister Coleridge, you are a clever man. Are you clever enough to save your own life?"

"I was doing what they paid me to do," mumbled Coleridge, holding his jaw. "I can't—"

Pastore fired another shot.

"And then there were two," he said. "What do you say?"

"You're going to kill us either way," said Kudowski. "Why give you the satisfaction?"

"Let me sweeten the pot," said Pastore. "There are different ways to die. When we had this place built, I made sure that there were thermite charges secreted in every wall. All that's going to be left when I'm done is a pile of smoking rubble. Burning to death is a bad way to die. The two of you deserve to die badly."

"I was right about your kind," she said. "You're animals. Every one of you."

"Well, my body count is considerably higher than yours," he conceded, "but that's because I've been around longer. Oh, what you might have accomplished over the next few decades. Mengele was an amateur by comparison. Last chance to talk."

Sam finished loading his gear into the van. He turned to see Tito and the surviving shepherds sitting on the ground before him.

You guys took yourselves out of the battle, said Sam. *That took a lot of strength. Thank you.*

What happens to us now? asked Tito.

You're free to go, said Sam.

Go where? asked Tito. *We aren't pets. If we go wild, they'll hunt us down.*

Boss? said Arnie. *We can't leave them.*

Sam looked at the rest of his team, then sighed.

Get in, he said to the shepherds. *You'll have to ride two to a cage and share water dishes.*

They were inside before he finished the sentence.

Alison came out with the others, carrying a carton loaded with computers.

"Where's Pastore?" he asked her.

"Salvaging what he can from the labs," she said.

"What are you going to do?" he asked.

"Can't go back to Augusta," she sighed. "Joe's gonna help me relocate. Might be a good idea for you, too."

"I'm not leaving," he said.

Buenaventura put her suitcases in the truck, then came over to Sam.

"This is my card," she said. "You're right: I'm a lousy therapist. But, you need to talk to someone, and I doubt there's another psychiatrist alive who knows werewolves like I do. Please call me, Sam. I want to hear your dreams."

"I'll think about it," he said, pocketing the card. "Thanks."

She squatted to face his team. "Is it all dogs, or only the ones you train?" she asked.

"All dogs," he said, "but mine are the best."

"You are extraordinary," she said to them. "It was a privilege to know you."

They wagged their tails.

She smiled sadly and climbed into the truck.

Pastore came out, carrying one more carton. "We need to talk," he said.

"All right," said Sam.

They walked away from the others. The sun was setting, and the moon, a large sliver past being full, was low in the sky.

"You find out anything useful?" asked Sam.

"Some," said Pastore. "Nothing I can take to a subcommittee. Let's just say that I no longer believe that the Department of Homeland Security has my back."

"Figured that," said Sam. "Kudowski was completely unimpressed when I said I was reporting to them."

"I want you to know that there will be another large check heading your way," said Pastore.

"For services rendered? Mission accomplished?"

"I'm saying that no matter what, I got your back, Sam."

"Do you? Do you really?"

Pastore looked at him impassively. "You got something you want to say to me, soldier?" he asked.

"I had some time to kill before you got here," said Sam. "I decided to look at McKenna's copy of the Book of Wolves."

"And?"

"And I'm not in it."

"No," said Pastore, "but you knew that. You knew that because you've had the Bogey Man's copy ever since you killed him."

"I knew it because it took Coleridge's vocal gadget for them to make me. If I was in the Book, then they would have looked me up from the start. You sent me knowing they wouldn't find me there."

"Of course," said Pastore. "I've kept a few werewolves out of it. That's the info Tennant was trying to—"

"Which leads to the very good question of how the Bogey Man was able to find me," said Sam. "Because he sure didn't get my info from Kudowski."

"Yeah, about that," said Pastore. "He got that from me."

"From you," said Sam. "You set me up to be killed by the Bogey Man."

"No, I was trying to set up the Bogey Man to be killed by you," said Pastore.

"Bullshit."

"Hear me out, Sam. I told you I was working on an informant by way of a couple of intermediaries. It wasn't clear if he was good or not. I gave him your info as bait, hoping they'd go after you."

"They nearly killed me—and my dogs."

"But they didn't. I was counting on you taking them out."

"You might have warned me!" shouted Sam.

"I did," said Pastore. "You got that urban legend about the Bogey Man, what he did, the poison he was using, the recommended antidote."

"I got that from a newsgroup that a bunch of us set up online," said Sam.

"I know," said Pastore. "I was one of them. Barker32. I posted the story."

"Jesus," said Sam, shaking his head. "You like to play games with living pieces, don't you? You almost got me killed, you sent me in here so Tennant could go looking for your precious disk, you set up your people here for a massacre, and you got Carson killed."

"I'm sorry about Carson, Sam," said Pastore. "If it's any consolation, I took out Tennant myself."

"What now? Are you going to keep this super-soldier project going? I already destroyed the processed werewolf material. Will you set up another lab and kill more of us for the new batch?"

"I am going to destroy every trace of that project," said Pastore. "You have my word—"

"Your word means nothing," shouted Sam.

"Let me tell you something, Master Sergeant Lehrmann," said Pastore. "Do you want to know why I chose you for this mission?"

"Because of my dogs," said Sam, "and because you didn't have anyone you trusted in your own organization."

"I had people," said Pastore. "Committed, skilled people—but I chose you. I could have come up with another reason to get you out of the way so we could find that disk, but I wanted you to come here."

"Why?"

"Because you are wasting your gifts hiding in that doghouse. You've always had the potential—"

"To be a great werewolf? Is that what I should be?"

"Yes, Sam. A great werewolf. You needed to find out what we really are, what makes us tick. You need to know why we're special."

"I thought this place was supposed to find a cure."

"We don't need a cure," said Pastore. "There's nothing wrong with us."

"Most of the human race would take the opposite position."

"Every species is afraid of the one that's going to replace them."

"Is that the plan?" said Sam. "How do we do that? Bite everyone? There's several billion of them and a few thousand of us. Each of us can only turn one person a month—assuming they're willing, which is generally not the case—so I really don't like the odds here."

"Yeah, you're not ready for everything yet," said Pastore, "but that shitstorm I was talking about? Still coming. You'll have to choose a side when it arrives."

"Are we done?"

"Not quite," said Pastore. "I brought these for you."

He handed him the carton. Inside were the EM pulse generator and the vocal stress analyzer.

"What am I supposed to do with these?" asked Sam.

"These are useful toys," said Pastore. "I would rather they weren't used by my stab-in-the-back government. I'm thinking that someone with access to the werewolf population of this country may want to get the word out that they are being treated as suspects in their homeland, and that they should do something about it."

"Do what?" asked Sam.

"Get organized," said Pastore. "Or change their identities and run. It can be done."

"That would make your database obsolete," said Sam.

"Yes, it would," said Pastore.

He stretched, grimacing in pain, then looked up at the moon in the night sky. "There it is," he said. "Does it ever call to you, Sam?"

"I'm a fucking werewolf," said Sam. "Of course it calls to me."

"A pulse unlike any other in the universe," said Pastore. "Coming from twelve points laid out like a giant clock. I want to find out what's going on up there."

"Send me a postcard," said Sam. "We're done. Dogs, inside."

The dogs jumped into the van. Sam hesitated, then put the carton in with them.

"I'll send someone to pick up the van," said Pastore.

Sam got in the driver's seat without replying and drove away.

Pastore watched until he disappeared, then rejoined the others.

"Give me the keys," said Alison. "You're in no shape to drive any more today."

He handed them to her, then climbed into the passenger seat.

As they drove through the front gate, he felt a tap on his shoulder. He turned to face Ms. Whitmore.

"What will I tell everyone?" she said. "About my job?"

He pulled out his cellphone and keyed in a number. A second later, a dull boom echoed behind them.

"Tell them the place closed down," he said. "Where can we drop you?"

Sam took the interstate home. Arnie rode in the passenger seat, occasionally standing on his hind legs and looking out the window.

How's the tail doing? asked Sam.

Hurts, said Arnie.

We'll get you to the vet first thing in the morning, promised Sam. *Hey, Otto?*

Yes, Sam?

I heard some of what you were saying to the shepherds when you were in that cage. Are you gonna explain that to me?

The other dogs looked at the Weimaraner.

It was all nonsense, Sam, said Otto. *Something I made up to get them to back off.*

Sounded pretty convincing.

It's the spooky eyes, said Otto. *Gets them every time.*

CHAPTER 18

Every dog in the place jumped Sam the moment he walked through the door, knocking him down and pinning him under a happy canine heap. They bombarded him with questions until his brain was ready to burst, but Arnie silenced them with a single bark. The dogs turned to argue with him, then saw the bandage on his tail and the respect the other dogs from the van gave him. Without quite knowing why, every one of them assumed a submissive posture.

"Hello, soldier," said Mona, watching from by the pit. "Good to see you."

"Good to be seen," said Sam.

She walked up with a look that he knew all too well.

"I smell like dog," he warned her.

She ignored the warning. "Sorry they weren't in their cages," she said when they came up for air. "They were too excited. I gave in."

"Not a problem," he said.

Okay, everyone, he said. *Arnie will tell you everything, but not until you get inside.*

The dogs scrambled into their cages. Sam showed the shepherds where they would stay, then hit the switch that locked them all in for the night.

Wait, said Olga. *Who will be the night dog?*

Arnie, who should it be? asked Sam.

Arnie scanned the group.

Ignatz, he said. *For tonight, anyway. Then, I'd go with the twins, alternating.*

Sam let Ignatz out. *Keep everyone safe,* said Sam.

Yes, Boss!

"How is Nicky?" he asked.

"Vet says she'll live."

"One good piece of news."

"What do you need right now?"

"A shower and a good night's sleep," he said.

She put her arms around him.

"I've got a shower," she said. "Can't promise you the other part."

"I'll settle for what I can get."

"Good night, dogs," said Mona.

There was a collective bark. Then, Sam turned off the lights and locked up.

In the morning, Mona drove with him to the warehouse and took Arnie to the vet. Sam fell back into his usual morning routine, but his mind kept wandering. Around eleven, Sally rode up on her bike.

Hi, Sam, she said as she entered.

Hey, Sally, he replied.

Then he looked at her, stunned, as she grinned from ear to ear.

"You can speak dog," he said.

"Yup," she said. "So can you. How cool is that?"

"Until now, I thought I was the only one who could," said Sam. "To think that in all the places of the world, the two of us would end up here. Weird."

"Sure is," said Sally, "and you're a werewolf, speaking of weird. What's that like?"

"Okay," said Sam, turning to the dogs. "Who told her?"

"I did," said Mona, coming in with Arnie, who sported a new bandage on his tail. "After what she saw—after what she did—I thought she was entitled to know the truth. And, she's smart enough not to blab."

"Seriously, who would believe me?" asked Sally. "Now, about that raise."

"Done," said Sam. "No medical benefits, though."

"Cool," said Sally. "Now, explain to me how you left to sell five dogs and came back with nine."

"Talk to Arnie," said Sam. "He tells it better. Besides, he's the hero."

Come on, Arnie, said Sally.

Holy shit! exclaimed Arnie. *Listen to you.*

Arnie, you're gonna have to tone down the language now that she can understand you, said Sam sternly.

Oh, that's going to cramp his style, laughed Olga.

"Keep an eye on the place for me," said Sam. "I'm going for a walk with Mona."

He took her out into the woods, along the same path as the last time they had been there. They came to where Sam had carved the heart in the tree.

"It's here, isn't it?" she asked him. "The Book of Wolves. Where the arrow in the heart is pointing."

"Buried six inches below the surface," he said. "I knew you'd figure that out."

"Are we going to help the other werewolves?" she asked.

"We?"

"Have you thought about what I said?" she asked him.

"I have," he said. "I want you to think about it some more. If you're still set on it, then the next full moon is in three weeks."

"Doubt I'll change my mind."

"Mona, I put us all in danger by doing what I did," said Sam. "If you become a werewolf, that danger will only increase."

"But I'll be able to defend myself better, won't I?"

"Guess so."

She kissed him.

Boss! called Olga. *That sheriff is back.*

"Shit," said Sam.

Boudreau stood by the wall of the pit, holding his hat in his hand, and watched with amusement as Sally put the new shepherds through their paces.

"Sheriff," said Sam as he came in.

"How do, Mister Lehrmann," said Boudreau. "I wanted to have another chat with you. Would you mind stepping outside for a sec?"

"Sure thing," said Sam, his heart racing.

Mona watched as they went outside.

"You remember Officer Wilkins," said Boudreau, "and that there's Officer Cole. They've been doing the primary work on those quarry fellers."

"Hi," said Sam.

The officers nodded.

"Now, what I'm about to tell you is gonna be part of a press conference we're holding later this afternoon," said Boudreau. "So I'd appreciate it if you kept it under your hat until then. Don't want no one to steal our thunder."

"You got it," said Sam. "You caught the guys who did it?"

"Not exactly," said Boudreau. "But, we ID'd the last victim, and he turned out to be a serial killer, name of Clarence Taylor. Know the name?"

"Can't say I do," said Sam. "Serial killer. Jesus. How many did he kill?"

"Twenty-one that we know of," said Boudreau. "Had a pattern. Always killed during the last full moon before Christmas."

"Any idea why?" asked Sam.

"Well, we found out his sister had been killed during a full moon on Christmas Eve twenty-two years ago," said Boudreau. "Gruesome death: got herself clawed apart. They never closed the case, neither."

"Poor thing," said Sam.

"Here's the part that we ain't releasing," continued Boudreau. "He had pictures of his next victim on his desk."

"Really? Who was it?"

Boudreau handed one to him. Sam looked at it.

"That's me," he said, his heart sinking.

"Knew that," said Boudreau, "but this next one is where we go off into the truly bizarre."

He handed Sam another, also with a telephoto lens. It showed a werewolf emerging from the warehouse.

"What did he do, Photoshop that in or something?" asked Sam.

"Not according to Officer Cole here," said Boudreau. "She's our resident computer expert. So, we have what looks like a werewolf, and I know, I know, I emphatically know that there ain't no such thing as werewolves. Only, for every one of his victims, he had similar pictures."

"So what's your point, Sheriff?" asked Sam.

Boudreau leaned forward until his face was inches away from Sam's. "My point, Mister Lehrmann, is that I still have an unsolved case involving four men torn apart by a pack of trained dogs, and, as crazy as it may sound, I think that these fellers were hunting and killing werewolves. And, I think you were his next chosen victim, but you managed to turn the tables on him. And, if that was the case, I would say that that was justifiable homicide under Georgia law and I would close this investigation. But, I can't say that unless I know how it went down."

"Do you really think they would let you close a quadruple homicide by saying it was self-defense by a werewolf?" asked Sam.

"I would certainly try to make them understand," said Boudreau.

"Sheriff, quite frankly, that's the craziest part of all," said Sam. "No disrespect."

Boudreau looked at him sadly, then put his hat back on. "You understand that I will continue my investigation until the killer is brought to justice," he said.

"I understand, Sheriff," said Sam. "Best of luck to you."

He watched as they drove away. Mona came out and joined him.

"You're still a free man," she said.

"Ain't no such thing," he said.

"We're low on gas," said Wilkins as they passed through Calhoun a few days later. "Shall I pull into Andy's?"

"Good a place as any," said Boudreau. "Gonna get me a Cherry Coke. You want one?"

"Sure," said Wilkins.

Boudreau got out and waved as Andy came up.

"How do, Andy?" said Boudreau. "Men's room clean today?"

"Clean every day, Sheriff," said Andy as he started filling the tank.

"Be right back."

There was a used car lot next to the gas station, separated by a chain link fence topped with razor wire. As Boudreau walked to the men's room, a German shepherd kept pace with him on the other side of the fence. When he came out, the dog was still there, matching him step for step. There was something familiar about its collar. He moved closer to the fence for a better look. The dog growled and bared his teeth in warning. It was missing one.

Boudreau strolled over to the front of the lot.

"Hey, Sheriff," said a salesman, coming out quickly. "In the market for a ride?"

"Not at the moment," said Boudreau. "Wanted to ask you about that dog in back."

"Oh, Errol?" asked the salesman. "Hope he didn't bother you."

"Showed his teeth, that's all," said Boudreau. "Missing one, I noticed."

"Yeah, well, the ones that are left can still rip you a new one," laughed the salesman. "He's a good dog. Only bites if he has to."

"Got him at Lehrmann's, didn't you?"

"Sure did. How'd you know?"

"Recognized the collar. Had his tag on it. When did you get him?"

"February."

February, thought Boudreau. *After the deaths of Taylor and company.*

One of the bite marks was from a dog with a tooth missing.

Boudreau wandered back to the car.

"No soda?" asked Wilkins.

"What?"

"Thought you were getting a couple of Cherry Cokes."

"So I was," said Boudreau. "Got distracted. Be right back."

He went into the little convenience mart, bought them, and came back.

"Thanks, Sheriff," said Wilkins, opening his while turning onto the road. "What distracted you?"

"Nothing important," said Boudreau, taking a sip. "Damn, that's good on a hot day, ain't it?"

EPILOGUE

GINNY SAT IN THE PASSENGER seat on the second Jeep ride of her life. It was the last week of September. The summer was still in full force, and she was sweating more than she wanted to be.

This time, she was ready when Kerry veered off the road. When they pulled up to the gate, they both got out to inspect it.

"See?" said Kerry triumphantly, pointing to the padlock. "Still shiny. No crime scenes today."

"Too bad," said Ginny. "Maybe Officer Wilkins could do another strip tease for us."

"Worth seeing the whole show, lemme tell you," giggled Kerry as she unlocked the gate and pulled it open.

"No! You didn't!"

"Aw, he was sweet," said Kerry.

"You have to tell me everything."

They chattered away as they drove down to the quarry.

"I really appreciate you helping me," said Kerry as they began setting up the tables for the sorority outing. "Missy's still limping around. I think it's just for sympathy. I swear, that ankle healed three weeks ago."

"She'll be milking it through Christmas," said Ginny. She looked out at the water and shivered.

"What is it?" asked Kerry.

"I can't believe we were swimming around, all happy and carefree, while there were four dead guys rotting away underneath us. Might be bits of them still down there."

"Come on, it's been raining all summer," said Kerry as she threw some plastic covers over the tables. "It's all been recycled, or whatever it does."

"But it's creepy. We swam around in dead guy soup."

"Ever swam in the ocean? Or a lake?"

"Well, sure."

"Then you swam with dead people," said Kerry. "I mean, think about it. All those ships that sank, all those drowned people. Not to mention all the dead fish, dead whales, dead lobsters—"

"Yuck."

"Dead clams, dead plankton . . ."

"Will you cut it out?" shuddered Ginny. "I'm only swimming in pools from now on."

"Where the brats pee?"

"Stop," ordered Ginny. "Let's get those chairs out. It's getting dark."

By the time they were done, the sun had set.

"Sorry it took so long," said Kerry, "but I know it's gonna be a big hit with—"

"Quiet," said Ginny, staring out into the woods.

"What?"

"I heard something moving."

"It's the woods, Ginny," said Kerry. "There's always critters running around."

"You got that gun handy?"

"Seriously?"

"Look, I don't want the sorority to be liable if one of the girls got bitten by something rabid."

"Ridiculous," snorted Kerry.

"I am serious," said Ginny. "There was this frat up in Virginia—"

Something large hurtled out of the woods, bounding straight at them.

"Kerry!" shouted Ginny.

Then it flew by her, its claws flashing for a moment in the moonlight.

"Wha—" moaned Ginny, blood starting to pour from her stomach. She collapsed.

The thing paused. Kerry snatched at the box holding the .45, pulled it out, and pointed it unsteadily at the creature. It moved towards them slowly, drawing itself up to its full height.

"Kerry," whispered Ginny. "Shoot it."

The thing stopped and bared a fearsome set of fangs. Kerry tried to steady her aim.

"For God's sake, shoot it," urged Ginny.

The clouds rolled off the full moon, and Kerry could see the creature's eyes.

Eyes that she knew like her own.

"Hey, sis," said the werewolf. "Miss me?"

Kerry lowered her gun.

"Kerry?" whimpered Ginny.

"Hey, big brother," said Kerry. "Welcome home."

"Good to be here," said the werewolf. "Who is your lovely companion?"

"This is Ginny Cavalieri," said Kerry.

Ginny looked up in terror as the werewolf stood over her.

"How do you do, Ms. Cavalieri," he said. "So nice to make your acquaintance. My name is Tom Cheller."

Then he bent towards her, fangs gleaming, his head blotting out the moon.

ABOUT THE AUTHOR

A LAN GORDON IS AN AUTHOR, lyricist, librettist and story-teller. His Fools' Guild Mysteries, starting with *Thirteenth Night,* now comprise eight books and four short stories and have been translated into many other languages. His short fiction covering several genres has been published in a wide variety of magazines and anthologies, including the Sherlock Holmes-inspired anthology *For The Sake of The Game, Jewish Noir, Wolfsbane and Mistletoe* [featuring the debut of his werewolf, Sam Lehmann], *Queens Noir, Asimov's Science Fiction, Ellery Queen Mystery Magazine,* and *Alfred Hitchcock Mystery Magazine.* His musical theater work has been performed across the country and has earned him numerous awards, most notably the Kleban Prize from New Dramatists. On the rare occasions when he tells the truth, he has won numerous Story Slams at The Moth and has been a featured performer on *The Moth Radio Hour* on NPR. He is a graduate of Swarthmore College and the University of Chicago School of Law. Alan lives in New York City. For more, visit *www.alan-gordon.com.*